Early Birds

By Janetta Fudge-Messmer

Angela,

Always enjoy the journey!

Janetta Fudge Messmer

ACKNOWLEDGEMENTS

The first person I need to thank isn't an actual person. She's our precious pooch named Maggie. After Ray and I adopted her, we thought we heard her say one day, "Please sell everything, buy an RV and let's travel the USA. I want you to spend more time with me." And that's the real reason we're on the road.

Others I must thank are my parents. They were always behind me, cheering me on in whatever I wanted to do. They told me more than once to keep at this writing thing. I wish they were here to see the unbelievable journey I'm on with this new book.

I can't forget my hubby, Ray. He's my partner in crime. Friend. Confidant and the person who isn't afraid to tell me what I've just read to him stinks. It's amazing, he's still able to stand after making such a comment. ☺ Mr. Ray, you're the best.

Thanks to my writer friends too. Couldn't have done this without ALL of you in my life. Even though it's taken me a long time to get the first book to print, you've been there for me. I have to give a special shout out to Kristl Franklin and Janice Thompson. Two ladies who have mentored me through the years. Thanks for your patience!!!

And to the ones who helped me whip *Early Birds* into shape – thank you. You know who you are and how much I appreciate your editing skills.

Last, but not least, thank you Cynthia Hickey at Winged Publications for making my dream come true.

Thanks a bunch everyone!!!

CHAPTER ONE

"Y ou want to do what in an RV?" Betsy couldn't believe her husband's pronouncement. And out of the blue, no less.

"I want to retire and travel around in an RV," Ben put down the morning paper as he repeated the bombshell. Then smiled when he reached down and picked up their 13-pound pooch. "Matilda, tell your mama you want to see the U.S.A. in a Chevrolet...or maybe a Ford dually, pulling a 5er."

Lord, is this really You? An RV, of all things."

Betsy could only stare at Ben after his out-of-character comment. Then she countered with, "But honey, you can't quit your job. You're only 59 years old."

"Matilda and I have been talkin—"

"Okay, Benjamin Stevenson, I've heard it all now. You're telling me you and our dog have been discussing our long-range plans." Betsy shook her head, hoping this would wake her up from the bizarre dream unfolding in front of her.

Ben placed his two hands on Matilda's black and white head and turned her to face Betsy. "Mom, you and Dad should quit your jobs and spend more time with me."

Betsy couldn't help but laugh at Ben when he pretended to

talk through their newly-acquired Boston terrier mix.

"Matilda told me she wants us to retire, sell our house and buy an RV."

"And I'm going to take you to the doctor this afternoon." Betsy dried her hands on the yellow towel, hanging on the oven. "Because you've been working *way* too hard."

"That's exactly right and why I should quit my job so I can spend more time with my girls. Think about it. Now we can travel around in an RV with Rose and Larry."

Half of Betsy's insides shouted, "He's gone off the deep end." The other half screamed, "Hallelujah. My prayers have been answered. He's finally come to his senses and wants to quit his job."

"...and another thing, Bets, look at all the material our retirement and subsequent travels would give you for your writing."

Betsy nodded her head. "Mr. B. we'll discuss this later. Right now I need some time to think and pray about all of this."

"Important we get the Lord's take on it. I'll take Matilda out for her morning walk." Ben opened the front door and turned. "Betsy, so you know, I've been praying about this for a while. It's like He's putting everything into place."

Except the part where you tell your wife what is going on.

Betsy watched her husband close the door then rushed into her office. First thing on the agenda, call Rose. Her best friend, who'd been bugging them to hit the road, would want to know the latest development.

Ever since the Wilford's bought their 5th wheel a couple of years ago, they'd hounded them to get one too. Rose commented the other day, "Wouldn't it be fun—the four of us, crisscrossing this great land of ours?"

"Rosie, you might have gotten your wish."

The fourth ring told Betsy that Rose either lost her phone or ventured out for the day. No need to leave a message. Her friend would check in when she got back from who knew where. While Betsy had the phone in her hand she called her mom, getting the same result.

No one's home for me to tell our earth-shattering news to.

This time she left a message—a very vague one. No need to give her mom a heart attack. Betsy hung up and did her usual when exciting, or in this case, stunning news abounded. She flipped open her laptop and wrote in her journal.

Yes, she'd better document what went on, 'cause from the sounds of things, there'd be plenty of things to write about. As Betsy typed, joy bubbled up inside of her. When she lifted her fingers off of her keyboard, she sat back in her office chair and marveled at the outrageous idea.

Really, Lord.

Betsy couldn't get over the fact what her hubby proposed fit exactly in what she'd hoped and prayed for. At least the part of Ben getting out of his job sooner than later. The RV part—not totally sold on it. Not sure she'd ever jump on the idea.

She recognized Ben needed out of his job or the stress would do him in. She'd listened for way too long how he and the others in the office battled with their CEO. Most times Mr. Greenspan shot down ideas saying, "I can see too much cost overrun already. Do a feasibility study."

Betsy commended her husband for sticking it out this long. Not that she hadn't recommended he get out when their marriage started to suffer. His response, "I can't. Gotta work until I'm 65. Can't retire on nothing."

Ben put in his time. Sometimes 80-plus hours a week. Betsy remembered she'd teased him once, "I'm going to make you a t-shirt that reads: Over-and-above-the-call-of-duty-kinda guy." Ben didn't find it funny.

"My love, you are the go-to guy. But after today's news, Mr. Greenspan will have to do it without you." Betsy chuckled. "When all we see is the impossible, God can and will do amazing things. I believe He did it today."

Betsy turned her attention back to her computer, scanning the words she'd typed. They needed a few tweaks, but for the most part they were perfect for her blog. Betsy copied and pasted the text and titled it: *PREPOSTEROUS PROPOSITION.* An apt heading for the announcement of the century.

Thinking about their Bible study group and her writer friends' reaction to their latest newsflash made her laugh. "They're not going to believe this. Oh, and their comments, I'm sure some will bring the house down."

Betsy reread her blog again. This time out loud.

Yes, I've been hit with a preposterous proposition and I'm not sure if I'm dreaming or my hubby is NUTS. Let me fill you in on what transpired. Ben waltzed into the breakfast nook, as he does every Saturday morning, but this fine day he announced. "Let's retire, sell our house and buy an RV."

Alrighty then!!! I'm glad I didn't have a mouth full of coffee when he made his big announcement. Or he'd been wearing it along with his sweat pants.

To say the least, I was surprised since my hubby's not one who springs things on me. Normally we talk things to death before we make a decision on anything. But not this time. He stated his case then told me he and the Lord (and Matilda) had been discussing it for quite some time.

I sat there stunned while Ben said things were falling into place. The funny thing is, I'm overjoyed with the idea (for the most part – an RV, I'm not so sure. ☺)

I've prayed for a long time for a change to happen. For both Ben and me to dream once again, like we used to. To trust in the Lord and His plans for our lives. To have the courage to step out in faith.

Today's proposition told me our Father has us on His radar. He cares for you and me. His love knows no bounds.

I'm sure there's more to come on this subject. I'll keep you posted.

Love ya!!!
Bets

PS: Sorry to break the BIG news without a warning. Hope you were all sitting down and hadn't taken a drink of anything. ☺

When Betsy finished reading the blog for the third time, she put it in the *Pending* file for a date one week later. She had to wait until Ben told his job about his upcoming retirement. Another reason: Didn't want the masses...*Yeah, right...*to read it before she told Rosie.

Speaking of which, where is that woman when I have BIG news to tell her?

~

Ben and Matilda strolled around the neighborhood and he couldn't remember a time he'd enjoyed their walk as much. He'd have broken out in a dance, but his neighbors might call the authorities.

But after he'd laid out his plan, he felt 50 pounds lighter and a couple inches taller. However, he should have prepared Betsy for what he'd been praying for over the last three months.

Never seemed a good time. Until today. This morning he decided to blurt it out and see what happened. Other than her shocked expression, Betsy handled it pretty well. Ben thought she might throw something at him since he blindsided her.

Similar to the way she... "And we all know how that worked out." Ben turned the corner. His pooch followed.

The spring in his step from earlier left him. Now all Ben wanted to do was take back all the nasty things he'd said to his wife when she announced, "I'm going to write for a living. Not find another job. I'll make money, Ben. You wait and see."

She didn't make money and that fact sent him into a complete meltdown. That and his job. He couldn't put his brain around it or her new career. Every chance Ben had, he made sure Betsy saw how unhappy her proposed plan made him.

"And now I expect her to understand my crazy idea of buying an RV and traveling. Even if we have the money to do it."

Ben turned down Locust Street and headed home. He had some explaining to do and hoped Betsy would open her mind to the possibilities. Then he laughed. No worries there. His wife, the dreamer, would grab on with both hands and run with it. That's why he'd married her in the first place.

"Hey Ben. Matilda."

When Ben's neighbor from across the street called his name, he knew he'd be tied up for a good half hour.

If Betsy needs me, she'll call.

He walked up to Jeremy and Matilda plopped down next to him. Almost like his pooch knew the conversation could take a while.

CHAPTER TWO

"Rose, are you sitting down?" Betsy toyed with the straw in her coffee mug.

"Well, I better be. I'm driving."

Rosie's signature snort/laugh combination filled Betsy's office, causing her to almost drop her phone.

"Then I won't keep you. Get home as fast as you can. I have something to tell you."

"What?"

"I'm not talking to you while you're behind the wheel. It's not safe."

For you or the other drivers. Rosie, you can't drive when you're NOT yapping on your Bluetooth.

"I'm pulling into my drive right now."

"Turn off your car. Don't want you to hit the gas pedal and end up going through the garage." Betsy laughed at the image that conjured up in her mind.

"Oh, Bets, you're a funny one today."

"Yes, I am. Have you turned your car off?"

Betsy heard what sounded like someone fiddling with keys then the humming sound in the background quit.

"Done. Now what's so important you couldn't tell me on the road?"

"You are still seated, aren't you?"

"Elizabeth Lynn Stevenson do I nee—"

Betsy didn't let her friend finish her sentence. In the same way Ben broke the news to her, she told Rose about the RV idea.

Silence filled the next five seconds. Then the reason Betsy had put her phone on Speaker happened. Her friend, Rose, let out a whoop and holler. If she could have seen it, must have shaken the Anadarko Building a few miles away.

No amount of talking could contain Rosie and the words that commenced—half weren't logical or legible from her end. Then Betsy caught a pause in Rose's rapid fire dialog and thought she better jump in quick. "Girl, you have to take a breath."

"Okay. I'll take a break, but I'm sooo excited. I can't wait to tell Larry."

Betsy chuckled at her best friend's exuberance. However, that's not what Betsy would call the feeling which churned inside of her. Fear. Doubt. And enough 'What if's' to wallpaper the Biltmore.

Lord...

"Hon, I hate to cut this call short. I've got lots more questions, but my ice cream is melting. Mr. Wilford prefers to dip his, not drink it. Why don't you guys come over for dinner later?"

"Sounds good. Hey, Rosie, if you can—don't tell Larry. Let's surprise him."

"Girl, even if I told Larry—he wouldn't hear a word I said, since his nose is buried in his computer. Those games...oh, never mind. I won't tell him."

"Thanks. See you tonight."

With dinner plans in the works, Betsy started to straighten up her cluttered desk then changed her mind. Her coffee needed refilled. On the way to the kitchen she glanced at the clock on the mantle. "1:30! Bet Jeremy kidnapped Ben and Matilda. Better give him a call."

~

Betsy heard the back door open and turned from the microwave. "There you are. Thought maybe you'd already started your travels without me."

"No, Matilda said we needed to wait and see if you wanted to come along on our big adventure." Ben unhooked the dog's leash and she scampered over to her normal spot—the kitchen rug.

"I told you we have a smart dog and she deserves a t.r.e.a.t." Betsy spelled it, so as to avoid getting caught in the middle of their terrier's leaps and the cabinet they kept the goodies in.

Betsy opened the door, undetected. "So far so good." Then reached in to get Matilda's favorite. "Here you go, bud."

The dog jumped up and down then sat on the rug with her little paw raised, ready for a shake. Betsy touched her paw before she laid the treat on the rug and said, "Get it." Matilda took it and munched on the morsel.

Ben sat down at their kitchen table, motioning for Betsy to sit as well. "We have some things to talk about."

"Want a cup of coffee? I was heating some when you came in."

Without waiting for an answer, Betsy poured two cups and brought them over to the table. Before settling into the padded chair, she took the pad of paper off their wine stand in the corner. "Just in case."

"Just in case of what? Do you want evidence of what I say? Use it against me when you have me put away for coming up with insane ideas."

"Oh, you have nothing to worry about, my dear." Betsy scooted her chair closer to Ben and rested her elbows on the glass top. "No, I won that award when I said I was going to write. Not get a job."

"Then we're even." Ben leaned over and gave Betsy a kiss. "Two whoppers, for sure."

"I'll agree with that." Betsy chuckled at her husband's response. A welcome change from his usual tirade when she tried to joke about their past infractions. "Anyway, smarty pants, I got the pad so we could start making a list of things we need to do around the house."

"So you're sold on the idea?"

"Not entirely, but we've got to start somewhere with...this...preposterous plan of yours."

Ben tapped his finger on the pad of paper. "What do we need to do, chief?"

"The carpets need stretched. We need to touch up the paint before we can sell this place. Have you thought about—"

"Sell the house?"

Betsy loved when her logic kicked in before Ben's. "Yes, dear, if we're going to do what Matilda told us to do, we need to get going. Time's a wasting."

Ben put his arm around Betsy and drew her to his side. "God smiled down on me the day He introduced us."

"Enough of the mushy stuff." Betsy smiled and half-heartedly pushed him away. "Remember that when we're in the middle of all this. It'll come in handy. And by the way, we're going to the Wilford's for supper tonight."

"Good, I don't have to cook."

"And neither do I." Betsy clapped her hands together. "Now are we ready to get back to making our list?"

"I've got a question for you? What do you think I should do first—stretch the carpet or... give notice at work?" Ben laughed.

Betsy jotted something down on the piece of paper. "That reminds me. I already wrote a blog about your big announcement. But don't worry, I didn't publish it. You need to give Mr. Greenspan your notice and we need to make some calls to family before I do."

Ben ignored her phone-call comment and stared at her. "You wrote a whole blog while we were gone on our walk?"

"I was writing in my journal and the next thing I knew I had a piece of brilliance." Betsy laughed. "Had to write how the Lord's setting everything into place."

"He's done a lot of that lately."

"Looks like it. And since this isn't the first time we've made a move. We'll look at renting a storage unit later. First thing you need to do is give your notice."

Ben watched her write "storage" down on the piece of paper. But his mind went back to Betsy's earlier comment. He didn't want to make any calls. Better to leave Brian out of it. Advice from his older brother almost made him want to put a halt on this before it began.

"Helllllloooo. Anyone home?"

Betsy's voice brought Ben back to reality. "Yep. I'm right here."

"Are you sure?"

"I'm back, but I have another question. Why not get a storage unit this week? Getting one would make our life easier. Then we can put stuff in it we know we're going to keep."

"I think we're rushing things. Anyway, the next thing on the list should be what you can't do."

"What can't I do?" Betsy's comment surprised him and she had his full attention.

"Even though you joked about stretching the carpet, it's a job for a professional."

Ben pretended to plunge a knife into his chest and gasped, "I'm...not...a..."

"I'll ignore the theatrics."

"I learned from the best."

"Can we focus here?"

"Yes, *we* can."

"We also need to get someone out for the broken window and...and... that's about it. Sweetie, this should be easy."

Ben couldn't contain his laughter any longer. Once again his wife had surmised their task of packing up as a simple—nothing-to-worry-about event and tied it up in a cute little bow. Or in Betsy's case, her rose-colored-glasses world took over.

"Why are you looking at me so strange?"

"Dear, you have no idea what it takes to downsize from a 2500 square foot home into an RV, which Larry told me is around 350 square feet."

This is going to be fun to watch. Ben said the last part to himself. Didn't want to get his bride riled up.

CHAPTER THREE

"Ben, I know what it takes to move lots of stuff into storage. And how to live without our things for over a year. Remember, we did it 11 years ago."

"Then I think we DO need to go get a storage unit."

This time Betsy gave her significant other 'the look' and walked to the sink. Coffee cups in hand. "Benjamin Stevenson you are scaring me. You need to reel it in. It hasn't even been 12 hours since you dropped your bombshell and we're packing up the house and moving tomorrow."

"That's a bit of an exaggeration."

"Could be, but we need to stop and pray. What does the Lord want us to do? When we're clear on that, we can proceed." Betsy tore off a paper towel and put it on the counter. "We can't move into *storage* tonight anyway."

"Why's that."

"Dinner. Remember? Oh, and I need to text Rose and find out what time."

Ben joined Betsy at the sink. "Guess I was moving a bit fast. Thanks for the reminder to pray. Don't want to get ahead of the man upstairs."

Betsy gave her husband a kiss then walked to their leather couch and texted her friend. Within a nano second a return text appeared, which she read out loud. "6:00 o'clock and bring Matilda."

Ben scooped their pooch up in his arms, "I won't let Baby hurt you. I promise."

"Put the dog down and quit filling her head with bad things about the Wilford's Shih Tzu. Baby isn't like that at all. She's a yapper, but...not evil," Betsy said as she looked over the back of the couch.

"No, I'd say that...that...thing is possessed."

Betsy chuckled at her husband's assessment, but wouldn't agree demons controlled the little thing and said as much. Sort of. "Ben, I think Baby is...is...crazed."

For a second time, in less than 10 minutes, laughter filled their living room. Ben came and sat on the couch next to Betsy and took her in his arms. "We better settle down and pray. It's 4:30 and we need to take the 'perfect' one out for her evening stroll."

That statement got them going again. Eventually they prayed, but Betsy guessed God Almighty thought they were both off their rockers. And she hoped He grinned from ear to ear.

~

Betsy almost jumped out of their car when Ben parked in front of the Wilford's house.

"I don't know why you're so excited. Larry already knows about our plans. You did tell Rose. Or did you forget?"

"I'm hoping for once she kept quiet and lets us tell him our big surprise."

Ben's raised eyebrows told her he didn't believe it could or would happen in a million years.

"You never know." Betsy rang the doorbell and had to agree with her hubby. Rose couldn't keep this information under wraps. Her chubby cheeks would have exploded.

The door swung open and Larry stood there in his normal attire: Texan sweatpants, Astros shirt and flip-flops. To finish off the ensemble, their dog Baby sat in his arms, yelping at the top of her lungs.

"Quiet down, mutt," Larry kept shushing the dog as he backed up to let them in.

"Mr. Wilford, I see you dressed up for—"

Rose stood behind her husband, motioning—in not too subtle of a way—to nip it. Which she did. And then it hit her: Rose hadn't told Larry about their big plans.

Will wonders never cease?

"Hi guys. Come on in. Dinner's ready and sitting on the table." Rose scooted them down the hallway into their dining room. "Oh, I fixed some food for Matilda too. It's in the kitchen."

Ben put their dog on the tile floor and the four of them sat down. Rose prayed what Betsy would classify as the quickest, most-to-the-point prayer she'd ever heard.

Larry glanced at his wife and cleared his throat. "What's the rush? They've tasted your lasagna before and it's nothing to write home about."

"Bobby Flay would tend to disagree. He said the other day on his show, '"This meal is for those special occasions with the ones we love.'" Rose smiled. "Anyway, you old coot, you wouldn't know if I served you shoe leather and called it Filet Mignon."

Everyone at the table got a chuckle out of Rose's retort. Larry, not as much, but he joined in. Then he took a couple of bites of his lasagna. After he swallowed he said, "This stuff is good."

"Thank you, dear." Rose moved her chair closer to Betsy and stared at her. "Now is one of you going to tell him what you're about to do?"

Betsy pointed to Ben. "This is all his. He needs to tell Larry."

"Lar, do you want to go with us to find an RV? We're going to sell everything and get on the road. Like you guys." Ben hummed a little of *On the Road Again* by Willie Nelson then picked up his fork and took another bite of lasagna.

Rose sprung out of her seat and gave Larry a kiss on his cheek. "Isn't this the greatest news you've ever heard?" She planted a second kiss on his forehead and sat back down again.

Betsy smiled until she spied Larry's expression. The shade of pale and the silence, which filled the Wilford's dining room, shouted only one thing—someone appeared less exuberant about their news than the other three at the table.

"Did you hear what I said?" Ben wiped his mouth with his napkin.

"Yes...I heard." Larry pushed his chair away from the table and got up. "We can go look at RVs, but we won't be traveling with you."

Ben laid his napkin on the table. "Why?"

"I...put...our RV...up for sale on Craigslist this morning." Larry went and sat down in his recliner.

As if on cue Baby let out a howl like never before. Betsy wanted to join her, but instead watched Rosie for her reaction. She didn't have long to wait.

"Please tell me I didn't hear you right?" Rose stood up. "You put OUR RV up for sale on—"

"I did. I'm done with messing with it. I already have someone interested in it."

Betsy gave Ben one of her 'you-need-to-do-something-quick' glances after witnessing Rose's clinched fists. A sure sign that the water's boiling and the teapot's about ready to explode.

"I don't know what to say, Larry." Ben leaned back in his chair.

"There is nothing any of you can say that will change my mind."

"Oh, I doubt that." Rose grabbed her plate and deposited it in the sink. "Larry, if you know what's good for you, you'll come over here and sit down. Betsy and Ben—you stay put. I'll be right back."

The loud clumping sound down their hallway told Bets she'd gone into their office. After some slamming of doors, her friend reappeared with a paper in her hand, which she waved in front of them like the American flag.

"Here is what will change your mind."

"What do you have, Rosebud?"

Oh there's more trouble brewing. Larry calls her this name when he's not a happy camper. Betsy almost choked. *Happy camper...*

"This little piece of paper is the title to our RV. Would you looky here—it has two names on it. And one of them ain't signing it."

"Betsy, we should help Rose clean up. Then head home." Ben got his plate and started toward the kitchen.

"I think that's a superb idea."

"I don't. Sit down."

Betsy and Ben almost collided with each other as they went to their chairs. Neither looked at the other.

"Sounds like today has been a day of bombshells." Rose put her hands on her hips. "I'd say Ben's news is a tad easier to swallow. But this. Larry, I don't know what you call this." Rose sat down. "The way you've been acting lately—I think you're coming down with... Low T."

All form of seriousness left the dining room after Rose's diagnosis (or her usual misdiagnosis) of her hubby. Betsy began to breathe a little easier. The disaster had been diverted. For the moment, at least. Or until Ben and her left to go home.

Oh, I'd love to be a mouse at the Wilford's later.

Larry dried his eyes and Betsy could tell he wanted to say something, but more laughter erupted. This went on for five minutes. Then Larry proclaimed. "Yes, my...dear you could be right. It is Low T. Low Tolerance for friends who decide almost too late...to get an RV."

"So does this mean you're not selling ours? Please. Please. Please."

Ben and Betsy got up and stood next to Larry and together they chanted, "Please. Please. Please."

Larry's head bobbed forward and back, indicating to Betsy they'd won. But she wanted to make sure. "Mr. Wilford, is that a yes?"

He sat straight in his chair and took out his phone. After pressing a few keys Larry answered, "You guys won this battle. I took our RV off Craigslist. Not sure why I put it on in the first place."

A choir of "thank yous" and hugs filled the yellow-striped dining room. Betsy gathered all the dishes and she and Rose went to work on cleaning the kitchen. They left the guys to plan the who's, what's, when and how's of the four of them traveling together in two RVs.

Betsy rinsed the dishes and Rose put them in the dishwasher. Her quietness and the extra banging told her that Rosie was still somewhat miffed. Betsy didn't blame her—surprises like they'd received today could almost buckle a person's knees.

Again Betsy wished she could sneak in later and see how this development unfolded. Rosie's 5 foot 2-inch frame might look innocent enough, but as the saying goes, "dynamite comes in small packages."

CHAPTER FOUR

Ben laughed when his wife told him on the way home that she'd like to be a mouse and visit the Wilford's later.

"Can you imagine?"

"No, Betsy, I can't. But with Rose's belief in a loving God and One who does miracles..." Ben laughed. "She will have prayed throughout the evening that He'd stop her from killing him after we left."

"Amen!"

"I'm sure the same thought crossed your mind with my big announcement this morning." Ben reached over and touched Betsy's hand. "Hon, I am sorry I didn't tell you what I'd been praying about."

"Me too."

"The only thing I can say, I kept it quiet...'cause I didn't believe another possibility existed out there for me. For us. That money isn't..." Ben left off the rest of the sentence.

"I'd say, "ye of little faith", but since I'm suffering from the same illness I can't say much."

"Huh."

"Promise you won't get mad if I bring up something?"

This time Ben noticed Betsy left words unsaid, but he knew the script and how it would read: *Rehashing junk that needed to stay buried.* That thought made his chest tighten and the urge to let his wife take over driving so he could walk home almost took over.

"Trust me, it's nothing bad."

"Go on, Bets, I won't get angry at my *mostest* favorite wife." Ben focused his eyes on the road ahead and hoped he sounded convincing.

"Yeah, right. Anyway, both of us need to quit doubting and trust Him for this change."

When he pulled into their driveway and hit the garage door opener, Ben waited for more wisdom, but nothing else came. Except for the sweet smile his wife gave him after he parked their car and shut it off. The one he'd seen more today than in a long time.

It is well with my soul.

Ben wasn't sure where the line of the hymn came from, but his heart doing backflips had more to do with Betsy's smile than the old song. He smiled and caressed her arm, which still rested on the center console.

"I love you, Bets."

"Love you too...and you better take Matilda for her walk. Looks like she's ready."

Ben's attention shifted from his wife to their pooch, who scampered around in the back seat. After she settled down, he grabbed Matilda's leash off the floorboard and put it on her.

While he stood at the end of the driveway, he heard the now-familiar sound in the empty lot. Matilda must have heard it too. Her whines and whimpers greeted the small herd of deer grazing in the open field next to their house.

Soon the animals would scatter for parts unknown, but for tonight Ben rejoiced in the gift God gave him a glimpse of.

Yes, Lord, it is well...it is well with my soul.

~

Oh how Betsy wanted to say more to Ben, but had kept it

short. For a change. No need to say more words. There'd been plenty in the past. No need to reflect on what should have happened. Or how someone should have handled it. No need to try and explain something that's unexplainable.

Smile. Love. Healing.

"A ways to go, but we're on the right track."

"Are you talking to yourself again?" Ben tapped on the side window.

Betsy opened her car door and stepped out, realizing she'd sat inside the car the whole time Ben took Matilda for her last walk of the evening.

"Were you sleeping in there?" Ben reached down and let Matilda off her leash.

"No. Just contemplating life."

"Is that so? How about we 'contemplate' a treat of some kind?"

The minute Ben mentioned 'the word', Matilda skipped around again. No amount of talking would calm her down.

Ben opened the door into their house. "What time is it, Mats?"

The dog raced inside and Ben and Betsy followed. When they got to the kitchen, their precious pooch laid on the rug, waiting for her bone.

"Don't know when she learned that, but it's adorable." Betsy got a Milkbone out of the cabinet.

"Unlike another dog we know."

Betsy swatted at his arm as she went by him. "Be nice."

"You want some ice cream?"

"No. Any Weight Watcher treats?" Betsy covered her mouth then said, "T.r.e.a.t.s. in there?"

Ben handed her a frozen two-inch square brownie. Within seconds the cellophane wrapping littered the counter and Betsy had consumed half of the chocolate dessert. "Yumm. Yumm. Yumm."

"Do you even taste that thing?" Ben asked while he licked his spoon, making his question almost unrecognizable.

"You're not supposed to talk when your mouth is full." Betsy stuffed the rest of the brownie in her mouth and said. "Didn't your mama ever teach you that?"

Ben's one eyebrow lifted. "I'm not sure what you said, but what I could make out—the answer is 'yes'."

After it appeared her hubby licked the finish off his bowl, Betsy watched him sit it down for Matilda to have a tiny taste.

Is there anything left, Mats?

Betsy kept quiet. No need to spoil a father/daughter moment. Instead she went to lounge on the couch, putting her feet up on the ottoman. Ben joined her a short time later, scooching in as close as he possibly could. Until Matilda entered the picture.

Without an invitation, or a spot to land, she jumped up and took her place right in the middle of their laps.

"Remember when I said I didn't want kids, Ben? Said they'd come between us." Betsy made a Vanna White move with her hand. "See, I was right."

"Oh, Mom. You know you love me."

"I do. Both of you." Betsy tousled Ben's blond hair, making it stand on end. Then she popped up off the couch and said, "I'm cold. How about I turn on the fireplace?"

"Matilda and my cuddling aren't enough for you?"

"Yes. But I love to watch the flames...even if they're fake."

"Oh, you do know how to set a mood." Ben moved Matilda over, giving Betsy room to sit down again.

"Well they are...plastic. Or something like that. But they reflect as if they're real."

"Kind of sounds like Hollywood."

Betsy sat up. "We do get off track, don't we?"

"A little. Anyway, I've been thinking, Bets. The first thing I need to do tomorrow is finish filling out the papers to get this retirement thing going—since I heard it can take two to three months."

"That long? Can't we leave tomorrow?"

"No. Wish we could, but we'll need that long to get all of this stuff packed, sold or donated." He motioned around their living room with his right hand.

"Ain't that the truth? And it's too much to think about tonight." Betsy stood up and turned their fireplace off. "Come on, Matilda. Tell your papa it's time to go to bed."

"Already?"

Betsy grabbed Ben's hand and they headed to the bedroom. Her phone beeped on the way. Laughter filled the hallway as she read Rose's text out loud.

"No bloodshed at the Wilford's. And it's RV or Bust. Excited to get "on the road" with you guys. Idea: let's call ourselves the *Early Birds.*

Betsy texted back, "Love it and love you!!!" Then she plugged her phone in and remembered she still needed to talk to her mom.

Tomorrow.

CHAPTER FIVE

W hen 4:30 pm hit, Ben couldn't get out of the door and into his car quick enough. And call this day a name he couldn't say in public. What got him the most—he'd never found time to work on the retirement paperwork. Lunch, when he wanted to work on it, a complete blur.

Ben told Betsy that morning, "I'll be able to get the papers finished in the next couple days and submit them Wednesday."

Now the end of the week made more sense, since he'd brought a briefcase full of work with him, with a tomorrow deadline.

Ben's car phone went off. "Hey, Larry."

"Did I catch you at a good time?"

"I'm heading home." Ben backed out of his parking space and turned right on Research Forest Drive.

"Wanted to say, you guys sure surprised me with your news."

"I could say the same."

"I plead the 5th and remember I'm suffering from Low T." They both laughed.

"Your wife's a funny lady."

"Ya. Want her?"

"No, I'm happy with mine." Ben glanced to his left before merging on the feeder road.

"So am I. Love my Rosie."

When Larry finished his sentence, Ben didn't hear anything else, so he asked, "You still there?"

"Ben, I'm curious. What changed your mind?"

This time Ben didn't say anything. He wanted to say the words that would convince him to finish filling out the papers and submit them. "Larry, I'm done with all of it. It's time I put God and family first in my life."

"Glad you came to your senses."

"But until my last day, which I don't know when that is, I have a boatload of work to finish up. Brought most of it home with me tonight. Hope Betsy doesn't need me for anything."

"Don't count on it. If she's like Rose...anyway, a briefcase full of work should be incentive enough to get the heck out of your job."

Ben nodded then realized Larry couldn't see him. "Thanks for listening...and for not selling your rig."

"No problem. Ben, I've got a piece of advice: Relax. Don't want you to have a heart attack before we take off. Talk at ya later."

Ben clicked off his Bluetooth when he pulled into the garage. Then he shut the door, only to reopen it again when he saw Betsy and Matilda come out the door of the house.

"Hey, how are my two favorite girls?"

"Pretty good. This one's excited to see you." Betsy put Matilda down before she leapt from her arms and handed Ben her leash. "Here you go." She gave him a kiss and went back inside.

Matilda did her duty then Ben stopped and got his briefcase out of the back seat of his SUV. He reclosed the garage door before going inside the house. The minute the door closed behind him, Betsy yelled from the direction of the kitchen.

"I'll be right there." Ben let Matilda off her leash and heard Betsy say something else.

He thought about saying, "What?" But chose to leave the long-distance conversation until he saw her smiling face. He dropped off his work in his office/man cave and took a few deep breaths, hoping they'd help him relax.

After a minute, he'd calmed down. On his way to the kitchen, Betsy must have heard him and said, "You'll never believe the deal I found on a storage unit today." She told him the amount then picked up a spoon and stirred something in the crockpot. "We need to check it out tonight."

Ben almost laughed. He'd told Larry he hoped Betsy wouldn't have other plans for him this evening—on top of everything else he had to do.

"Are you sure they said $65.00 for a 10" x 15". Normally they're $80.00 to $100.00."

Betsy tossed him the piece of paper she'd written the information on. "If we sign for a year, it's $65.00 a month and we need to do it by tomorrow at 7:00 pm."

God himself held Ben's tongue with both hands, keeping him from saying a retort that wouldn't be conducive to peace on earth. All the while Betsy chattered on. Not letting him say anything.

"It's such a good deal and look at what I got packed to—"

"Can you give me a minute, Bets." He picked up the paper off the table she'd written the notes on. "If this is what you said it is, I don't have to do anything right this very second. Let me sit down. Please."

Betsy left him alone, which surprised him. In the past, *oh, there are those words he hated,* she wouldn't leave him be. Whatever had happened in her day—she wanted to share or read to him one of the stories she'd written and would submit...after his nod of approval.

No breathing room.

But today she did. Ben laid his head back and must have dozed off.

"Hon, I made you some hot tea. Supper's about ready. Not sure it's eatable, but..."

Ben almost knocked the tea out of his wife's hand when he sat up in his chair. "Betsy, I am so tired of you putting down your cooking and ANYTHING else you do. Give me a break."

The glare Betsy gave him before she went to the kitchen could have curled his hair if he had more than an inch to curl. Ben prayed the Lord would rewind the last five seconds of his stupidness.

Nothing happened. Ben took that as a sign to figure out how to get his size 10½s out of his mouth. Then it hit him.

Humor.

He got on his knees and "walked" all the way over to where Betsy stood at the stove. His almost 60-year-old knees screamed the whole way across the tile floor, but he had to do something.

When Ben got to the stove, he put his head on the side of Betsy's leg and clasped his hands in a praying stance. "Bets, please forgive me. I'm a jerk."

No response from his wife while she stirred the crockpot again. Then she moved to the refrigerator. So did Ben. Still on his knees.

Is that laughter I hear? Ben could only hope, so he stayed put. "Would you...take...these to...the...table?"

Ben took the two bottles of dressing Betsy handed him. Then she closed the fridge and added. "And when you get back—"

He couldn't look up at her or he'd lose it too. "Sure thing." Ben made his trek and put everything on their glass table, without incident. This go around, his knees cried out in pain, but he didn't care.

When he turned to go back to the kitchen, he spotted Betsy. Or he should say—he saw her backside. The rest of her stood in their pantry. The noises coming out of the tiny room resembled nothing he'd heard before, but they made him chuckle.

Ben decided his knees had seen enough action for one day and he sat right in the middle of the kitchen floor. Matilda came over and joined in the fun, licking him square in the face and Ben let her have at it.

And, he couldn't remember when he'd been the first to calm

the storm, but it felt good.

CHAPTER SIX

"What you gawking at?"

"You." Betsy shut the pantry door and stared at him. "And...I'm ...wondering...how long does one have to stay in prison for justifiable homicide?"

"I don't know, but if you help me up I'll google it."

Betsy walked over to Ben and held her hand out. When he got up she said, "You do know you're nuts. That's all I can say."

"I know. Now who are you going to kill?"

Betsy took off her apron and flung it in his direction. "Someone I love very much."

"Rosie?"

This made his wife laugh. "Heavens no. She's my saving grace. It's you."

"Me?"

"Don't act so innocent." Betsy went over to get bowls out of the cabinet. "Oh, by the way, the only thing that granted you a stay of execution. Your comedic routine. Mr. B. That's got to be the funniest thing you've ever done. For as long as I've known you."

"Glad you liked my performance." Ben stepped away from

the stove. "The one before it...not quite as stellar."

"I'll have to agree with you. But I did hit you, again, with my exuberance the minute you waltzed in the door."

"That's no excuse for taking my day out on you, even if it was a doozer."

"I'm sorry, bud. Why don't you sit down and I'll bring over the 'delicious' tidbit I've cooked up?" The minute the words hit the open air she put her hand over her mouth. "Sorry."

She noticed Ben didn't say anything to her latest comment. Didn't need to—he'd said enough the first time and it still stung. And Betsy had to accept his apology and go on. Not carry it for days like she normally did.

Betsy grabbed the bowl of salad, the red beans and rice and sat them in the middle of the table. "Dig in."

Her hubby sat in his normal spot and appeared pleased with the meal she'd cooked. She sat down and took a spoon full.

Hey, maybe I should watch the Food Network more often. Rosie sure raves about it.

"This is wonderful, Bets."

Everything in her wanted to shout, "You're just being nice after our fight." Instead she changed the subject and said, "So...how was your day?"

~

For the next 20 minutes Ben ranted and raved about his Monday. Then he sat back in his chair. "On top of everything, Betsy, I brought work home and I'm not sure I can get it all done. Along with getting the last of the retirement paperwork filled out."

"Is this a good time for me to add my two cents?"

"Take your chances." He reached out and squeezed Betsy's hand.

"This decision to sell everything isn't supposed to add stress, but I can see it has. Already. In three days." She smiled at her husband. "About storage, I don't need you to look at it tonight. It'll work for what we need."

"You don't want me to go check it out?"

"No, I'll make sure it's not sitting in a valley, it's air-conditioned and not too far away."

"I'm impressed." Ben stood up and went to stand next to Betsy. "I do have one request—when you are packing during the day—don't pack everything. We'll be living here for three to six more months. It still needs to be livable."

Betsy chuckled.

"What part of that is funny? Remember, we can take our time and go through things. No need to rush." Ben gave her a sideways glance.

"You bet. Now don't you have work to do?"

Ben and his faithful companion, Matilda, headed down the hallway. But before they got too far he stopped next to their dining room. "You did all this today?"

"Sure did. I even had time to submit a story to *Chicken Soup*."

Ben couldn't believe all the boxes he saw piled against the far wall. *She got all this done in one day. And still had time to do other things.* His harsh comments from earlier came back to him. Almost like a punch in the stomach. How could he have been so cruel?

His short fuse never took into account the things Betsy did right. As usual, she had embraced this new idea of his, and any others he'd had over their 32 years of marriage. Never questioning. Enthusiastically joining in with wherever Ben wanted to go.

"And the sooner we can do this, the better."

"Ben, are you talking to yourself?"

"You caught me. And I'm going in right now and get those retirement papers done. All of them. Mark my word, you'll be able to send out our big announcement blog no later than tomorrow." He jumped up and clicked his heels.

"That's why I love you."

Those words spurred Ben on for the next three hours. He answered questions, went over plans for a new high rise and signed letters. When he closed his briefcase and picked up his retirement papers, he checked to see if he'd left his eyeballs on his desk. They ached and so did his lower back.

He turned off his office light and flipped on the hall light. When he did, Ben almost collided with Betsy. "Hey. What are you doing? I thought you'd be long gone by now."

"Got going on a movie and texting Rose."

"Why didn't you call her?"

"Takes too much time."

"And texting doesn't."

"No. With text we stay on subject. Just so you know, Rose is coming over tomorrow."

"That took you two hours?"

"No, silly. I watched a movie. I only texted her a couple of times."

"Let me see your phone. I bet you guys went on for days." Ben tried to snatch Betsy's phone as he took the short cut through the kitchen to get to their bedroom.

"And I'd say that's an invasion of privacy." Betsy caught up with him and gave Ben a hug from behind.

He put the papers down he'd been carrying under his arm and took her hands and turned her to face him. "Now where is your phone?"

Betsy broke free from his grasp and ran. He chased Betsy into the bedroom, forgetting retirement, selling their home or any thought of an RV. The only thing on his mind—how much he loved Elizabeth Lynn Stevenson.

~

"What's this?" Betsy picked up a stack of papers the next morning and yawned.

"Your ticket out of here?"

"Don't you mean, 'Our ticket out of here?' I'm not going without you."

"I'd like to see you drive a big Ford dually with a 5th wheel behind it." Ben came over and ruffled her hair.

"I could say the same for you. Have you ever driven one?"

"Can't be any worse than the old motorhome we had." Ben picked up the soy milk and poured it on his cereal then walked over to the table. "And, Bets, those are the retirement papers you're holding in your hand. Signed. Sealed. And to be delivered to Mr. Greenspan today."

Betsy went over and hugged Ben and congratulated him. His smile assured her everything would work out fine. Her hubby went back to his Cheerios and Houston Chronicle. She went to the laundry room to put in a load of whites.

Would it all be okay, Benjamin? What if...she didn't know where it came from? But trepidation hung on her like a thick, winter cloak, making her doubt their grand plan. For the umpteenth time.

The verses in Proverbs she loved came to mind. *"Trust in the Lord with all your heart and lean not on your own understanding; in all your ways acknowledge him, and he will make your paths straight."*

"Even in an RV, Father?" Betsy laughed and walked out of the laundry room, leaving the pile of whites for later. "I said that out loud, didn't I?"

"Yes, you did." Ben took his bowl to the sink and held his hand out. "Papers please. Gotta run. Don't work too hard today."

"No worries there." Betsy and Matilda followed Ben to their back door and gave him a kiss. "Have a great day. Love ya!"

CHAPTER SEVEN

Betsy took Matilda out, forgetting she hadn't put shoes on. "Hurry up, Mattie. Mama's toes are a little chilled." Their pooch appeared uninterested, and tugging on the leash at 6:30 in the morning didn't rush things along.

Standing in the grass somewhat helped, but now her feet were wet. Ben had watered. *I do love South Texas. Beginning of May—and you need to water your grass.*

Matilda finished and they came in and Betsy closed the garage door. On her way to the door to the inside she glanced down at her outfit. The University of Colorado sweatpants and a Denver Bronco shirt.

"I might live in Texas, but my heart's in Colorado." Betsy took a gander at her attire. "And, I'm also starting to look like Larry."

She decided mimicking a 68-year-old's getup couldn't be good, but for the moment that's what she had on. Betsy opened the door and Matilda ran in, straight for her morning fare.

Betsy did the same, grabbing a bagel out of the fridge then sat down at the table, waiting for the familiar beep on her phone. The one where Rose would tell her she's running late.

'The Journey Begins' tone sounded and Betsy smiled at the

sound of the brand new ringtone. Before it went to voicemail, she swiped the screen and said, "Hello Rosie."

"I wanted to let you know I'm on my way. I've got one more stop to make."

"Don't you dare?" Betsy threatened her friend.

"You know you want one."

"Yes, I do...but my thighs have sworn off Randy's Donuts."

"So have mine, but the smell of their apple fritters always overrides it. I'm putty in their hands. Bye. See ya in a few minutes."

Betsy hit the 'end call'. Didn't wait for Rose to do it, since she tended to forget to turn her phone off. All the time. One day they'd both forgotten and her friend heard a heated argument Betsy had with Ben, concerning her writing career.

Or lack thereof. *That one was fun to explain. And they still want to go RVing with us.*

Rose arrived in record time with hot apple fritters in hand. Matilda met her at the door, wanting to see what Rosie brought.

"Mats, let her in the door. I'll give you some later."

Betsy put a couple of pieces in the dog's bowl then went and topped off her coffee cup and poured one for Rose.

"Don't give me any. I'm cutting out caffeine for a while."

"Why?" Betsy could feel another diagnosis coming and Rose came through.

"I'm suffering from I.B.S. Irritable B—"

"I know what I.B.S. stands for and I'm not talking about that area of the body when I'm relishing one of my favorite foods." Betsy took a bite and sat back and slowly chewed the fritter.

"Anyway, WebMD says to lay off caffeine and alcohol if you suffer from it."

"Rosie, I wouldn't worry about the al...keee...hol. The little bit of wine we get at communion isn't enough to get a gnat drunk."

"I'm just telling you what the website said." Rose picked up her apple fritter and pointed it at Betsy. "And, don't give me any of your lip."

Betsy tried to grab the fritter from her friend's hand, but

Rose's movements made it impossible to get a good shot at it. This made Betsy laugh and it got Rosie started. At one point one of her snorts made a sleeping Matilda startle, which brought more laughter ringing through Betsy's eat-in kitchen.

"Sooooooo. You said on your text the other night. You didn't kill Lar…"

"Oh, that's old news."

Betsy stared at Rose. "You not killing your husband for almost selling your RV is 'old news'?" She touched her friend's forehead. "Ouch. You've got a fever."

"Another symptom of —"

"Rosie, we're not going down the tummy-trouble highway. I'm simply asking, as a friend, what happened?"

"The Lord happened. After you two left I wanted to cut Larry's legs off and beat him with the stumps. However, I weighed the options, with the Father's guidance, of course, and decided to have fun with my 'whole' honey."

After Betsy quit laughing she asked, "Did he say why he put your RV up for sale?"

"He repeated what he said the other night. But there's more to it. Those casino games have got a hold of my man."

"I'm not sure of that, but I did love his expression when Ben told him we wanted to buy an RV."

"Priceless. Now don't you think it's time to get busy?"

That's exactly what they did for the next two hours. Rose made boxes and Betsy filled them. At 1:45 Rose put up the 'time-out' sign and said, "I'm pooped. Let's take a break."

"Great idea." Betsy surveyed the scene in front of them. They'd gone a little too hog-wild and Ben would wonder if Hurricane Ike hit their home again. "We better slow down and take some of these boxes we're donating to the Pregnancy Assistance Center."

"They're sure to make loads of money for their thrift shop with all these things."

One item Betsy loaded into Rose's truck wouldn't be put in the store to sell. The wooden rocking chair, she'd inherited from an old friend years before, would go to one of their new moms.

"You're fine with this. Right?" Rose tied a rope around the one leg of the rocker.

"I've prayed about it and know it'll get a good home."

Ben and she had made peace on the subject of not having kids many years ago. The Lord had chosen them to bless other people's kids instead. But for some reason, she couldn't part with the rocking chair.

Until now. Time to clean out and start fresh. Betsy pulled on the rope to check if it was tight then put two boxes Rose had brought out next to it.

"You're sure about this?" Rose touched the rocking chair and asked again.

"The center will have much more use for it than it sitting in a storage unit."

~

When they came in the door of the pregnancy center, carrying the weathered rocking chair, the women behind the desk stood up and one said. "Please tell me you're donating this beautiful thing?"

Betsy nodded. "I'm so glad you'll be able to use it."

"You have no idea." Both women said it as they came around the counter and gave Betsy a hug and thanked her.

"You're welcome. I couldn't be happier with my decision to give it away." Betsy turned to Rose. "You ready?"

They left with a chorus of "thank yous" as they walked to Rose's truck. Rose backed out and got on the feeder road and stayed on it past Betsy's street.

"Are you going to where I think you're going?"

"Yep."

"Sonic, here we come."

They arrived and Rose ordered for them. "We'll take two Route 44 Cherry Limeades and a small order of Tater tots. Please."

"You know me too well." Betsy reached for her purse.

"It's on me. You deserve a treat after what you just did. Are you glad you gave the chair away?"

"You have no idea. The last memory of it for me is rocking in it for hours and praying our marriage would survive."

"It worked."

"That's why I knew it was time to let go and let someone use it for what it was intended for—rocking a babe to sleep."

"You're going to make me cry."

"No need for tears. The Lord knew what He was doing when he didn't give us our own little one. I would have left him or her in Wal-Mart and then wondered what I did with them. Can you imagine that phone call?"

"Girl, I don't know about you." Rose fumbled in her wallet, coming out with a five-dollar bill. "Bets, I do love your sense of humor."

"That's why we get along so well."

"Speaking of getting along—have you told the Bible study group or your writer friends your news?"

"No, I plan to when I send out my blog. You know me—I like to keep people on their toes."

"I'll second that...oh, you are going to tell your mom before then, aren't you?"

"I tried to call—oh, there's our food."

The roller-skating server, named Betty, handed Rose their drinks and sack. Rose picked up the money off the floor, where it had fallen, and said, "Thanks, dear. Keep the change."

"All of it?"

"Every bit of it."

"Thanks and hurry back." Betty waved as she rolled off to help other customers.

"Now back to your mom."

"I tried to call her on Saturday morning, but she didn't answer. Then it was too late when we got home from your place. Sunday and Monday came and went. Figured she'd call me back." Betsy picked up her phone to put a reminder in.

"Why don't we call her right now?"

"Good idea. I'll put it on Speaker."

"Hi Bets."

"Hello Fran. It's Rosie. How's Florida?"

"I'm loving it. Wish Betsy's dad could have seen this."

"Mom, I'm not sure he would have enjoyed hanging out at the pool."

"Hon, we do so much more than that. If your husband ever took you on vacation, you'd find out what I do down here. What's going on with you two?"

"Larry and me...boring. On the other hand...Ben and—"

"I'll take it from here. I do have some news. Are you sitting down, Mom?"

"Do I need to?"

Rose took the phone out of Betsy's hand. "Might be a good idea, Fran."

Bets retrieved her phone and said, "Ben told me on Saturday he wants to sell the house, buy an RV and travel."

Complete silence filled Rose's vehicle then Betsy's mom said, "He's taking you and Matilda with him, isn't he?"

Betsy almost choked on her Cherry Limeade. "Of course he is."

"Good. Then you can come down here and hang out with me. All of you. Rose and Larry too. You can park your RVs at the resort I'm at. I'll send you the info."

"That would be great."

"Betsy, I'm sorry I gotta run. Pickle ball is about ready to start. Great news. Talk to you soon."

"Bye, Mom from me and Rose." Betsy talked into her now-dead phone.

"Your mom is a pip."

"That she is."

Betsy's mom never ceased to amaze her. An 88-year-old who could pass for 65, loved life to the fullest. Something she, herself, needed to do more of—once they retired. Again the thought of living in an RV full-time sent her almost shaking out of her skin.

But the fact her mother had asked IF Ben would take his wife with him. What an absurd question? Betsy had never told her mother they'd separated three years before.

Didn't want to worry her. Still it bothered Betsy she hadn't shared with the one person always on her team. No matter what.

"You ready to head back to the house? We've been at Sonic long enough."

"Matilda probably thinks I ran away from home."

"Larry and Baby are napping. I could leave home and neither would miss me."

"They wouldn't know what to do without you." Betsy reached over and touched her friend's shoulder. "Anyway, I need to run to the storage unit. Pay up before the 'deal of a lifetime' is no more."

When Rose parked in front of the house, Betsy got out and ran over to the driver's side and opened the door. "Let's get this over with."

"Sometimes, Bets, your humor isn't so great."

Betsy watched as Rose got out of her truck and came over and gave Betsy the hug she expected and could count on every time they left each other's company. This one occurred right in the middle of her street.

"Now, Bets, don't you feel better knowing that if we never see each other again, this is your last memory of me?"

Betsy laughed and said. "You're morbid."

"But you still love me." Rose waved as she hopped back in her dually and drove off.

"With all my heart, dear. With all my heart."

Betsy unlocked the front door and let Matilda out of her crate to go outside. Then she put her pooch in her prison again and headed to A Plus Storage. The pile of paperwork from the storage place reminded her of the ones they carried home after closing on a house.

Sign your life away and get keys to your new abode. In this case a lock and two keys. Two more things to keep track of. Then a brilliant idea hit her—put one key in each of their vehicles. Whichever one they brought to storage, they'd always have a key.

Sometimes I do amaze myself. She had another thought. One concerning her writing life. Betsy needed to get home, sit in her chair and work on the blog some more—before she posted the big event.

CHAPTER EIGHT

"Thank goodness it's Friday. Bets, I'm home." He heard
something when he came in the front door, but couldn't figure it
out. Upon further investigation, the noise came from Matilda. "I
wondered why you and Mom didn't meet me at the door. "Do I
have news for her?"

Ben opened the latches on their dog's crate and out she shot.
Not sure her excitement came from seeing him or him getting her
out of captivity. He let Matilda run off some steam then he picked
her up and carried her into the bedroom.

"You sit right there while I change." He put her right in the
middle of their king-size bed and went to his closet. First thing off:
his tie and jacket. *Not too much longer.*

The rest of the clothes Ben took off went in the dirty clothes
or hung on hangers. He snatched a t-shirt and pair of jeans off the
shelf. When he finished getting dressed he went to stand next to
the bed. "Mattie, it won't be long now. Just three or four more
months...or unless I decide to use my vacation days and get out of
there sooner."

"Who's getting out of what sooner?"

Ben hadn't heard his wife, but grabbed Betsy the minute she

stepped into their room. He couldn't wait. "What would you say if I told you we could be on the road in three and a half months, if everything works out." He twirled her around a couple of times.

"I'd say we've got work to do."

"What you and Rosie got done this week looks like we're ready for something."

"The storage unit is awaiting our arrival. Oh, and why I'm late. I had to go sign a piece of paper they forgot to give me the other day."

"Before I forget—I'm sorry it took until Friday, but you can send your blog. Or whatever you do with it. The boss got back and I turned in the papers. I put my retirement date down as of August 22."

Betsy's hollering drowned out anything else he might have said. When they bought the house, the builder said they used double-pane windows. If not, he hoped their neighbors wouldn't call the cops from the joyful noises coming from his wife.

"Congratulations...and it's about time. I've had a hard time sitting on this news for almost a week."

"You done good, my dear." Ben chuckled. "Your badgering helped too. But now the fun begins. How about we put some boxes in my car and make a trip to storage."

"You start. I want to send my blog." Betsy left the bedroom, with Matilda on her heels.

Must be supper time.

Ben followed the duo out the door, stopping in the kitchen to get their pooch some food. Afterward, he picked up two boxes off the kitchen table, marked 'craft...storage', and carried them out to the garage.

Or as Ben had started calling it—the toss-everything-you-don't-know-what-to-do-with room. Along with all of the tools, lawn equipment, trash/recycle bins. On and on and on. A job he looked forward to as much as he would a root canal.

This weekend. That's my plan.

"Ben, I've got an idea."

"Could you enter a room before you start talking?"

"Can't help it. The conversation in my head has to come out."

"What's your idea?"

"Glad you asked." Betsy walked to Ben's SUV and opened the back door. "Since we have to eat something, why don't we stop at Taco Bell on our way?"

"Now you're talking." Ben glanced at the doorway. "Looks like Matilda is ready to go."

"Always."

He piled boxes in his vehicle, but made sure he gave their 13-pound princess plenty of room to breathe. Ben closed the hatch. "We're almost overflowing."

"You can give me something to carry."

Ben stopped and stared at her. "How would you eat your 7-Layer Burrito?"

"Got a point there. Let me get my purse."

Ben pulled out of the garage after Betsy got in. On their way down their street, their neighbor waved. "Oh, I've got to remember to tell Jeremy what's going on. I'll do it this weekend."

At Taco Bell he ordered Betsy her normal. He stuck with what he always ordered too. A stuffed burrito. The machine squawked and Ben hoped the person said what he ordered. He took a ten out of his wallet and moved forward.

Ben paid and pulled in one of the parking spots. In between bites he told Betsy about his boss's reaction to him turning in his retirement paperwork.

"Bets, I've never seen anyone turn so red. I didn't know if I should run and get the defibrillator thing off the wall. Or wait."

"Did he finally say something?"

"I wish I had a tape of it. When he figured out it was true, I wasn't sure he'd survive." Ben put down his burrito and spoke in a monotone voice. "Ben, you know I don't like practical jokes. After getting off of a 21-hour flight...this isn't funny."

"Betsy, he got home Wednesday. Today is Friday. Anyway, he kept looking at me. I didn't know what to do, except get up and leave his office."

"Did you?" This time Betsy put her burrito down and eyed

him over her glasses.

"No, but I wanted to. He asked me "why" at least five times. I told him, 'Sir, I've written out the reasons in the paperwork. It's time I spend more time with my wife." Ben looked at Matilda. "Mats, I didn't bring you into the conversation—didn't want him to send for security."

"Probably a good thing, but it sounds like you handled it like a pro."

"Hope so. At least I'm not running out on him. He's got me for a few more months." Heartburn set in when he said those words. "Want an ice cream to finish off your delicious meal?"

"Sure."

Ben pulled around again and ordered two soft-serve cones. He handed Betsy hers and then headed out to storage. By the time they got to the unit, his heartburn had diminished. "Mats, you want the rest of Dad's ice cream?"

Her ears perked up and Ben scooped out a spoonful for their furry daughter. While he ate the cone, she licked the spoon clean. "Now it's time to get busy."

"Yippee." Betsy took the key and lock out of their ashtray. "Here you go."

"Glad you thought to do that." Ben got out of his SUV and opened the hatch. "We'll stack these against the wall. Next trip we'll bring your cedar chest."

Betsy took the box Ben handed her and deposited it where he'd instructed. Ben went in behind her and put the box down. "Two down—three thousand to go."

"Such a funny guy."

Humor wasn't his intent when he said it. Ben eyed the empty 10 by 15 unit. Looked like enough to hold everything. Then they went home and brought two more loads. After the last load, Ben stood in the middle of the unit and questioned, "Why didn't we go with a 20 by 20?"

"Again I say, 'ye of little faith.' Get busy and work your magic." Betsy pointed at her cedar chest. "Always want to build a base for the boxes to sit on." Betsy mimicked him to perfection.

"Oh, you're the funny one now."

"Are you ready to move the chest or not?" Betsy smiled and tapped her foot.

"Yes, ma'am."

They moved it into place. On the far wall.

In all of their other three moves, he'd found putting the cedar chest as the base worked the best. Solid—no shifting. Like a foundation when he built a building.

"This will stay put. For however long we're in storage."

Betsy walked over and swatted Ben's arm. "How about we don't worry about that right now. I'm a tired pup. I'm sure Matilda is ready to get out of the back of the car too."

"Can't do anymore tonight anyway. Need my ladder to stack more on top of those boxes." Ben gave the middle section a push and he could see no movement from any of them. This made him happy. "Looking good."

"Never a doubt in my mind. I'm thinking the 10 by 15 will be fine."

"I'll have to agree with you."

"See you tomorrow, Mr. Storage." Betsy gave one of her waves, fit for the queen, as they left.

Ben chuckled as he turned on the feeder road.

"You laugh, but we might as well name it. We'll be spending more time here than at home in the next three months."

CHAPTER NINE

How true Betsy's words became. Each day for the next week, when Ben came home from work, she had more things boxed up for them to take to storage. Also, along one wall in the living room, she'd left three boxes open for more things: Throw away. Donate. Give away.

"Give away." Betsy almost did a happy dance when she picked up the empty box.

"What are you talking about?"

"This reminds me. We should take our furniture over to our Bible study's garage sale they're having in June. It's sure to bless the people who need it most."

"Great idea. We'll stick it in storage until then."

"If you haven't noticed, Ben, we're running out of space"

"How about we talk about this tomorrow. I've got work to do in my office." Ben walked down the hallway. Halfway there he stopped and turned. "Bets, have you checked on your blog this week? You haven't said anything about the comments."

Blog...Comments...Oh my goodness!

Her hubby's remark made Betsy forget all about moving, storage or boxing anything up. "No, but I'm going to check right now."

When Betsy sat down at her desk and typed in her blog address, she almost fell out of her chair. Over 100 comments popped up.

If there's that many here—what about Facebook?

Betsy hadn't touched social media after she hit the send button last Thursday or Friday night. "Whatever day it was."

A click on the Facebook icon told her she needed to pay attention to those who followed her blog and she needed to write her own comment.

This very minute.

But before she did that, she needed to talk to Rose. Ask her why she, of all people, kept her mouth shut about all these goings-on. Betsy picked up her phone then put it down on her desk. "No, girlfriend, stay on task."

"Bets, I can hear you."

Ben's voice came from across the hall and made Betsy want to take a break from the toil of answering all of her fans. She laughed. "Who am I kidding? They're writing 'cause they're as shocked as you were when Ben dropped his bombshell."

"You sure are entertaining yourself in here." Ben came to the double doors of her office.

"Mr. B. come over here and take a seat."

He did and Betsy proceeded to tell him about all the feedback from their announcement. "Look at this one. It's from Janet. One of my writer friends, 'I'm so jealous. ☺ But you two deserve this. The Lord is blessing you. Go have the time of your life. Live the dream He's put in your heart.'" Betsy wiped away a tear. "Hon, they are all like this one."

Ben hugged Betsy. "Does seem He's giving us back the years we battled with each other. A new beginning."

She could only nod her head. The lump in her throat made it impossible to say anything else.

Yes, a new beginning. Bless You, Father!

~

Saturday morning Ben woke up at the first hint of daylight. As hard as he tried, he couldn't go back to sleep. Unlike the love of his life, Betsy's steady breathing, with an occasional snore thrown in, told him she'd visited La La Land and do not disturb her.

If I turn over?

That didn't do anything, but move Matilda over a few inches. Ben gave up and slipped out of bed as quiet as he could and got dressed in his tattered jeans and old white t-shirt. Off to the garage, after he stopped to heat up a cup of coffee.

A sore back and more boxes than he knew what to do with, Ben could check the garage off the list Betsy made him. He went inside the house. About halfway down the hallway, Ben heard his wife say, "Hey, maybe when we get on the road...I'll become a chef."

He tried to stop from laughing, but didn't succeed. "You become a cook. Someone who's always putting down their cooking. Not sure it'll happen."

"Why do you always seem to pick the most inopportune times to walk in on me?"

"I do have a knack for that, don't I?" Ben picked up Matilda. "You can always say you're talking to our pooch."

"Guess I could." Betsy wrapped up a coffee cup and put it in a box in front of her.

"All I can say, dear." Ben crossed the kitchen and gave his wife a hug. "You do brighten my day."

Betsy gave him a peck on the cheek before she leaned on the counter. "Making much progress in the garage?"

"Come see." He took her hand and led her to the area of his blood, sweat and tears the last two hours.

"Amazing!"

Every shelf he'd built stood empty. Boxes he'd filled stood against the wall, ready for their trip to storage. The only things left was their lawn equipment, which still hung on the south wall of their garage. He'd ask their realtor if the new owners wanted any of them.

That IS when they hired a realtor. We forgot to add that to our list.

"Looks great out here. Are we ready to go to storage?"

"Whenever you are." Ben started to load up his vehicle.

~

When Ben lifted the door to their storage unit, Betsy remembered their conversation from the night before. "Sweetie, we have run out of space. Our furniture is NOT going to fit in here. Even for one day."

"Do we need to go through some of these boxes?" He took down a box labeled 'kitchen' and started going through it. "Let's make sure we're not keeping stuff we don't need. Or could donate."

"I've got a better idea."

"I'm ready."

Betsy saw her hubby had braced himself. His stance and expression read, "My right-brained wife can and does come up with wacky-tabakky ideas."

"Trust me. This won't hurt." Betsy smiled. "Since we move some of the same things every time we come, why not get another unit? Put the items we're going to sell and the tools you need to go through in that one. It'll give us more room to get organized."

Ben gave her an "I'm-thinking" look, but she could almost see the wheels inside of his head churning.

"So, Mr. B. what do you say about getting another unit?"

"It's money we don't need to spend...but it does make the most sense. I'll run to the office and see if there's a 5 by 5 unit close to this one."

After Ben left, Betsy walked over to their car and sat down. "Matilda, I'll bet you are as glad as I am that we're doing this." Their dog tilted her head as if she understood every word. "Pretty soon we'll be on the road and loving every minute of it."

"Are you talking to yourself again?"

"No, as a matter of fact, Matilda and I were having quite a conversation."

"Hope no one heard you." Ben came up behind her and gave her a squeeze and kiss on her neck.

"Hey, no funny stuff, mister. They have cameras on us at all times."

"Ask someone who cares," Ben said as he turned Bets around and planted a kiss on her lips. Then he stepped back and looked up. "Hope they got that one on tape."

Matilda barked and they both stared in her direction. "I think our pooch is jealous?"

"Hon, she's a female. She doesn't like it when I show affection to anyone but her." Ben picked up their dog and petted her. "It's okay, buddy, sometimes I have to show your mom some loving. You'll have to learn to live with it."

"And you think I'm nuts?"

"A little...but your idea to get a second storage unit. Outstanding. We now have the unit down there." Ben pointed to one two doors from where they stood. "It came open yesterday. Can we say the Lord's looking out for us? Again."

"Seems so."

For the next hour Betsy helped her hubby carry or, in some cases, drag the items they'd try to sell to the other unit. Also, with his assistance, they moved his tool boxes. All five of them. She didn't have a clue what he carried in them, but her muscles ached afterwards.

"I better leave these out so I can get to them. Decide what I need to take on our adventure."

"Good idea."

Betsy headed back to the 10 by 15 unit and grabbed the office chair and rolled it to the other unit. No need for this in an RV, since she wouldn't have a designated office space.

Either the bed or the couch will become my desk.

Ben told her on one of their trips to storage. "Space is at a premium for both of us, Bets. 5th wheels come with basements, but I don't want to fill it to the rim with items we'll never use."

"Like some of my stuff I might want or need."

"Betsy, what are you mumbling about?" Ben asked when he walked past the door.

"You know me. I'm always talking to myself. Most times

when I've..." Betsy hoped he wouldn't ask her to finish her sentence. She didn't want him to know she struggled with leaving her desk behind.

The thing I'll miss the most.

Betsy loved to spread out when she wrote. Where would she put her Bible? What would she do with the slips of paper she jotted ideas on? Would she even have the room she needed to write when they settled in their new RV?

Again her new friend, doubt, crashed in on Betsy, causing her to want to give up. Ride the computer chair back to their house and forget this ever happened. But something stopped her when she rounded the corner of the 5 by 5 unit. Ben sat on the cold concrete floor of the unit with tools strewn all around him.

Oh, Father. I'm sorry.

Betsy sent up an arrow prayer, asking for forgiveness for her selfishness. Her hubby needed to make some drastic changes too.

"Looks like you're having as much fun as I am."

"I don't know what to take."

Ben's sad face broke Betsy's heart and she sat next to him. "Neither one of us have any idea what we have room for until we buy whatever it is we're going to buy."

"I know. Just thought it'd be easier." Ben got up and helped Betsy off the floor. "There's so much..."

Ideas to solve their dilemma swirled around in Betsy's head. What if instead of buying an RV, they could keep their home and follow Rose and Larry in their car. Stay in hotels where they stopped.

The song *Money, Money, Money* by Abba joined the party and Betsy realized the absurdity of hotel hopping each night. Along with all the cash they'd spend if they went down that highway.

"Ben, I've got another great idea. Actually two of them. We need to find a realtor and go shopping for our new home."

"I couldn't agree more."

Betsy smiled at her hubby's quick response, and while Ben

closed up the two storage units, she sent up a second prayer. *Lord, can You help us find the perfect RV? If it's possible, could it have so much space we are able to take everything we want.*

With her prayer prayed, she took her phone out of her back pocket. Betsy chuckled while texting Rose. Then she opened Facebook to put the same message on it. Certain it would make everyone laugh.

She hit status and typed in: *We are officially looney toons – can anyone say, "2 storage units?"*

CHAPTER TEN

Ben hoped his evening wouldn't include a trip to storage. He and Betsy had taken at least one load each night for the last week and a half. Tonight he'd like to put his feet up and browse the RV's sites he'd found online. Not do anything else.

When he walked in the house, Ben greeted Matilda on his way to put his briefcase down in his office. Until he noticed something of importance missing. His desk. The spot where it once sat—now empty. As well as the blank wall where his flat screen had hung. A box, marked TV, stood over in one corner.

"Betsy?" He yelled and waited for his bride to show up. She didn't. Ben glanced around his barren room and couldn't believe what he saw. But when he ventured out into their living room, Betsy's exuberance with this move stopped him in his tracks. Their 60-inch flat screen TV sat on the floor.

"This has gone too far. We need to talk." Ben went in search of Betsy and found her in the back of her closet. He coughed to keep from startling her.

"Oh, hi. I thought I heard something, but I've been busy in here." Betsy motioned at the two bags of clothes.

"You think?" Ben held out his hand to help her up.

"No, I better do this on my own." Betsy got on all fours and backed out of the corner of her closet, before having room to stand. "There."

Ben wanted to continue their 'discussion', but her gray hair, in every direction but the right one, made him laugh out loud.

"What's so funny?"

"You. Take a look in the mirror."

Betsy moved past him and said after checking out her reflection, "Do I get the award for *Sexiest Woman Alive* tonight?"

"Always and you get...something for clearing out my office. You've been busy."

"I thought you'd be glad I got some of the stuff out of there?"

"Sweetums, I'm thrilled we're making headway, but we still have to live here. Until we put the house on the market." Ben reached down and picked up Matilda.

"About selling our house. Alene came by this morning and the paperwork is on the table."

Ben petted the dog, which gave him time to formulate the thoughts rambling around in his head. When he got a grip he asked, "So what did she say the house is worth?"

The smile on Betsy's face told him the good news before she uttered, "$200,000.00."

"Are you serious?"

Betsy walked over to Ben and gave him a big kiss on the cheek and nodded. "Alene told me we shouldn't have any trouble selling our house. Our price range is what everyone's looking for."

He couldn't believe the amount and took Betsy's hand and danced her around their bathroom. "Thank you Exxon for moving to the area and it means one other thing."

"What's that?" She stopped her husband in the middle of a dip.

"I'm married to a remarkable woman who gets things done."

"Was there ever a doubt?" Betsy quit dosy doeing and snuggled in Ben's arms. "It also means we have lots to do to get this house into shape to sell."

"Aye, Aye, Captain. But first we need to eat something. How

about an omelet?"

"While you cook, I'll work on the front closet and clear it out."

Ben whipped up the ingredients for a frittata and put it in the oven. This would give him 20 minutes to locate what Betsy had done with his office stuff. Knowing her, she'd stuffed it in one of her office boxes and it now sat out in storage.

Or in a box to go to our new RV. The one we haven't purchased yet. Gotta love her, Lord.

On his way to his office he caught a glimpse of Betsy. Her rear end stuck out of their hall linen closet. Ben watched as she tugged and pulled at something. Whatever she wanted must have come loose when he heard a scream and she sat on the tile with a blanket on her lap.

Ben roared, but his wife didn't skip a beat. She stood up and wrapped the blanket around her shoulders and said, "What are you grinning at, old man?"

"Hey, I'm not old. I'm only 59 and three quarters."

"More like 59 and seven-eighths. I'd say you're slapping elderly." Betsy hobbled down the hallway, pretending to use a cane.

"Everyone should be as lucky as me – living with a comedian." Ben picked up a box. "And not a very good one at that." He opened the door and went out into their garage.

This time Betsy laughed at their interaction. It'd been a long time since they'd been able to banter back and forth. Or enjoy each other's company and not end up in an almost knock down drag out fight.

Too many demands and long hours had taken its toll on Ben and their marriage. And only by the grace of God and prayers from friends and family had it survived. They'd witnessed a true miracle, but this one with Ben quitting his job and them going on the road...

Father, You've shown us how BIG You truly are."

Betsy took the blanket off her shoulders and finished folding it. "Rose will love this." She tossed it into an empty box marked "Rose". "Yes, this is perfect for my crazy friend."

"You about ready for supper?" Ben asked when he came in from the garage.

"On my way."

~

On Friday night, Ben sat at the kitchen table with Betsy. They listened to Alene go over all the paperwork. He still couldn't believe they would clear so much on the sale of their house. Their realtor said, "That's how the market is going right now."

They signed on the dotted line and decided the showings would begin in two weeks. Ben took Matilda over to Jeremy's house to talk about his backyard. On his way down the drive he said, "I promise I'll be back in less than a half hour, Bets. In plenty of time to go RV shopping."

An hour later, and plans finalized on the backyard, Ben whistled when he and Matilda came in the house.

"You're sounding mighty happy, my sweet baboo."

"I don't know about you, but I'm seeing the light at the end of the tunnel."

Betsy gave him one of her "I have no idea what you're talking about" looks then put words to her expression. "What I'm thinking is you had a conversation with yourself and I heard the end of it."

"You're right and sorry it took so long at Jeremy's. The two of them are coming over next weekend and we'll finish the brick in the side yards."

"Always love it when we finish tasks when we're selling a house." Betsy held up her hand. "Sorry, Ben, that sounded sarcastic."

"No need to apologize. It's the truth. But I do have some good news and some bad news."

"Give me the good news first."

"I've got less than two months left at work." Ben smiled and walked over to Betsy, who stood in their living room. "Then I'm officially retired."

"What's the bad news?" Betsy moved closer to him.

"I've got less than two months left at work then you'll have me around 24/7. Think you can handle it?"

"I'm willing to give it a try."

Ben leaned down and gave Betsy a kiss she could write about in one of her articles. Which she'd do, if she ever finished with packing and took time to write.

"Hello. Is anyone home?"

Matilda let out a bark when Rose's voice came down the hallway. Bets broke away from her hubby's arms, but before she got too far, she patted his backside. He turned and smiled and mouthed the words, "I love you."

"Love you too."

"Are you guys smooching in here?"

"Something like that."

Ben chuckled, which Betsy knew would egg her friend on— but for whatever reason Rose didn't make any other comment. She just stood next to Larry. Both had their arms crossed.

"What?" Betsy questioned.

"Are we going today or should we give you two some quiet time to..." A snort escaped from Rose.

"No, we're fine and ready to go RV shopping."

~

Larry took them to three different RV places. After perusing the third dealership, Ben saw the scowl on his friend's face. His expression screamed he'd rather find a rattlesnake in his underwear than continue camper shopping.

That perturbed Ben, but one look at Rose told him—she's not happy and said, "Larry, I don't know what's wrong with you, but you need to tell your face to wake up and smile."

Rose stepped out of the Cedar Creek 5th wheel and proceeded to glare at her husband. "And as my mama used to tell me, 'If your face froze that way, you could scare a dead man.'"

Ben saw the smile on Larry's face, but turned his attention to their salesman's reaction to Rosie's statement. The man stopped on the top step of the camper and started to laugh. At one point, Ben thought he might have to give him mouth to mouth.

"Tom, you better breathe or one of us is going to have to

catch you when you fall."

The salesman walked down the rest of the stairs. "I've never heard that saying before. I'm going to use it on my kids tonight. Now, back to RVs. Found any you like?"

"Ben, I'm not telling you what to buy, but we love this one." Larry gestured toward the one they'd all come out of.

"We'll be the talk of the town," Betsy stepped back up on the retractable stairs. "Rosie, we'll be matchy matchy."

"No, this one is a year newer and has curly cue designs on the curtains."

Tom chuckled. "It's not the technical term, but it works."

Ben followed his wife into the Cedar Creek again. "As you like to say. Is it a keeper?"

Betsy didn't answer him, but he watched her as she touched the countertop on the center island. Ben still couldn't get over the design. Who'd have thought you'd ever have such a thing in an RV.

"This is the one, Ben. The dark cabinets and everything else. I love it." Betsy came around the island and kissed him. "If you agree—we've found our new home."

"Hey guys. We've bought ourselves an RV," Ben yelled from the door then checked to see if other customers heard his loud peal. No one paid him any attention. Didn't matter. He loved the place too.

"So are you ready to go inside and sign the papers?" Tom put his hand out for Betsy when she came down the stairs.

"Thanks." Betsy took a hold of his left hand, appreciating the extra help. Way too many steps in one day. But when she hit the bottom stair she let loose of Tom's hand and sprinted up the steps again. "You guys go ahead. I need to look at something first."

She wanted to go see where her soon-to-be-desk unit would sit. On the far wall where the couch sat now. Perfect. Betsy didn't know what they'd do with the hide-a-bed, but she'd bet the family farm—if she had one—it would decorate someone else's RV.

The color of the couch could only be described as a

combination between baby poop and a hue of beige/yellow, with a little brown thrown in. Even if Betsy had room, she wouldn't have kept the hideous piece of furniture. "I'm not sure Goodwill would take it."

"Helllllllooo in there."

Betsy heard Rose's voice. "Come in and join me."

Rose came up the stairs and plopped down on one of the dining room chairs. Then she stood up again, pointing in the direction of the couch. "I'm not sure what you're doing, but I hope it has something to do with that thing. It's...it's..." She threw up her hands. "There are no words for it."

"Rosie, to finish your sentence, it's atrocious. And, it's history. And it's where I want Ben to build my desk."

"Are you sure about getting rid of the couch?" Rose tapped her finger on the side of her cheek.

"Sure as the day I was born. This puppy's gone and the sooner the better."

Rose raised her hand in the air again and shouted, "Praise You, Jesus."

"Amen, brother. Oh, I mean sis—""

A loud knock on the side of their trailer stopped Betsy in mid-praising and Rose walked over to the door.

"If you two are done having church in there, Tom needs you to sign some papers." Larry peered inside the RV. "And I need to get home so I can register my game bonus. It has been four hours.

"We're on our way." Betsy headed down the stairs, but noticed the not-so-happy-look Rose gave her hubby. Rosie made it clear she didn't like him spending money on computer games.

"Just to let you know, Ben won't be in the office. He signed the papers right before he got a text on his phone. Went outside to call someone." Larry took Rose's hand. "We'll meet you at the car when you get done."

Betsy wondered about the phone call, but figured Ben would tell her when he finished. Twenty minutes later she laid the pen on the desk and took the keys from Tom's hand.

"Thanks Betsy." Tom opened the door to his office and they

walked into the showroom. "Oh, and be sure to tell Ben there's no problem with us keeping your RV on the back lot until you need it. But the way the housing market is going, it shouldn't take too long."

"We sure hope it sells fast." Betsy walked to the door then turned and waved at Tom. "Thanks again."

When she got in the SUV, Betsy could see a slight tinge of red on Ben's cheeks and the deep breaths shouted something's amiss. "I'm sure you don't want to talk about work, but we've just spent a sizeable chunk of change in there. Your mood isn't buyer's remorse. Is it?"

Ben took his phone out of his side pocket. "No, it's not buyer's remorse. It's my boss. I'll read you his text."

"Bets, you're not going to believe this."

"Hush, Rose. Ben doesn't need your assistance."

"Sorry."

"Anyway, Mr. Greenspan wrote: "Change of plans. Yours. Got a job. Will pay $30,000. Completion October. Retirement will have to wait." Ben put his phone on the seat.

Betsy remained quiet, staring out the window. When she spoke she asked, "What are you going to do?"

"He's going to tell him to..."

"Rosebud," Larry's one-word response shut her up.

"Betsy, I'd like to tell him something, but I won't. One thing's for sure—I'm sticking to the retirement date I turned in."

"We need to pray about this. $30,000 is a lot of money to pass up."

"We need to pray, but the Father, Himself, will have to come down and tell me I'm sticking around for five more months. Not happening."

Rose gasped. "Mr. B. I'd keep my voice down. The Lord can and WILL direct your path. And don't you forget it."

Larry added, "She's right. I'm not putting my nose in here, but you've had His leading up to this point. Don't take the reins now. The Lord still knows what He's doing."

"You're right. Just had to vent." Ben reached over and patted

Larry and Rose's shoulders. "Yes, it'll all work out. It always does."

CHAPTER ELEVEN

"Betsy, you are never going to believe what happened?" Ben asked the open-ended question the minute his wife came in from grocery shopping. "We have a contract on the house for full price. It's a cash deal. They want to close in four weeks."

Betsy stared at him as if he'd sprung an extra appendage. All coloring faded from her face and she dropped the bags in her arms.

Ben rushed to Betsy's side and steadied her. "Hon?"

"How could it sell? It's not listed yet. Please tell me it isn't true." She turned around in a complete circle. Ben could only assume she looked at their home, which stood in total disarray.

"Alene said she brought someone over and they loved it. Bets, this isn't anything we haven't dealt with before." He said this to convince himself, as well as his wife. "Yes, we'll get this organized in no time."

"I sure hope you're right. We've got a lot to get out of here." Betsy reached down and picked up the oranges which had rolled out on the floor when she dropped the bags.

"Not to worry, my dear."

But Ben did exactly what he told his wife not to do as he went out to grab the other sacks out of the car. When he came back in, he glanced around at the boxes littering their living room. Along with them, two cans of paint waited for someone—him—to finish an accent wall.

Ben shook his head, hoping the motion would clear away the doubt which started to bombard his mind. Panic wanted to take over, but then he realized what had just happened. They didn't expect to sell for months. Now it sold before it hit the market.

"Bets, the Lord's done it again."

"You're absolutely right. Why do we doubt?"

"Don't know. Guess we're human." Ben laughed. "Right now I'm going to head over to Larry's and see if he wants to go truck shopping."

"Sounds like a plan since we'll need one sooner than we thought."

~

Betsy didn't want to question the Lord's quick answer on the sale of their home. However, right then she wanted to shout something unchristianlike at her hubby for coming up with this harebrained idea.

But she kept her mouth shut as Ben walked out the door. Betsy stood staring into space and the compelling thought of following him to inflict bodily harm on him crossed her mind. "Hon, this time I'm afraid we've bitten off more than even we can chew."

She put away the rest of the groceries and resumed her job of sorting kitchen stuff and putting items in boxes to go to the camper. Even though they weren't living in it—today's news told them they'd be moving into it sooner than planned.

Which sparked a question she needed to ask their realtor. Betsy wrote on the notepad she kept on the counter: Alene – leaf blower, lawn mower and other lawn gadgets.

"I don't think the RV parks will expect us to keep up our own lawn when we stay at them." Betsy put the pen down and laughed. "No, they take care of those kinds of things. Or, I hope they do."

A vision of a lawn mower sticking out of one of the compartments brought on a chuckle, which made Betsy remember something else. She needed to call her mom and Rosie and tell them their good news.

"Rosie, you're never going to believe this, but we sold the house."

Betsy could only explain her friend's reaction as a mixture between a fit of giggles and an occasional snort. Rose finished off with a loud shriek. Loud enough to peel one of the oranges she'd picked up at the store earlier.

"Quiet down, Rose. You about broke my ear drum."

"Sorry. Next time I'll remind you to put it on Speaker."

Betsy moved the phone to her right ear and rubbed the left one. "I wish you would."

"Can't believe you sold your house. The Lord is wanting you guys to get on the road."

"Speaking of 'on the road'..." Betsy paused. "Have you thought about how...how..."

"How we'll get along?"

"Doesn't it concern you?"

"Heavens no. We'll be okeedokie. You and me—we'll keep busy doing...what retired people do. Whatever that is. The guys, they might drive themselves nuts, trying to find things to do."

"I'm not worried about Ben. Since he's such a handyman, he'll go up to people in the RV parks and ask them if they've got a leaky faucet."

Again Rose did her giggle/snort combination. Thankfully she'd left off the shriek this time.

"Rosie, I better scoot. Gotta call Mom to tell her." Betsy glanced at her watch. "Oh, and has Ben shown up yet?"

"He's pulling in now."

Betsy tried to call her mother, but it went to voice mail. "I'll try later when I'm finished boxing up the kitchen." She taped a box and the *Mission Impossible* theme song started to play inside her head.

"Help, Lord."

~

"Do you ever feel like we're out of our minds for doing what we're doing?" Ben took a bite out of his burrito and laid the rest on his wrapper.

"Every day."

"Seriously?"

"But that's not always a bad thing. I think it keeps a person motivated to get the job done. Like with my writing. If I don't have a deadline to send in a submission, I'm sunk. I wouldn't get anything done otherwise."

"This isn't about your writing. It's about our life."

"Oh, is that right?"

Ben shook his head 'no' and wished he could take the words back. "I'm sorry, Bets. I didn't mean it the way it sounded."

Tears filled her eyes as she stuffed the remainder of her 7-Layer Burrito into the bag. "Benjamin, I know you didn't. But we're under a lot of stress right now and maybe we need to spend more time praying than talking."

"I couldn't agree more. And, again, I'm sorry."

"You're forgiven...this time." Betsy winked. "Don't let it happen again."

Ben smiled and squeezed her hand, knowing his wife joked with him. But her statement held some truth too. They had hurt each other over a period of time and were still healing. Another reason they needed this change.

"Change is a good thing."

"Ben, you're having a conversation with yourself again?"

"I was, and what I told myself, "We need to get this show on the road."

"Sounds good. However, there is the job off—"

"The ever-looming job offer. How about we get out of here? We've got lots to discuss." Ben grabbed the Taco Bell bag and on their way out of the store, he tossed it in the trash container.

"Go on out to the car. I have to make a pit stop."

Ben chuckled as he made his way to the car. Even though

they were only five minutes from their house, Betsy made her usual stop. Her excuse for why she did it: They might get stuck in traffic and what would she do then?

After he settled himself in the driver's seat, Ben waited for Betsy. Within minutes she appeared and must have noticed him staring at her. Next thing he knew she did a dance across the parking lot. Oblivious to the two other cars in the parking lot and the people staring at her.

Ben watched his wife get in their car and said, "Not sure where that came from, Betsy, but it was fun to watch."

"Someone's phone rang. It was the *Dance the Night Away* ring tone. Now it's in my head."

"And in your dance steps as you came out of there." Ben placed his index and middle finger on the dashboard and moved them as if they were dancing.

"Stop it." Betsy swatted at Ben's hand. "I thought we had more important things to discuss than my dance steps."

Ben laughed. "Those need some discussion, especially when done out in public. Don't want your picture showing up in The Villager newspaper."

"The front page, I hope...dancing, danc—"

"For right now we'll leave that possibility alone." Ben pulled out of the parking lot onto Lake Woodlands.

"So what about the job offer, Ben? Lots of money to turn down."

"Almost too much to not take advantage of." Ben stopped at the red light at Six Pines. "Bets, it would pay for a lot of campgrounds."

"It would. But what is the Lord saying to us?"

"Our house sold in less than a month."

"Check."

"We found the RV of our dreams."

"Check."

Ben got a kick out of Betsy's answers. Always one to make a list and mark it off. "Last, but not least, friends who are expert RVers who we can tag along with."

"Check and who almost sold their own RV before we could hit the road."

"Don't remind me."

"Sorry. To me it's still kind of comical and amazing how it all worked out. On the day you announce your big plans, Larry put their RV up for sale."

"Good point."

"Anyway, back to what we were discussing. The job offer is great, but do you think the Lord is worried about the cost of campgrounds?"

Betsy's obscure question hit Ben right when he pulled into their driveway. He put their car in park and faced his wife. "No, He isn't concerned about tomorrow or whether we can pay for an RV spot. All He wants is our hearts. Not us fretting over our 401K or bank accounts."

Betsy reached over and gave Ben a lingering kiss. At that moment, he wouldn't have cared if a crowd of a thousand surrounded their car. This dance he'd be happy to share. She touched Ben's cheek. "So, have we made a decision?"

"I believe we have." Saying those four words almost seemed to take the weight of the world off of his shoulders. Another thing—Ben loved Betsy with all of his heart.

Who needs an extra $30,000 when you've got love?

Ben opened the garage door and pulled inside. "There is still one thing, Bets."

"What?"

"We still need a truck."

"Ben, everything else has fallen into place. This will to. Until then, we'll keep praying."

"Agreed. Now I need to rescue the princess from her crate."

Ben and Betsy went in the door and he released Matilda and she almost leapt into his arms. "See. She missed her dad."

"No, dear, she needs to go out."

He waltzed out to their front yard. Off in the distance the deer munched on the grass in the open field. This time Matilda didn't pay any attention to them, but Ben loved seeing them each night. Reminded him of his childhood. His brother.

The one he should call...in a few weeks.

~

Ben couldn't believe three weeks later he still hadn't found a truck and voiced his frustration to Larry. "It seems like I've called or we've gone to every dealership in the Houston area and there is not one Ford F350 available."

"How about we drive out to Cypress again? See if my buddy has anything. I'm sure he would have let me know if he'd gotten one in. But let's give it a shot. I've got a couple things to do. I'll give you a call when I'm done."

Ben hung up and he didn't care if they had to drive to Kansas to find one. He needed a dually truck. He and Larry had looked at 12 to 15 trucks. Every one of them had something wrong with them or they sold before they could make it to the dealership.

Never failed when Ben found an item he wanted to buy—the rest of the populace seemed to want the same thing. He began to question if he DID get the cart (RV) before the horse (truck).

Ben's phone buzzed and he answered it, "Hello, Mr. Greenspan. How are you?"

"Fine, but I'm not sure how you will be after I tell you I need you to come in tomorrow at 8:00."

"Saturday? Sir, I...can't. Lewis Hauling is delivering my 5th wheel at 9:00 in the morning."

"Is that MY problem?"

"No, it isn't." Ben took a breath. "But I can't change my plans at this late date."

"Betsy can handle the delivery. I'll see you in the morning." Ben heard some paper rustling in the background. "This is the least you can do since you took today off and you're baling on us on Monday."

Again the Lord held Ben's tongue from saying the unsavory words which came to mind. After a deep breath, he answered his boss, "I'll be there..."

With bells on.

He wanted to add the last part before he hung up, but didn't.

Better to leave his job with his professionalism in place. Not childish pettiness.

"Turn the other cheek Benjamin Stevenson."

Ben recited the snippet of verse, hoping it'd change his bad attitude. It didn't. "Yea, yea, yea. I've turned the other cheek and where's that gotten me?" Ben got up out of the chair and stood in the middle of their almost-empty living room. "Father, this is Yours. I'm done."

Matilda tilted her head.

"Yes, your dad is talking to—"

Ben's phone beeped. "That was fast."

"I hope you're ready to go. My friend has a truck and he said we need to get to Cypress as fast as we can. I'll be over in ten minutes."

Ben laid his phone down on the kitchen counter. "This day is looking better and better." He grabbed a paper towel, the only thing he could find to write on, and jotted a note to Betsy. No doubt she'd return from her writing group before he got back with his 'new' truck and he didn't want her to worry.

When he put the pen down he chuckled. Not about his confidence in finding a truck, but about Betsy and his conversation later. About him having to work in the morning.

"Matilda, Mama's gonna have a fit when she finds out she has to handle the big move all by herself." Ben smiled at the pooch. "And you're not going to like me either. Come here. You need to go in your crate."

With Matilda safe in her cell, Ben waited for Larry. If it'd been much longer he would have worn a hole in the carpet in Betsy's office, waiting for him.

When he got in his friend's SUV, optimism ran through Ben's veins like a stream in the Blue Ridge Mountains after a good rain. He told Larry as much on their way to the dealership.

"I know you're excited, but if you don't sit still, I'm stopping at the next convenience store so you can use the little boy's room."

"No you're not. You keep driving. I've got a truck waiting for me."

"I sure hope so."

Larry pulled in and waved at a salesman. The portly man stood next to a bronze and beige dually.

Ben opened the door, realizing at the last minute his friend hadn't come to a complete stop. "I'd say I'm in a hurry. Sorry."

"All right. I'm stopped." Larry put the SUV in gear and got out.

"Hey, Lar. Good to see you."

"Ben, this is Steve. Steve this is Ben."

"Larry, your friend doesn't care who I am. Let me open the truck before he breaks into it." All of them laughed.

Ben could feel his cheeks reddening and he took his hand off the door handle and turned to shake Steve's extended hand. "Good to meet you."

Steve shook his hand then hit the button to unlock the dually. "There you go."

Ben opened the door and he could almost hear the Hallelujah choir. He'd researched this exact truck online. A dually king cab, long bed, fully loaded with only 50,000 miles on it. It also had a 5th wheel hitch and a tonneau cover.

"Is this for real?" Ben asked when he got out of the driver's seat and opened the back door. For some reason Matilda popped into his head. A perfect place for her when they're traveling.

The salesman shook his head. "Our mechanic checked her over and she's in perfect condition. Only one owner."

"I've heard that before." Ben stepped back from the truck and crossed his arms.

"So have I, but this one is...is picture perfect." Steve moved over and wiped something off the fender with his handkerchief.

Larry came up and glanced inside. "I'd believe him if I were you."

"What's the price?" Ben almost hated to ask. Afraid the 'too good to be true' would come and kick him in the teeth.

Steve took a piece of paper out of his jacket and announced the price. The one Betsy and he had agreed upon.

"Larry, come over and pinch me. I do not believe this."

"Love to." Larry acted like he would gladly do what Ben suggested then he stopped when a man walked up.

"Guys this is Shorty. He's the one who checked out this truck."

"Man, if I didn't already own one of these." He pointed to a row of pickups and smiled. "It's the red one. Like I said, I'd buy this one."

"Sold." Ben headed to the office. "Well, are you guys coming?"

For the next half hour, he filled out paperwork and wrote a check that could choke a horse. Done—he'd bought the truck of his dreams. He couldn't wait to see Betsy's face. She'd, without a doubt, rejoice he'd found one and would quit talking about it.

"Then her jubilance would come to an abrupt end," Ben said as he drove home. "When we discuss me working tomorrow."

Again when he thought of her reaction, he smiled. First Betsy would offer him their first born, which they didn't have, not to have to do it. Or her second tactic—putting her abilities down.

"I can't do it, Ben. I'm sure I'd send the driver to the wrong spot. Or worse, I'd send him to the wrong park."

Ben laughed as he exited off the freeway at Woodlands Parkway. In less than five minutes he parked the dually in the driveway and hit the call button on the steering wheel and said, "Call Betsy."

"Yeeeeessssss!"

"Come see the newest addition to our family."

No answer. Just a click. Ben got out of the cab of the truck and waited. He didn't have too long to wait. The outside light came on and Betsy flew out the front door. Oohs and ahs followed as she walked around the pickup.

"You done good, sweetie." Betsy came over and gave Ben a hug. One which told him she approved.

"Glad you like it. Get in the passenger side and I'll take you for a spin."

"Can I shut the door first?"

Ben got in and started the truck. The distinctive rumble of the diesel engine filled the neighborhood. The noise would alert the neighbor kid. Todd told Ben when they worked on the yard, "I want dad and me to find an old truck. One we can restore for when I go to college."

Knowing Todd, he already had most of the money saved from mowing lawns. The contribution Ben made to the young man's fund, after he helped him lay two pallets of bricks over two long weekends, sweetened the pot even more.

Ben's back still hurt, but right now all he had on his mind, taking his dually out with his honey. The one who hadn't materialized yet. But when she did, she carryed Matilda, and talked on the cell phone.

"Mom, I've got to run. Ben's taking me for a ride in his new toy. Can you hear it?" Betsy let go of their pooch and both jumped in. "I'll talk to you tomorrow, after the monster is delivered."

Ben couldn't have written the script for a better segway into the conversation they needed to have. But what she said next, after she got off the phone, floored him. Again he thought he heard the angels in heaven singing. This time at the top of their lungs.

"Hon, before I forget, your boss called. When I answered, it seemed to catch him off guard." Betsy put on her seatbelt. "He said to tell you to come in to work tomorrow."

"He called you?" Ben's grip on the steering wheel tightened as he backed out of their driveway.

"Guess Mr. Greenspan called the wrong number. I know you know this, but he sure is a grumpy old man.

"And..."

"And." Betsy touched her hubby's arm. "Ben, don't worry about the trailer. The guy delivering it will get it handled. What's the worst that could happen?"

Lots of scenarios flashed in Ben's mind, but the one overshadowing all of them—his wife said she'd take care of it.

Those few words made his heart beat a little faster and, if truth be told, shocked the living daylights out of him.

CHAPTER TWELVE

Betsy waltzed into Starbucks with a spring in her step. RV moving day and Ben would be present and accounted for. No work for him afterall. Thank You, Jesus. He'd answered her fervent prayers.

After she received her Skinny Latte and one black coffee, her attention turned to her next stop. Crescent Moon RV Park. There she'd meet her hubby and Joe from Lewis Hauling.

When she rounded the curve into the park, she praised the Lord she'd kept her mind on driving. Not off somewhere else. 'Cause right smack dab in front of her sat a rig and two trucks blocking the entrance to the park.

"Don't these people know my trailer is being delivered today and I don't want to miss a second of its arrival?"

Betsy disliked sitting in traffic on I-45 or in an RV Park and she almost honked. Then realized she owned the recreational vehicle that stood in her way. What gave her the first clue: a temporary license plate and Cedar Creek splashed across the back of the honking thing.

Something else which told Betsy the monstrosity belonged to her—Ben, with Matilda on her leash, strolled up to the side of her car. He signaled her to open her window. When Betsy got it down about 12 inches, the first thing that came to mind fell out of her mouth, "What's taking him so long?"

"Well, hello to you too."

"Sorry. Oh here's your java."

"Joe said since he's brought other rigs in, the park's letting him take it in. Won't be long now." Ben stood with his hands in his pockets.

Frustration laced Ben's explanation and Betsy couldn't blame him. The whole morning had to have made her hubby crazy. First he thought he had to work. Then he didn't.

Mr. Greenspan called right before Ben headed out. If the phone hadn't been on speaker, Betsy would have called 9-1-1. Ben's face got redder with each word his boss said.

"Ben, there's no need for you to come in. Jack finished everything last night. Since you're deserting us, he's my go-to guy."

He hung up the phone and walked out the front door with Matilda. Betsy left him alone and now, while they waited for Joe to park their RV, she kept quiet too. Not adding molasses to the mustard.

That was a Rosie if I've ever heard one.

Betsy texted the Rosieism to her best friend and put her phone in the back pocket of her jeans. When she looked up, a man came out of the office and moved his arm in a 'forward ho' motion in Ben's direction.

"Time to move." Ben picked up Matilda and ran past the man to get in his 'new' dually.

Not sure her husband saw it, but Betsy gave him a 'thumbs up' anyway and let the caravan go ahead before she joined them. From a distance she wished she'd left her phone out. The perfect photo op loomed in front of her.

Betsy parked near their site and got out of her car and gazed in awe at the man's expertise as he pulled their rig forward. He put his truck in reverse and brought their RV in for a landing on the concrete pad. His exactness left her to question if Ben would have the ability to move their RV from Point A to Point B.

Of course he can. Didn't he tow a 6-place snowmobile trailer almost every weekend for 15 years? "This can't be any harder."

"Is that right?" Ben came up and stood next to her.

"Yes, it is. You'd have this puppy aligned in no time. What took this guy so long?" Betsy joked.

The wide-eyes and tilt of Ben's head told her that Joe, their RV deliverer, stood within earshot. Betsy covered her mouth and wished she'd learn to curb her jesting for more appropriate times.

One of Ben's looks, given for her foot and mouth disease, usually bothered her. But today, she welcomed it. The last thing Betsy wanted to do was hurt the gentleman's feelings. Specifically, the one assisting them with moving their RV.

Her devotional from yesterday came to mind. *I might be the only Jesus they ever meet.* Betsy hated it when her conscience reminded her that her mouth over-rode her brain.

"Sorry, Lord...and Ben too."

Betsy held out hope Joe hadn't heard her, and over the noise of his diesel engine she concluded he hadn't. When the man finished unhooking his truck from the RV, she went over to Ben, who had taken out their checkbook to pay him.

Instead of leaving well enough alone and letting her husband handle it, Betsy decided she'd ask a simple question. "Joe, do you give lessons on 'The Tips and Tricks of How to Park an RV? I know Ben could use a few. Maybe me too.'"

The two men looked at her. Their expressions told her they thought she'd fallen on her head sometime in her life. Joe verified it when he answered her question, "No, ma'am, I don't. My liability insurance won't let me."

His Texas accent and professionalism lent validity to what he'd said. Betsy didn't pursue her inquiry any further, but walked to her car. Certain Ben would have something to say about her stupid question when he finished with the transaction.

Much to her surprise, Ben didn't mention anything about her earlier faux pas after Joe left. But chatted on and on about their new home on wheels. After a tour around it, Ben said, "Hon, I don't know about you, but I can't wait to stay here full time."

"Neither can I."

"For right now we need to head home and get busy. Let's take the truck."

Betsy moved her car in front of the 5th wheel then walked to the pickup and opened the door to the dually. Her assessment of the step up today—it's a long way up there.

"Grab the handle."

Betsy hoisted her wherewithal's up into the leather seats. The minute she sat, Matilda came up and stood on the padded console between the seats. "Hello, girl. How do you like your special perch?"

Their dog cocked her head as if to say she approved. "Mats, I'm with you. I like the view from up here. People can see you coming. Unlike my compact car."

Ben got in the truck. "You two ready to head to the house to wrap this up?"

"Ready as I'll ever be."

Betsy watched Ben. Even though the truck had a back-up camera, he checked behind him three or four times and said, "Want to make sure all is clear."

"Don't want you running over our neighbors."

"That wouldn't be a good thing." Ben put the truck in drive and something beeped. "Hello, Mr. Greenspan."

"Benjamin...I...hum...I owe you an apology."

"Sir, I—"

"Let me finish, Ben." He coughed then went on. "I'm sorry for what I said earlier. Totally out of line."

Ben glanced at Betsy and he shrugged his shoulders.

"I've watched you over the years, son. How you're there when I've needed you." The man laughed. "Ben you're my go-to guy, not Anderson. We'd all die of thirst before he figured out how to put the bottle of water in the cooler. The pip squeak would have to reinvent it first."

Laughter came out of the speakers and this time Ben and Betsy joined him. In all the years her hubby had worked for him,

Betsy never knew the guy had a sense of humor. Fine time to find out when Monday's Ben's last day.

"Ben I want you to know if this venture doesn't work out, you've always got a job here. I'm proud of you for putting your beliefs and family first. We'll miss you. I'll see you Monday. Goodbye."

After Ben clicked off the call, silence filled the cab of the dually. For the first time in a long time Betsy's word count diminished to zilch. When she peeked over at Ben, his mouth stood open but nothing came out.

"Bets, am...I...I...dreaming?"

"No. We've witnessed another miracle."

"I think you're right."

"We need to start praying for him." Betsy took her phone out and added, "Pray for Mr. G." in her notes. "I need to text Rosie. She'd love this turn of events."

"You can't...they're still on their cruise."

"That's right. Guess cyberspace will hold my texts until they land. When are they getting back?"

"Tomorrow sometime."

The rest of the ride Betsy almost took her phone out again to text Rose, but then decided to keep it tucked in her pocket. Instead, she watched Ben. His grin broadened with each mile.

His high spirits reminded her of the Ben from a long time ago. The one who lived for the next adventure. The one so full of life she could hardly keep up. The one who she'd prayed to return. In His own amazing way, the Lord answered with an out-of-this-world miracle.

Once they reached the house, they spent the day taking the last of their belongings from the house to the RV and to storage. Matilda stayed in the air-conditioned truck—out of the way— while they accomplished the monumental task.

On their last trip to storage, Betsy announced. "Ben, are you up for another of my great ideas?"

"Not sure."

"You'll love this one. Look around. We can give up the two

other units. The rest of this stuff will fit in a 5 x 10."

Ben took the keys for the units from Betsy's hand and said. "I'll be right back. Then we can finish this up."

For the next two hours they consolidated everything down to the items Betsy and Ben couldn't part with. When Ben put the last box inside and closed the door he said, "Hon, there's room to spare. We better go to the house and see if there's anything else."

"I'm sure we'll find something hidden somewhere." Betsy smiled.

At 7:00, Betsy stopped in the middle of their large living room and shouted, "Ben, look. We're DONE. Glory be to God."

Betsy parked her backside on the empty floor after her proclamation. Ben joined her, along with Matilda. Her hubby leaned over and gave her a kiss. Their pooch licked her ear. "Wow, two kisses."

"Bets, can you believe we did it?"

"No, I can't. But it sure looks like the RV is our home tonight. There's nothing left here." Betsy glanced around one more time. "Oh, there is a roll of toilet paper."

"There are some cleaning supplies under the sink in the kitchen." Ben motioned with his foot.

"How about we come over tomorrow and clean. I'm too tired tonight." Betsy's stomach grumbled. "Did you hear it? It's telling us it's Taco Bell time...then let's take it to the RV?"

Ben took Betsy's hand and when she stood, he enveloped her in his arms. "Bets...I couldn't have done this without you. Thanks for your help." He leaned down and gave Betsy another kiss. One for the record books. Almost as an afterthought he added, "Oh, and I love you too!!!

Betsy laughed when she saw the big grin on her husband's face. Yes, the man she'd fallen in love with, and married, had returned.

Glad the workaholic is gone.

"What's with the sour puss look?"

Betsy smiled and decided to keep the answer to herself and said, "I'm dreading all the work we have waiting for us at the RV."

"Well, let's get cracking. It won't finish itself."

"Remember we're going to grab Taco Bell."

"Yep."

Ben and Betsy went to the garage. Before Betsy had time to close the door, her husband set a tile cutter on her lap. "Don't have room in the back seat" was all he said when he got into the dually and backed out.

Instead of complaining, she texted Rose the latest news. "I know you're still on the ship, but welcome home. We're staying at the RV tonight. YEAH!"

CHAPTER THIRTEEN

B en drove in silence along Six Pines on their way to their favorite fast food joint. He still couldn't believe Mr. Greenspan's call, but Betsy's expression, before they'd left the house, bothered him more.

Did she want to make this change? Or did she go along with it since he'd suggested it? Part of him wanted to ask, but tiredness from their full day kept him quiet.

Ben didn't want it to end in an argument. For whatever reason, when he brought 'something' up, what he wanted to say never came out right. He almost laughed when he remembered what Betsy said about her frequent slips of the tongue.

"Sometimes, dear, when my words hit the air – I don't know what happens. They seem to take on a life of their own and sound like a complete idiot said them."

"That's what I'm saying—"

"What?" Betsy chuckled. "Guess we do learn things from each other, even after all these years."

"We'll never quit learning, my dear. Or I hope we don't." Ben pulled up to the order window. "Hon, what do you want? Your normal? Or something else."

"Tonight I'm going to spice it up a bit. Get me a Mexican pizza."

Ben spoke the order into the speaker and when the person repeated it, he smiled. Again, nothing coming from the small box resembled what he'd told them. But when he received their food, everything they'd ordered sat in the bag. Along with the hot sauce he'd asked for.

"We can call this our 'first official dinner' in our new home." Betsy opened the bag. "Hope they gave us napkins. Oh, they did. I'm not sure we'd locate them at the RV."

"How about plates?" Ben smiled as he leaned over to look in the bag.

"No, silly...that's what laps are for...if they're...not holding tile saws."

"Not for long." Ben pulled out on the side street and made it to the RV Park in short order and parked next to Betsy's car. Before he gave her time to move, Ben came over and opened up her door, relieving her lap of the saw.

Betsy put Matilda's leash on and they got out of the truck. "Sure glad we don't live any farther away. I'd have permanent marks of her paws on these pups." She massaged the top of her legs.

Ben laughed at his wife's comment and took the bag of food from her. "You ready to eat?"

"I'll go in and grab paper—"

"You'll never find the plates. We can use the wrappers."

Betsy sat down and Ben joined her on the same side of the picnic table. The minute he did, the seat greeted him with a creaking noise, which caused him to jump up and go to the other side. Fast.

"Good idea, dear, don't want the table to break or tip over." Betsy dug into her Mexican pizza.

Ben bit into his Black Bean Burrito and devoured it in seconds. Then crumpled up his wrapper and put it in the sack.

"You ready to get busy?"

"No, but it won't put itself away." Betsy stood up and went over to the RV, then turned to face Ben. "Are you coming tonight?"

"I'm right behind you. Got to get Matilda."

Before Betsy could open the door to their RV, Ben had it handled. "If I wasn't carrying Mats, I'd carry you over the threshold."

"No you wouldn't. Don't want you to hurt your back. We've got too much work to do."

Ben put Matilda down and looked around their tiny abode, wondering where all of the stuff they'd piled inside would land.

Betsy and Ben spent until midnight putting their things away. Their bedroom closet proved the most challenging and a discussion almost ensued when Betsy tried to switch sides on him.

"Ain't happening, my darling. Sweet, adorable wife. You said you wanted the left side. I have it in writing."

"But I don't like this turn-style thingy. The hangers hang up on your clo—"

"That's what hangers do." Ben couldn't believe he'd been so quick with a humorous retort. But from the look on Betsy's face, she didn't find it quite as funny. Not one little bit.

Betsy tapped her watch and closed the closet door. "I'm not in the mood for a wanna-be comedian right now. What I'd like is sleep. We can talk about this tomorrow."

Ben nodded in agreement and shut the drawer he'd stashed his underwear in. "You're absolutely right. We'll settle this in the a.m."

Later, when they went to bed, Ben couldn't sleep. He kept going over all the extras their RV came with. And the soon-to-be desk unit for Betsy. He couldn't wait to surprise his wife.

Soon. Very soon.

~

A phone rang and Betsy couldn't remember where she'd left hers the night before. Ben pointed at the kitchen island on his way out the front door. She hurried and answered it. "Hey, girl. You're back. What's going on?"

"Not much. How was your first night in the RV?"

Betsy tried to stifle a yawn, but knew she hadn't done a good job when she tried to speak through it and it came out as a squeak.

"That good?"

"Rosie, hold on. Ben's trying to tell me something."

"Hon, I got to run by the house. Check things in the light. I'll be back around 9:30. Then we'll head to church."

"I'll be ready. Love ya!" Betsy blew a kiss to her hubby who pretended to grab it and put it to his lips.

"I'm back, Rosie. Actually, Mats and me slept like a log. That is when Ben laid still for a minute. I'm not sure if he got any sleep at all last night. I do have to say he's entertaining when he did go to sleep. His moans and groans were almost musical."

On the other end of the phone Rose did her normal snorting sound when she heard something funny. Betsy got tickled and both women ended up laughing. When Betsy got her amusement under control and poured a cup of coffee, she asked her friend, "So how was the Caribbean? What islands did you see this time? Did you have fun without us?"

"I'll never go on another cruise without you again."

"Yea, this no email, no texting, no nothing for days is for the birds."

"Amen...but I did learn something while we were gone."

"What's that?" Betsy took a sip of her coffee and tried to pay attention to her friend's call, but her eyes kept finding pretties in her new home.

"...and so you know, Larry doesn't have Low T after all."

Betsy praised the Lord she'd swallowed what she had in her mouth while gawking at the RV's décor. Or she would have made a mess all over the place.

"Rosie, we already knew he didn't."

"I still questioned it, but now I know what he's got."

"Dr. Wilford, what is your diagnosis?" Betsy went over and put her coffee cup on the table, bracing for what her friend might say next.

"Since he was on the ship and couldn't play his games all day—my concensus is he's suffering withdrawal symptoms from G.A. The exact same symptoms he displays when we're at a campground that doesn't have good internet service."

"What in the world is G.A.? Is it contagious?" Betsy glanced at her arm to see if she had a rash or bumps anywhere.

"G.A. is Gaming Addiction. Not sure that's the official name, but Larry's suffering from it. Big time."

Betsy chuckled at her friend's diagnosis. "I have to disagree. Not our level-headed engineer?"

"I'm glad you find this so amusing." Rose humphed. "Let's ask him the next time we're all together. I'm banking he'll admit it's the reason he wanted to sell our RV. So he could play, play, play his games any time and not fight with poopy internet service on the road."

"I'm still not sure it's what Lar has. Maybe it's..." Betsy couldn't come up with a name of a disease.

"See, it's got you baffled too. And since we're discussing serious matters, how did it go when Ben told his boss he was leaving? That he's not taking this last job on?"

"Ben said he'd never seen a person's face turn that color before."

"Did he have to give him mouth-to—"

"No, but there's more. Lots more." Betsy toyed with Rose and loved every minute of making her wait for the news.

"Go on."

Betsy didn't dwell on what happened two weeks ago. Instead, she told her friend about the phone call they'd received from Ben's boss the day before. No detail left out. She added a little more flash—always the truth—where the story needed some sprucing up.

Then came the best part...*Drum roll, please. The end of the st—*

"The old coot will never change."

"Don't be so judgmental, Rosie, I saved the best for last."

Betsy told her the happy ending, which all writers delight in.

Rose inhaled and Betsy thought for a second her friend swallowed her tongue. But she soon continued, "The geez—oh, I mean Mr. Greenspan. Can't believe he said all those nice things."

"You never know what an influence you are in someone's life until something like this happens."

"No, and I need to remember when my patience wanes while I wait in line. People are watching me."

Betsy laughed. "When you say it out loud, sounds kind of creepy."

Rose made a noise which sounded like a hiccup and a chirp. "Only sounds scary to someone, you, who's a writer. And doesn't let too many people in too close."

Oh how Betsy wanted to change the subject, but knew her friend wouldn't let her. Might as well play along. "What are you talking about, Rosie, I tell you everything. To you, my life is an open book," Betsy accentuated the last sentence with the same Texas drawl as she'd heard their RV mover use.

"I'll believe that when pigs fly. Anyway, I'm glad it went well with Ben's job. Makes leaving a lot easier."

"I agree." Betsy ignored Rose's comment about bovines and appreciated her friend changed the subject from talking about her.

"When's the closing on the house?"

"Next Wednesday. I can't believe it's almost here."

"The *Early Birds* will be on the road before you know it."

"We can't wait." Betsy noticed the time. "Gotta go and get ready for church and if I have time—write my next installment."

"You have an installment loan?"

"What? No, not an installment loan. I need to write my next blog."

"You want me to proof it before you publish it?"

"Nah. It's always perfect." Before her friend could comment Betsy said, "Bye!"

She took the phone from her ear, but before she hit the end-call button she heard Rose cackle on the other end.

Thank You, Lord, for my friend. I love her.

"We better enjoy Rose and Larry, if we're going to travel full time with them… and I'm pretty sure he's not a gambler."

Betsy rushed into the bedroom and changed then came out and picked up her laptop and carried it to the ugly couch. Then went and retrieved her cup of coffee.

Two out of the three necessities to complete the task at hand.

The third requirement, the most important in her book, came next. Prayer. If she failed to start with it, nothing came out as planned. Before bowing her head, she jotted her blog idea down on a pad of paper then picked up her Bible.

The underlined passages in Matthew 6 reminded her of what their pastor spoke on last Sunday. The "do not worry about your life" verse stopped Betsy and how the set of verses fit her life like a glove.

The words for the next blog hit her and she began to type. About the time she'd typed the period on the second sentence, the front door opened and Ben came in. Their dog bound over to the door and greeted him.

"I love you, too, Mats. Your mom, on the other hand, seems less enthused." Ben came over to the couch. "Hon, how'd you sleep last night?"

Betsy picked her fingers off the keyboard and stared at her husband. Lots of words came to mind to answer Ben's question, but none had anything to do with sleep. However, the thought of throwing something at him, for disturbing her writing, sang a tune in her head.

But all she had to throw was her Bible and computer. And she'd rather not sacrifice either one.

Pray, Betsy, pray!!!

In her heart she knew the Lord wanted her to thank Him for Ben. But the only prayer Betsy could muster—to herself, of course, *Oh Lord, please tell me this isn't how RV life is going to be?*

Ben stared at her. And after Betsy calmed down, she answered. "I slept better then you did, apparently."

"Not saying much. Are you about ready to go to church?"

"Yes," Betsy's answer went with a glance down at her computer. The one she'd been typing away on until...

You knew he was coming. He's not to blame.

If she repeated the phrase enough, there'd be hope for her husband's wellbeing. No need for an ambulance. But they needed to talk about her writing and how it would work, living in the RV full time. Set some kind of boundaries?

But they'd talk later. Ben hurried Matilda into her crate then stood at the open door, waiting for her. Which she did after she put her computer on the table next to the loveseat.

All the way to church, and while they walked into church, Ben went into why sleep eluded him. Betsy could see why he'd had a problem. The mechanical side of him overrode any sensibilities. Even the desire to sleep.

"I'm sorry. Hope you have better luck tonight." Betsy sat down in the pew and decided she couldn't stay miffed at a man who hadn't gotten enough shut eye to keep a bird alert on his perch. Betsy chuckled at the image in her head of a canary hanging onto its roost with one claw.

Ben sat down. "Are you entertaining yourself at my expense?"

"You could say that. I'll tell you when we get home." Betsy put her arm in the crook of Ben's bent elbow.

"After you tell me the cause of your amusement, do you want to see what options our RV has?"

Betsy smiled at what sounded like a pick-up line, but the extras on the rig rang her bell. But what would get her over-the-moon excited, her own place to write. Which she did not have.

Yet.

For the hundredth time since Ben brought the subject up about buying an RV, Betsy questioned their sanity. But, today, the craziness flew out the window when she convinced herself she'd talk to her husband about the desk unit.

Her own space.

At the end of the service, when they walked out to the foyer, Betsy wondered if she'd heard the sermon. The desk planning process wrecked havoc in her head. She made a note on her phone to listen to Pastor Montgomery's podcast. See what she missed.

"Betsy, I've been trying to get a hold of you for a week."

Debbie touched Betsy's arm, which caused her phone to slip out of her hand. The youth pastor, standing next to her, caught it before it hit the concrete floor and said. "I knew football would come in handy." Dave laughed and walked away.

"Betsy, I'm sorry I about took out your phone."

"Nary a scratch, Debbie. How are you?" Betsy reached over and hugged her petite friend.

"I'm fine, but I was concerned you'd already skipped town and didn't say goodbye."

"Not a chance. We're looking forward to next Saturday's going-away party. Except for when it's time to say goodbye. I hate that part."

"So do I. Anyway, I texted you and Rose about all of us girls doing lunch on Tuesday. Want to get together as much as we can before you leave."

"Thanks for the reminder. I'll put it in my phone." Betsy clicked on her calendar, but changed her mind. "Debbie, with the move, I'm not sure I'll remember to look at my phone. One day I couldn't find Matilda. Thought I'd packed her in a box."

Debbie's laughter filled the foyer. "You didn't, did you?"

"No, but she wasn't having any of moving that day. She went and hid in a closet. It was the last place I looked for her."

"Too much activity can stress out a human. I'd include pets too. Be sure to take some time away from it and veg."

"Will do. I better scoot. Ben wants to show me all the bells and whistles on our new RV today and I better not keep him waiting." Betsy hugged her friend again then met her hubby at the side door.

CHAPTER FOURTEEN

The ride home resembled the one a few nights before. Quiet. Ben didn't ask and Betsy didn't share the funny he'd heard from across the foyer. Maybe when they finished with the tour of the undercarriage of their Cedar Creek—she'd tell him.

After they got to the RV Park, Betsy went in and released Matilda from the confines of her crate. She tied her up outside and Ben began showing her the inner and outer workings of their new RV. Even as a female, the hoosiewhatsits and thingamajigs intrigued her.

And she couldn't have been happier her bud answered her many questions. Except the last one. The one she might have thought humorous, but wished she kept her mouth shut the minute it came out. "Hon, when are you going to build on the addition?"

"Addition?"

Betsy saw Ben take a step back and his shoulders drooped when he repeated the word. At that moment all intelligent or witty responses failed her. She had to find a way to let him know she needed a 'me' space. A place, if she sat in the particular spot, not to interrupt her.

"My statement needs a little clarification."

"I'd say it does." Ben plopped down on the bench of the picnic table and picked up Matilda.

"How about I get us a glass of sweet tea and some cheese and crackers and I'll tell you what I *should* have said."

"I can't wait to hear this."

Under normal circumstances, Betsy would be fuming at Ben's sarcastic remark, but today she deserved it. She went inside and all the while she got their light lunch together, she berated herself. "When are you ever going to think before you talk?"

She brought out the tray and sat the goodies on the outdoor table. Betsy waited until Ben filled a small plate with the snacks and took a drink of his tea before she spoke. This gave her enough time to pray and get her apology in order. Didn't want to muss up the make-up speech.

"Please forgive me for my unnecessary comment. I'd like to say I know what you're thinking, but I'm sure I'd be way off. But I know it hurt you and I'm sorry. Let me tell you what I meant to say."

"I'm listening."

"When you left the RV earlier today I started to write my blog. When you came back, you opened the door and started talking. I know you weren't aware of what I was doing. When it happened, I couldn't help but wonder how I'm going to write in such a small space."

Ben sat there with his arms crossed. His deep breathing told Betsy he wanted to say something, but decided to nod instead.

She asked, "Can I continue?"

A muffled "yes" gave her the go ahead. "All I'm saying, I want time to get my blog done."

"Seems fair."

"Since we're in agreement, I'd like to make a suggestion. For both of us."

Her hubby took a long sip of his sweet tea before he answered, "Go for it."

"When either one of us is working on their laptops, let's

promise each other we'll ask the other if we can disturb them before we start chattering. Would that work?"

A slow smile broke out on Ben's face. He got up and sat next to Betsy and said. "Works for me too when I'm surfing the web and don't want anyone interrupting me."

"Glad you like my idea."

"I do. Now don't you have a blog to write?"

Betsy kissed her hubby and bound up the three steps into the RV, knowing she hadn't broached the subject of the real "addition" she wanted. The topic of the desk would come at a later date. Not too far off, she hoped.

~

RV LIFE AND WEDDED BLISS

I mentioned in my last blog that we (hubby, pooch and me) are making a MAJOR change. Well, we've made the leap into RV life. This is the second day and we're loving it!!!

Before making our big move, lots of discussion took place. What to keep and what to put in storage? What to sell and/or give away? How are we going to fit all of the stuff we're taking into a 350 square foot 5th wheel?

It's funny – that was the easy part. What we've found most difficult is the two of us and how we live life inside of our small abode.

For those of you who have followed my blog for long, you've learned from me my mouth sometimes overrides my brain. Today I had such an occasion with the person I share the new RV with. But I'm happy to report hubs and I lived to tell everyone we solved the problem and no one got hurt in the process. ☺

The issue we needed to tackle—a touchy one. And, because I opened my mouth when I shouldn't have, it became complex too quickly.

But I realized the errors of my way and apologized. Did I hear a gasp out in cyberland??? I can hear some of you yelling, "You're telling me I have to apologize?" If forgiving is a foreign object in your marriage, rethink your thinking.

My apology set the stage so we could talk about the offense. In a more rational way (sweet tea and cheese may have helped a little too). Saying "I'm sorry", calmed what could have been a raging storm.

.Problem solved. Solution found. Praise the Lord.

Since hubby and I are living in a much smaller space, this tiny tweak will make our life easier and more enjoyable. Wedded bliss will once again be the norm in our home (in our case, RV).

If you haven't noticed, marriage is a funny thing. My advice: Take care of it, say you're sorry—when it's needed, and nurture the bond God placed in your heart for each other. When you do, it will blossom and grow.

Until next time and more RV adventures!!!
Bets

Betsy glanced out the window, after hitting the Publish button, and smiled. Ben and Matilda sat in one of their lawn chairs, snoozing. With no need to bother them, she placed her computer on the end table and went to preheat the oven for dinner.

After putting the meatloaf in, Betsy set the timer before she went over and reread her blog. And, as usual, a thousand ideas on what she should have added to it bombarded her.

Betsy stared at the screen and let out a sigh. "I should have put the part in about wanting a desk. Ben would have read it and found out what I want. I blew the perfect plan."

She could almost say verbatim how the conversation with Ben would go if she asked for a desk.

"You want what?"

"I want a desk. A built-in one would fit perfectly where the couch is."

"But there's a couch sitting there."

"I know. But when we give it to Goodwill, we'll have room for my new desk."

Betsy rehearsed her speech out loud and it sounded as stupid as it did when it rambled around in her head. "Ben will never agree to such a thing." She closed her computer and put it on the entertainment center this time.

"Is it safe to come in?" Ben peered into their RV before he stepped inside. "Hope so. Sure smells good in here."

"Come on in. You ready for dinner?"

Betsy set the table, while Ben got Matilda her supper. The two of them sat down to her one and only specialty dish. As she listened to Ben's prayer she, too, sent up a prayer of thanksgiving for how the Lord had steered their discussion earlier in the day to calmer waters.

"In Jesus' name. Amen!" Ben picked up his fork and devoured half of his slice before he took a break.

While she ate, Betsy made a mental note. She wanted them to make sure they prayed through each room of the RV. Like they'd done when they moved into their last house. What a difference it made.

Also, without prayers of family and friends, they wouldn't be together today. Let alone, getting ready for the journey the Lord had orchestrated. Betsy wanted to make sure their heavenly Father dwelled in their new home, as well.

"As for me and my house we will serve the—"

"You amaze me, Bets. Out of the blue you just say something."

"Guess you know what I'm talking about and I think we should hang our favorite plaque over this slide." Betsy pointed above her head and recited the whole verse this time. 'As for me and my house we will serve the Lord.' Ben, the verse helps me...us..."

"Keep our eyes on him. And while we're at it, we need to have Rose and Larry over so we can pray over our new place."

The lump in Betsy's throat kept an answer at bay. But love flooded in for her husband and what the Lord had done in his life. Their life, in such a short time. She managed a "thank you" and got up and carried their dishes to the sink.

As Betsy put them in the water, she chuckled since she'd only walked five steps to get to her final destination. If she'd thought about it, while she sat at the table, she could have leaned to her right and put them in the sink—without getting up.

The joy of a small abode. I think I could get used to this arrangement. With a desk, of course.

~

Ben came over and stood next to Betsy. Towel in hand to dry the few dishes his wife handed him. But every so often she'd have to nudge him to take the item since his mind wandered to the project he needed to do.

After their "discussion" earlier in the day—he needed to get busy and get Betsy's desk done. But with them living in such close quarters, his surprise would take a little bit of maneuvering.

One good thing, Ben had already gotten their friends in on it. Larry let him use their garage to store the board he'd bought for the desk top. Along with storing the two file cabinets he purchased which would hold the newly-stained plywood. Rose stated she'd keep her mouth shut and plan a girls-day out.

The stage is set. Almost.

"What are your plans tomorrow?" Ben asked when he put the last plate up in the cupboard and shut the door.

"Rose is picking me up around 8:30 and we're going to spend the day doing girl stuff. Nothing that would interest you."

Yes, the plan is in place.

"What's with the smile?"

"I'm a happy guy. Remember tomorrow's my last day at work." Ben hoped his wife would quit questioning him. No such luck.

"I know it's your last day, but I still think you're up to something else."

"Heaven's no!"

"Mr. B., you don't lie well."

Ben picked up Matilda and came over closer to Betsy. "Mom, we hope you have a wonderful day with Aunt Rose and I'll be good in my c.r.a.t.e. while you're gone."

"There is no hope for you, but whatever you have up your sleeve – it better not take up any square footage in this RV. We've pretty well filled it the way it is."

Betsy went to their bedroom to read. Ben looked at his watch. Almost time for *The Good Wife* and the other show he could never remember its name.

"See you in a couple of hours, dear."

Ben emailed Larry and they planned out their day. He said Rosie was ready. With all the plans finalized, he flipped on the show and put his recliner back to enjoy the two shows.

CHAPTER FIFTEEN

The horn tooted and Betsy gave Ben a hug as he sat at the table, eating breakfast. "Enjoy your last day at work. Tonight we'll go celebrate."

"Can't wait." Ben picked up his bowl and put it in the sink. "I think I should have worn jeans and a t-shirt instead of my suit."

"Behave. It's only eight hours."

"Which will be filled with a going-away party where everyone tells me how wonderful I am. The only good thing, it'll take up part of the day."

"You be good."

"From what old man Greenspan said – I'm a model employee."

Beep! Beep!

"Gotta go. Love ya!

Ben smiled. "Love ya, too and I'll be good!"

Betsy gave him a goodbye kiss, grabbed her purse and flung open the door. Which almost knocked Rose off the bottom step.

"Well, I was about to send in the police."

"Oh, you know Ben – he had to tell me a story." Betsy came down the stairs and gave Rose a hug.

"Better get used to it, sweetie. As the saying goes, "Now you have less paycheck and more husband." Rose chuckled at her own comment as they headed to her car and got in on their prospective sides.

"It'll be interesting. But no need to worry today. We've got a whole day together to have fun and spend some money."

Betsy had her eyes on some books on writing. The only problem – again – due to their smaller dwelling, where could she put the extra teaching tools?

"Rose, I'm reading too much on writing and not writing enough. And now that we're living in the RV, I need to quit buying so many books?"

Her friend put her car in park again and turned and stared at Betsy. "Woman, I'd say buy them if you need them. You can also download some on your tablet. But, Bets, I do know one thing. God has opened up an opportunity for you and you don't even know it yet."

"Yea, whatever. Can you prophesy over me at breakfast? Right now I'm hungry."

Rose put her car in gear and backed up a few inches before she stopped again. This time she stared straight ahead. "You can discount what I say, but He's up to something with you and your writing. And a..."

Betsy ignored her friend's unfinished sentence. "All I can say, I hope He's up to finding us some food pretty soon."

"How about breakfast at IHOP Miss Sassy Pants?"

~

At the restaurant the hostess directed them to a booth and they sat down. The young woman's excited arm movements reminded Betsy of a flight attendant giving her pre-flight spiel. Only this time she had menus in hand and flung them in their direction.

One missed Rose's nose by inches and Betsy leaned back in time to avoid having her head severed from the rest of her body. A bit of an exaggeration, but no doubt the plastic would have left a mark.

"Can I get you two ladies some coffee? Oh, and I'll be your waitress. When you're ready I'll take your order. If there's anything el..."

Betsy watched the woman walk away without taking their order and chuckled. "Either she's had way too much coffee or she's worked the last three night shifts without a break."

"Whatever it is, we need to make sure their insurance is paid up. The menu she swung in my direction got so close to my nose, I could read the fine print on the way by."

"Quiet. Here she comes."

"I see her. You can quit kicking me under the table."

"Hello again. My name's Camille. Are you ready to order?"

Betsy thought they better get their food in writing before Ms. Menu got away again. "Yes, I'll take Stuffed French Toast and coffee."

"Double that."

"Coming right up." The waitress/hostess left without the menus, which Rose tried to hand to her.

"You're having java? I thought you gave it up."

Rose put cream and sugar in her cup. "On girl's day out it's okay to drink coffee. It won't bother my I.B.S.—"

"I. B. SO not caring about your stomach problems, Rosie. Don't you say anymore or you'll ruin my breakfast before we get it."

"I can see you're a caring individual today." Rose put the napkin on her lap and added, "If you're interested, I've also heard all calories are removed too...but...your little snippy comment tripled them."

"So I shouldn't make smart-alecky remarks on my birthday either?"

"Right you are and if you continue them today, you won't get..." Rose covered her mouth.

"Get what?" Betsy eyed her friend.

"Never mind."

"Here you go, ladies. Enjoy."

Betsy thanked the waitress then turned her attention to

Rose. Her tablemate had already dived into her French toast, stuffing her mouth with the delectable-looking fare. A bite waited on her fork.

"Well…what is it I won't get if I don't quit sassing?" Curiousity about got the best of Betsy, but she'd wait. Rosie would spill the beans soon enough.

"A thosnd cowreies."

"What?"

"A thosnd cawreis."

"Girl, I think you said, 'a thousand calories', but I'm not sure. You better tell me what's going on."

Rose nodded and tried to say something else, but instead of words – she snorted. At which point Betsy lost all hope she'd find out anything until Rosie gained control once again.

She glanced around IHOP and spied their waitress. Camille, too, needed to curb her enthusiastic laughter. The tray she carried with one hand swayed to and fro, alerting everyone within a ten-foot radius they'd better move or a stack of pancakes could fall on their head.

As always, Rosie jumped to the rescue. After she laid her fork down, of course. This time she caught the wobbly tray in mid-freefall and put it and its contents on an empty table before she turned and said, "There you go, sweetie."

Camille gave Rose a hug and the restaurant's patrons who witnessed the near catastrophe stood up and clapped. A few chimed in with a "Woohoo" or two, causing the two to blush. Betsy loved when her friend's helpfulness got noticed, even if it embarrassed her a bit.

"Thank you, ma'am. I better get this food out before someone starts booing me. Hungry people can get mean." Camille laughed again, but this time she had complete control of her tray of food.

"You done good, Rosie." Betsy took a bite of her French toast.

Rose settled in and picked up her fork. "Nothing you wouldn't do. I just happen to be faster today." Another snort escaped.

"Only 'cause you were closer to the action." Betsy waited for

Rosie to look then reached her fork over to take a piece off Rose's plate.

"Oh no you don't. Give that back to me."

"Can't...I already ate it." Betsy popped it into her mouth and smiled.

"And I'll have to put up with this when we're on the road. I'm not sure my I. B.—"

"Rosie, I. B. still not wanting to hear about your ailment. But I do have a question." Betsy put her fork down and asked, "Mrs. Wilford, do you honestly think this RV thing is going to work?"

"I have no doubt in my mind." Rose took a big bite and settled back in the booth.

"I'd say I agree, but I have one concern." Betsy told her about her stupid comment to Ben and how they came to an agreement, without mentioning the addition of a work station. "But I still want to ask him about us putting a desk in the RV."

Betsy had gotten the last word out and Rose started to choke. Not the kind where she needed to give her friend the Heimlich maneuver. More like the time you tell somebody something and they know something they aren't telling you.

"Okay, Rose, fess up?"

Rose sputtered and swallowed a couple of times. For theatric's sake, Rosie wiped her mouth, finishing with dabbing each side of her lips.

"Bets, nothing's up. But I do know the bookstore awaits our credit cards. When we're done there, and if we have time, we can hit Hobby Lobby."

Betsy watched the twinkle in Rose's eyes get bigger the more she yapped. About nothing. If she'd been Pinocchio—her nose would have extended to downtown Houston. Betsy realized no amount of prodding would get anything out of her friend. But there would be another chance.

"Since you received a standing ovation today – I'll buy breakfast." Betsy reached in her purse to get her wallet.

"Heaven's no. It's on me. I'm so full of benevolence today it's spilling over. Anyway, it's my turn." Rose tapped her fork on the table.

"You're full of something, but I'm not sure what." Bets laughed then looked down at her watch. "Rosie, do you know what time it is?"

"No."

"We've been here for almost three hours."

"Time flies when you're saving lives and limbs."

"Go on believing that, sista. Let's pay and get going. There's books to buy."

And secrets to find out from Rosie when she's not paying attention to what she's saying.

Betsy and Rose hit Barnes and Noble around lunchtime and the rest of the afternoon flew by as they perused their favorite store. Betsy picked up too many books, reasoning her writing needed a shot in the arm.

While on her book-collecting frenzy, she'd hand Rose books she didn't want and they'd retrace her steps to put them back in the correct spot. Betsy observed more than once the task took on a characteristic of someone doing a balancing act. Of sorts.

Rose kept glancing at her watch, while leaning over to tuck the book into the spot it belonged. Finally, Betsy couldn't take it any longer and leaned over. "What are you doi..." She stopped when an obnoxious noise took over the air waves. "Is that your phone?"

After digging for a while, she answered it and Betsy could tell the subject of discussion had something to do with her.

"Sounds like a plan. I'll get her, oh I mean it, home A.S.A.P."

"Rose, you are up to something and I'm not sure I like it."

"Trust me, sis, you're going to love it." Rose took a hold of Betsy's elbow and rushed to the front door.

Betsy peeled her friend's fingernails out of her arm and said, "Rosebud, can we hold up? I need to pay for these books."

"Oh, I wondered what all the beeping was about."

The store alarm rang in the background, even after Betsy took the merchandise from Rose's outstretched arms. Once at the counter she laid the books down and searched for her debit card, which she found at the bottom of her purse.

While she waited for her receipt, Betsy looked around and saw Rose. Her friend stood smack dab in the middle of the front door. Unmoving. Unwavering. Unaware she'd blocked one of the exits out of the mega store.

Betsy waved frantically, hoping Rosie would get the drift she needed to get out of people's way. But her deer-in-the-headlight stare told Betsy, "Nobody's home and I don't hear the incessant ringing of the store alarm."

Yes, the one still going off from when Rose tried to drag her out of the store without paying. Betsy wanted to leave the counter and rescue her friend, but the clerk handed her the receipt. She signed it, grabbed her bag and nabbed Rose. Together they hurried to the car.

Once inside the vehicle, Betsy couldn't contain her laughter any longer.

"What's so funny?"

"You. All Barnes and Noble needed to do was put a book in your hand and call you a display."

"Oh, aren't you funny."

"I am and if I could get a hold of the security camera footage, you would too." Betsy continued to chuckle, stopping when she heard a beep. "Rose, is your phone going off or is it still the alarm at Barne—"

"Hush and buckle up. You're in for...never mind." Rose put her car in drive and headed out of the mall parking lot.

Betsy fastened her seatbelt and took Rose's advice. Didn't want to distract her when her friend drove. They might end up in the ditch and she'd never find out what was going on.

~

"Larry I can't thank you enough for this." Ben wiped down the top of Betsy's new desk and arranged the mesh pen holder for the third time.

"You're welcome. Now would you sit down? You're making me and Matilda nervous." Larry pointed to the dog. "See?"

The Boston terrier mix sat right in the middle of the floor, looking up at Ben. Every so often she turned her head from side to side, as if she listened to their conversation.

Ben ignored his pooch and said, "What's taking them so long?"

"You just texted Rose. She will drive as fast as the law allows."

"Which worries me."

"Don't blame you. I'll pray she gets Betsy home safe."

"Please do. Don't want our work of art to go to waste." Ben sat down on the loveseat and waited for the ladies. And prayed for Rose to put her foot into it – for a change.

He'd ridden with Larry's wife and would classify her driving a little above a snail's pace. All of them joked – "You never count on her getting anywhere fast or on time."

Today, Ben wanted Rose to drive faster and get Betsy home to see her surprise. *And, boy is this new 'addition' to their RV going to surprise her.*

The girls arrived 15 minutes later. When Ben heard the Wilford's car pull up, he sprung into action. The first thing, he put Matilda in her crate. To keep her from jumping around. He laughed. When Betsy saw her new desk she'd be doing enough of that herself.

"Can we come in?"

Ben heard Rose's voice and went over and opened the door. "Come on in."

"Go ahead, Betsy."

Betsy took a step into the RV and Ben pointed to the front of it, where his wife's gift sat. He heard a gasp then nothing for a few seconds.

"It's perfect." Betsy walked over and touched the top. Then she turned and gave her hubby a kiss on the cheek.

Those two words and getting a kiss told Ben he and Larry had done well.

"Think we'll leave you two alone." Larry took Rose's hand and led her to the door.

"Call me." Rose made a gesture of a phone to her ear before

her husband guided her down the stairs, closing the door behind them.

Ben stood behind Betsy and watched her as she opened drawers on the filing cabinets and checked out all the gadgets around her laptop. His heart swelled every time he caught the smile he loved so much. At one point he thought he caught her wiping a tear away on her face.

"How did you know?" Betsy said, still facing the present she'd received. "This is perfect.

"I'm glad you like it."

"I don't like it, hon." She spun around. "I love it."

Betsy came over and kissed Ben. One he wouldn't forget for a long while. A little bit of lumber and a few hours' labor and his wife's a very happy lady.

Go figure.

"You want out of your crate, girly?" Betsy unhooked the door and Matilda performed her usual routine then settled down with her chew toy.

"Hon, I have to show you something." Ben took Matilda's crate and wheeled it under her desk. "We can put it under there when it's not in use and when we leave, we can pull it out and Mats is in the middle of the living room."

"Love your ingenuity. Especially the wheels on the bottom of her crate."

"Makes it easier to move. Also, the file cabinets—one for each of us gives us more storage. Which we need."

"You thought of everything."

"No, Larry, Mr. Engineer, did. He finished it while I was at work today."

"I'll have to give him a kiss the next time I see him."

"We'll see about that."

Betsy smiled. "So how did your last day go? I want to hear everything."

"Glad I wore my suit. They had quite the party for me. Mr. Greenspan got up to speak and said almost the same thing as the other day." Ben loosened his tie. "Bets, I had no idea I'd made such an impact on my boss or the people I worked with."

"God works it out that way so we don't get such a big head." Betsy snuggled up next to her hubby.

"It blows my mind what some of them said." Ben wiped at his eyes.

"I wish I'd been there."

"You had more important things to do. We had to get you out of the house so Larry could complete this masterpiece. Now it's time you sat down and got the feel for your new workspace."

"You sure?"

"Positive."

For the next two hours, Ben watched Betsy at her desk. Like a child on Christmas morning, she touched and tried out her new toys. No one else existed in her world for the time being.

She didn't even notice he'd gotten up to start dinner. Not until she turned around and said, "Something smells wonderful. But I thought we were going out to celebrate."

"We'll do it some other time. Are you hungry?"

"I'm starving."

"You should be. It's 7:00." Ben stirred the spaghetti and sauce together and checked on the bread in their convection oven.

"I've been sitting here for over two hours?"

"Yep and I'll bet you touched every item on your new desk a couple of hundred times, while perched there." Ben laughed at his own joke.

"I can't believe this. Honestly, Ben, this is the exact desk I envisioned in this spot. How did you know what I wanted? We haven't talked about it."

"Bets, I knew you missed the desk you had in the house and all the space to spread out. So when we agreed on the RV, Larry and I went to work on the design. Hope you don't mind we took out the couch."

Betsy almost fell over. "Are you kidding me? I hated that couch. The color reminded me of a color somewhere between baby poop and tangerine."

"Guess I shouldn't have worried so much about getting rid of it."

"No, and anyway, if someone wants to come stay, they can sleep on the airbed."

"Hotels are good too. Now are you ready to eat. I'm starving." Ben filled a couple of plates and carried them over to the table. They bowed their head and Betsy prayed, thanking the Lord for her new desk and Ben's retirement.

"Amen. Oh, and could You bless this food to our bodies. I almost forgot. Amen!!" Betsy ended the prayer then twirled some spaghetti with a piece of roasted chicken breast on her fork and stuffed it in her mouth.

"Looks like someone was hungry."

Betsy reached over and patted Ben's hand. "Thank you for this special present and...for this tasty meal." She picked up her fork again and spun more pasta on it and took a big bite.

"You're welcome." He wanted to add more – but decided today he'd revel in the fact Larry and his act of service hit it out of the ballpark.

"Mr. B. do you want any more spaghetti?" Betsy went to pick up her plate.

"No, I'm stuffed." Ben took her plate and carried it to the sink. "I'll clean up."

"You've done enough. Let me." Betsy tried to scoot Ben away from the sink.

"I hear your desk calling your name. Anyway, don't you have a blog to do?"

Betsy smiled. "I do have some ideas I need to jot down before I forget them."

"Then get over there before you do. I've got the kitchen covered."

Ben went to work and got it cleaned up in record time. And from the goings on at the door, Matilda needed to go for a walk.

"Ready to go, buddy?"

When their dog stopped and sat still, Ben leaned down and put on her leash. Before he opened the door he asked Betsy. "Hon, you want to go with us?"

"I'll stay here."

That didn't surprise him and off they went for their evening stroll around the park, leaving Betsy to get some writing done.

CHAPTER SIXTEEN

Betsy's heart overflowed as she typed. Today's events spurred the sequel to her last blog on *Wedded Bliss*. Her fingers almost couldn't keep up as she poured out her heart.

ANSWERED PRAYER

"When you think He's not listening. That the Lord is nowhere to be found – He's right next to you. Our Father in heaven hears our prayers."

Keep praying for those circumstances in your life.

Tears streamed down Betsy's face as she continued to write. God's love poured forth and she sat in the middle of His blessing. The desk, being one of the biggest ones, meant so much to her. How could a mere sentence convey the true meaning of this gift?

"He hears your prayers. I don't know how much more I can say. You are loved. He cares for you. And He will never leave you."

Blessings,
Bets

Betsy closed her laptop and stayed seated at her desk, never noticing she sat in total darkness. But His light, illuminating in her heart, overshadowed anything else around her. She sat and rejoiced in God's love. Amazed at the gift He, Ben and Larry had given her.

"You asleep in here?"

Ben's voice startled Betsy and she sprang out of her chair and flipped on the light. "No, I'm sitting here admiring my desk." She took a seat on the loveseat.

"I'm not sure how to take that statement." Ben smiled while he took off Matilda's collar.

"No worries, my dear. It passed inspection."

Ben came over and planted a kiss on the top of Betsy's head before joining her on the loveseat. Matilda squeezed in between them—in her normal spot and fell fast asleep.

"Think she's out for the night," Ben said after a yawn.

"I'm about ready to call it a night myself. How about you?

"At 9:00?"

"We can catch the early news or..." Betsy got up and picked up their snoozing pooch and headed for the bedroom.

"All of a sudden I'm feeling extremely tired." Ben shut off the living room light and followed his wife.

~

"What are you going to do today? Gonna tackle another HGTV project?" Betsy asked Ben while he got dressed the next morning.

"Like your side of the closet?"

"Nah, I'm liking the turnstyle deal much better. Once I started to use the plastic clips. Works better than hangers."

"Well then, I'm not sure what's on the agenda. Probably need to go over to Larry's. Clean up from the desk project." He finished buttoning his maroon polo shirt. "But the first thing I need to do..." He reached over Matilda, who lay in the middle of their bed, "is tickle my wife."

"No, you don't." Betsy flung her legs over the side of the bed and got up before he had a chance to do anything of the sort. Her laughter filled the bedroom as she gave him a big hug and kiss. "You know I love you, bud?"

Ben pushed her away and gave her a sideward glance. "Me thinks you only love me for my gifts and talents."

Betsy nodded. "And don't forget your resourcefulness. That's on the top of my list." She opened their closet and took out a pair of blue jeans and a black and white tee and walked into the bathroom.

"You can call me MacGyver," Ben yelled. "If you're ever locked in a room and you have 30 seconds of air left – call on me to bail you out of the jam."

Betsy couldn't figure out why Ben spoke at a higher volume, she'd only moved 12 feet from their closet, but kept it to herself. "You're absolutely right. You're the man." She turned on the shower and shut the bathroom door, drowning out any more conversation.

Or any chance of more tickling. Unless Ben wanted to get drenched from the shower nozzle Betsy held in her hand. She waited. Nothing out of the ordinary happened to interrupt her hot shower.

~

Ben chuckled when he heard Betsy's retort and the shower running. Oh how he wanted to join in, but decided breakfast called his name louder. He'd fix them an egg sandwich and hashbrowns.

While he heated up some coffee he thought about their conversation. They'd had this talk more than once about his different attributes. Those situations where Betsy said he always came up with the most sensible solution. Or as Betsy called it: his resourcefulness.

"That people at work took advantage of. Sometimes getting credit..." Ben stopped when he thought of the day before. He also let go of the death grip he had on the measuring cup he'd sat in the microwave. "Nothing more to worry about. I'm retired. Thank You, Lord."

Betsy's laughter told Ben she'd heard some of his tirade. Leaving the coffee to cook, he strolled over to the steps and glanced up. This time he chuckled. His wife stood in their bedroom in all her glory, with only a towel wrapped around her head.

Ben whistled one happy tune. Then his eyes scanned the thermostat to check the temperature in the RV and commented, "Is it hot in here?"

"No. It's just an old man who's delusional and obviously half blind." Betsy smiled as she waltzed past him into the bathroom. Before closing the door all the way, she said, "You sure have been talking to yourself a lot lately."

"Matilda and me were having a discussion." Ben heard the beep on the microwave and went over and took the coffee out. "Hey, Bets, I've got an idea. How about I fix us an egg sandwich this morning?"

Betsy opened the door and came down the stairs fully dressed. "I have a better idea. Let's go to Einstein's and have a bagel? We can run over to Rose and Larry's afterward and help you guys clean up?"

"I'll give Larry a call on the way and tell him what we're doing." Ben poured the coffee into their mugs and handed one to Betsy.

She put her coffee down on the counter and took Ben's hand. "You know since you're retired you don't have a schedule. Have you thought about that?"

"Oh, yea. I think I'm going to like this spur of the moment living."

Six months ago Ben couldn't have fathomed he'd ever retire, but now he couldn't imagine otherwise. Why he hadn't listened to Betsy and Matilda sooner, he'd never know. But Someone, his Lord and Savior, got through to him before he keeled over and died from stress.

"Mats, I'm sorry, but you have to go in your c.r.a.t.e. for a while." Ben wheeled it from under the desk, watching Matilda try to avoid the inevitable. "I promise when we get on the road we'll work on you staying out of it."

With Ben's comforting words and a bit of nudging, Matilda walked in by herself. Even though reluctance of doing the unthinkable sprang to attention on her tiny face.

~

"Poor thing." Betsy patted the top of the crate. "It's okay, we won't be gone long."

"Bye, Matilda. See you later."

Ben closed the RV door and Betsy followed him to the truck and heard him shut the alarm off on his key ring.

"Want to drive?"

"No, I'm good."

"Hon, sometimes you have to jump to find out if you can swim. In this case, drive to see if you can handle this thing."

"No comment." Betsy watched her hubby as he started the dually. Seemed pretty simple. No switches or a scary clutch to operate. Turn the key and back it up. So why couldn't she convince her brain she could drive it.

Or steady her fast-beating heart whenever she thought of taking the thing out. Betsy had been praying for her fear to go away. To get behind the wheel and do it. She also needed to *just do it* in other areas of her life too.

"What kind of bagel are you getting?"

Ben's question took her away from chastising herself and onto bagels and cream cheese. "Hope they have the power bars or whatever they're called."

"If they do, let's get some extra and freeze them." Ben pulled up at Einstein's and went inside.

While he got their order, Betsy called Rose to see if they could come over later.

"Sure thing. We're not doing anything other than our normal, getting ready to hit the open road with our two best friends."

"I've got an idea, when Larry and Ben get finished cleaning up, we can help you guys do whatever you need done." Betsy saw her husband come out of the bagel place, carrying two big bags. "Rose, we might be a while. We're at Einstein's and it looks like

Ben bought out the store."

"Oh, a bagel sounds good."

"We'll be right over."

Ben got in and proclaimed in a loud voice. "They had your bars for half price and I bought them all. They're day old, but it shouldn't be a problem." A smile of accomplishment lit up his face.

"I do have a concern. Is our freezer in the RV big enough to hold all of them?"

His expression told Betsy he hadn't thought this endeavor all the way through and she smiled at him. "Sweetie, I called Rose and mentioned bagels and she said she was hungry for one. Told her, "We're on our way.""

"Maybe they'll take a few of these off our hands."

"You might want to stop and get Matilda. You know how we get when we're over at Larry and Rose's."

Ben took the back way to the RV Park and when Betsy went inside to let Matilda out of her crate, their dog did her normal dance. "Come on, we're going over to visit your friends. Hope Baby doesn't bug you too much."

No worries. Matilda doesn't let yappers bother her. She yips once and they know who's boss.

"Not sure, but I'd say we have a Type A personality dog. I'll have to tell Ben."

By the time Betsy put Matilda in the backseat of the dually, she'd forgotten her profound thought about their dog's personality trait. What interested her—her cinnamon raisen power bar.

And she didn't see a need to wait until they got over to the Wilford's. Betsy glanced at the bag. She could have more than one since they had plenty to go around.

CHAPTER SEVENTEEN

"Lar, how about we go out to your shed. Get the place cleaned up?"

"Got it done this morning."

"Yes, so he could go play those stupid games on his laptop." Rose picked up their empty plates and napkins. When she got behind Larry's chair, she poked the back of his head and stated. "The G.A. is out of control."

"Unless you're doing an exorcism or cutting my hair, quit touching my head. Also, sweetie, quit diagnosing me. I DO NOT have Low T or G.A. Whatever that is. Quit! Leave me alone." Larry swatted at Rose's hand.

She moved it away and carried the plates to the sink. "I'm right. You've go—"

"Rose, I've got something alright, but I'm not sure there's a cure."

This got everyone laughing. Even Rose, who clapped her hands and soap suds covered everything around her. The snorts began.

"As I was about to say before I was interrupted." Larry moved his chair away from the table. "Ben, we should look at the tools we're taking. No need to take duplicates when we get going on our adventure."

"You're right and don't look now, but you've also got a friend."

Matilda stood on her hind legs, her front paws on the side of Larry's chair. "What's on your mind, Mats?" He petted the Boston mix. The minute he did, the Wilford's Shih Tzu, all 10 pounds of her, started yelping at the top of her lungs.

No one said anything for a minute then Ben spoke up, "Larry? Rose? I'd say your dog could use some serious meds."

"You are absolutely right. Rose, write that down. We need to get something from the vet before we leave. Or the RV parks are going to ban us from staying there."

"They won't want you to stay either. Your G.A. makes you unsociable as well. Yes, you need some drugs too. Those psycho...psychedelic drugs."

Betsy watched the two men get up from the table and walk out. Their uproarious laughter could be heard from behind the closed door. She'd bet her life on the fact they carried the conversation about Baby and Larry's supposed G.A. farther than it needed to go.

"Hello Betsy."

"Sorry. I was imagining what the guys were talking about. Also, sorry about Ben's diagnosis of Baby. It's none of our business."

"He's right. She does have an attitude. What she needs is obedience school."

"Great idea. Matilda and Baby can go together."

This brought a round of noises from Rose that Betsy hadn't heard before, which caused tears to roll down her face.

"Betsy, your dog...is the poster child of how...everyone would want their dogs to behave." Rose continued to snort and pointed to the corner of their living room. Matilda sat there with a smile on her face.

"Honestly, I don't know why we were so lucky. Oh, I mean, blessed to find her. She's an incredible dog. I need to write a story about her."

"She's not the only one. I've been dying to tell you your latest blog about your new desk was...spot on. Have you checked how many comments you've gotten on the blog and on Facebook?"

Betsy shook her head "no" since she'd taken a bigger-than-normal bite of bagel. Also, while trying to answer Rose, she tried to keep Matilda off of her lap. It worked until Baby came over to antagonize her. For no apparent reason. Again

"Baby, leave Mats alone. Go outside and bug your dad."

Betsy watched the Shih Tzu go out the doggy door. Then she turned her attention to her own pooch who strolled over to Baby's pillow and laid down.

Rose said, "Go for it." and Betsy knew Matilda kept one eye open to see when the 'enemy' would return.

With both dogs settled, Betsy took a drink of her coffee then asked her friend, "Did my blog make sense?"

"And then some. I can't believe you haven't read your comments. Girl, I sometimes wonder about you." Rose reached over and picked up her phone and pushed on the screen. "Here, read them."

Betsy scrolled through and read each of the comments. Most hit 'like'. Others thanked her for the timely post. But the ones which brought tears to her eyes said they'd prayed, some for years, and still waited for an answer.

One woman's post shouted at Betsy and she couldn't stop the tears. At the end the person wrote, "You make it sound so easy. You pray. Viola. The next day you get what you want. WHAT ABOUT ME? What's your advice for a loser like me?"

Betsy handed Rose her phone. "Don't think you read this one. Please tell me I didn't sound like the answer was wham bam. Did I?"

"No, but sounds like this woman wants them ASAP. The only answer you can give is the one you hear from above. I'd say before you answer her, you need to spend some time with your heavenly Father. Find out what He wants you to say."

Rose lifted her phone as if it offered the answer. "Betsy,

Tljscorned needs His love and you're the one elected to show her how much He loves her.

"This is not what I signed up for when I started writing the blog."

"I'm sure it's not, but for whatever reason He's used you for the last three years."

"But I'm not equipped or smart enough."

Rose gave her one of those looks—like her mother used to. Betsy knew she'd belittled herself once too often.

"All I can say, girlfriend, it's not you. It's the Lord. He's giving you the words to write and He'll give you the answer Tljscorned is searching for."

Betsy hung her head then went over and hugged Rose. "Now to a lighter subject—do you want to share a bagel with me?"

"I thought you'd never ask."

She and Rose scarfed down their half, but Betsy's didn't taste as wonderful as the first two. Her heart and mind kept going to this woman's comment.

What do You want me to tell her?

"I know you are fretting over there. He'll give you the answer. He always does." Rose reached over and gave Betsy's hand a squeeze.

"I hope you're right."

"I'm always right." Rose then stuffed the rest of the bagel into her mouth, causing her cheeks to protrude like a chipmunk.

Betsy didn't want to encourage her, but couldn't contain it. "Rosie, you make it very hard to have a serious discussion when you do things like that." She blew up her cheeks to mimic her friend.

"Made ya laugh, didn't I?" Rose swallowed and continued, "You were getting too down in the mouth about all this. Remember, the joy of the Lord is my strength. Amen and Amen!!!"

Before Betsy could respond to Rose's comment, the Wilford's back door opened and the guys came in, all smiles. Baby followed them in with non-stop barking and an ear-piercing noise Betsy wasn't sure had a name.

Larry came and stood next to his wife's chair. "Rosebud, if you don't do something with this pooch—me, my LowT and G.A. are moving to...Boise...Idaho."

Rose stood up, all five feet two inches of her, and pointed at his chest this time and said, "Idle threats will get you nowhere, mister. Go ahead and leave without me."

"Really?" Larry pulled out the chair next to his wife and sat down, motioning Ben to take a seat. "Sit down, you don't want to miss this."

"If you take off, Lar, Baby and me will hitch a ride with Ben and Betsy. I don't have a problem sleeping on their loveseat. It reclines." Rose took a breath. "Or, I'll get a pad and sleep on top of Bets's new desk."

Betsy couldn't pick out who in the group laughed the hardest, but it stopped when, out of the blue, Matilda started chasing Baby. The two ran around Rose and Larry's living room at break-neck speed. If the Shih Tzu stopped, Matilda growled and the chase began again.

"Where did that come from?" Betsy's stared at their pooch.

Ben chuckled. "I don't know, but if Larry goes to Boise. I'm going with him. Leave you two with these maniac dogs."

"No way." Betsy got up and hugged Rose and grabbed Ben's hand. "We need to get home. We've outstayed our welcome."

"Never. Come any time—especially if you bring bagels," Larry said.

~

Ben glanced over at Betsy on their way home. Her nose buried in her phone and her thumb scrolling back and forth. He waited for his wife to tell him what interesting thing she'd found.

Nada.

Not good when Betsy stayed quiet for too long. He wondered if Rose and her got into it? No! They all joked around when they left the Wilford's house. He hoped he hadn't done anything, but knowing his record on saying the wrong thing. Anything's possible.

Matilda, move over, I'm moving in the crate with you.

Ben laughed and the minute he did, he knew he'd have to explain what he found so funny.

"And you think it's strange I talk to myself. I'd say you're weird. I've caught you chuckling more than once over the last month."

"It's because I'm such a happy guy...now that I'm retired."

"You should be happier getting out of there, but tell me what was so amusing a second ago. Trust me, I need something to cheer me up."

"Well then you'll find great humor in this. I'm sitting here wondering why you weren't talking. I said to myself, 'Self, am I the cause of her not talking? Just one day after I gave her the huge surprise. Then I told Mats to move on over I'm joining her on her doggy bed.'"

"After that explanation, I'd say you're on some of those 'psychedelic' drugs Rose was talking about?" Betsy laughed.

"Maybe. Hey, didn't I also hear something about obedience school before we headed out the door?"

"I'm not sure what they agreed on—other than Boise. But could you do me a favor, the next time we go over there, please leave your opinion about their dog at home."

"Will do...but their mutt brings out the worst in me." Ben chuckled again. "And, what about our quiet, almost comatose dog? What came over you?" As if on cue Matilda came up and plopped down on the center console. "I think Rose feeds Baby spicy food and Mats ate some."

Ben thought he heard a little laugh, but Betsy didn't comment. Must not be as funny as he'd thought. "Enough about the pooches. Tell me what's going on with you."

"It's about a comment on my blog."

"What'd the person say?"

Betsy took out her phone and read Ben the complete post. He took a quick peek at his wife and saw her wipe away tears. "What did Rose say to do?"

"Pray."

"She is one smart cookie. Tonight in our prayer time, if it works for you, we'll spend some time praying about it, too."

"Thanks, I need all the help I can get."

"Want to stop at McDonald's for some ice cream."

"Before supper?" Betsy reached over Matilda and squeezed Ben's arm.

"You need a little pick-me-up."

"I think you're right."

CHAPTER EIGHTEEN

Betsy wanted to shout from the tree tops, but her hollering had nothing to do with her soon-to-arrive ice cream cone. What her happiness had to do with—Ben referred to their 'prayer time'.

Together. Something they'd started after Ben came home. An almost sacred time to keep their restored marriage on track. Each night Betsy couldn't wait to pray. It became almost as important as breathing to her.

When they'd settled in bed, Ben prayed for Betsy and for the words she needed to say to Tljscorned. His prayer warmed her heart with its short, to the point delivery. No beating the request to death. Just the facts. Nothing more.

After they kissed and all got snuggled in, Betsy—now the one who couldn't sleep—lay there praying and worrying about what to say to the person who commented on...on...*Facebook.*

The second the word hit her, Betsy scooted out from under the covers, grabbed her phone off her side table and went to the living room. Darkness greeted her, but the open blind reminded her she'd come out half dressed. Clad in a tattered tee and undies.

Betsy's saving grace—if there's a Peeping Tom, they couldn't see in the tinted window if they wanted to. She chuckled at her random thought while she closed the shade and turned on the light.

Once settled on the loveseat, nothing mattered but letting Tljscorned know someone cared. No words of wisdom or great epiphany popped into her mind when she clicked on the person's name. But when Betsy hit Message, her testimony began to pour out.

Only a snippet tonight. More would come later. When Tljscorned trusted her enough to give her an email address or phone number.

Father, I'm not qualified. But You are.

Betsy hit Post at the top of the page, realizing the second she did she'd exposed her heart to a total stranger. A person who could ridicule, condemn or...a smile crossed Betsy's face...or accept God's love in the words sent.

She laid her phone on the desk and it came to life almost before she had her hand off of it. Betsy glanced at Facebook and read a Message from Tina. Tljscorned.

I don't know how you can get to know a person in one simple paragraph, but it's as if I've known you all my life. Your journey is ahead of mine, but so much of what you said fit—as if you were writing MY story. Thank you for sharing yours with me. And so you know, Betsy, I want your happily ever after.

Again, Betsy put her phone down, wanting to take a minute to absorb what Tina wrote. No, she hadn't spilled the beans on her life, but she'd opened the door to share more about Ben and her struggles.

Did she want to go down that highway and relive the heartache of betrayal? Did He truly heal her, them, of the hurts enough she could help another person through their story? Did Betsy want to...

For some reason Rose's comment from the other day came to mind. "Betsy, you don't let people in."

"I don't have a choice this time." Betsy picked up her phone and typed a second note to Tina, telling her she'd write more to her in the morning.

"Can't leave you alone for a minute and you're up playing on your phone." Ben stood at their bedroom door.

Betsy got up and met Ben at the stairs. "Larry's been showing me some of the games he plays. Kind of fun."

Ben gave her a sideward glance. "That's not what you were doing, was it?"

"No, I couldn't sleep." Betsy yawned and took Ben's hand. "I'll tell you about it when we get back in bed."

"Glad the Lord prompted you tonight."

"So am I." Betsy snuggled closer to her hubby and told him what she'd written.

"Sounds good. My advice...keep praying."

"Trust me. I will. Goodnight, bud. Sleep good."

"You too."

Snoring met Betsy's ears within seconds and she smiled. Never took Ben long to hit the zzz's and before turning over to catch some, she sent a prayer up to her heavenly Father, thanking Him for the man next to her and this opportunity.

~

Can you believe we are almost one step closer to hitting the road?" Ben buttoned up one of his favorite shirts. He looked at Betsy, certain she'd tell him to remove the tropical attire he now donned. She didn't.

Until they came down to breakfast. Over coffee and a bowl of cereal his wife peered over her glasses and announced. "You're not wearing anything with palm trees to closing."

Ben marched back to their bedroom and put on a polo shirt. When he came down he decided to rib her a little. "You do realize, since I'm retired, I'll be wearing those shirts more often." He saw Betsy's eyes widen, which made Ben backpedal a tad, "But not every day."

"Goodie. And I can wear my capris sweatpants *whenever* I want. This retirement thing is going to work out fine and dandy."

Ben dropped the shirt subject like a hot potato and finished eating his cereal. No need for either one of them to go down the wardrobe boulevard. Today they'd close on their house and smile all the way to the bank.

Less than two hours later Ben and Betsy strolled out of Star Title with an envelope full of signed paperwork and a cashier's check, safe in his shirt pocket. He teased, "Now that we're into money, sweetums, what do you want to do first?"

Betsy stopped right in the middle of the parking lot and gave Ben a kiss then answered. "Go buy two one-way tickets to Rio. First Class, of course."

"What about the RV?" Ben put his lower lip out in a pout, pretending his wife's statement crushed him. "Is that what you want to do?"

"No, Mr. Stevenson." Betsy gazed up at her hubby. "What I want to do is get on the road with you, Matilda, Larry and Rose. I'm ready to get this party started."

In place of answering, Ben spun Betsy around three or four times. Then he stopped. He heard a sound, almost musical, but not quite, coming from her. Concerned he'd twirled her too many times in celebration, he took her arm and asked, "Bets?"

Betsy puckered her lips again and all Ben could figure out— she tried to...whistle. But nothing came out, but spit. Next, she began to hum. With one sour note after another, Ben heard fragments of Willie Nelson's tune, *On the Road Again,* resounding for all to hear.

Thankfully they'd reached the truck and Ben opened Betsy's door for her to get inside. "Sounding good, hon."

In the confines of the dually. Utterances like that could bring out wildlife that are extinct.

Before he could catch himself, Ben chuckled. This time, though, he decided to cut it off at the pass. "Bets, I wasn't laughing at you. Trust me." He couldn't see his reflection, but hoped his expression spoke sincerity.

Must not have, Betsy crossed her arms in the passenger's seat. "I've been practicing for weeks. Why can't I whistle?"

Ben had trouble answering. Clear to the soles of his feet. He wanted to say, *You can't hum either,* but kept quiet and did the next best thing. He whistled Willie's song...perfect pitch, perfect tone...and perfect melody.

When he finished, his audience of one didn't appear to appreciate the rendition as much as he did, so Ben finished his repertoire with the Oscar Meyer song.

"Sometimes, Benjamin Stevenson, you have the compassion of a...a." Betsy stuttered.

"Compassion of a dead horse." Ben smiled at his choice of animals, but his wife remained stone faced. "I'm sorry. Trying to be cute."

Betsy laughed. "A dead horse? Think you could have done better than that. Not sure they have a need for compassion. Like some human being I know."

Ben shifted the dually into drive and pulled out of the parking lot. "Whatever you say, dear. You are absolutely right, dear." He spoke in a monotone voice, making sure his words came out slow and easy.

Betsy put her hands in the air. "Praise Jesus. I've waited so long to hear you say that."

"And it's just in time for when we hit the road." Ben took a chance and started whistling again. This time Betsy joined in— singing On the Road Again at the top of her lungs.

"This traveling thing is going to work.

As long as you don't whistle, hum OR sing, it will.

CHAPTER NINETEEN

"Yes, we're hitching up and moving out a week from today. On the road again." Betsy sang the familiar song and it seemed to tickle her mom, on the other end of the phone.

"You're getting into this RVing thing, aren't you?"

"Mom, I can't wait and Ben is chomping at the bit. He's ready to get out of Dodge."

"I thought you lived in The Woodlands?"

"We do. It's just a saying." This time Betsy chuckled. "Gotta get going. Debbie is throwing a going away party and since I'm one of the reasons for it—I don't want to be late."

"Have fun."

"Love ya!!!" Betsy put her phone on the bed and tried to decide what to put on. The turny thing she hung her clothes worked like a charm—once Ben had found the clothesline clips. Now she could twirl the deal around and have no impediments.

Bets picked out her usual capris and t-shirt and finished getting dressed at about the time she heard the door open.

"Hello. Is it safe to come in?"

"No writing happening today. I'm getting ready for the luncheon."

"And the guest of honor is looking good."

"You're too kind." Betsy always appreciated Ben's compliments and said so when she came down the stairs. Along with, "Hey, did you and Matilda have a nice walk?"

"We did, but I'm telling you, I don't like the park's doggy area." Ben unhooked Matilda. "I heard one guy say they call it the 'snake pit'."

"That's not good." Betsy poured a cup of coffee. "Want some?"

"Nah, I'm fine."

"We better keep our pooch away from there." Betsy joined Ben at the table. "Don't want one slithering up next to her while she's doing her business."

"I'm sure Mats wouldn't be too keen on meeting a snake face to face either."

"Can we change the subject? This one gives me the heebie jeebies."

Ben laughed. "So, when are you leaving for your party? How long do you think it'll last?"

About the time Ben finished asking his questions, Betsy's phone wiggled across the table. "Rosie's on her way to pick me up. About how long the party will last—not sure. When women get together..."

"Matilda and me, we'll figure out what to do without you. Could go to a real dog park."

Betsy chuckled. "Ben, you said the 'word'. She's ready." Their pooch's ears stood at attention and the jumping began.

"One of these days I'll learn her buzz words. Oh I almost forgot. I'm picking up Baby and taking her and Matilda to Camp Bow Wow. Then Larry's teaching me how to drive this thing." Ben took the leash off the hook again. Matilda came over and sat while he put it on her then Ben glanced at Betsy. "Text me."

Betsy stood in the doorway and almost started laughing. *Text me? What a hoot.* She wanted to ask him if he'd actually see it since his phone stayed in his pocket most of the time. Unless it rang. Then she hoped he heard it.

"Ben, I'll let you know when we're headed out the door."

He gave her a thumbs up and Betsy watched her two best buds get in the dually and head south. Right after he left, her other best friend pulled up in the spot Ben had vacated, honking to beat the band.

Almost waking the dead.

Betsy put her finger to her lips and shushed her friend. Rose immediately took her hand off the horn and yelled, "Sorry."

"I'll be right there." Betsy grabbed her purse off the chair and went down the stairs, stopping to lock the door.

Betsy got in Rose's vehicle and decided to tackle the honking thing head on. "You do know they're going to kick us out of here if the blaring noise doesn't stop every time you come in the park."

Rose ignored Betsy's comment and backed her car out of the spot. Her snub continued, while they got on the I-45 feeder road. Nothing Betsy did got a rise out of her friend. Poking her in the ribs, be it ever so gentle, so Rosie wouldn't wreck their vehicle didn't work.

The next thing Betsy tried—she stuck her tongue out and gave Rosie a mouth-wiping raspberry. Yes, her driver's license said 58 years old, but sometimes a person had to pull out the big guns to get a response. None came. Not even Rose's typical snort.

"Hello, is anyone home? We've gone almost a mile and you haven't said a word. What's wrong with you?"

Rose turned right on Research and after she straightened the wheel she glanced at Betsy. "I'm not talking to you or Larry. First he hurt my feelings. Now you. Everyone is telling me to shush."

"I'll agree my shushing tactic might have been a little harsh. I'm sorry about that. What got Lar on the wrong side of the law?"

"He told me I talk too much? Then I told him I would definitely be going with you guys. But now you turn on me." Rose glanced at Betsy again. Tears began to fall in torrents and her driving turned from bad to worse.

"Rosie, it'd be a good time for you to pull into Sonic and tell me all about it."

Betsy watched the proceedings from the passenger side, but

couldn't grasp how Rose got her sedan parked in one of the restaurant's narrow spots. Without hitting the order do dad.

After Bets regained the ability to speak she said as she unbuckled her seatbelt, "Tell me what happened."

"I...asked...Larry...if" Another wail escaped.

Betsy opened her purse and handed Rose a handful of Kleenex and imagined her friend's anguish had something to do with her husband's love of playing games on the computer. And said as much.

"Thanks. No, my angst doesn't have anything to do with gaming. For once." Rose wiped her eyes. "I don't know about Ben, but Larry wouldn't know logic if it came up and gave him a million dollars."

"Not sure what you're talking about, but Rose I do have a question. Why should Larry shushing you stop you from going with him? We already know you're a jabberer."

Rose's face, splotchy from her recent outburst, broke into a huge smile. "Exactly! Why ever am I crying over Larry's comment. It's nuts since I feel God bestowed upon me the gift of gab. It states in the Bible to use your gifts. You've seen it."

Betsy loved when her friend had a light-bulb moment. You could almost see it above her head, shining bright. "Now that we've solved the reason for your overabundant chitchat, what about Larry's lack of logic?"

"He wants to leave at the crack of dawn on Wednesday and get to Boulder, Colorado by Friday. Of the same week. Have you ever heard such...such craziness?"

"You do remember who I'm married to?" Betsy could recall many trips where Ben drove through the night to get somewhere. "Rosie, if you didn't already know it—it's a guy thing."

"Uh huh, but the two of us are going to get our fellows to slooooooooooow down. Smell the rutabagas."

"It is roses...Rose. Where you come up—"

"Never mind."

"And, from the sounds of things, the *Early Birds* better have our first meeting before we take off next week. Make some plans."

"Bets, that's the most logical thing I've heard all day."

"Since we've solved all the world's problems, there's only one thing left to do."

"Could it be us leaving to a going-away party?" Rose laughed and slapped the steering wheel.

"Heavens no. What we do need to do is order a Route 44 Cherry Limeade to celebrate all the bright ideas we came up with today."

While they waited for their order, Betsy watched Rose powder her nose and apply an ample coat of red lip gloss. About five minutes later the two drinks arrived. Rose paid for them and pulled out of the parking space and out on Research Forest again.

Betsy glanced at her watch. "We've got plenty of time. It's only a quarter to 2:00. Unless you—"

"Drive as slow as I normally do."

Betsy chuckled when Rose finished the sentence, but in reality she wasn't in the mood to joke around. Too many things skipped around inside her head. The biggest one—saying goodbye to her friends.

"Did someone steal *your* happy this time?"

"Thinking about goodbyes." Betsy shifted in her seat. "You know I don't like them. No, it's not forever and we'll be back here to visit. Please tell me again why Debbie is doing this?"

"She wanted to send you off knowing how much you're loved."

"Rose, I'm a terrible friend. I don't even look at my blog, Facebook or emails when people make comments."

"If I wasn't driving I'd have to contemplate back handing you." Rose extended her hand over towards Betsy and continued, "And, you're forgetting someone you've helped."

Betsy thought for a second. "Oh...I forgot Tina." She smiled at Rose. "I suggest you keep your hands and your eyes on the road. I don't want to die before you get us to the paartea,"

"Contrary to your beliefs, Bets, which are flawed, you're an outstanding friend. Sweetie, I know it firsthand."

"You lie, but you're going to make me cry."

"Then I guess we're two peas in a pod."

"And if you don't slow down and turn on Debbie's street, we're going to be two peas in a pod who are late."

Rosie made the left on Indian Springs in time and parked her car. Then looked at Betsy. "Normally I'd say, 'the Eagle has landed'. Today it's 'the two old peas have arrived'. She opened the driver's door and laughed all the way to Debbie's front door.

Betsy followed close behind her friend, trying to quiet her cackling with every step they took. As usual—to no avail. Rosie kept on until someone opened the front door. Then her mouth dropped open.

"What's the matter?"

"Look at the sign!"

Betsy's eyes followed Rose's hand to the banner hanging across Debbie's second-story walkway. It read, "Bon Voyage Betsy and Rose. We Loooooooovvvvveeee You Both!!!"

"They included me too." Rose stood in the spot and stared.

All the ladies laughed then gathered around them. Everyone tried to talk at the same time and hugs came from every direction. When the crowd let them move into the dining room, happy tears fell. Betsy saw a table filled with food, but what brought the tears – one of Bonnie's cake creations adorned the middle.

Betsy had always wanted a delight from Nana's Cakes and Cookies, but used the excuse, "Too many calories." Then she remembered Rose and her conversation at IHOP. On special occasions – goodies have no calories.

"Are you thinking what I'm thinking?"

"Rosie, I'm counting on it," Betsy said as she loaded up her plate with almost everything on the table, excluding the olives and guacamole.

"Those won't kill you." Rose put an olive on her index finger and popped it in her mouth.

"I'm saving room for cake and cookies."

"Yea, right."

Betsy picked up a glass of sparkling punch and followed Rose to the loveseat next to the fireplace.

"Do you need anything?" Debbie asked, holding out extra napkins.

"One of those, so I don't spill anything on your new carpet." Rose took two and handed one to Betsy.

"Debbie, this is too much and you also invited my writer friends."

"Ben gave me your list."

"Sneaky, but I'm glad you did it. Thank you." Betsy stabbed one of the Vienna sausages with her fork, but before she put it in her mouth she said, "Can you believe we're leaving in a few days."

"Where are you headed first?"

Betsy laughed when she heard two or three voices chime in together with "Colorado". The answer she'd given fifty times before.

"Along with Colorado, I'm on the hunt for the Largest Ball of Yarn." Rose took a sip of her punch. "It's on my Bucket List. Anyone know where it's at?"

A lot of "I don't know" or "Check google" rang out from the gaggle of ladies. But Sherie, who sat on the chair next to them sighed, "Can I hitch a ride? I need some inspiration for my newest book, which is set in the Rockies."

"Come on. We've got a fold-out couch." Rose said between bites.

"Don't tell me twice or I'll leave right now and pack my bags."
A ball of yarn?

Betsy hadn't heard about Rose's interest in the anomaly. But in her book, talk of Colorado ranked higher than their search for anything to do with string. She also savored the delectable finger food Debbie served them.

And...the thought of showing the place she adored to Ben for the first time. This made Betsy almost giddy with excitement. She could only imagine his reaction to Colorado.

"What are you all smiles about?" Rose stood up and started to collect plates.

"Can't help myself when we get on the subject of my favorite state." Betsy chuckled as she handed Rose her plate.

"If it was up to Larry, we'd wave at the *Welcome to Colorado* sign on his way to the nearest campground...at midnight. No less."

She went on about their earlier discussion in the car and some of the ladies made suggestions on how to slow their husbands down. Rose said, "First thing: They need to slow down. Smell the...the...petunias. Or was it a poinsettia?"

After the laughter died down, Gloria from their Sunday school class stood up. "Rose, it's *smell the roses*. But with you—it can be any flower you want."

Rose smiled and put the dishes she'd collected on the kitchen counter.

"With all the world's problems settled, I believe it's time for dessert." Debbie motioned towards her dining room. "Does anyone want a piece of cake? A cookie?"

Betsy wasn't sure how *roses* and *dessert* went hand in hand, but she didn't bother trying to figure it out. Instead she went with the crowd of women who now congregated around the table filled with goodies.

"Don't forget to take pictures." Betsy took her phone out of her back pocket and snapped two or three of the cake and cookies Bonnie decorated for them. "Perfect. Just perfect."

After what seemed like a 100 flashes, Bonnie cut into the special cake. The 5th wheel camper, with the words *Cedar Creek* written across the top, soon resembled more crumbs than butter crème cake.

"I've never tasted anything like this."

"Do you have cards? I want you to make one of these for my daughter's shower."

The accolades continued while Betsy took a bite of the piece of heaven on her plate. Only six months before, Bonnie had announced on Facebook she'd make cakes and cookies for anyone interested. Today's praises sounded like her new baking business would be a sure-fire hit.

Debbie escorted Betsy and Rose back to their seats with a plate of cookies and a basket in tow. "These cards are for you."

Bets took one and handed one to Rose. They opened the pile of cards from their friends and all the while she nibbled on cookies. When she finished reading a card and had eaten the cookie, Betsy would reach for another...of each.

"Get those things away from me. I can't stop eating them. UNCLE!"

"We're taking some of them with us when we leave." Rose held an RV shaped cookie up in the air. "This will be what I use to get the guys to make more stops on our way to Colorado."

"To smell the pon—"

"Sorry to interrupt, but the only flour, F.L.O.U.R. we're smelling here is what went into these stupendous cookies." Rose chomped down right in the middle of one of them and smiled. Then she wiped off her mouth and said, "Yum."

"Yum is right." Betsy saluted her with the half of cookie she held in her hand. "You guys went to too much trouble here. And the gift cards. WOW!!! We'll never have to buy coffee for the rest of our lives."

"Told you in the car you're special. I can't wait to get on the road with you and Ben." Rose reached over and took the half-eaten cookie out of Betsy's hand. "We're going to have so much fun."

"I can see that."

If they'd been alone at Rose's house, Betsy would have chased her friend down and taken her cookie back. But today, at Debbie's, she'd let the cookie thief get away with it. This time.

Later in the afternoon, on the way to the kitchen to see if she could support the clean-up crew, Betsy hugged at least a dozen of her friends. "I'm so glad you came. And Bonnie, bless you for the cake and cookies. Out of this world!!!"

"Yes, and please keep making them." Rose bit into her cookie. This one shaped like the sun.

"I will. Blessings to you guys on your travels."

Another hug for Bonnie then Betsy turned to Debbie and Sharon and said, "Can we he—"

"No, today was you and Rose's day. We're almost done in

here. See."

Betsy scanned the counters and agreed with Sharon. "You sure know how to throw a going-away party. For sure."

"Amen," Rose added when she came up and stood next to Betsy.

"Glad you two enjoyed it." Debbie took the trash bag out of the container and sat it on the rug then turned to face them. A tear escaped down her cheek. "We wanted to send you off with a bang."

"You accomplished that and then some. Thank you." Betsy hugged Debbie and tears ran down her face as well. "I hate goodbyes and thanks for including Rose." The last part she whispered.

"I hate goodbyes too." Sharon wiped her eyes. "But it'll only be a few months...or so. We hope."

"We'll be back." Betsy imitated Arnold Schwarzenegger to try and lighten the mood.

"Keep your day job." Rose picked up her purse and flung it over her shoulder.

"You better keep writing. I love your blogs."

"Thanks. I plan on it."

"Debbie, I'll make sure she continues to write. And now we better scoot since Betsy will want to write a blog about our big party."

Betsy got her own purse and said, "Yes, we better. Larry and Ben will think we stopped to smell the...what was the flower. Petunias? Poinsettias?"

"Oh, peshaw."

Rose's remark caused the four of them to lose all sense of time and rational. Snorts from every direction, especially from Rosie's side of the kitchen, led the parade down happy street again.

Betsy got control of herself and took a hold of Rose's arm and headed them to the front door. She turned to thank their hosts again, but before the words left her lips, Debbie and Sharon had Rosie and her in a four-way hug.

Sharon broke away from the circle. "You tell those husbands of yours we don't like that they're taking you away from us."

"Sunday school will not be the same without you two," Debbie added.

"You can count on it." Rose gathered them back into another embrace.

While enfolded in her friends' arms at Debbie's front door, Betsy chuckled, imagining a camera aimed at them. Similar to the last show of *Mary Tyler Moore* when the group tried to say goodbye. In the end all of them, still hugging, headed to the door. The last frame, Mary shuts off the light and the show ended.

Betsy took a step back and said, "Rose and Betsy make their exit. Stage right."

"We love you." Debbie and Sharon chimed in together.

"Love you too." For the third time Betsy snatched Rose's arm. This time they made it out the door.

"See I said you were loved." Rose opened up her car door.

Betsy got in and looked over at her best friend. "Looks like I could say the same for you."

"And, I'd say it was pretty cool." Rose started her car. "Bets, there's another neat thing about this afternoon."

"Something else?"

"Now we have an excuse for the guys to slow down. To smell the...the coffee. Starbucks and Colorado. Here we come." Rose hollered a "Woohoo" as she put her vehicle in gear and headed out of Briarwood Estates.

Betsy seconded the motion. Coffee and Colorado ranked #3 and #4, after her love for the Almighty God and Ben, of course.

Oh, Ben...I better text him and tell him I'm on my way. Almost four hours later. Yes, women do carry on.

CHAPTER TWENTY

Ben's back pocket vibrated, alerting him a text had arrived. He read it to Larry, "The girls are on their way home." He went back to his phone and wrote a quick note.

"Don't forget to tell them to meet us at our house?"

"Just did."

Ben typed, backspacing when he'd misspelled a word. His wife, always the editor, caught even the tiniest of errors. To her defense, she'd saved him more than once when he had her proof something for work.

"Are you writing a novel over there?" Larry opened his window.

"No. Fixing my boo boos."

"As I was saying, the way Rosie left this morning, she'd rather go to your house...that is, RV to live."

"Why's tha—" Ben stopped his sentence when he had to scramble to pick up their purchases. They'd fallen over when Larry's back tires hit the curb as he pulled out of Home Depot's parking lot.

"Got to get into practice driving this thing again."

"I know what you mean." Ben situated the bags in the front

this time. "However, your lessons this afternoon with the RV sure made sense. All I need to remember is look before I leap. Or in this case, before I pull a 38-foot trailer behind my dually."

"Right you are and have Betsy watch for curbs. Unlike someone else I know." Larry cleared his throat.

"I'll ignore your snide remark, but it's a good point about Betsy." Ben laughed. "She loves to tell me how to drive."

"Amen!"

"Now what's this about Rosie moving in with Bets and me?"

Larry filled him in. Ben laughed at the part where he'd told Rose she talked too much. "How's that working for you?" He decided to steal Dr. Phil's famous line.

"About as well as when you told Betsy, "I think it's time you be quiet."

"You had to remind me?"

Certain memories needed to fade, but the 'be quiet' one would live on. Along with the one when the Christmas tree holder fell out of the rafters in their garage and grazed Betsy's neck. Tears streamed down her face...until he uttered, "Ready to go to Wal-Mart."

Funny how life worked. Items falling on his wife became insignificant when his words of wisdom hit the airway. Betsy took them as fighting words and if someone asked Ben, he couldn't remember if they'd made it to the superstore, or not. Not important now.

One day Ben hoped he'd learn putting his arm around Betsy solved more problems than sharing his agenda at inopportune moments. And their travels might teach him how to show compassion to others, specifically the woman he loved. How to walk in someone else's shoes for a change.

"Hey, Lar. Are we going to have another lesson? Or two. I'm up for three before we take off. Bets said she might be interested in coming along too. Get a few tips."

"Good for her, but I won't tell Rosie. She's told me there's not an instruction I could give her that would get her to drive. Back to lessons. Got church tomorrow. Let's shoot for...Monday. Yea, in the afternoon. No. Won't work. Tuesday's better."

The day before we leave.

Ben wanted to ask Larry, "What's the hesitation all about?" but instead answered, "Whatever works for you." No need to start their travels off on the wrong foot.

He glanced down at his phone, after he felt a vibration. Betsy had sent him a second message. "Early Bird meeting in twenty minutes. Be there or be square".

Ben couldn't believe the Lord's timing. Pretty sure what bothered Larry would come out tonight. He'd wait and see. Rose had ways of making her husband talk.

~

But first the women had to grab a cup of coffee and yak their ears off about the fun time they had at their going-away party. Betsy pulled out a handful of cards from her purse and fanned them out. "Look at these Starbucks cards our friends gave us."

"When they run out, we can register them online with our own money, of course." Rose picked up her mug and took a drink. As she sat it down she said, "I'll go in after you leave and register it. Must keep the coffee flowing. Larry, I'll need the credit card to do it."

Ben noticed Larry's face whitened with his wife's statement. Almost the same shade as the night he tried to sell their RV.

Rose seemed right on top of it too. "Mr. Wilford, either you're having a heart attack or the beans had better spill on why you look as if you've seen a ghost."

Larry leaned his chair against the wall. To any who watched, Ben thought his friend's coloring returned to normal with each breath he took. No words had emerged yet, but along with pinker cheeks, he could almost see Larry's mind churning at break-neck speed to come up with something to say.

God, please don't let it be about him selling his camper again.

"Rosie, before you do that, I have a confession to make. I can't give you my card. I..." Larry stopped and stared at his wife.

Ben glanced at Betsy and saw she'd stuffed her Starbuck's cards back in her purse and sat up straighter in her chair. Almost like she braced for the same thing he feared.

"I refilled my coins on my favorite game and cut up all of my cards. Even the Starbucks card."

Everyone has said things move in slow motion when something unexpected occurred. It's true. Time stood still until the unthinkable happened. Rose stayed seated and said, "Don't worry about the card. I have my own. Not sure where it's at, but I'll find it."

Larry, along with everyone else, stared at Rose. Then he spoke, "Did you hear what I said?"

"Heard every word. You've admitted you have G.A., which is a HUGE answer to prayer. Oh, and Larry, I also forgive you for telling me I talk too much. Decided it's a gift from God. Can't do anything about it. Now can we continue with the first meeting of the *Early Birds?*"

Not sure what happened, but Ben left it alone. He decided his friends could grapple with their issues after they left. Then he thought about when... or if...his next driving lesson would happen?

No time like the present to find out.

"Sounds like we're putting things out on the table. I've got one for you, Larry. I'm scared spitless about driving the dually with Artemis the Albatross behind me." Ben stopped and glanced at his table mates. They all looked at him this time.

"You? Scared? Ben Stevenson?" Larry's eyes brightened. "You did gulp loud enough for the driver next to us to hear."

"I did not. Anyway, I'm curious as to why we can't practice a few more times? Only Tuesday morning? The day before we leave?"

"What?" Both Rose and Betsy rang in.

Then Rosie took over. "You're retired. What's so urgent...oh my goodness..." Rose put down her coffee cup. "Larry, I'm telling you right now. I'm locking your tablet in the storage shed. Never to see the light of day until we get back from Colorado."

"At this moment, I'll let you." Larry got up and walked to the end table and picked up a black leather case. Next he reached in his pocket and brought out a key ring. "Here's the shed key. Take it before I change my mind."

Rose went over to Larry and gave him a hug. "I'll do it later. Thank you."

"Well I don't know about you, but I'd say our first meeting is going quite well. Don't you guys?"

"Bets, if I hadn't witnessed your helpful input on many occasions—I'd say your last statement makes me question if you've heard a word we've said."

"I've heard every word, Ben. No, we haven't gotten much done at our first meeting, but we cleared up some serious issues and we spoke the truth in love. In my opinion, the *Early Birds* are ready to hit the road."

Ben smiled at his wife. Always the optimistic one in the group. If anyone could see the bright side of things, Betsy could. This evening, he thought, she'd received her PhD in the area of optimism. Something they could all learn.

"Are you up for one tomorrow?" Larry laid his tablet and keys on the bar area.

"How about 1:00?"

"I'll meet you behind Sam's."

"Say goodnight Ben. It's time we hit the road. For tonight, that is." Betsy got up and carried her coffee cup to the sink. "Rosie, don't forget to Google *Largest Ball of Yarn*."

"What? We aren't stopping there?" Larry stood with his hands on his hips.

"I wouldn't count on it, dear. I'll check it out later, Bets, but first I have to get my hugs."

Ben took Betsy's hand and tried to advance them to the Wilford's front door, but Rose wouldn't let go of his wife. "Say bye, Rosie."

"Oh, you! Bye and know I love you two."

"We know, Rosie. You tell us all the time."

"Are you coming tonight?" Betsy stood and tapped her foot at the opened front door.

Ben turned and realized his wife waited for him now.

"Always. I'm ready to go with you. Anytime. Anywhere."

"See, Larry, Ben's ready to see the yarn. Lighten up."

"You guys are weird."

Laughter resonated behind Ben when he closed the door.
Bets, I'm more than ready to get going.

~

ON THE ROAD AGAIN...FINALLY

"It's official—we are ready to go?" Ben came up and stood
next to the dually four days later. Wednesday. Their agreed-upon
departure date. Betsy joined Matilda in the front seat of their
truck, after she parked her car in the Wilford's garage.

Anticipation and a bit of disdain covered his wife's face and
Ben heard her say, "Would you tell Rosie to hurry up?"

He surmised his wife had lost her patience somewhere in the
last forty minutes, but didn't want their friends to hear her
sassiness. Ben waved his arm inside the cab to quiet Betsy down.
The movement worked for her, but Matilda took it as a sign to
come over and lick his elbow.

"Thanks, Mats." He wiped his arm off on the side of his t-
shirt. "Oh, look Betsy, Rose is coming out of the house and she's
heading your way."

Betsy got out of the truck. "Good morning, Rose. We about
ready?"

"She better be." Larry yelled from next to his truck. "Come
on, Rosebud, times a wasting."

"I know. Wanted to give Ben and Betsy a hug."

Betsy and Ben stood next to her. They both gave her a big
hug since she wouldn't leave until they did. No use arguing with
their friend. Rose never got in her vehicle without acting as if it
would be the last time she saw them.

"Rose would you get yourself over here. You'll see them again
at lunch when we stop and eat." Larry got in the cab of their
truck. The engine idled.

"Okay, you old poop head. I'm coming. Bye other half of the
Early Birds."

Ben watched Rose try to hoist her backend up in the pick-up.

Without the sideboards he concluded she wouldn't have made it. His mom flashed in his mind. She'd made a "special" stool to bring along when they picked her up in his truck. By attaching a string to it, Mom could bring it in after she sat down. Perfect.

Larry's flailing arms and Betsy tapping him on the arm alerted Ben his mind had wandered. He responded with a wave of his arm and the foursomes were off for Colorado. Their first stop, on what Ben could only imagine, an adventure of epic proportions.

His biggest concern, Larry leading the way. He loved his friend, but as long as he'd known him, when he drove, he never got anywhere without some kind of mishap. The main reason why, he ignored signage and wanted to get to Point B before nightfall.

On his last lesson with Larry, on how to park the 5th wheel, Ben mentioned they needed to take their time getting to Colorado. "This is my first time and I want to see as much of it as I can."

Also Betsy's insistence on the subject prompted him to ask for an extended time. Something she said to him about smelling some kind of flower. That one caused him to lose some brain cells. Ben assured his wife Larry would slow it down.

Ben put the thought of their ETA and if or when Larry might have to turn around out of his mind. No need to worry until it happened. Then he turned to Betsy. "Well, we're on the road. Can you believe it?"

"I was beginning to wonder." She fidgeted in her seat.

"You don't have to go to the restroom, do you? I'm not stopping five minutes after we get on the road."

"No, dear, I'm just so excited." Betsy took off singing the Pointer Sister's No. 1 hit.

"Don't you think it's too early for that song?"

"Never too early for disco. Anyway, aren't we forgetting something?" Betsy took a piece of paper from her lap. "I ran out the lyrics to *On the Road Again* and made them big enough for you to see them as you drive."

"Are you serious?" Ben didn't know why he asked the

question. The song had been their mantra on every trip they'd ever taken.

"Here you go. I wanted to get all the words right this time." She handed him a sheet and there on the page were the words to Willie's song, as she'd promised.

"Matilda, are you going to sing with us?" Ben petted their pooch.

"Come on, Ben, we're almost to the highway. Let's get to singing before we hit I-45."

> *On the road again –*
> *Just can't wait to get on the road again.*
> *The life I love is <u>making music </u>with my friends*

"Oh, I almost forgot, we need to get on the CB and get Larry and Rose to sing with us."

"You are kidding, right? This isn't something they'd want to do. Anyway they don't know the song." Ben tried to reason with his wife so she wouldn't get her feelings hurt when they turned her down.

"Oh, yes they do. I gave Rose copies of the lyrics the other day and told them to practice, practice, practice." Betsy grabbed the mic and spoke into it. "Breaker, good buddy..."

"You've seen *Smoky and the Bandit* too many times. But you've got the right idea." Ben followed Larry's rig onto I-45, heading north. He took the mic from his wife and spoke into it. "Wilford's, copy. Can you hear me?"

"Copy, 21. Hey, buddy, sounds like you got this thing figured out." Larry's voice echoed inside the cab of the truck. Matilda's ears perked up at the sound of the radio.

"Not too tough. I'm turning this thing over to Betsy."

"She wants to sing the song, doesn't she?"

"Larry Wilford, you settle yourself down. We are going to sing the song." Rose's voice came across loud and clear. "Here we go, honey, this one's for you.

On the road again –
Just can't wait to get on the road again.
The life I love is <u>making music</u> with my friends

Ben tried to watch the road and follow the words on the page. The four of them made a sound, somewhere between a squeal and a fog horn. He wanted to laugh, but knew how much this meant to Betsy, so he continued to sing at the top of his lungs.

And I can't wait to get on the road again.
On the road again…

Goin' places that I've never been.
Seein' things that I may never see agai
And I can't wait to get on the road again.
On the road again –

Like a <u>band</u> of gypsies we go down the highway
We're the best of friends.

"Wait. Hold on." Rose's voice crackled on the radio. "That's my most favorite part of the song. *"Like a band of gypsies we go down the highway. We're the best of friends.* The four of us. Praise the Lord and pass the turtle soup."

"Amen, sister!" Betsy shouted.

Ben took the mic from his wife's hand and spoke into it. "Don't know about you, but we've done the song proud. Now it's time for some peace and quiet."

"Couldn't agree more. Signing off, good buddy."

"We were just getting good."

"Yes, we were, but when Rose mentioned *praise the Lord* I realized we hadn't prayed before we started."

"Oops. Do you want to start?"

"Since I can't close my eyes—it's better if you pray."

Betsy laughed then got going on praying for safety, security and for God's hand to lead and guide them on their travels. Ben loved to listen to her prayers—they were always without premise and always full of enthusiasm.

Unlike his. He felt uncomfortable every time he prayed, but had to admit praying every night with Betsy, it had gotten easier to open up and share his heart.

When Betsy finished praying, he added a couple of sentences and ended it with an "Amen!"

"Prayer always makes me feel better." Betsy put the paper on her lap in the pocket of her door. "Now it's official. We are on the road."

"Next time let's—"

"I know. Next time I won't include Rose and Larry. This is our song – not theirs."

Ben agreed. They'd sung the song for years. He couldn't remember a vacation, even when they flew somewhere, one of them didn't break out in song before they pulled out of their driveway.

Precious memories. And we're on the road to make more.

This made him smile and along with the fact his wife could barely contain herself in the passenger seat. He'd never get over that suggesting the RV thing would make her happier than she'd been in years.

"And, Ben, without a doubt this RVing idea is the best thing you've ever come up with," Betsy announced this while rummaging through the glove compartment. "Did you put the charger for the GPS in here? We're probably going to need it, if we continue to let Larry lead."

Ben didn't know if they could get any more on the same page. They'd been at odds for so long, that this change of heart on both of their sides could only be classified as another miracle.

One they needed in the worse way. He sent up a silent prayer as he drove down one of Texas's major highways.

CHAPTER TWENTY-ONE

Contentment etched every inch of Ben's face when Betsy glanced over at her hubby as he drove their new rig. The dimple, she could see, made her smile. She hadn't seen it often, but over the last few months its appearance sent her heart all aflutter.

And in those months, the love for the man she'd married over three decades ago grew stronger. No doubt there were still things they hadn't pulled from underneath the proverbial rug and talked about, but their pastor had sent them out on the road with tools to discuss the hard stuff. Once and for all.

"When the time's right," he'd said. "You'll know when you're ready to start talking about things."

But not today. Not on the day their new life journey began. Betsy decided to change the direction her mind teetered. Away from what they needed to talk about sometime and the rejection letter she'd received on Tuesday.

"How's it going over there?" Betsy asked, hoping to get her mind on what mattered today.

Ben smiled, but kept his eyes straight ahead. "I'm doing peachy."

"I'm glad." Betsy almost laughed. What would she have done

if he'd said he needed her to drive? Not an option yet. Maybe with more practice.

But making small talk with Ben kept her mind off the one thing she'd rather stuff deep down inside. Rejection.

As always it seemed to happen at the most inopportune times. Yesterday. The day before they planned to leave. A rejection came in the self-addressed-stamped envelope. Betsy ripped it open, hoping—praying for acceptance for the article she'd sent in for the Valentine issue.

Their love story.

"Your article does not fit our magazine."

Those words prompted Betsy to take the steno pad out of the side pocket on the door of the truck. She wrote those seven words. Then she added, "What does fit?"

In her mind their love story personified Valentine's Day. Tenderness. Tears. Transformation in Christ. Betsy smiled. *It does fit and it's perfect.* As fast as her pen could write her thoughts, Betsy penned more of her testimony. The words she would share with Tina.

Ben's voice broke in, which stopped her frantic scribbling. "What you doing over there?"

"Jotting down some ideas for my next blog."

"Remind me to read it when you're done."

"Ah huh."

"Breaker 21 – are you ready for lunch?" Larry's voice caused both of them to jump then they laughed.

Ben pushed the side button. "We are. Lead the way."

"That's a scary thought." Betsy covered her mouth, hoping Ben had let go of the button so Larry didn't hear her comment.

"You're fine. I let go after I answered."

"Phew, I'm glad. Don't want to hurt the old guy's feeling on our first day on the road."

"Knowing Larry he'd already put the mic down, trying to figure out how to park. Pretty sure he doesn't want to turn around. Or make me have to do it. Right now I need the wide, open spaces."

Betsy looked out the windshield and chuckled. The parking lot sat almost deserted on Wednesday afternoon. "Bud, you and Larry could do figure eights out there. If you can't move this bad boy out here and get us back to I-45, we need to head back to Houston.

He joined in his wife's gaiety after they exited the cab of their truck and he got a glimpse of the two rigs parked outside of Taco Bell. The only two, which were theirs.

"Your hubby picked the perfect place to pull in," Ben told Rose before he picked up Matilda. "Now it's time to turn on the generator to air condition the RV while we eat. Don't want you dying of heat out here."

Rose nodded. "Larry's doing the same. Wish we could put Baby and Matilda together, but the RV we picked might not live through the moment." Her signature snort ended her suggestion.

Your dog...not mine. This thought he kept to himself.

"Rose tells me you can't go a day without your fix of Mexican food," Larry said when he walked up.

"You ladies discuss my eating habits?"

Rose grabbed Betsy's arm and they both headed into the building.

"I'll bet it's a bathroom break."

"I'll second it." Larry closed the door to his truck and went inside.

Ben walked in and up to the counter to order—since he knew what they wanted. They're in a rut. Then he changed his mind. *No, I'm not. I'm going to get something totally different today.*

He decided their new adventure deserved a little shaking up. A Mexican pizza sounded good to him. Betsy raved about it when she got it all the time. "Today I'll give it a try."

"You are scaring me, dear." Betsy scooted up next to him. "Standing in the middle of Taco Bell, talking to yourself.

"Been living with you too long not to pick up your bad habits." Ben laughed, but hoped no one heard his reasoning out loud.

"What do you guys get? This is our first time," Larry said as he came out of the men's room.

"Are you kidding me?" Ben couldn't believe he hadn't taken Larry there in all of their running around.

"Mr. Stevenson, normally our palates desire a few steps up the food chain than this." Larry elbowed him in the ribs.

"Well then, Larry and Rose, you haven't lived until you've tried their smothered burrito or black bean one. Betsy, on the other hand, loves their Mexican pizza and 7-Layer Burrito." Ben hadn't told any of them he'd decided to change it up a bit.

And he couldn't wait to see his wife's expression when he announced his choice of fare. "Go ahead, you two. Think outside the bun." Ben used Taco Bell's slogan to his advantage. Groans followed.

Rose and Larry got in line and both ordered the Mexican pizza. Ben heard Rose say, "It looks like the better of two evils."

Ben headed to the counter. "Double their order, please."

The young man stared at him as if he had something hanging out of his nose. Ben reached in his back pocket and removed his handkerchief and wiped it, but the 16-year old still stood with his mouth open.

"Two Mexican pizzas...please." Betsy's voice and theatrical arm movements awoke the other patrons waiting in line. They all turned and stared.

"Two Mexican pizzas. That'll be $7.58."

Ben took out his wallet and paid then decided the next time he changed his order, he'd say what he wanted — not try to be cute.

They sat down at the table and Rose said, between fits of laughter, "You should have heard Larry after all of us quit singing. He and Baby carried on for five more minutes."

"I did not. It was more like Rosie singing to high heaven. I'm sure Willie's ears were burning. Or should have been."

"Order 612."

"Oh, that's us, Rose." Larry walked up and got their tray. On his way to the table they called Order 613. "Let me get it for you."

Ben stared at the new menu item. No clue what to do with it.

From the look on Rose and Larry's face, they didn't know either. They, too, stared at the square box after they'd opened it.

Betsy must have picked up on their confusion. "Here, since you're all novices, let me show you how it's done." She picked up one of the slices and took a bite. "See it's pretty simple. Just to warn you – if they put too much sauce on it, you'll have to eat it with a fork. Too messy."

Ben followed his wife's lead and took a bite of his first slice of Mexican pizza. "WOW!!! This IS good."

"Would I steer you wrong?" Betsy picked up her second piece.

Rose and Larry stared at them, but the smile on their faces told Ben he'd won them over to his side.

"I hate to admit it, but Taco Bell will become one of my regular stops from now on."

"That's good, Larry. Our budget will thank us at the end of the month when we stop going to those high priced places you like to frequent."

"But steak...seafood..."

"You'll adjust, sweetheart." Rose reached over and gave Larry's arm a squeeze.

"Like you're a pro at this new lifestyle?" Betsy questioned her friend.

"I am. I lied about visiting Taco Bell. This is about the third or fourth time I've been to one. I heard Bets shouting their praises and took a chance. I'm hooked on these things." Rose took a piece in her hand, foregoing her fork this time.

"And what about you, big guy?" Betsy turned to Ben. "What brought a change in what you ordered this time?"

"Our new adventure. Decided it was time. I agree with Rose. I'll be back."

"Dear, on your death bed, you'll ask one of us to bring you Taco Bell."

"What I meant – I'll be back for this pizza. And Lar, if you visit more often, it'll give you more money to spend on your gam—"

Rose gave Ben a look that could singe off the hair he hadn't even grown yet. He glanced at Betsy, but even she deserted him. He watched her get up from the table and walk in the direction of the condiments.

So much for thinking she'd get him out of this with her wit and overflowing optimism. No, he'd have to do it on his own. "Rosie. Larry, I'm sorry. Didn't mean to bring up…" The right word slipped his mind, so he shut up.

"I thought the same thing." Larry gathered up some of the trash littering their table. "Anyway, Rose will find a place for the extra cash I've been frittering away."

Rose held out her hand as if she waited for her husband to give her some of the money on the spot. Larry chuckled, but Ben could tell it lacked its normal enthusiasm. Oh how he wished he'd gone to use the facilities before stupid fell out of his lips.

"Hey, what's with all the long faces?" Betsy returned to the table and started to pick up some of the clutter.

"Here, I've got it." Larry stood up and finished the job he'd started.

Ben glanced at his friend, trying to catch his attention to give him a sign. What he'd do, he didn't know. But he had one question—how could someone spend money on a casino game? Not on Ben's radar.

Larry? A serious gambling problem? No way.

Ben made a mental note he'd talk to Larry and they'd continue to pray for him. For all of them.

~

Betsy picked up her drink and followed everyone to the door. "Are we ready to hit the road?"

Larry stopped in the doorway. "Yes, but you're not going to make us sing the song again, are you?"

"Nope. You're off the hook. However, tomorrow's another day."

"Yeah."

"Larry, behave yourself. If Bets wants to sing the stu…I mean, sing a song. We'll do it."

"Thanks." Betsy winked at Rose then dropped the cup in the

155

trash can. "Go on a head, I've got a stop to make."

Ben raised his eyebrows at her and Betsy said, "Go on. I'll see you in the truck."

Betsy wanted to apologize to the teenager who had taken their order. The old adage of "you don't know what someone is going through" kept pestering her after she'd yelled at the kid. He must not have understood what Ben meant. But it was no excuse for snappiness on her part.

"Excuse me. Excuse me." Betsy leaned into the counter, trying to get the young man's attention.

"May I take your order?"

Keeping her voice low, she said, "No, I've already eaten. I wanted to tell you I'm sorry for yelling at you earlier."

After Betsy said the words, she noticed the young man's eyes brightened. The smile on his pimpled face showed a slight dimple on his chin. A little Kirk Douglas going on. Handsome indeed.

"Thanks." He continued to look at Betsy. "Have a nice day."

"You too." Betsy turned around and caught up with the other three, who stood outside in the September heat.

"We were deciding who was going to come in and get you. Thought you fell in."

"No, I had a couple things to take care of."

"T.M.I. Don't tell me anything else." Ben put his fingers in his ears.

Rose and Larry nodded their heads in agreement then Larry said, "Looks like we're ready to go."

"You lead the way, Mr. Wilford," Rose said as she took her husband's hand and led him in the direction of their RV.

"I will, but please tell me again we aren't going to sing the song, Betsy?" Larry shouted over his shoulder.

"Why not? I thought we did a splendid job for our first time together."

"Betsy, I'm not sure if I didn't hear a band of truckers say they were going to swear off of their CB until we landed in Colorado. That's how bad we sounded."

"Fine." Betsy pretended to sulk.

Rose came up and gave Betsy more hugs. "Now don't you feel better?"

"Never bett—"

"Come on ladies. There's miles to be made."

"Don't worry about him, hon, we'll sing the song," Ben said as he carried Matilda back to their truck from their RV. "Like we agreed this morning."

"I can always count on you." Betsy settled in and Matilda came and sat on her lap.

Before they broke out in song for the second time, Betsy watched Ben as he followed Larry out of the still deserted parking lot. All appeared to run as planned until Larry zigged when he should have zagged and got into a pickle.

The Wilford's trailer and the light pole almost became one. But Ben honked in time, since he'd seen it coming. Their friend stopped and straightened out without causing any damage to their trailer or anything else.

"Wow! That was a close call."

Ben got on the CB. "You alright up there, good buddy?"

"We're all in one piece. How about we get out of here before another light pole comes out of nowhere and tries to take us out?"

"Right with ya."

Betsy couldn't stop laughing at Larry's comment. Ben joined in and she thought at one point he might have to pull over to get control of himself.

"Do you need to stop?" She asked her husband, who kept wiping at his eyes.

"No, I'm fine. I just can't get over Lar. He's a funny guy."

"He is and I'll bet those two will keep us in stitches. Or, at least, I'm counting on it."

"Bets, are we going to sing, or not? Matilda and I are waiting." Ben reached over and touched their dog. "See what I mean?"

"Okay. Okay. Already."

CHAPTER TWENTY-TWO

Mile after mile her hubby drove their dually through the Lone Star State. Trees, cities medium-size and small flashed like picture postcards as Betsy glanced out the window. In a few days her eyes would behold something she'd longed for and what her soul needed. Her mountains.

Colorado.

But first they'd make some stops in between. Betsy hoped they'd land long enough for her to catch up on emails and texts. One in particular. Tina's. She'd tried two or three times, but no service. Betsy picked up her phone one more time.

Service. Betsy sent a text to Tina, since she'd forgotten to do it before they left. Her excuse: too busy getting ready to go. In truth—she still needed to get better in the friend department.

'Cause right now I'm failing at it Lord.

"We've landed."

Betsy watched Larry as he drove into a Wal-Mart in Wichita Falls, Texas and parked. Ben pulled in right behind him. They got out of their trucks and Larry said, "We'll be back. Need to check to see if we can land here for the night."

A few minutes later Ben and Larry came out with another

man. "You are more than welcome to stay here. My names Randy Moore. I'm the manager. If there's anything we can do for you, don't hesitate to come in. We're open 24 hours a day, so security is not an issue."

"Randy, we appreciate your hospitality." Rose answered for all of them.

"Welcome to Wichita Falls." The man walked back towards his store.

"I'm going to like this camping at Wally World." Ben smiled. "It's free and they also throw out the red carpet."

"Can't beat free. Now, how about supper?" Betsy gestured over to a Taco Bell. "Do we want it for supper, too?" A chorus of groans told Bets they vetoed her idea.

"Not me. I opt for BLTs. I'll make them." Rose turned and went inside their RV.

Betsy couldn't have been happier with something else to eat for a change. Without an invitation, she opened the Wilford's camper door and waltzed in and said, "What can I do?"

"Sit there and look pretty while I put out the kitchen slide. Oh, and keep Baby company. Then you can slice up the tomatoes."

She tried to talk to their dog, but Baby's continuous yapping caused her to want to yank the dog's chain, ever so gently, but then the commotion stopped. The sound of the slide caught Baby's attention and she shut up.

Betsy watched her friend push a button behind a cabinet door and said, "Like magic, the kitchen becomes larger. I don't know about you, Rose, but that never ceases to amaze me."

"Me, either. And it quiets Baby down."

But not for long. The barking resumed until Rose threw her dog a treat. Then she got in the refrigerator and handed Betsy two ripe tomatoes and a knife. "Here you go. Slice them tomatoes thick. Larry likes 'em that way."

"Is this one thick enough?" Betsy moved the knife over from the first slice.

"Looking good."

Betsy cut them and put them on a plate Rose had given her. The smell of bacon filled the small space and she couldn't wait to sink her teeth into her BLT. After, she'd think of an excuse to go to their RV to write Tina a longer note.

"Didn't know it took so much concentration to cut a fruit."

"A fruit?" Betsy put her knife down. No use cutting her finger off when she told her friend she barked up the cuckoo tree.

"If you watched the Food Network, you'd know this valuable piece of information."

Betsy almost choked at Rose's suggestion. The channel *was* fast becoming one of Betsy's favorite. *But tomatoes a fruit?* She had to find out. "They're a fruit...why?"

"They have seeds. Like cucumbers." Rose smiled and turned the heat down on the bacon that sizzled in front of her.

"Good to know. I'll make note of this new information. Could turn into a blog. Never know." Betsy laughed.

"Would make for an interesting read." Rose came over to the table and put the plate of bacon in the middle of the table. "Oh, and how's your correspondence with Tina going? You haven't said much."

"Funny you should ask." Betsy gave Rose the Reader's Digest Condensed version of what she'd written earlier on their way here. "I told Tina I'd email more to her later tonight."

"You're on the right track." Rose brought over the bread and mayo. "When in doubt—a testimony is always the way to go."

"I wasn't sure for a while, but today confirmed it."

"God's in the business of settling things for us." Rose winked. "My advice, after supper we'll keep Ben occupied, playing a card game or two, and you get yourself over to your RV and pray. See how the Lord wants you to continue helping Tina."

Betsy appreciated her friend's encouragement. "I'll do that. Thanks."

"You're welcome. But first you need to eat to give you strength." Rose smiled. "And while I set the table, do you want to hunt down the guys."

Betsy went out and found them staring into the basement

compartment of each of their RVs. "Anything the matter?"

"No, we're checking on how my, I mean, our tools weathered the road. Seems they did fine."

"Good. Are you guys ready for dinner?"

"Yes, we're starving." Larry answered for both of them.

Betsy tried to keep her mind on their conversation, but lost track a few times while they ate. Not much need for her to pay attention since the guys did most of the talking. The subject of the day—RVing.

"Why don't you go on, Betsy? The men will help me with the dishes. Ben, you're staying over here. Your wife has some heaven business to take care of and she doesn't need you bugging her."

"Alrighty then. Don't want to interfere with that." Ben put his plate in the sink and gave Betsy a kiss on her way out the door.

"I'll call you when I'm done."

"Want me to walk you over to the RV."

"I'm fine."

Betsy went to the truck to get the pad out of the door then over to their 5th wheel. Ben had put their living room slide out. She took her Bible off of her desk and sat down.

Betsy clicked on Tina's name again and typed the words she felt the Father had given her.

I, too, was abandoned. After 28 years of marriage. I was told to make decisions on my own. I didn't know how to do that or where to turn. But my Father in heaven did. He asks us to turn to Him. BUT, like a fool, I still held on to unforgiveness. Even after we reconciled, and all seemed fine, I carried this burden. Yes, the Lord healed our marriage, but I found out I had to let go and forgive my husband for leaving me and the hurtful words he said. And ask forgiveness for the ones I'd said to him. Tina, I couldn't have done it without Him in my life. After years of trying to do this thing called marriage on our own—we've finally given it ALL into our Father's hands. He is the only One who can heal our hurts.

Tears ran down Betsy's cheeks as she typed the words. When she finished, she hit send and waited for Tina's response. Betsy whispered a "Thank You" to the One who continued to show up every day. She couldn't imagine her life without Him.

When she didn't get a text back from Tina, she shut the lights out and went over to the Wilford's RV. They smiled when she came inside and no one asked her any questions, which Betsy appreciated. Later she'd share what she'd written with Ben.

~

Sunshine greeted them on their travels to Trinidad, Colorado. Another pull in and park spot. This time at a small campground. Since it'd been a long day, Betsy suggested they hit the sack early. "Tomorrow we'll get up at the crack of dawn and be in Colorado Springs in a couple hours."

All of the *Early Birds* agreed. Especially Ben. His neck, arms and shoulders screamed, "Stop. Now." After driving 483 miles he wanted nothing more than a shower and the evening news.

The hot water hit his back and Ben could feel the tension begin to wash down the drain. He flexed his hands. They ached from the hours he'd held the steering wheel.

I need to relax and not worry so much.

His normal twenty-minute shower ended in ten. No need to fill up their tank. Ben toweled off and attempted to get dressed in their tiny bathroom. With the door closed, he found it almost impossible and couldn't figure out why he'd shut the door and he blamed it his tiredness.

"News is getting ready to start."

Ben finished tucking in his shirt and ambled down the two steps to see Scott Pelley's face splashed on the screen. The sound muted for some reason. He reached for the control, turning the volume up as he sat down. Matilda joined him on the loveseat.

"How about popcorn for dinner?"

"I'm too tired to chew." Ben muted the commercial.

"I'm pretty tired and...not very hungry either."

Ben stared at his wife for a moment, which gave his last brain cell time to kick in and NOT ask, "Why are you so tired? Wouldn't think sitting on the passenger seat would wear you out. Sweetie."

Even with the loving sentiment at the end, Ben bet his wife's ire would trump his exhaustion. He kept his mouth shut and watched the news. Or he tried like mad to do it.

"Hon, it's time to go to bed."

"I'm watching the news."

"It's been over for an hour." Betsy laughed as she stood up. "Come on Matilda. Time for bed."

Their dog followed them upstairs and settled in the middle of their queen-size bed. Her norm every night. Ben snuggled as close to Bets as their precious pooch would allow and relaxed once again, falling right back to sleep.

CHAPTER TWENTY-THREE

"It's 7:00 bells. All is put away. We've hugged Rose and we're on the road again. Hon, you ready to sing our song?" Ben asked his wife, but got what sounded like a growl. "Matilda, do you want to sing with your sweet, adorable, patient, kind, long-suff—"

"Morning people should come with muzzles. Your saving grace, brother, is I love you with all my heart and we're in COLORADO."

Ben focused on the road ahead, but peeked at Betsy once in a while. Every time he did, her eyes stared out the left side of their truck. He heard her say her favorite phrase. The one she'd said a thousand times since they'd arrived. "My mountains."

The contented smile on her face tugged at Ben's heart. He'd taken her away from all of this beauty. He wondered if she'd totally forgiven him for taking her from Colorado and moving her to Houston, Texas.

Glad it's behind us. Literally and figuratively.

Ben grimaced at the thought. 'It' encompassed more than a location on a map—it also included a time neither Betsy, nor he, wanted to relive.

"We're almost there," Betsy announced. "Rose said Larry will take the Manitou Springs exit, but I'm sure he'll alert you."

A half hour later Larry's voice crackled across the CB. "Hello, Ben. We're going to a park we've stayed in. They're open and cleaned up after the mudslides. Follow me."

"Been doing it for 933.4 miles. Why change now?" Ben joked.

Without a hitch, Ben and Larry got their RVs parked, leveled on the cement and the slides out in less than fifteen minutes.

"I don't want to jinx anything, but that was too easy."

Rose came over and swatted Ben's arm. "Mr. Stevenson, when did you become superstitious? I'd say you need to get on your knees and pray the evil spirit away."

"Let's go inside the RV and you can pray over me. But we need to keep it down. Don't want our neighbors to find out." Ben hooted.

"I'm not getting anywhere near you. You devil-possessed person." Rose danced around the fire pit, acting as if she warded off flying objects. Or something along those lines.

"Yes, Rosie, an evil spirit had a hold of his brain for all those years he worked in management. They let loose of him when he retired."

Ben came over and gave his wife a hug. "Remember I'm not the only one possessed in this crowd. Look over there."

Their good-natured teasing continued until Larry let Baby out of the cab of their truck. Then yelping, louder than Ben had heard in all of his years, came out of the ten-pound pup. Rose went into high gear and grabbed the mongrel and headed to their RV.

"Obviously obedience school didn't—"

"Ben?"

Betsy put her index finger to her mouth and Ben decided not to finish the rest of his sentence. Sometimes the best thing to do—leave it alone. Realize they're out on the road with a lunatic dog. The one they owned: precious.

"Matilda. Come." The Boston terrier mix scampered to the end of her leash and sat down next to the picnic table, where Ben had sat down.

"I'd say more training's in order," Larry said then leaned back in his chair and put his hat over his eyes, signaling to all he'd reached the end of his rope too.

Rose came out a minute later, carrying the now-quiet Shih Tzu. "She must have smelled something she didn't like."

"Rose, admit it. Your dog is the one possessed. The rest of us, including Matilda, are running on all our cylinders. This one," Larry pointed to Baby, "not so much." He once again reclined in his chair and put his hat over his face.

"Well, I never." Rose turned and went inside their RV again.

"You want to go for a walk, hon?" Ben went over and undid Matilda's leash. "I'm sure there's a coffee shop around here."

"A great idea. We'll pick up one for you guys too."

"Make it strong."

As they walked along Cypress Street, the scent of pine and juniper greeted Betsy. A sure sign Colorado welcomed her home. The early morning chill in the middle of September signaled the start of fall. In Texas, heat hung on until November.

"Ben, why were we so fortunate to find such a well-behaved dog?"

"I don't know, but I'm so glad she's almost perfect...like her parents."

Ben's off-the-wall comment must have tickled Betsy. She stopped right in the middle of the sidewalk and started to laugh. When two men walked past them, they smiled and nodded their heads.

They reached the coffee shop, which the owner aptly named *Wake Up.* Remnants of the mudslide from earlier in the month cluttered the parking lot. Since they had Matilda, Ben picked their pooch up and opted for the walk-up window.

"What'll you have?"

"We'll take four Bold roast." Ben wanted to add some small talk, but couldn't figure out how to bring up what had happened to Manitou Springs.

"We're sorry to hear about the mudslides."

Ben appreciated his wife's forthrightness and attention to detail at times. Now being one of them and he added, "But it looks like you've gotten it pretty well cleaned up."

The woman pointed at a bulletin board. "This is what our place looked like a month ago. Last year's fires caused the problem with the mud. When the rains pounded us, there was nowhere for the burnt trees, debris and water to go." She poured their coffees.

Betsy stepped forward to look at the photos. "It must have been awful."

"You can still see the damage and how much we had to clean up. Almost brought us to our knees. But the Lord reminded us to keep going, which we did, and reopened in less than a month. Here you go."

Ben paid for the coffees and thanked her. Betsy assured the store owner as they left the window, "We'll be praying for you."

~

As they neared the corner where they needed to cross, Betsy stopped and turned to Ben. "Wow is all I can say!" Then she took off, chasing Matilda.

"Hey. Hold up. We have to wait on the traffic light."

"I planned on it, but your dog is doing her best to do otherwise. She's spotted a squirrel." Betsy saw it in the bushes and knew nothing would deter Matilda from trying to break free to get to the furry creature.

Ben came to Betsy's rescue, taking the leash from her white-knuckled hand and handed the coffee off to her. "Matilda, you know better than that. Relax. Anyway, you're no match for a squirrel. They climb trees and you don't."

Betsy chuckled. More from the vision in her head of their black and white dog scaling a tree like a cat. "I'd pay good money to see her do it."

"So would other people."

"We better get to training her then. America's Got Talent is look—"

"Light's green."

Betsy put Hollywood and fame out of her mind as they walked. And did her best to keep her eyes on the road so she wouldn't trip. The red rocks of the Garden of the Gods jutting up all around them lured her attention away.

Her family came and stayed in Manitou too many times to count during her childhood and two times in college. Betsy never got Colorado out of her mind or heart. Then when a job opportunity came at age 22, she jumped on it with both feet.

The mountains became her home. Forever, she'd hoped. Two years later she met Ben at a business conference. Their long-distance relationship lasted a year before they got married. Love took her away from her favorite place.

The best part of the move, she'd gotten to spend her life with Ben. The man who now stood staring at her.

"Hon, are you coming today?"

"I'm reminiscing. Don't bug me."

Betsy loved to watch Ben when she made one of her absurd comments. Then she laughed. Even she thought this comment classified as crazy. How many people did she know admitted their thoughts went awry on occasion?

A list of her writer friends from Houston came to mind and she smiled. Those ladies brainstormed or plotted a new story every time they met. As long as Betsy had known them, she still didn't know how some could have so many ideas.

Might be because they wrote fiction and she wrote nonfiction. Real life. How she saw it. And from the wide-eyed look on her hubby's face, his brain saw something different in her earlier comment.

Betsy stopped walking and asked. "What? You're giving me a strange look again."

"Dear, all I can say is—you're the only person who can turn a 15-minute walk into 30 plus and now our coffees are cold."

"I have one answer for you. No...two. Colorado and your wife are having a moment. Anyway, bud, we have microwaves to heat up our coffee."

"Got a point there."

They reached the campground and Baby greeted them with her usual barking and carrying on. The Wilford's dog sounded like she could tear them apart, if given the chance. Matilda backed away and did everything in her power to leap into Ben's arms.

Ben picked her up and said, "Sorry it took so long, guys. I'll heat up the coffees. Be out in a minute."

Right then Rose got up from one of the lawn chairs and shouted, "Baby, you need to hush." She reached down and scooped their dog in her arms and gave her a treat.

Betsy shook her head. "Rosie, why do you give your dog goodies when she misbehaves?"

Her friend turned to her. "Because she's cute. And—"

"Baby is adorable, but her incessant barking isn't." Betsy couldn't believe she'd been so bold, but it needed said. And she said it.

Larry sat up. "She's right, Rosebud."

Rose sat down on one of their chairs and appeared to have lost her best friend. Betsy took the seat next to her and reached out to touch Rose's hand.

"Oh, now you want to make up. After calling my dog rabid."

"I did not say you have a diseased dog." Betsy glanced over at Rose, hoping to see a grin or hear a snort from her. But no alms of peace emitted from her friend.

I should learn to keep my mouth shut too. And pray.

Silence followed, which verified she should have zipped her lips. Best thing to do, send up prayers for the Wilford's mutt and for their friendship to survive Betsy's bluntness.

The only saving grace, during the almost four minutes of stillness, Ben brought out their now-heated up coffees and handed them out to everyone. Then he went and plopped down in one of the empty canvass chairs.

The hush resumed until Rose crossed her arms and announced, "So, Bets, what you're saying is the obedience training didn't seem to work?"

Betsy looked at Rose when she heard the familiar sound coming from her friend and they both almost fell out of their chairs laughing. That would have been fine, but Baby took one look at them and joined the party.

She climbed on Rose then jumped over to Betsy's lap. Each move brought more yelps and a commotion from Baby - almost as if she'd been beaten. Her shenanigans brought Larry and Ben out of their chairs. Doing anything and everything to quiet the mutt down.

Betsy stood up and stared at a woman who'd come out of the Registration office at the end of their row and said, "Uh oh."

She voiced the short warning to her RV mates, hoping they'd seen the same thing as she had. The scowl and all-out fury on the woman's face told Betsy the welcome-wagon lady wasn't coming for a visit. What she would be bringing...the inevitable eviction notice...they didn't want.

For some strange reason, Betsy had an insatiable urge to leave and said so, "Excuse me, but I need to go check on Matilda."

"You are doing nothing of the sort," Rose whispered and pinched her arm.

"Ouch." Betsy rubbed her forearm. "Guess I'll be staying. But we've got to do something." Then it hit her. She motioned for Larry to come over. "Take Baby in your place and stay put. Ben, you go in and get Matilda. Then come back out."

"Why."

"You'll understand in a second." Betsy watched the guys do as they were told and prayed her seat-of-the pants idea worked. If it didn't, they would need a new place to park their RVs tonight.

Dragon Woman arrived and in between her taking gasps of air she yelled, "Someone better explain what all the racket was about and who is responsible for it."

At that precise moment, Ben walked out of their RV carrying Matilda. He must have understood what Betsy had up her sleeve because he'd put their precious pooch in her little t-shirt which read, "Me Cute."

Betsy also noticed he stayed near their door and kept the shirt hidden. Again Betsy almost lost it and she heard her friend Rose snort. Praise be to God she caught it in time so it sounded like she'd suppressed a sneeze.

"Well, there are three of you standing here and I don't hear any of you explaining all the hubbub."

Ben waltzed over with Matilda, her t-shirt visible for the world to see and said, "Ma'am, Baby's having problems adjusting to RV life. We're new at this recreational vehicle thing. Could you possibly give us some pointers on how to help her?" Ben turned their dog to face the woman.

"Oh my goodness. This is who made all the fuss?" She reached out and took Matilda in her arms and started making all kinds of noises. Baby talk and some things Betsy had never heard before. After a minute, words came out of the woman's mouth she could understand.

"Adorable. Simply adorable."

While she cuddled Matilda, Betsy watched the woman's smile. They'd won the battle. Then she verified it when she said, "There's no worries with this one. Anyway, I see this all the time. They're scared. If you need me to watch this cutie, don't you hesitate? Bye now."

As the woman went back the direction she'd came, Betsy decided she loved her hubby a whole bunch. And if they handed out Academy Awards for Texas drawl, he won it hands down.

She came over and joined Rose, Ben and Matilda and they hurried into the Wilford's RV. Before Betsy got the door closed, all of them burst out in the most riotous laughter she'd ever heard from the four of them.

"Hush, you guys she's not...out of ear shot...yet," she stammered and if she didn't quit slapping her leg, she'd have a bruise on it tomorrow morning.

"I only have two wishes." Rose flailed her arms around like she had something caught in her throat. When she settled down she continued, "That the Almighty forgives us for lying and He has a video of this when we all get to heaven." Rose let out a snort that almost brought the trailer to its axles.

"Quit. We've got to quit talking." Larry folded his arms. "My stomach is killing me."

No one said anything for a few minutes then Betsy spoke up, "Soooooo, are we calling Matilda - Baby 1?" She asked as she picked up the real Baby.

Baby barked for a solid minute before Rose got her under control. "Guess her answer is she wants to keep her name all to herself."

"That's fine. I'm sort of partial to Matilda. We do have to remember, until we leave here, the dogs have made a switcheroo."

"Be quiet. No more talk of dogs. Let's fix dinner." Larry dug in their refrigerator and came out with a selection of salamis and cheeses. "Grab the crackers, Rose. I'm ready to eat."

The evening ended and they hadn't made it to Garden of the Gods. *There's always tomorrow. Today I wouldn't trade for a million dollars.*

"Bets, you ready to head to our place?"

"First I have to ask, are we going to make it out of the RV Park tomorrow? To see some of the sights?"

"We'll finalize our plans in the morning."

"Earlier than later," Betsy told Rose.

"Bright and early, for sure."

Betsy reached their RV and Ben came behind her and had Matilda tucked under his left arm. If anyone saw him they'd think he had a serious weight problem around his middle. Not a dog hidden inside there.

"I hope the woman isn't watching us. Does she have surveillance cameras?"

"You never know. She did have that look about her."

"Yes, I did see her beady eyes. I saw something else too."

"What?"

Betsy went up the stairs and into the RV. Ben followed. She turned and gave him a kiss. "What I saw is you're quite an actor. What you did out there...your performance deserves an award. A little white lie, yes, but it was splendid."

"Let's say when I thought of the crazy t-shirt, I wasn't sure it was going to do the trick, but it worked out great.

"Ben, I don't know how any of us kept a straight face."

"Me either." He went to the cabinet. "Want a couple of

cookies?"

"Sure. Then let's veg and watch some HGTV." Betsy put her side of the loveseat back and picked up the TV remote.

"Hon, I'd rather have some quiet." Ben handed her two oatmeal raisin cookies and sat down. "Acting wore me out."

Betsy turned on the TV and music came out of the speakers. "Some romantic music for the three of us to relax to. Come here Matilda. Oh, I mean Baby. Oh this is going to get confusing."

Ben patted the side of his chair and their pooch jumped up. "You do know her cuteness got us off the hook, don't you?"

"I've always told you from the day we picked her up at the animal rescue that she's a special gift from above. This afternoon her charm and your ingenuity got us out of a boat load of trouble. And if I haven't told you two today—I love you bunches and bunches."

"Love you too."

Ben put his recliner back and soon Betsy could see his even breathing—a sure sign the soft rhythm of the music and their busy day had lulled him to sleep. But she saw something else. He wore the same expression he had when he got home from work.

Something's eating at my sweetie and I bet I know what it is.

CHAPTER TWENTY-FOUR

"Hon, you want some breakfast?"

Betsy heard Ben's bellowing from the kitchen, but stayed snuggled under the covers for some extra shut eye. She figured since her hubby woke up early—it must be 8:00 or 8:30. She glanced over at their clock on the wall and almost rolled out of bed.

"Why didn't you wake me?" Betsy questioned Ben after she got out of bed and between swishes of the toothbrush in her mouth.

"I came in a couple of times, but you looked so peaceful. I couldn't bring myself to wake you. Anyway, I love watching you sleep."

Betsy took a look at her reflection in the bathroom mirror. Must be true love, if her beloved said he enjoyed seeing what she saw. She rinsed out the toothpaste and came down to sit at the table. "Thank you, but..."

Ben gave her his famous sideward look and she left the rest off the record. No need to start the day putting her appearance down. Self-deprecation didn't get her anywhere. Anyway, the verse she read yesterday told her to think about things that were noble and true and...

Betsy couldn't recollect the rest of it and decided in her quiet time she'd look it up and write the verse in her Bible.

"Here you go."

Ben sat a cup of coffee and a bowl of cereal in front of her and Betsy took a bite of the granola. With her mouth still full of the clusters she asked, "Are you ready to see the sites today?"

"As soon as you get dressed."

Betsy took another bite and while she contemplated what to wear, she watched Matilda. Didn't matter if their pooch got eight hours of sleep or four - she always got up in the morning, went out and did her business then came in and went over to her bed and fell fast asleep. Again.

"Ben, she's got the life. Sleep, eat and poop." Betsy took a sip of her coffee then sat it down. "If I believed in reincarnation—I'd want to come back as a dog in my next life. "No worries. No cares. No need to write. My paws would be too big to hit the keys, anyway."

"One thing's for sure, if I laid all twisted around like Matilda does, I'd need a chiropractor."

Betsy nodded her head and got up from the table. "That's true." She walked over squatted next to Matilda's bed. "Mats, you're not going to like us much. You have to stay in your c.r.a.t.e. for a while today. Mom and Dad are going scooter-pooping."

Matilda yawned and stretched and gave Betsy, what she took as an understanding look. Understanding in the sense their pooch knew what the spelled-out word meant. Their pup got up out of her bed and headed to the bedroom.

If history repeated itself—no amount of coaxing would bring her back into the living room where 'it' sat. Not even the mention of getting a treat.

"Wait until we're about ready to leave before you roll the crate out." Betsy whispered. "We don't want to traumatize her any more than we have to."

Ben rolled the crate back under the desk. "When do you think you'll be done?"

"Give me ten minutes." A not-so-becoming thought dangled at the edge of her throat, but again she kept quiet.

"I'll go over and tell Larry and Rose."

Ben gave Betsy a kiss and headed out the door, leaving her to figure out her attire. But first she took her Bible off the desk and sat down in her recliner with one goal in mind. To find the verse she'd thought of earlier.

When Betsy found it, she touched the page and read the verse out loud:

"Finally, brothers and sisters, whatever is true, whatever is noble, whatever is right, whatever is pure, whatever is lovely, whatever is admirable—if anything is excellent or praiseworthy— think about such things."

When Betsy finished, she waltzed over to her computer and sat down to write her newly-discovered blog idea. Her fingers typed, "It's one thing I put myself down, but it's another to lie to the woman last night."

"Done. For the time being." Betsy shut the lid and hurried upstairs to get dressed, with less than five minutes to make something happen. In record time she put on an outfit and combed her hair and no one suffered damage in the process.

Unless you counted their pooch Matilda, who still lay across their bed, shaking all over. Betsy left her alone and went to get the crate out. "Mats, come on down. I've got a treat for you." She went over and got one out of the drawer. "Matilda?"

Their dog stayed upstairs. Betsy gave her a couple more minutes then went and picked her up. Or tried to. Matilda lay on her back as limp as a wet noodle. "Come on, girl. I'm sorry, but it's time for you to get in your crate. We won't be gone long."

After putting Mats away, Betsy exited the RV and whistled a happy tune. The idea for a blog accomplished and Colorado under her feet, what more could a girl ask for? The only thing – a trip to see the Garden of the Gods.

With all of that on her mind, she almost tripped over Larry when he stepped out from underneath their basement compartment. "Sorry, Lar. Didn't see you there."

"Not a problem."

Betsy smiled at her friend, but Larry seemed more concerned at closing the storage area than being run over. Once he locked the door, he turned to face her. "Bets, I wish I had what you have. Never a care in the world."

Huh?

For some reason, it didn't seem as if her legs wanted to hold her up. Before they gave out, Bets circled around the picnic table and sat down on one of the lawn chairs. Not sure whether to laugh or cry at what Lar said.

"Are you okay?" Larry hurried to her side.

"I'm fine. Your comment caught me by surprise." Betsy took a deep breath. "If you'd read the notes to my last blog I wrote, you might look at me in a different way."

The second those demeaning words left her lips, she wanted to rewind them. The verse she'd read five minutes before clobbered her.

Whatever is true, noble...

"Bets, maybe the devil's fooling you into believing something you're not." Larry stood and brushed something off his jeans. "

"You could be right." Betsy hugged her friend. "Thanks."

"Now it looks like we're ready to go to the Garden of the Gods."

"I'd say it's about time you two quit yapping." Rose came over next to them. "Ben and I thought you were going to talk for days."

"Takes time to solve the world's problems." Larry smiled at Betsy then took his wife's hand and headed towards their truck.

"Are you coming, Bets?"

"I'm right behind ya."

On the way to the truck Betsy thought about their conversation. *And one other thing...why was Larry looking in our basement compartment? Very strange.*

~

"We'll sit in the back." Rose adjusted the seatbelt. "Larry, you did make sure Baby's secure in her crate, I hope. Don't want the park to find out we tried to pull the wool over their eyes."

"Or, we're a bunch of liars." Ben blurted out.

"Say what?" Larry asked as he got in the driver's side. "Who pooped on your parade this early in the morning?"

"Let's get going and we'll talk about it later."

Larry left and took them to the Visitor's Center at Garden of the Gods. Ben didn't say anymore on the topic he'd brought up and noticed no one else did either.

They hadn't gotten in the door when Betsy motioned for Ben to come over. "This is what I was telling you about."

Out in front of his wife, in her right hand, Betsy held up a row of postcards. They were almost as tall as her. Ben leaned over and peered at them. "I'm assuming this is what we're going to see today."

"Exactly. I can't wait."

Betsy's enthusiasm caused the postcards to wave from side to side, while still in her grasp. Since Ben thought they might not make it too much longer he suggested, "Why don't you go and buy them, hon?"

"I do believe I will. These will go with the ones I have from when we came in the 60s and 70s."

Ben's family never traveled anywhere. Instead, they went to his uncle's farm and worked all summer. Hard work, but the experience gave him a chance to learn what it meant to work for a living. He wouldn't trade those years and what they taught him.

Then Sundays, his grandmother took him, his brother and cousins to the small church in Durham, North Carolina. Changed his life. Forever.

"Let's get this show moving. We've got the post cards bought and watched the video, which I've seen a dozen times. What's next?" Rose announced to everyone when she came out of the restroom and rejoined Ben and Betsy. "Where's Larry?"

"I'm right here."

"Ben, I better run in here before we head to the chapel."

While the other two went out to their truck, Ben waited for Betsy. A ritual they'd done since they first got married. *Guess she's afraid I'll get lost.*

The one time he left the designated spot, he thought he'd have to call an ambulance for Betsy. She'd tried to find him in the crowd and couldn't. The incident happened before cell phones, so she had the person with the microphone call out his name. Not something you want done as an adult.

From that point on, he'd stayed glued next to the public restroom his wife went into. And as always, his wife came out with a new friend. He let them chat and they exchanged emails. Then Betsy walked up to him and said, "Ready?"

"I know you are." Ben took her hand and they strolled out to find their friends.

Larry drove around the red rock formation and Ben decided the pictures on the postcards Betsy purchased dimmed in comparison. All around him stood magnificent grandeur only the Master could have created.

Ben chuckled at Betsy. More than once she made Larry pull over so she could take a picture. The one at the Balanced Rock made him nervous. While he stood under it, Ben hoped the boulder above his head stayed in place.

Then it hit him, his wife's 58 years old. The photo Betsy's dad took of her, in the same spot, happened 52 years before.

Doubt it's going anywhere.

After coming down off the rock from their photo op, Ben suggested they stop and eat. "Rose fixed some sandwiches for us before we left this morning."

"I'm with you." Larry glanced at his wife. "Where's the cooler?"

Rose went to the rear of their truck and opened the tailgate. "While you were out fiddling under the RV, I grabbed it and put it back here."

Larry's face turned a shade of red before he said, "Here, let me get that for you." He hurried to the back and took out the cooler and carried it a short distance to a picnic table. By the time he returned, so had his normal coloring. "What have we got in here?"

Rose pushed his hand away and lifted the lid. "Who wants tuna salad and who wants egg salad? The chips are in the bag. Oh, I left them in the truck."

"We've got them." Betsy put the snacks on the table and went to the cooler and grabbed a bottle of water. "I'll take the egg salad. If there's any left."

"Plenty to go around." Ben took one out and handed his wife a foil-wrapped sandwich, marked 'egg' and sat down.

Betsy joined him then shot up off her seat and asked, "Anyone need anything to drink? I got mine and didn't ask anyone else."

"Sit, sit, sit. We've all got something to drink." Rose sat across from Betsy and opened a can of soda.

"I don't," Larry said as he joined his wife. When he started to get up again, Betsy told him to, "sit, sit, sit," trying to sound like Rose.

"That was a terrible imitation of me." Rose took a bite of her sandwich then swallowed. "And, if anyone is wondering why, it needed more of a Texas twang."

"I thought it was spot on." Ben laughed and gave Betsy a hug when she returned to the table.

"Coming from the Best Actor winner from last night's performance at the RV Park, I'll take it."

Ben watched the three of them after Betsy's comment. If they weren't cracking up as much as the night before, it was a close second. He got up and walked to the cooler and waited for them to settle down.

When they didn't, Ben decided he had two choices—leave them alone or step in and take charge, which Betsy said he excelled in.

Here goes!

"Hello. Excuse me." Ben stood next to the table. "To my crazy wife and her two nutty friends, who are making fools of themselves at the Garden of the Gods, can I have your attention?"

"Guys, what hubs is trying to say is, 'Come on—straighten up.'"

Ben appreciated Betsy's assistance and within seconds the three of them quieted down. They looked at him with a smile on their faces. He took a seat at the picnic table again.

"Guys, I don't want to spoil our fun, but my performance last night wasn't funny. We lied to someone. When we get back I'm going to the office to apologize." Ben watched his table mates. "Lying's not my style."

"Mine either." Betsy leaned over and gave Ben a kiss. "I'll go with you."

Larry pointed over at Rose. "Funny you should mention that. We talked about it last night. Sorry for laughing today. It is, and was, inappropriate. Count us in too."

"And we'll bring Baby along." Rose added.

"Oh, including her ought to fix things right up."

Ben laughed at his one liner and the other three joined in. Well, most of them did. Rose's chuckles and snorts weren't as boisterous as before. When she picked up their trash and asked, "Are we done here?" He knew their site-seeing tour might have ended sooner than planned. He needed to make amends.

"Rosie—"

"No need to apologize. I know I have a dog...that...that's...I'm not sure there's a name for it."

This time all of them cracked up. Rose's statement told Ben and everyone else their day was back on track. If not, he would have had another female to contend with. And no one wanted to mess with Betsy Stevenson when it came to her favorite place on earth - Colorado.

"Larry, put this puppy in gear and hit the road." Betsy grabbed the cooler and put it in the truck. Then got in and said, "Let's go."

Their friend drove a short distance and when he turned right, Betsy came to the center of the bucket seat and said, "Pull over. This is it."

When Ben spotted what his wife hollered about, his mouth dropped open. Nothing Betsy said or the photographs he'd seen prepared him for the sight of the tiny chapel, standing across the field in front of him.

"Hon, this...this is a replica of the church Grandma Stevenson took us to." Ben got out of the truck and rushed ahead of everyone else to read the inscription on the stand outside. Sweet memories of the special place washed over him. The wall around his heart he'd kept closed for too long burst. Tears ran down his cheeks.

For the last ten years he'd turned his back on his brother, blaming him for what he'd said or not said. Ben had also turned his back on the love of his life, Betsy. And when everything fell apart, he'd turned his back on God.

Standing there, outside the small church, Ben dried his tears and realized something he should have known. He wasn't in control of anything. God always would be. He needed to reconnect with Brian again and love Betsy the way God intended him to.

Lord, connecting with Betsy. Easy. Brian...I'm not so sure.

CHAPTER TWENTY-FIVE

Betsy viewed her husband's reaction to the little church as she stood next to the truck. She wanted to go to him, but left him alone. No need to chat with him about the first time she'd seen the chapel and how it had touched her heart.

From the looks of his tears, the church touched him too.

"Hey, there's a trail back behind here. Lar, let's go take a look. Catch up with us when you're done."

Betsy smiled at Rose as the couple walked towards the rocky path. Love for her sweet friends grew by leaps and bounds at that moment. When she saw they'd disappeared behind the church, Bets strolled up and stood next to Ben, making sure she did it without fanfare.

"Hon, this is amazing."

"Glad you like it."

"It's almost like they took the church Grandma took us to and shrunk it. The placard gives a name of someone. I'm not sure he would have had anything to do with the one in Durham. I'll have to check."

Betsy smiled. "I'm sure Google or one of those other places will head you in the right direction."

"Yep." Ben sat down on the bench and took out his phone.

"Are you going to start your investigation now?"

"No, I was checking the time. Don't want to miss the office hours at the RV Park, so we can talk to them."

Betsy sat down next to him, "I'm sorry I didn't get a chance to talk to you about all this. As usual, I was too busy with my own stuff..."

She stopped before she said any more when she remembered Larry's comment from earlier. *Maybe he's right. I'm believing something I shouldn't.*

"You do seem to entertain yourself." Ben stared at her.

"Why do you say that?"

"We're talking along and then you quit. It's as if you're in never, never land."

"As I always say, 'Come live inside this body for a day. I'll bet you'd want out before an hour went by.'"

"No hon, I'd stay there long enough to find out why you always, yes, always, put yourself down."

Betsy shrugged her shoulders since she couldn't come up with a clever comeback. About that time an epiphany hit her. Is there a response which would convince anyone that the truth she believed about herself outweighed what the Father said about her in His word?

"Betsy, this place is absolutely beautiful."

Rose's voice stopped Betsy in mid-thought and she saw their friends as they came around the corner of the church. "And with the aspens and pine surrounding it, it almost tickles my toes. Thanks for showing it to us."

"I have to agree on most of what you said." Ben stood up. "The 'tickles to my toes', I'm not sure. Are we ready to head to the RV?"

Larry nodded. "We better. Our pooches are probably crossing their legs by now."

"And speaking of which, Rose do you want to hit the—"

"Yes, ma'am. I do."

"I'll swing into the Visitor's Center on our way out." Larry got in the driver's side and everyone else followed.

With their pit stop accomplished and the four of them in the truck again, Betsy leaned up and touched Ben's shoulder. "Lar, before we take off can we pray about our meeting with the lady at the RV Park?"

"Can do."

Larry grabbed Ben's hand and soon their circle inside the Wilford's dually sounded like a prayer meeting at the chapel a few yards away. Betsy's heart soared when she peeked and saw the smile on her hubby's face.

This is the day that the Lord has made. Let us rejoice and be glad in it.

~

Ben stood in front of the registration desk with Betsy, Rose and Larry. His friend carried Baby, and for some strange reason she didn't make a sound.

"Good afternoon. May I help you?"

Ben glanced at the woman's name tag. "Marilyn. I think you can. I, no, I mean we, came down to apologize to you."

"For what?" She gawked at them and her eyes came to a stop on the dog. "Who is this?"

"It's the real Baby." Ben wanted to say more, but the words caught in his throat for some reason.

"Baby?" The woman's forehead scrunched together. Almost as if she tried to process a difficult math problem. Then she must have gotten it. "Baby...No...The cute black and white is. You told me."

Baby started her customary yapping and leapt out of Larry's arms as if on a mission. She headed in Marilyn's direction, behind the desk. When she got around to her, she stood there. Not a bark in sight.

"Yes, Marilyn, I told you a lie last night. The dog we showed you is Matilda, our pooch, who isn't a barker. When we saw you coming, we decided to pull a fast one. That's what happened and I'm sorry for lying to you. I'm also sorry for Baby making such a racket."

"Me, two."

"Me, three."

"Me, four."

Marilyn stared at them and a smile broke out on her face the size of the state they'd left the month before. "Well, whoever came up with the idea sure has my vote. And this little princess," she picked up Baby, "I can't believe she could make that much noise."

As if to prove Marilyn wrong, Baby started up with some high pitch yelps. Ones Ben felt certain Denver and surrounding areas heard.

"As you can see, she's got a healthy set of lungs." Rose reached over and took Baby from her. "This is after she attended obedience school."

Marilyn laughed, "I've seen and heard worse. This one doesn't hold a candle to one I had last week. Howls at midnight. Frantic calls at 12:01. Don't you worry. Go on now!" She motioned them toward the door.

"You're not mad at us?" Ben asked.

"No, I'm not. But I do appreciate your honesty. Don't get much of it anymore."

"We've learned our lesson," Rose added.

Ben heard laughter coming from the office when they made their exit. Relief washed over him when he realized they could continue their stay at the Springs RV Park.

"Yes, my grandmother would be proud of all of us for coming clean."

"Preach it, brother."

Larry's comment was met with more giggles. Baby must have liked it too. She joined in with some loud barks and a tiny growl.

"Girl, I wish some of Matilda would rub off on you." Rose petted her pooch.

"Perfection only comes around once and we've got her."

"Betsy, your hubby is telling another lie and it could be detrimental to his wellbeing."

"How's that?"

"As I told you yesterday, one of these days the Lord is going to zap you. I'm just saying. And, I don't want to be standing anywhere near you when He decides to take you out."

Their laughter brought strange looks from the other RVers as they made their way back to their own spaces. Ben waved at them as they passed, but didn't care if they gawked. Along with making amends for Baby's behavior, Ben would remember the day for something else too.

Today he realized, thanks to a little church at the Garden of the Gods, he needed to make a phone call to someone he hadn't talked to in years.

~

On the way back to the RV, from the registration office, Betsy suggested Rose and Larry come over for dinner.

"No, we're going to stay in tonight and try to work some magic on our little bundle of joy."

Rose's description of Baby screamed for her to say something else, but Betsy left it alone. Ben and Larry did too.

The rest of the way, Betsy enjoyed the quiet. Gave her a chance to hear and see one of her favorite things about Colorado. The hand of God at work. The aspen leaves, shifting from shades of green to touches of yellows and reds fluttered in the late afternoon breeze.

Autumn...a time to let go of the old...be ready for what's to come.

Betsy got so caught up in gazing at the colors, she jumped when Rose poked her and said, "We'll talk to you in the morning. Oh and if Baby does anything miraculous—you guys will be the first to know."

"We'll pray for you and her. Keep us posted." Ben turned toward their RV.

Betsy followed Ben up the stairs. When they got inside, her hubby made a right and went up to their bedroom. She tilted her head, like Matilda did when she seemed perplexed.

Do dogs get befuddled?

Betsy let the random thought go. Along with letting Ben go

where he wanted to in their RV. She went over to Matilda and asked their dog a dumb question as she released her from the crate, "You ready to get out of there?"

Matilda sprung out of her cage and after a few frenzied laps around the kitchen island, their dog came to the loveseat for some cuddle time with Mom...and Dad.

Where's Ben?

"Hey, bud, there you are." Betsy saw her husband walking down the stairs and said, "Do you want to go with me to take our princess out for a walk?"

"Sure."

While Ben got a bag, Betsy hooked the leash on Matilda's collar and said, "Come." In a split second the dog scooted out the door and wrapped the leash around one of the lawn chair legs.

Ben smiled as he came down the steps. "Here let me have it."

Betsy gladly handed the leash over, knowing full well she could handle their little mutt, but Matilda loved her dad more and stayed in step with him a whole lot better than with her.

They walked around the park, stopping to say "Hi" to their neighbors. She heard someone say something about a 'flood' somewhere. But Betsy's mind only wanted to pay attention to the beauty surrounding her. Tomorrow, the predicted rain, would make them stay inside their RV.

Again nature didn't disappoint her. Along with the sound of the aspen leaves rustling in the background, a thought came to mind. She wanted the world to stop so she could cherish this almost perfect day.

"Ben, I don't know about you, but I sure want to come and spend more time here. Not in the winter, but May thru this time of year would make me happy."

"I can tell it agrees with you. Haven't seen you smile this much in years."

"Didn't find much to smile about in Hous..." Betsy stopped the not-so-kind comment and wished her words hadn't hit the air.

"You're right about that, sweetie." Ben took Betsy in his arms and gave her the biggest hug. Then he planted a kiss on her lips—

in front of God and anyone watching at the RV Park—which almost buckled her knees.

When she caught her breath she said, "Well, mister, I'd say that should put a smile on any girl's face."

"Yesiree and you are the only girl for me."

Any negative thoughts swirling in Betsy's head seconds before disappeared. Or questions why her husband had gone up to their bedroom after their visit to the Garden of the Gods evaporated. Love ruled the airways.

What a fantabulous day!

~

Ben had no idea why he did what he did. Especially in such a public place, but any embarrassment he may have felt disappeared when he saw the glow on Betsy's face. His exuberance must have surprised her. She hadn't uttered a word since he put the lip lock on her.

Her quietness could also have to do with the fact he never showed affection in public. Hand holding only. Something he learned from his dad. If his father gave Ben's mother a kiss in front of the family, it was on the cheek. Hugs...unheard of.

For some reason that seemed wrong and he vowed to change a lot of things from this point forward. With the Lord's help, of course. He hoped Betsy and everyone else would like the new-and-improved Ben Stevenson.

"You doing okay?" Betsy stared up at Ben.

"I think I am."

"You're not sure?"

"Not really, but are you ready to come along for the ride."

"Haven't turned you down yet."

"That's what I'm talking about, my love." Ben knew from the look on his wife's face she thought he'd hit the crazy button again.

Sweetheart, you'll get use to the new me. Give it some time.

"Hon, look over there." Ben pointed to the sunset, reflecting through the trees. "Or, what we can see of it."

"A grand finish to an absolutely wonderful day."

Betsy put her arm around his waist and Ben smiled. They

continued their walk around the park and when they got up next to their RV he said, "Mats, you ready to go inside?"

Their pooch did a few jumps before she settled down and Ben picked Matilda up and carried her inside.

"What are you doing?"

"Since I didn't leave a light on, she could miss a step."

"Hon, you crack me up. It's not even dark yet."

"Wait there. I'll turn the outside light on for you. I know how you tend to trip on occasion."

She waltzed up the stairs, without incident, and gave Ben another subtler kiss. "Sometimes I would say you take better care of Matilda then you do me."

"I told you I'd turn the light on for you. That was thoughtful, wasn't it?"

"Very and speaking of which, do you want to tell me about why you went upstairs when we got back from the Garden of the Gods?"

Ben wondered why it had taken Betsy close to an hour to ask. He'd let her suffer a while longer and not say anything.

"Well, spill it."

"I...I..." Ben smiled. "I went up and prayed for Baby."

Betsy stared at him again then touched his forehead. "Now I know something's wrong with you. What did you do?"

"I emailed Brian."

CHAPTER TWENTY-SIX

"You did what?" Betsy wrapped her arms around Ben's neck and squeezed. "I'm so proud of you."

"Don't get too excited yet. He still has to answer me."

"We'll pray he does. And, while we're at it, we'll say a prayer for Baby too."

"After I fix supper."

"Deal."

Betsy wanted to do a couple of cartwheels at her hubby's news. More prayers answered. Almost. She also wanted to chuckle at Ben's kindness for her and their pooch. Him admitting his soft side made her want the wonderful day to go on forever.

But even with her "rose-colored glasses" mentality, Betsy knew tomorrow would come with whatever it came with. After a dinner of soup and sandwiches, she turned on the news and as they watched it she asked Ben, "Is this what the gentleman next door was talking about?"

"He said they're calling it the '1000-year flood'."

As they watched the coverage of the flood ravaging Boulder and the surrounding areas, Betsy wept for the town she adored. Some of the buildings and landmarks she recognized lay in ruin.

"Ben, I can't believe this is happening. All I ever wanted to do was show you Boulder. Colorado. Now it's destroyed."

Ben reached over and wiped a tear trickling down Betsy's cheek. "I'm so sorry, hon. We need to pray."

"And find out, ASAP, what we can do to help. There's got to be something we can do." Betsy glanced at the TV. "Ben, they're talking again. Turn it up...please."

"At the end of the newscast, we'll put up a list of places which need help. Stay tuned," The female anchor said.

While they waited, Ben prayed. Betsy listened to her hubby, but kept an eye on the screen. Not wanting to miss Channel 9's list.

As promised, at 10:30, a list of websites appeared on the screen. Betsy let go of Ben's hand and hollered, "It's on. Be sure to write them all down."

"You can also go to 9News.com for the complete list."

"Thank the good Lord." Ben tossed the tablet on the desk and sat back in the loveseat. "I'm not sure I could have written that fast."

Betsy appreciated Ben's attempt at a joke, but she knew neither of them thought any of this was funny. She went over to her computer, typed in the station's website and followed the link.

"Everybody and their brother must have done the same thing I did." Betsy rested her elbows on her desk and waited. "There it goes." One click and their printer came to life.

She got up and handed Ben the two sheets of paper and he said, "We need to head out tomorrow."

"I agree. Boulder needs us more than us playing Tom and Terry Tourist for another day or two. And the blog I wanted to write can wait."

"I'll call Larry. If he's watching the news, he has a plan brewing in his head." Ben stood next to Betsy.

"Sort of like someone else I know." Betsy smiled despite her broken heart.

Ben picked up his phone and punched some numbers in and

said, "Hey Lar, you been watching the news."

"I vote we change our plans."

"I'll be right over." Ben hung up and walked to the door. Before he opened it he turned and said, "See you later."

After her hubby left and Matilda settled into her bed, Betsy appreciated the solitude. A quiet time to pray for the tragedy unfolding in Colorado. If and when she finished, she'd write the blog she'd made notes on.

But for now—Betsy turned to Psalm 121 and read the words out loud.

> *I lift my eyes to the hills—*
> *Where does my help come from?*
> *My help comes from the Lord,*
> *The Maker of heaven and earth.*
>
> *He will not let your foot slip—*
> *he who watches over you will not*
> *slumber;*
> *indeed, he who watches over Israel*
> *will neither slumber nor sleep.*
>
> *The Lord watches over you—*
> *the Lord is your shade at your right*
> *hand;*
> *the sun will not harm you by day,*
> *nor the moon by night.*
>
> *The Lord will keep you from all*
> *harm—*
> *he will watch over your life;*
> *the Lord will watch over your coming*
> *and going*
> *both for now and forevermore.*

Tears fell on her opened Bible. Betsy wiped them away

before closing it. Sitting in the stillness, she still couldn't believe what she'd seen. The devastation. Lives changed forever.

"Father, my heart aches for everyone affected in this horrible tragedy. Please watch over the people and the rescue workers. Keep them safe. Lead the four of us where we're needed most. Oh, and before I forget, please open Brian's heart to write Ben back. And, Lord, Baby needs You too. Could You do something with the noise she makes? In Jesus name. AMEN!!!"

Betsy laughed at the part about Baby, but knew the Lord understood her peculiar prayers. "They might be weird, but they're from the heart. Now it's time to write." She clicked on the file she'd opened earlier. Once again her fingers flew across the keys as she referred to the notes.

Hey All:

First off—I want to ask everyone to PRAY for the flooding in Colorado. The people in Boulder and the surrounding areas need our prayers too. The news said they also could use some volunteers.

Seems like it's been forever since I wrote in my blog. The *Early Birds* have been on the road for a week and what a time it's been. Some trials and tribulations have weaved their way through our journey. Nothing serious, but ones which opened my heart and mind to different possibilities

Some of you are saying—that's a good thing. It's about time. ☺ But I have to warn you this eye-opening post could go on for days when I start filling you in on all the changes taking place.

But first, I suggest you get a cup of coffee (or tea) and sit back. Delight in God's word:

"Finally, brothers, whatever is true, whatever is noble, whatever is right, whatever is pure, whatever is lovely, whatever is admirable—if anything is excellent or praiseworthy—think about such things. Whatever you have learned or received or heard from me, or seen in me—put it into practice. And the God of peace will be with you." (Philippians 4:8-9)

These two verses are a mouthful, but I want us to stop and read it again. I'm not going anywhere—so read it aloud and think about what the verses say.

What did they say to you?

In my case, the Lord shouted the first part, Philippians 4:8, loud and clear into my soul. If you haven't noticed, I'm one of those who puts themselves down any chance they get. I also don't take a compliment well.

Another sore spot, I'm always telling myself I can't do this or that. I'm sure some of you have opened your Bibles and are quoting a popular verse back to me. "Betsy, you can do all things through Christ who strengthens you."

Yes, I can and thank you for your encouragement. But (and it's a big one), until I allow Him to do a work in me, I'll stay as I am.

Belittling. Bemoaning. Badgering myself over and over and over...

Can I get an AMEN?

But, there is a solution and it's in Philippians 4:8. (Note: The reason I didn't include verse 9, as I did above, it comes later.)

I told you this blog would be lengthy. ☺

My way of talking and the way I think about myself is wrong. NEGATIVE. God's word tells me (us) to keep our mind on, *"whatever is true, whatever is noble, whatever is right."*

Where in the text does it say anything about slamming ourselves? When I asked you to read it again—was there anything in there about using self-deprecating humor in any situation? What about poo-pooing a compliment? It's like we're telling the other person we don't deserve whatever they are bestowing upon us.

Oh, and the subject of telling ourselves we can't do something—it isn't anywhere in the verse. Trust me, I've tried to find it. It's not there.

I read these verses before, but for the first time they penetrated my heart. They touched the parts where I have believed the wrong things for way too long. They told me I had better ways to think.

They turned my life around...to face my Savior. About time, I'd say.

He's been telling me in His word that what I've been putting my thoughts toward all these years is, and was WRONG!

I didn't realize until the other day how slow of a learner I am. This isn't a put down. But if it took me all these years to learn this powerful lesson. I'm overjoyed He got through to me.

Now before you think I'm holier than thou, I'm not. Still need lots of work. But, the Lord showed me the error of my ways and pointed me in the right direction. Now, I'm also asking for prayer to stay on this path.

As you read this, remember WE ARE LOVED and are daughters (and sons) of the King.

Philippians goes one more step. Paul tells us how to do it.

Let's follow our Father's instructions and dwell on things that are true, noble, pure, lovely, admirable, excellent and praiseworthy...

And for the second part of my loooonnnngggg post of how to get it done, read Philippians 4:9. The verse tells me if I think on these things, I will have PEACE.

Glory Hallelujah. All I have to do is change my thinking and He will give me calm, quiet, harmony.

How many times have we (I) prayed for these things? I know I've spent most of my life asking for the peace that passes all understanding.

Well, I'm happy to report I (we) have the answer. It's all in the way we think.

So, today, I hope you will spend some time with your Savior, asking Him to change where your mind goes. The Lord is there to show each of us the way. All we have to do is open His word and find what He has in store for us.

Blessings.
Bets

PS: A reminder – please PRAY for Colorado.

Betsy reread her words and then posted them. When she hit the Enter key Ben returned and she said, "Good timing" and turned her chair around.

"You're done! I've only been gone a little over an hour."

Betsy spun back around and glanced down in the corner of her computer. "I'd say it's closer to two hours. It's 8:30."

"Oh. I guess checking out maps...and..."

"And what?" Betsy came over to sit next to Ben.

"Eating brownies Rosie made takes time. Here's one for you." He took it out of his shirt pocket.

Betsy unwrapped the dessert and took a taste. "Wowzer, what a great way to end the day."

"Want to watch a little TV?"

"As long as it has nothing to do with the flood. *House Hunters* sounds good."

The next hour Betsy lost herself in other people's desire for a new home. Before the last episode finished, Betsy turned it off and yawned. "I'm done watching. Right now it seems wrong to watch someone elses search for a new home when others have lost theirs."

"I agree." Ben got up and put Matilda's leash on and opened the door to let their dog out.

"Before I forget, Ben, when are we getting up in the morning?" Betsy thought she better ask in case they wanted to pull up stakes in four or five hours.

"Larry said we'd leave around 10:00. Miss rush hour. Arrive in Longmont about 12:30 or 1:00." Ben brought Matilda in and unhooked her. "Not sure you know this, and I forgot to ask Lar, why doesn't Boulder, a university town have an RV Park?"

"They used to have a KOA off of 55th, but it's been gone for 25-30 years." Betsy headed up the stairs. "I'd like to have in my bank account what they sold the property for. Can anyone say, 'A cool million.'"

"Or two mil. It's your turn to pray."

Betsy smiled. "You should start. I could go on for days about the flood. End up not getting any sleep at all.

"I'll take my chances."

CHAPTER TWENTY-SEVEN

Betsy strained to see the mountains, but the cloud cover going up Monument Hill limited her from seeing even a hint of them today. For a second or third time she prayed, *Lord, please calm the storm.*

Both of them had prayed for the floods when they'd gone to bed the night before, but Betsy thought another prayer couldn't hurt. Too much rain in such a short time. And the headlines read the storm had started to subside, leaving wide spread devastation along the Front Range.

"Sorry you can't see your mountains today," Ben's voice interrupted her thoughts.

Betsy took one more look out of the front window before she answered. "I've been checking to see if there's a break in the clouds where one can peek through. But nothing yet. I'm sure once we get to Longmont, we'll see Longs Peak."

"The news this morning said the front has moved through, heading to Nebraska and Kansas. Now the cleanup begins."

"Do you or Larry know where you're going to help?"

"We'll check the list from last night and with the area churches. See what they need."

"I'm sure they'll have plenty for you guys to do."

"With us out of your hair, you and Rose can figure out what to do to help. Matilda and Baby will protect the RVs while we're all gone."

The minute Matilda heard her name, she got up from her bed and stretched. Then came and lay down between them on the padded console. "I believe Baby could protect the Wilford's 5th wheel with her barking. This one would go with the bad guys and lick them to death."

Matilda got on Betsy's lap and started licking her hand. "Ben, I believe our dog understands every word we say."

"I don't doubt it. She definitely has t.r.e.a.t. down."

"Breaker 21, can you hear me, good buddy?" Rose's voice sounded on the CB.

"You do know you can say "Breaker whatever," don't you?"

"Yes. I like to make it official...good buddy." Rose snorted before she let go of the mic.

Ben pushed the button. "What's on your mind?"

"Larry's hungry and wanted me to ask if you are too."

"Right in the middle of Denver, Colorado?"

"And there's a problem with that?" Larry questioned.

"Good buddy, you do know I've never been to Denver in a car, let alone driving this monstrosity."

"You'll be fine. I won't steer you wrong."

Ben put the mic down and he put both hands on the steering wheel in the 10 and 2 position. "That's not what I'm afraid of. What scares the bejeebers out of me is when you get us lost and we have to turn our rigs around.

"Hon, remember, he's been doing this a long time. So far Larry's done fine."

"The light pole back in Texas would tend to differ with you."

"You do have a point."

Betsy watched the road, wondering where they'd exit. No easy on, easy off exit came to mind. But she'd sit back and trust their friend and hope Larry knew a perfect stop for their rigs.

While she sat, she took in the sights all around her. The new

Mile Hi Stadium loomed in front of them. Betsy laughed when Ben took the slight curve on I-25. The road looked like it would run right into the stadium, but at the last second, it skirted to the right of it.

While Betsy pondered the optical illusion, a few miles later she noticed Larry put on his turn signal to take them on Highway 76 to find food.

That works.

~

Much to Ben's shock and amazement, Larry found a place for both RVs. They pulled into the truck stop, on the north side of Denver, and Ben put his dually in park. "Mat's, we'll be right back. No need to put you in the RV. It's cool enough here."

Betsy put on her jacket. "You do know it's steaming in Houston right now. Going to take me a while to get used to wearing a jacket again."

"And long pants." Ben surveyed his bare legs and decided he better change into a pair of jeans. "I'll be right with you."

He caught up with the other three and they sat and ate at the Denny's restaurant next to the truck stop. The country skillet Ben ordered came with biscuits and gravy. One of those stick-to-your ribs kind of meals.

I'll eat a light supper. Don't need to gain more weight.

Ben glanced at his wife and the Wilford's. They, too, could take up a walking program. Or lifting weights.

Oh, so much for political correctness.

He kept his thoughts to himself and the four finished their hearty meal. As they made their way to the counter to pay, they jockeyed with each other as to who would take care of the bill.

"It's our turn." Rose took the receipt.

"Saw you had the RVs out there. Where you headed?" A trucker asked when they stood at the cash register.

"Longmont. We stayed at an RV Park on the—"

"You're not staying there this year," The man interrupted Larry before he moved away from the desk. "Everything from Boulder to Longmont is full of people who lost their homes or can't get back to them."

In all the rush to get to Longmont, Ben couldn't believe one of them hadn't thought to call the park to find out. "Got any suggestions?" Ben asked the man.

"Ft. Collins. Probably the closest place. Gotta run. Good luck to you."

"Houston, we have a change of plans. Wal-Mart here we come."

Rosie's illogical remark about staying at the store with no hookups made Ben's chest hurt. Like at work. The doctor he'd talked to at his last physical said, 'You're not having a heart attack. Your body is telling you to relax. You're not in control.'" A position Ben hated.

For a split second he wanted to blame Larry, but stopped. Every news channel and newspaper covered the flood. And he had a cell phone and could have called ahead to check on the reservation.

"Got it under control." Larry pushed the front of his cell phone and stuck it in his pocket. "We've got a place on the outskirts of Ft. Collins."

"You're the man." Ben smiled. For the first time in his life, someone else took over and it felt good.

"We better get going before someone nabs our spot."

"Can't happen. They have my credit card to hold two places."

They got on the road and the closer they got to the Longmont exit, traffic thickened. Ben saw the reason for the delay when they hit the exit marked: Johnson's Corner. Water stood in the fields, almost up to I-25. Lookie loos stopped their cars to take pictures, causing a traffic jam.

"Have they never seen water before?"

Once again Ben realized he wasn't in control. Any more than when he drove in Houston's rush hour traffic. Today, with the albatross hooked behind them, Ben wanted the backup to disappear.

"Hon, this almost looks like the time people left before Hurricane Rita. Better pray for patience here."

"I'd say you had plenty of it when you found out about our accommodations in Longmont. Or lack thereof. You didn't freak out."

"You noticed." Ben glanced at his wife for a split second. "I did almost bite my tongue in half, standing there after the guy told us."

"Your face turned a little red."

"It did?"

"Yes, but for whatever reason you controlled yourself. Now I need to practice mine while you weave this puppy through all this." Betsy waved her arms, which raised Matilda from her bed in the back seat.

"Come here, little buddy. Maybe if I pet you I'll relax for our slow trip to China. Oh, I mean, Ft. Collins."

~

The clouds lifted over the Front Range. Hues of yellow, hints of red and orange splashed across the sky. The magnificent sight of 'her' mountains somewhat tempered the pain in her heart for the flood victims.

Betsy wanted to get a shot of her beloved mountains, but sat on the wrong side of the truck. Only one thing would remedy the problem. She'd get in the back seat and roll down the window and shoot away.

About halfway to accomplishing her goal, Betsy heard Ben, "You're not taking more pictures, are you? If you recall in our downsizing, we threw hundreds of pictures of the Colorado Mountains away."

Betsy ignored her hubby's comment and put her phone up to the majesty in front of her and hit the button. She heard a click and checked the picture she'd taken. A bit fuzzy, but it would work for a post on Facebook to remind people to pray for Colorado.

After taking a couple more, in case she got a better one, Betsy climbed back into the front seat and said. "Even though we've spent time in Colorado Springs, I forget how much the mountains fill my soul, every time I catch a glimpse of them. Must be what heaven looks like."

"With streets of gold thrown in, of course."

"Good buddy, Breaker 21, we're about 15 miles from our destination. Since I don't know what to expect – let's pull over in Loveland and I'll give the park another call."

Ben liked someone else taking the reins for a change and once the traffic thinned out, the tension in his shoulders disappeared. No more stress to get him riled. Until Larry's voice came back on the CB. "You're never going to believe this. We don't have a place to park tonight."

"What?" This time Betsy grabbed the mic.

"They said some workers came in and needed the spots for the next two nights. They'd have spaces for us at the end of the week."

Ben took the mic and held it in his hand, but didn't say anything.

"Got any ideas?" Larry came on and asked.

"Matter of fact I do. Since you have the GPS tacked to your dash and I still can't find my cord , check and see where the nearest Wal-Mart is. They were so nice to us the other night. Rosie, we'll give them another shot."

"You're the man this time."

"I am if they let us stay on their property."

Larry came on the CB a few minutes later and confirmed they could stay the next two nights at the superstore down the street in Loveland. "Head 'em up. Move 'em out."

"I'm behind ya."

Once again they homesteaded in Wal-Mart's parking lot. This time Ben, while they stood outside their RVs, announced he'd fix supper for all of them. "I'll make us my famous Tortilla Surprise."

"Surprise. Surprise. Mexican food."

"Yeah, yeah, yeah!!" Ben opened the door to go inside. "You know you love it."

Rose did state the obvious to anyone who knew him. They teased Ben that he had to have Hispanic blood somewhere in his lineage. But with the name of Stevenson on his dad's side and

Scott on his mom's, he doubted it.

"While you're making your magic, I'm going to run into the store. Want to come, Rose?"

After the ladies left, Ben put the kitchen slide out and started to cook. Since he didn't want to run them out of water, he did his best to clean up. Paper products became his go-to for his gourmet meal tonight.

CHAPTER TWENTY-EIGHT

"As always, dear, I compliment the chef." Betsy pushed her plate away, but took a couple of chips from the bag on the table.

"I knew we invited you guys along for a reason." Larry leaned back in his chair and adjusted his belt buckle. "But if I don't watch it, I'm going to have to buy bigger jeans."

"All low-calorie stuff."

"I'll believe that as much as if you told me your wife was driving this tomorrow." Rose grabbed a chip from Betsy's hand.

"Hey, watch it. Anyway, Rosie, we're not going anywhere until Saturday."

"She got you, didn't she?" Ben said as he picked up the paper plates off the table and chucked them into the trash. "Now are we ready to play some cards?"

The Wilford's left around 10:30 and Betsy put away the spices Ben left near their sink. She couldn't get over how clean he'd kept the place while cooking dinner. She'd tell him when she made it up to bed.

Betsy would also tell him about the text she'd gotten from Tina. Happy tears threatened to fall when Betsy had seen the message earlier, while they played cards. Then she shut off her phone, not wanting anyone to ask questions.

"You coming tonight?"

"I'll be there in a second."

After Betsy wiped the counter, she strolled up the two steps into their bedroom and said, "I'm done."

"I didn't make too much of a mess, did I?"

"No. Ya done good." Betsy undressed and put a pair of pj's on, joining Ben and Matilda in their bed.

Ben leaned over their pooch and gave Betsy a kiss. "Love ya."

"Love ya, too." Betsy lay on her back and tried to get comfortable. Not an easy task when a small dog attached herself to your hip. "Move over a little, Mats. You're crowding me."

"It's your turn."

Betsy laughed at the game they continued to play, almost every night, since they'd started to pray together. After a few weeks of figuring out who would pray when, they'd agreed she'd have even days, leaving odd days for Ben.

Tonight was even, making it her night. "Anything you want me to pray for you?"

"Safe travels and for the Lord to lead Larry and me to the best places to help with the flood."

Betsy prayed for her husband's requests and added a few for their families and friends scattered all over the United States. "I also ask for Your blessings on Tina and her situation. In Jesus' name. Amen."

"Tina?"

"She's the one I told you about. The one I've been texting and emailing since before we left on our travels."

Movement on her right told Betsy that Ben had rolled over on his back. The light coming through the window reflected his silhouette. Her hand reached over and caressed his face. "Hon, tonight she said what I've written her has helped her and their family."

"This surprises you?"

"Yes...but...I guess it shouldn't. The Lord gave me the words to say."

"How about we pray for Tina."

Ben took his turn and prayed. The thoughtful words he spoke about her new friend touched Betsy's heart. When he finished, she leaned over and kissed him. "Sleep good." She rolled over and went right to sleep.

~

Ben stood in the Wilford's living room, waiting. Larry put on his boots and kept reassuring his wife they'd be fine.

"You're sure Wal-Mart is okay if we stay here all day?" Rose questioned for the third time.

"Dear, I'm certain the nice gentleman I spoke with knows you and Betsy will be in there to buy him out of house and home."

"A comedian. Everyone needs one." Rose reached out her hand. "Here let me help you go to work. Oh, that has a ring to it. I kind of like it."

"Are you going to stand here and talk all day or are we going to go and get some work done." Ben grabbed his light jacket and headed down the stairs to his truck.

When Larry got in, Ben started to back up, but saw Betsy poking her head out of the door of their RV. He put his window down, "Bye. I'll see you in....I don't know. I'll call you later."

The miles between Loveland and Longmont were filled with the female's voice from Ben's GPS. He'd found the cord for it that morning and plugged it in. The closer they came to their destination, the faster her directions came.

"You're killing me, P.I.T.S."

"P.I.T.S." Larry laughed.

"Betsy gave our GPS unit the name when she got us turned around one time. It stands for Pain In The Shorts. I kind of like it." Ben followed the directions the GPS gave him. "There's the mall. Now all we have to do is find where they're set up."

That deemed easier than anything they'd done so far on their trip to the shopping complex. Signs the size of billboards directed them to where they needed to go. Soon they had papers in their hands to fill out.

Ben answered the ten or so questions and watched Larry do

the same. The line they'd gone to moved at a quick clip and in a short time they stood in front of a man who took the papers they'd filled out. He glanced at the questionnaire, then up to Ben.

"What's your background?"

Ben wanted to point to the papers in the man's hand, but refrained from doing so. Not the wisest way to get started. But Larry, on the other hand, gave his humor a shot at 8:30 in the morning.

"Well, sir, my wife would tell you I'm a jack of all trades, but the master of none."

Larry's bit of comedy fell on deaf ears. Ben could see the person behind the long table stayed stone faced. So to keep them from getting thrown out before they even got started, Ben came to his friend's rescue.

"We've both managed crews on job sites and can use most equipment."

"Thanks for volunteering. Go over to the next table. Doug will assign where and what he wants you to do."

They walked over to the man, and in less than five minutes, he had them assigned to a team headed to Boulder.

~

Ben parked his truck and got out. His eyes took in the enormity of the situation at the motel. Larry came and stood next to him and said, "Not sure, but this might be a gut job."

Doug came up behind Larry and patted him on his shoulder. "The family who owns this place hopes it's fixable. That's why we're here."

"Guess I should keep my opinions to myself." Larry's cheeks blazed a crimson color.

"I'm sure you're not alone in your thinking. Anyway," The foreman pointed at the hill behind the damaged structure. "Story goes a wall of water and debris busted out the windows and flooded the place. This week our job is to rip out the interior. Later, a crew will come in and redo the rooms."

"We need some heavy equipment." Ben took out his phone to Google rental places.

"Got someone trying to locate front loaders, Ben. Right now I need you two to go into the rooms and strip them down to the studs. Remove everything."

Ben picked up two hammers and a couple of shovels and handed one of each to Larry who said, "Let the fun begin."

Their 'fun' lasted until 1:00 pm when Ben heard someone shout, "Pizza." He straightened his aching back and leaned his shovel against a pile of debris.

"Lunch time."

Larry put his tools next to Ben's and they walked over to a folding table covered with boxes of different kinds of pizza.

"I'm not sure I have the strength left to pick up a piece."

"Here. Let me help you." Ben grabbed two pieces of pepperoni and tossed one on a paper plate for his friend. "Do you want me to carry them for you too?"

"I can manage."

They hobbled over to the nearest tree and stood and ate their furnished meal. Between bites Ben commented on their morning job, "Lar, I've never seen anything like it. Two or three feet of muck in each of the rooms. Amazing."

"This will take weeks and we still have the second and third buildings to go."

"Don't remind me. Not sure my body will hold up."

Larry held up his piece of pizza. "This will give us our second wind."

"That, and another piece...or two. Let me get them." Ben headed to the table and got them each a piece of Canadian bacon pizza. Larry stood talking to Doug.

"Good news, guys. United Rental said they'll have two front loaders here at 8:00 in the morning."

"That'll be a start."

Ben wanted to add to Larry's statement, "Two-donated machines won't do much."

And, after working on the place for close to four hours, he tended to agree with Lar's earlier assessment – they needed to bulldoze the place.

Larry and Ben finished their lunch and went to get their tools. Before they got too far, Doug introduced the owner's grandson to them.

"My grandparents built this in the 40s," Barry said. "Dug out the side of this mountain with picks and chisels. My dad and his brothers built the buildings, cutting each board. I've spent my life at this motel." He stopped, wiped his eyes and broke out in a smile. "I love this place."

After Barry left, Ben took in all the destruction around him. Again. He hurt for this family who'd build their dream in the side of a mountain. Now covered in yards of mud and debris. Could a crew of 20 dig out and save the property?

On their way to Loveland in the evening, Ben mentioned the two front loaders to Larry. His friend's response almost caused him to pull his dually over on the shoulder of Highway 287.

"Remember the story in the Bible. Jesus only had two fish and one loaf of bread. Or was it one fish and two loaves. I can't recall at the mom—"

"What are you getting at?" Ben interrupted his friend.

"What I'm trying to tell you is Jesus took those items and fed the 5000. Actually it was more like 25,000. In our case, He can take two front loaders and get this property cleared."

"I hate you."

"Why."

"I believe our wives' ability to bring the Bible around to real life is rubbing off on you."

"And that's a bad thing?" This time Larry stared at Ben.

"No, but I wish I thought more that way."

"You do, but you don't get out of the way to see it most of the time."

The rest of their trip Ben chewed on what Larry said. *I DO get in the way. I am a control freak?*

"Ben, if you concentrate any harder or frown any deeper, you're going to hurt yourself."

"Huh?"

"You heard me. I didn't think what I said would shut you up."

Larry laughed.

"As usual, you're right. I'm a person who likes to be in control. But, I've finally figured it out."

"Oh I can't wait to hear this."

For the next half hour Ben filled his friend in on what happened at the chapel in Colorado Springs. "Larry, going to the little church confirmed I need to make changes. Mend fences."

"With your brother?"

"I emailed him, waiting to get one back." Ben hesitated. "Reconnecting with him is a biggie, but my biggest concern is still my relationship with Betsy."

"The Almighty almost parted the Red Sea again for you two. And, the Lord got you to retire. HUGE!"

"Boy, you're full of it tonight."

"What?"

"Seeing the church hit me hard. How has Betsy put up with me all these years? Don't answer that." Ben laughed this time. "Larry, I'm an idiot."

"No comment."

"Thanks."

"That's what friends are for."

Ben drove towards their trailer in the parking lot. "Hey, Lar, got a question for you."

"Shoot."

"Want to stop in at Wal-Mart and get our wives some flowers? For some strange reason I'm in the mood to do something nice. They'd love them."

"Great idea. But we might want to pick up some smelling salts for Betsy. After she faints."

"I hate you." Ben repeated the phase.

Larry laughed all the way into the super store, but Ben had his mind on the mission he had to accomplish. Rekindle his romance with Betsy. The one he'd almost killed while they lived in Houston.

He'd also do his part to clean up after the floods devastating Betsy's first love. Boulder County.

~

"We ought to throw in some candy?"

Ben glanced at Larry as they stood in the flower aisle. "Candy?"

"Is there an echo in here? Yes. Candy. Do you think we should get some?"

"It's not Valentine's Day."

"Trying to be nice."

"Bringing chocolate into my house is never considered a kind gesture. Unless it's brownies." Ben picked up a bouquet of yellow roses. "This is the ticket to my wife's heart."

Larry reached down and retrieved a bunch of colored daisies and cradled them in his arms. "Don't care what you say Ben, I'm getting Rosie a candy bar. Then you can watch when she becomes putty in my hands."

Ben almost lost all control at his friend's statement. When he could speak again he stated, "Larry, I'll take your word for that one."

They took their flowers and one Snickers bar to the check-out counter and paid for them. Ben chuckled at Larry's smug expression. Almost like he told him he'd one upped him in the wife-wooing department.

Not a chance.

"We better get a move on." Larry picked up the sack the clerk put their items in. "Don't want the ladies to wait for this."

Ben wasn't sure if his friend referred to what he had in the sack or to himself. The way Larry strutted out of the store. He knew one thing—he wouldn't ask him anything as they made their way across Wal-Mart's parking lot.

CHAPTER TWENTY-NINE

From inside their RV, Betsy saw her husband and their friend. She questioned why Larry danced about. Then she spied the bouquet of flowers Ben carried, sort of, behind his back.

"I'll see you in the morning. Same time?" Ben held the door open, leaning out.

Betsy almost cracked up at the maneuvers her hubby tried to do to keep the flowers out of sight, while he waited, she assumed, for an answer from Larry.

"7:00 it is."

Ben closed the door and with the most adorable, almost shy expression, he tried to present the flowers. But Matilda got in the mix of things and almost caused him to drop the bouquet then he nearly tripped over her, trying to retrieve it.

Her hubby did catch the flowers and himself and presented them to her. All the while, keeping an eye on their dog.

What did I do to deserve these?

Betsy shelved the comment and went over and put her arms around Ben's neck, kissing him to high heaven. A much better option than putting herself down.

"I'll bring you flowers more often if I get this kind of

response."

Ben's comment, and the sound of his stomach rumbling, brought Betsy back to earth. She took the fragrant offering from him and gave his arm a squeeze on her way to finding the lone vase she'd packed.

Somewhere.

Betsy opened the cabinet next to the stove, but before she stood on her head to retrieve the glass container, she turned to face Ben. "Thank you."

"You're more than welcome." Ben pulled the chair out and sat at the table. "I'm tired and—"

"Hungry. From the sound your tummy made a minute ago, I'd say you're starved. You only took a sandwich and a bag of chips."

"Which reminds me. They're still in the truck. They supplied pizza."

"That was nice of them." Betsy leaned down and retrieved the vase and arranged the roses. Their scent, along with the already-scrumptious aromas happening in their kitchen, brought a smile to her face. And surprise when Ben hadn't mentioned the odd occurance.

His brain is overloaded with his gentlemanly gesture.

Betsy fixed their plates with another Food Network recipe she'd tried out and sat it in front of Ben without her usual comment. She took her chair and tasted the chicken dish and said, "Not bad."

Ben's smile and the inability to speak told her he approved of the entrée too. But after he took a drink of water he started to tell her about his day.

"The amount of debris left behind boggles my mind, Bets. I'm still not sure if we had twenty-five backhoes tomorrow they'd get the job done." Ben looked toward the window. "I've never seen Boulder, but what I saw today, it'll take a long time for them to get back to normal."

"The pictures on the news breaks my heart. They said the flood wiped some towns completely off the map. Ben, how is it possible water can do so much damage?"

And how can Rosie and I help to make it better?

~

The minute Rose stepped inside the RV the next morning Betsy said, "Okay, we had fun yesterday. Doing nothing, but pigging out on your brownies. What do you suggest we do for the flood victims?"

"First, I have to say hi to the little princess." Rose petted the now animated Matilda then poured a cup of coffee before settling at the table.

"Rosie I'm wait—"

"Sorry to interrupt, but I don't have a clue on what we can do to help."

"And I thought you knew everything." Betsy took her cup and sat across from Rose. "Let's spend this morning brainstorming. Work for you?"

"I thought that's what you and your writer friends did."

"It is, but it works for normal stuff too." Betsy took a drink out of her cup then grabbed her pen and opened her steno pad. "Ready?"

"No. I'm still bumfuggled about Larry bringing me flowers. It's been a few years."

Betsy glanced at the vase on her desk and smiled. "I was a tad surprised too. But it's even more special after hearing about their day and the news reports we saw yesterday."

"Terrible and they're saying more rain is predicted for the weekend."

"We need to keep praying that doesn't happen. But in the meantime, let's put our heads together and figure out something to do."

"I've got it. Bets, years ago I'd go to the store and buy chicken breasts. Fix up a bunch of marinade and put them in individual bags and freeze them. When I needed them, I'd take out a couple and we'd have them for supper. I called it my turbo cooking for the month."

Despite the hardships surrounding them, Rosie's last comment almost caused Betsy to run into Wal-Mart and ask if they sold oxygen tanks. She couldn't talk. When she caught her breath she asked, "And, Rose, flood victims, who have lost their homes, keep a freezer tucked in their back pocket to keep your bright idea in?"

"Miss Person-Who-Doesn't-Let-the-Other-Finish-Her-Sentence, what I was going to say—we'd get the chicken breast, fix them the way I used to and then make chicken sandwiches to take to the shelters they've set up."

"That makes more sense."

The two sat huddled at the kitchen table and mapped out more ideas. The one Betsy suggested—peanut butter and jelly sandwiches made Rose chuckle.

"Bets, even you have peanut butter and jelly on hand."

"Oh. Ha. Ha." Betsy wanted to add that her friend would be very interested in what her cupboards held. Her secret (i.e. her new love of cooking and Bobby Flay being the reason) would stay undercover. For the time being.

~

Friday morning, after they arrived at the job site, Ben and Larry checked with Barry to see what was on the agenda for the day. He pointed at the front loaders. "They arrived fifteen minutes ago. Along with those guys standing over there."

"Who are they?"

"Paul got a group from his church together last night. We've got them as long as we need them."

"Loaves and fishes?" Larry elbowed Ben.

"You got me on that one. Again, the Lord's timing amazes me. Extra hands. How about we go talk to them so we can get started?"

They hiked through the mud to the group and Ben introduced himself. "And this is my side-kick Larry Wilford."

With the introductions complete, Ben took charge of getting things going. Never once stopping to think the men might have questions. Or, their own ideas of how to do things.

He even took it upon himself to assign the front loaders, after a show of hands told him who could operate them. "Harry, you take this one. Jeff, this one's yours. But honestly I don't know how you'll fit." Ben smiled at the bigger-than-life red head next to the machine.

"You'd be surprised where I can tuck these things." Jeff shook his right leg and laughed. "My wife says I'm a pretzel."

Ben watched as Jeff finessed his way into the cab and it only took one try to accomplish the monumentous feat. "You did it?"

"Never underestimate a double-jointed pers—"

The engine noise of the other front loader drowned out the last part of Jeff's comment, but Ben didn't care. His mind had already started tackling the next task at hand. Ben went to locate his friend.

"Lar, we need to start picking up the trash and loading it into the roll offs. Try to stay on top of it."

Throughout the morning and into the afternoon the two lifted wet carpet, drywall and anything else and loaded it into the dumpster. Along with the job they did, Ben kept his eyes on what the volunteers accomplished in and around the motel.

Most of the guys hummed along at their prospective jobs. However, Ben spotted a group of five from the day before who sat more than they worked. When he'd had enough, he went over to them and said, "You need to get off your tails and do something. NOW!"

Ben wanted to laugh when he watched four out of the five scramble away like oil hitting a hot frying pan. But one stood his ground with his arms across his chest and asked, "Who made you boss?"

"I'm trying to get things done around here. How about you?" Ben's voice echoed across the muddy parking lot, but he could have cared less who heard.

"Have we got a problem over here?" Jeff stepped out of the front loader and went over to stand between Ben and the young man.

"No. I'm making sure work's getting done," Ben answered, his jaw taunt.

"Sounds good. That's why we're here." Jeff stepped closer to the young man and took a hold of his shoulder. "Son, I've got an idea. Oh, by the way, what's your name?"

"Christopher."

"Good to meet you, Christopher. My name's Jeff and you and I will get along fine. How about I teach you how to run this machine over here?"

Christopher couldn't get over to the front loader fast enough and into the cab. Ben wanted a few more words with the twerp, but smiled at how Jeff calmed the heated exchange. Grateful the big man stepped in when he did. Not sure how it would have ended otherwise.

"Thanks, man."

"Glad to help."

Ben went back to work and realized in two short days on the job he'd allowed the stress to encompass his life again. He'd spoken words out loud before he'd thought them through and he'd let someone push his buttons.

"You all right over there?"

Ben welcomed Larry's voice, which brought him out of his own head. "Yea, I'm fine. Just languishing in more learning experiences from above." Ben laughed. "Sure hope He's going to move on pretty soon."

"Don't count on it."

~

"Mom, you have no idea. The Lord is moving in mighty ways." Betsy shifted the cell phone to her left ear. "The smile on Ben's face last night, after he connected with Brian, made me want to do a happy dance. We're exactly where God wants us."

"Hon, I'm thrilled things are working out for you two. Prayer does work."

"Never a truer statement, Mom! Gotta run. Rosie's coming over. We're making up sandwiches to take somewhere." Betsy heard her mother's laughter and joined in. "That did sound strange, didn't it? I'm sure Rose knows where we're going."

As if on cue, someone knocked on her front door. "Mom, Rose is here. Talk to you on Wednesday. Love ya!"

Betsy opened the door and spotted Rose rummaging through their outside compartment. "I'd say good morning, but instead my first question would be: What are you doing in our undercarriage?"

"Looking for Larry's iPad."

"His what?

"I'm searching for his iPad, which I thought we left at home." Rosie almost climbed inside of the basement, standing on her tiptoes to peer inside.

"Before you tell me anything else. Give me a second and I'll help." Betsy held up her hand in front of her dog. "Matilda you've got to hold on. I need to put your leash on first."

Betsy closed their door and took Mats for her usual early morning walk, leaving Rose knee deep in tools and whatever else Ben put underneath their RV.

Please don't let her find it.

Her friend found it tucked behind Ben's plastic, three-drawer cabinet. Unfortunately, Larry carried it one step farther and wrapped it in a towel. But with eagle-eye Rosie searching for evidence, no stone—or iPad would be left unturned.

"Larry's a no good—"

"Don't say it." Betsy hooked Mats on her outside tether and rushed to her friend side. "There's probably an explanation."

"None I'm buying with the way it was strategically covered up and hidden. Lar didn't want me or anyone else to find it."

When Rose said those words, the image of Larry digging in their compartment while parked in Colorado Springs came to Betsy. "That's what he was doing."

"When? Tell me."

"Right before we went to the chapel at Garden of the Gods. I came out and almost mowed Larry down. Then I asked, to myself, what he was doing under there, but reasoned he was looking for a tool."

And, later, giving me a sincere compliment. I hope...

"Oh, he was looking for a tool. All right...a tool of sin and destruction."

"Or putting it away, so he wouldn't be tempted?" Betsy added, but wanted to laugh as she took in her friend's scowl. This won't end pretty and she could only imagine Rose and Larry's conversation later in the afternoon. The fury of a woman scorned.

This thought stirred in Betsy's mind when she pictured her friend's reaction. Rose's natural rosy-red cheeks would morph into a fire ball. Flames would shoot out of her unruly gray mane.

The only thing that could save Larry's life—Jesus' triumphant return. Or a trip to deliver PB & J sandwiches to the people of Boulder County.

CHAPTER THIRTY

Ben pulled his dually up next to his RV and shut it off. "Sure am glad today's done. I'm tired."

"Yelling will make ya sleepy." Larry laughed when he opened the passenger side door and got out.

"Guess I deserve that."

"We're all a work in progress." Larry shut the door and walked around the truck and stood next to Ben. "All I'm saying, don't be too hard on yourself."

"Are you going to give me a don't-put-yourself-down speech? The kind I give Betsy every so often?"

"If you need it, I'm available. But food's first on my itinerary before I get too philosophical."

"Wow! I'm impressed. You used a big word on an empty stomach."

"Wait until it's full and happy, I'm the 9th Wonder of the World...after the Astrodome and the Ball of Yarn Rosie wants to see."

Ben wanted to add more to their bantering, but Larry stared off into space in the direction of his own RV before he turned and asked, "Where's my truck?"

"Don't you remember? The girls' sandwich delivery service started today? They should pull in here any minute." Ben hoped so. The food Betsy had started cooking made his chops water even more. "I'm going in and wash up."

"Good idea. See you later."

Ben opened the door and Matilda greeted him out of her crate. "What's this?"

Their dog didn't answer with words, but her skipping around told Ben that freedom from captivity made for a pleased pup.

"I know, girl." Ben picked up and hugged Matilda, while he checked out the living room. Nothing out of place. Nothing chewed. Nothing to worry about. "Mats, it's time we trusted you to stay out of your c.r.a.t.e."

Ben put Matilda down then pushed the crate under the desk. He'd deal with his pooch later. Now he wanted to get cleaned up. Relax. Get a quick nap in before Betsy got home.

A loud knock stopped Ben's daydream about snoozing. When he opened his front door, Larry's expression told him sleep wouldn't be happening today. "What is going on?"

"Can I come in?"

Ben stepped away from the door and let his friend inside, shooing Matilda away so he wouldn't trip on the way in. "Sit down. Want some coffee?"

"NO! I need to do this before I change my mind. Here."

Before Ben could blink. Or in this case, defend his mid-section, Larry pushed something into it. The force caused him to lose his balance. As he regained his footing he said, "I don't know what's going on, but you better explain before I deck you."

"It's my iPad and I want you to smash it to smithereens."

"You want me—"

"Smash it before I change my mind."

"Sit down," Ben said it louder than intended, but it got the job done. Larry sat down at the table. "Now, what's your problem?"

"Rosie found my iPad." Larry slumped in his chair.

"The one she took and said you weren't bringing along...or

you'd die?" Ben joined his friend at the table and put the iPad on the seat next to his.

"One and the same. Ben, I tried to leave it there. But the morning we took off, Rose asked me to get something out of her closet. I moved a box and it stood there shouting, 'Take me! Take me!' I did and I hid it in your basement."

Unbeknownst to Ben, or Betsy, they'd been party to a crime. A tiny bit of amusement toyed with Ben's insides at the thought. But he stayed quiet. Not the time for any joviality. Instead, the dumbest thing fell out of his mouth. "My basement?"

"Yes, in your basement and I'd appreciate it if you'd wipe the grin off your face."

"I'm sorry. Go on."

"I hid it there and when I had a spare minute, without watchful eyes, I'd come over and play a few games. Ben, since we got to Colorado, I've gotten up in the middle of the night to play."

"In Wal-Mart's parking lot? Are you nuts?" Ben covered his mouth, knowing he shouldn't have said what he did.

"It's fine. I am crazy. For too long." Larry laid his head on the table and said, "I am loony. Last night I charged $65.00 for more coins."

Larry's last statement hit Ben in his gut as hard as his iPad had earlier, leaving him without a response. But he realized he didn't have to say anything. Ben needed to listen to his friend.

"When I put in my password and hit Okay, the Lord convicted me." Larry pushed his chair away from the table. "There I go telling a lie of my own. He's been pressing His thumb in my back about gambling for over six months. Boy am I a slow learner and also in deep trouble with my wife."

"Remember, we're a work in progress. To quote someone I know and love." Ben put his hand up for Larry to give him a high five.

He did and smiled. "Keep the jokes coming, but trust me when I say this, Rosie's doing more than delivering sandwiches today. She's planning my demise."

"How about we pray for a better outcome?"

~

Rose pulled into Wal-Mart's parking lot and Betsy chuckled. On their way home from delivering sandwiches, they'd made the decision to park closer to the front of the super store. Not out in the North 40, next to their RVs.

Their reasoning—twofold. After dinner they had a plan. Shop for water and other supplies they needed for Monday morning. The other reason, Rose said she wanted to park near to the door had to do with her hubby.

Rose had commented, "By now Larry's figured out I found his iPad. But, it isn't important anymore, Bets. These poor people we helped today and what they've lost is what I'm supposed to reflect on. Not anything else."

"That's for sure." Betsy thought the same thing. Or so she thought it was a thought.

"Were you having a conversation in your head again?" Rose snorted.

Betsy laughed. "Could be. Now are you ready to face your husband? Or, do I need to call Ben to warn Larry we're close? That he doesn't have to worry about you ridding him of the, how'd you say it, 'his instrument of sin and destruction?'"

"Girl, you do exaggerate and yes, I'm fine. I'm also humbled at how the Lord arranged everything. Impeccable. Couldn't have planned this day any better. Thank You, Jesus."

"Then you're ready to head to the RV?"

"You bet."

Rose led the way across the parking lot, whistling *Jesus Loves Me.* Betsy longed to join in on the chorus of her favorite song, but refrained. She hummed the tune in her head. No need to scare the Friday night shoppers back into their cars with the sound of her not-so-angelic voice.

"We're home." Rose whispered.

Betsy followed suit. "Call me later when you're ready to go shopping."

"Will do."

Betsy opened the door and almost fell back out when she saw

Larry sitting at their dining room table.

And why is Ben holding Larry's hand?

~

"In Jesus' Name. Amen!" Ben glanced up at his wife, after he finished praying for Larry. The smile Betsy wore told him she'd also had a great day. His, excluding his screaming match with Christopher, ended with prayer and praising the Father in heaven.

"Looks like you two were using your time wisely." Betsy reached down and petted Matilda.

"Hello. Anyone home?"

Ben heard Rose's voice and turned toward the door Betsy had left wide open. "Come on up, Rose. We're all here."

"Coming your way."

"Yea, we're here. Waiting for the firing squad to proceed."

Rose entered the RV and marched right over to her husband. A smile lit up her face. "No guns drawn tonight. I've put it in the Lord's hands—where it belonged in the first place."

Ben glanced across the table. It appeared his friend had taken a bite of a pickle. But before he could ask where he got it, tears flowed down Larry's face. Then Rose joined in. Betsy followed, with Ben as the last holdout.

For a solid minute the waterworks ran nonstop before Ben got up and grabbed the paper towels off the kitchen island. He ripped off a double-sheet for each of them and said. "If we don't stop, we're going to have our own flood in here. Don't know about you, but Boulder County doesn't need any more water."

Larry smiled as he wiped his eyes. He stood up next to Rose and gave her a kiss. "I'm still not sure what happened here, but I figured the only thing that would save me was Jesus coming again."

Everyone laughed at Larry's admission. Particularly Betsy. She sat on the loveseat and howled.

"What's so funny?" Rose came over and sat next to her.

"The exact words I said to myself when you found the iPad. Only thing going to save Larry is Jesus' return. Lar, I thought your days were...numbered."

"They were until we delivered sandwiches to Mary Miller. She saved you from certain doom."

Larry chuckled. "I need their address so I can thank them."

Ben saw the exchange between the two women when they both wiped at the corners of their eyes again.

"Larry, you can't. They lost their home and have nothing left."

"Nothing?"

"Mary showed us pictures. Their neighbors stayed behind and told them the force of the water pushed their house off its foundation, causing it to break in half. They said the wall of water carried off part of their home and it's now floating down the newly-formed river."

Ben stared at Rose then over to his now-subdued wife. Laughter no longer filled the RV as it had only a moment before. No one in their right mind could classify what they'd seen or heard today as humorous.

"Did you by chance get Mary's phone number? I'd like to see if we could do anything for them."

"Yes, whatever they need," Larry said. "We'll see what we can do."

"Right before we left she gave it to me and said they're renting a place in Ft. Collins." Betsy's eyes lit up. "Hope it's not too far from the RV Park we're going to stay at."

"We'll find out tomorrow." Larry took out his phone. "Ben, I forgot to tell you. Got a text from the Wild Rose RV Park and they've got our spots ready. What time in the morning do we want to head out?"

"Earlier the better, but right now could we discuss food. I'm STARVING!!!"

"I saw a Taco Bell around the corner from here. How's that sound?"

CHAPTER THIRTY-ONE

The mention of food sent Betsy's stomach grumbling. It also made her think of potato salad. Not sure why the particular food made its way into her head, but her mother's to-die-for dish sounded so good.

Later when she and Rose made it to Wal-Mart to get other stuff, she'd pick up the ingredients. Try her hand at making it, hoping it'd turn out. If not, it'd line the inside of the trash can.

Betsy ignored the negativity she'd spouted and watched Ben. He had come over to the loveseat and started to talk to Matilda.

"Now you be a good girl. We'll leave the light on and the blind up so you can see out. We won't be gone long."

"What are you doing? She's going in her c.r.a.t.e."

"No, we've moved past the prison. Somehow Mats got out of her crate today and met me at the door."

Betsy checked out the chair legs. *No teeth marks.* Her hubby's shoes, tucked under her desk, untouched. The pet bed all in one piece—not in shreds as she would have thought.

"Our little girl is growing up." Betsy snuggled their pooch. "Matilda, you be good. We love you."

Taco Bell's parking lot and lobby stood deserted. Except for the four of them. At 8:00 on a Friday night most people were out painting the town. In Betsy's case—she listened to the discussion of Mexican pizza versus $1.00 tostadas at the counter.

"We are all on budgets. You know."

Ben's comment brought a round of laughter as they decided on their evening meal. The worker, Betsy noticed, stared at his phone. His fingers flew across the keys. Texting?

Occasionally he'd stop. Soon his phalanges would start again at breakneck speed. The urge to poke the kid almost overtook Betsy, but she nipped the idea in the bud. They'd probably have to clean him off the ceiling after she startled him.

Or pay for a new phone after he dropped his.

Luckily Ben saved the Taco Bell employee and gave the young man their order. In record time they had their food—three Mexican Pizzas and two bean tostadas.

Betsy put her earlier thought of potato salad aside, picked up a piece of pizza and bit into it. With her mouth full of her favorite fare, she proclaimed, "Taaaaasssssstttttyyyyy"

"I'm with you." Larry took a slice out of the box in front of him, but before he bit into it he added, "I don't know how I lived without this on my menu."

"You were too busy playing..." Rose put her hand to her mouth then moved it away slowly. "I'm sorry. That was uncalled for."

"No, you're right. I did spend way too much time on those casino games. I also owe you an apology for all the money I wasted on them. I'm sorry." Larry touched Rose's hand. "I'm done with gaming. Ben's got my machine and I've asked him to smash it."

Betsy watched her friend melt right before her eyes. An answered prayer could do that to a person. Especially when they've prayed and waited so long for the situation to change. And Larry getting caught red-handed helped hurry things up a tad too.

Even in the midst of Larry's lie, Betsy knew Who had orchestrated it. All in His timing. Otherwise, Rosie wouldn't have budged off her high horse. Lar would have answered to her about his gambling issues.

But all of them found out the Lord had plans of His own. Plans which placed Mary Miller in Rose and her path earlier in the day. Plans to soften hearts and change perspectives.

Funny how He works sometimes.

This profound thought put a smile on Betsy's face. He does have His own way of answering prayers. Like saving their marriage with a dog and living fulltime in an RV.

Never in her wildest dreams. If she ever let anyone in on the whole amazing story, Betsy knew no one would believe it. Or publish something that included the menagerie of characters she now lived life with.

The very ones, excluding their pooches, who stared at her wide-eyed from across the table. Betsy ignored them and finished off her last slice of pizza, which had cooled off considerably.

"She lives in her own little world," Rose said as she held out a napkin. "Where a piece of cheese hanging off her chin doesn't matter."

Betsy took the recycled paper and wiped her mouth. "Better?"

"Don't like hanging out with people who drool."

"Ben, remind me next time to leave them at home."

"Not a chance, Bets. Rosie's my entertainment."

Rose smiled when she stood up and took their tray. "Bets, it's getting late. Let's go shopping."

"I'll try not to slobber on you in Wally World."

"I would hope so."

As Betsy placed their trash in the container, she chuckled at Rose. A flood could alter so much more than the landscape. It changed lives. For the good and in ways only He knew why.

Betsy and the rest of the *Early Birds* climbed in their truck. Ben pulled out of Taco Bell's parking lot. "Want me to drop you two at Wal-Mart?"

"Yes, I do." Rose laughed. "Less walking on these 60-plus legs."

Ben parked at the front of the store and unlocked the back doors and Betsy and Rose hopped out, "We won't be too long."

As Ben headed out, he put Larry's window down. "If you need anything, call...Larry."

Betsy could hear her husband's laughter as he drove away. Yes, it'd been another interesting day and she hoped the Lord would show them how to help their new friend Mary and family. To get them on their feet again.

~

Ben yawned on his way out of bed at the crack of dawn on Monday morning. The weekend—a complete blur. They'd unhooked, moved and parked their rigs at the park in Ft. Collins. He'd hoped for concrete pads, but mud ruled the day.

Ruts the size of semi-truck tires made for careful backing in of their 5th wheels. But they conquered the gulleys and settled into two spots next to the laundry room and showers.

Which Ben would use when he finished brushing his teeth. As he rinsed out his mouth he still couldn't believe the owner of the RV Park only charged each of them $550 a month. And this came after Rose and Betsy almost tackled him when they thanked him for the great spots.

Poor guy. He didn't know what those two were capable of doing when they aimed their attention at you.

Ben laughed when he took his towel and toiletry bag out of the cabinet. With Betsy and Rose, anything could happen. But, at the moment, he had a shower to take. When he opened the shower house door he saw his friend.

"Good morning, Lar. Ready for a fun day in the mud?"

"I'm up for something, but I've got a question?"

Ben stopped at the shower stall and turned toward his friend. "What's that?"

"Why do we clean up to get dirty again?"

"I don't have an answer, but it's something to ponder when we're knee-deep in..." Words escaped Ben and any that came to mind he shouldn't say.

"Anyway, I'll be ready when you are."

Ben entered the six by six stall and welcomed the hot water, streaming out of the shower head. Unlike the one in their RV. Depending on the water pressure at the park, sometimes you could almost spit faster and farther.

Today's shower—heaven on earth—and one Ben wanted to stay in longer. But decided he'd better dry off and get on the road before Larry came in to see if he'd melted and gone down the drain. Ben toweled off in quick order and returned to the RV ready to go.

Before he could get out the door, a slight problem ensued. Betsy, still in her pjs, wanted to tell him what the women planned for the day. His mind, still in somewhat of a fog, wanted to leave.

But no escape plan came to him. Ben thought the best thing he could do was use humor to stop the gusts coming at him at 120 m.p.h.

"Hon, I think it's time you quit talking."

Funny how something works one time and the next time you try it – not so much. After Ben said those few words, Betsy stomped up the two stairs with such force he felt certain the wood would splinter under her feet.

Matilda must have thought so too. She went after her mom. Everything inside Ben told him, "Run for your life." Before stupid took him out the door, God held his feet to the kitchen floor. Ben prayed before meandering up the same stairs Bets tried to take out a minute before.

When he hit the door into their bedroom, he stopped and had to cover his mouth to keep from laughing. Betsy had pulled the covers over her head and she lay like a mummy underneath it. That hit him as funny, but what made it even more hysterical— their pooch sat perched on top of her, staring down at the blanket covering Betsy.

Ben walked over and asked, "Can I take a picture of this?"

"Please do."

His wife's laughter from under their comforter told him he'd dodged a bullet this time. And it said he'd better hurry and take the photo, which he did right before Matilda jumped off. Ben put his phone in his pocket then peeked under the covers and said, "Want to see?"

"You bet," Betsy said as she hopped out from underneath their chocolate brown comforter like she'd been shot out of a cannon.

Ben chuckled at the sight. Betsy's short, gray hair stuck up in every direction. But a smile now replaced the earlier I'm-not-sure-you're-going-to-live-through-this-moment look.

Thank You, Jesus.

"Must be a little early for funny. Sorry."

"Got that right. Now where's the picture of our attack dog."

Ben took out his phone and clicked on the camera. "Here's the maniac." He turned his phone so Betsy could see what he'd seen. "Isn't she cute? Almost as adorable as her... her...dad."

"Almost, but not quite. She is adorable, for sure. Now isn't it time for you to go toil over a shovel?" She gave Ben a hug.

"It is." Ben didn't move. Then a knock on their door came and whatever thoughts he had of skipping work vanished.

"Better get the door. Larry will keep it up until you do."

Ben ignored his friend and hugged Betsy tighter. "How about we pick this up later when I get home?"

Betsy nodded. "I'll be here. Now you better let Larry in before he calls 9-1-1."

"You'll have to. I have to find my keys."

CHAPTER THIRTY-TWO

Betsy opened the door and motioned Larry inside. "Ben will be right with you. He's looking for his keys."

"That'll help us get out of the parking lot."

This tickled Betsy since they'd actually started their day at odds. Then, like Mighty Dog, Matilda came in and defused their argument—doing something so cute she couldn't stay mad at Ben any longer. She'd have to give her pooch an extra t.r.e.a.t. later.

"Are you ready?" Ben came down the stairs and took the coffee mug Betsy offered him.

"Got any more of that?"

"Sure." Betsy rummaged around in the lower cabinet again and found their extra insulated cup. "Here you go."

"See you tonight, hon."

Ben's handsomer-than-all-get-out wink and quick hug before he and Larry walked out the door left her breathless. Betsy went and sat at their dinette and again praised the Lord for what He'd done in their lives.

Then she texted Rose. "Get over here so we can get busy cooking." Betsy fanned herself since she was already overheated.

~

Larry's door wasn't closed two seconds before he turned and faced Ben. Enjoyment showed on every corner of his face. Ben could only imagine what went on in his friend's head. But he had one question for Lar. Can't a guy show affection to the little woman before he leaves for work?

Little woman. Ben laughed at his phraseology, knowing his *little woman* would hoot if he ever referred to her as such. He also ignored Larry's stare as he started the pick-up and pulled out of the RV Park.

"Ben, are you sure you're not coming down with the flu?"

"I'm fine. Why do you ask?"

"You're acting weird. Holding hands. Flowers. Shenanigans. You're turning into Mr. Casanova."

"Making up for lost time, Larry."

"Man I'm proud of you. Keep up the good work, but next time I'd rather not be privy to it. Old people kissing on each other doesn't seem right."

Ben almost ran off the road when his friend blurted out the comment and had to wipe tears from his eyes so he could see to drive. When he got control of the situation he said, "Larry, that WAS the funniest thing I've ever heard you say."

"Giving up gaming has its benefits. It's given me more time to work on my new career."

"Can't wait to hear this."

"Stand-up comedian."

"Lar, with Betsy and Rose by our side, you'll never run out of material."

"Son, you ain't too far from the pack either. Your Type A personality. A person who sells everything and buys an RV. I can see it now. Hey, we could go on the road."

Ben let his friend's job idea go without a comment. Larry, the die-hard introvert, would never stand in front of a crowd. Their wives, they could go on the stage together, and entertain a crowd.

The miles between the two college towns faded as the sun made its debut for the day. A sunny day for working. Rain long gone.

Ben pulled into the parking lot at the motel almost two hours later and turned to Larry. "We are on the road."

"We are what?"

"Back to what we were talking about. Your new vocation? You might have hit on something, but you do know you'll have to perform in front of people when you're doing it."

"Not happening."

"Thought so."

Ben and Larry exited his truck and were still laughing when Jeff walked up. "Hey guys. Ready to move more dirt?"

"No, but Christopher is?" Ben glanced at his point of contention from Friday and smiled. The transformation in two days floored him. The twenty something had pulled his pants to where they belonged and his now-clean hair hung in a ponytail.

Larry took off his glasses and cleaned them with his shirttail. "No way it's him."

"Christopher?" The red-haired giant walked over to him and stooped down to get eye level with the younger man. "I can't believe it. It is you."

"Yes, and I'm ready to get to work. But first, Ben, I owe you an apology." Christopher extended his hand. "Sorry for my attitude last week. Not too Christian like."

Ben shook the man's hand then patted him on the back. "I'm sorry too. Came on a little too strong myself."

Larry came and stood next to Ben. "Trust me, Christopher, the man upstairs and I worked on him all the way home Friday nig—"

"Guys, church is over. Time to work." Jeff moved to the other side of the front loader then turned. "Today?"

Ben watched Larry sprint to the stack of tools and picked up a shovel. Christopher scrambled over to the front loader and jumped on. Ben stood, unable to move until Larry came back over and handed him a shovel and said, "Here."

The two walked over to the dumpster. "Lar, I don't know about you, but I'd say we need to pray for him."

"Right now would be good."

Larry took the lead. "Father, we don't know what's going on with Jeff, but please give us Your words to say to him. To encourage him. In Jesus name. Amen."

Ben leaned the shovel Larry had given him on the dumpster and started to pick up pieces of drywall and splintered wood. With each piece he tossed in the trash, he kept seeing the fire in Jeff's eyes when they'd mentioned the Lord's name.

Father, whatever he's dealing with, please help him.

~

"Can you help me with this, Ben? Then I'm ready for a break." Larry brushed off the sleeve of his jacket.

Ben stopped and glanced at his watch. "Can't believe it's 10:00 already."

"Time flies—"

"Yea! I'm not sure about the fun part?" Ben picked up the end of the soaked two by four and they carried it to the dumpster and pitched it in.

Larry laughed when he sat down on a boulder. "All I can say is you're sure intent on picking up trash today."

"That happens when you're praying," Ben added when he joined Larry on the rock. "Hey, you want a water?"

"Sure."

Ben's muscles screamed bloody murder when he straightened up all the way. But he managed to hobble to his truck and grab a couple of bottles out of the cooler in the back seat. Right before he closed the door, Jeff walked up and he asked him, "Want one?"

"I'll take one and I owe you an apology. I was out of line. Got a lot on my mind."

"No problem." Ben handed him the bottle and opened his own, taking a long drink. He then poured some of the rest down his neck.

Jeff took his bottle and drank some of it then doused the front of his shirt with the remaining fluid.

Larry came running over. "I'll take mine before you decide to baptize someone else with it."

Ben laughed then took a quick glance at Jeff. From the look on his face, he'd seen the humor in Larry's comment and said when he quit chuckling, "That was a good one."

"Don't encourage him, Jeff. He's hard enough to live with."

Ben's comment got a strange look from Jeff and he appeared to mull it over before asking. "You two live together?"

"Heavens no. We're married and live in our own RVs." Larry opened and drank half of his water.

"Full-time?"

"Wife and I are full-timers. These guys still own a home in Texas. What about you?"

Jeff stared off as if he searched the sky for the words he wanted. He finally said, "Lost ours in the flood."

"Ah man, I'm so sorry."

"So am I, Ben."

"Is there anything we can do?"

"Count us all in." Larry moved closer to Jeff and smiled. "Betsy and Rose would want to come along, even if it's just to supply food and prayer support."

Jeff stared at the men before he crushed his water bottle and tossed it into the dumpster. "This can't be. No way."

"This can't be, what?" Ben asked, waiting for Jeff to continue. He kept repeating, "It can't be…"

"If you hum a few bars, we might be able to help you." Larry came over and sat down again on the boulder.

"I think my wife Mary met your wives last week in Longmont."

"Mary Miller?" This time Ben sat. Dumbfounded.

"That's my wife."

~

"Mary, we'll see you two later tonight." Betsy handed her new friend the address to the RV Park. "I know the guys are looking forward to meeting Jeff."

"Him too. I couldn't quit talking about you two ladies Friday night."

"That's understandable." Rosie snorted.

Betsy thought she saw Mary flinch and decided to explain. "Don't worry. It's a normal noise. You'll get used to it, if you spend much time around us."

Rose got going even more after Betsy's explanation. Mary joined in. In the middle of the mall's parking lot the three stood giggling.

"You ladies have no idea how good it is to laugh." Mary opened her purse and took out a Kleenex, wiping the corners of her eyes. "Not much joking since...Jeff...he's..."

"He's...up a...creek without a paddle."

The second those words left her lips, Betsy wanted the pavement to part so she could slip into the abyss. But nothing happened...unless you call two women gawking at her as nothing.

"Wasn't such a great analogy of what he might say, was it?"

"Not particularly, but I love how your mind works." Mary chuckled.

"That's why God made Betsy a writer. He gave her so much up there to write about," Rose gestured to her own head. "Sometimes some of the craziness comes out of her mouth. At the most unexpected times."

"Betsy, we must have the same problem. Only Jeff calls what I say a different name."

"Unrepeatable?"

"Rose, let Mary finish." Betsy could see she needed to talk.

"Jeff called me self-righteous the other day and asked how I could believe in a God who rips our home out from under us?" Tears streamed down Mary's face. "I wasn't preaching. I'm new at this Christian thing too and don't have the answers."

"No one would have a definitive answer for what happened to you," Betsy said as she hugged Mary. "Losing everything is above my scope of understanding, but I know God is in it and loves you."

Mary dried her eyes and nodded. "Tell my husband."

Betsy sensed Rose's comeback before her best friend said anything. Rosie never waited for a formal invitation to give her opinion. Or, as she liked to call it, share her faith.

"Dear, I'm going to ask you a question."

Betsy stared at Rose. *Only one. Where's your normal dozen?*

Rose leaned against the truck. "Mary, what made you walk down to the front of the church and accept the Lord's love and forgiveness?"

This time Mary gawked at Rose before she said, "My heart told me to stand and walk down the aisle. Proclaim Jesus as my Savior in front of everyone. Even though it didn't make sense, I knew He loved me." Mary wiped at her eyes again.

"This is what you go home and tell your hubby. No matter what happens. God loves you and Jeff."

"You go, girl." Betsy couldn't have said it better and decided it would be the topic of her next blog.

Mary laughed while she glanced at her arm. "Oh my goodness. I've got to go make some phone calls." After opening the car door, she spun around. "Thanks for listening."

"You're welcome. Now go." Betsy waved her hand at Mary. "We'll take care of fixing dinner."

"Are you sure?"

"Listen to Bets. Go get your calls made and leave this dinner to Bets and me. See you at 6:30. And we'll be praying for you."

"Thanks again." Mary waved as she drove away.

"You ready to go?"

For whatever reason Rose's question prompted Betsy to check the time too. "We better get going. It's after 1:00." Then she opened the door and got in the Wilford's pick-up and Rosie took off.

By the time they hit I-25, nothing else mattered to Betsy but home and the bag of potatoes waiting for her to peel for her mom's famous potato salad. A perfect get-acquainted dish and sure to please the palettes of everyone.

IF it turned out the way Mom made it. But if she ran into trouble, Betsy had her mother's phone number on speed dial.

"What has you so entertained over there?"

"Thinking about dinner."

Her best friend patted the side of her leg. "This is why these resemble a side of beef. I don't wait for meal time. I eat my way through the day to get to dinner."

"Amen to both and tonight I'll be consuming...please Jesus, please help me make it like mom's...potato salad."

"I don't know when this change in you happened with cooking, but if it tastes like hers, you'll be fighting off everyone for another spoonful."

"I can only hope."

CHAPTER THIRTY-THREE

A nagging thought kept Betsy company while she peeled the spuds. *Why didn't we stop and pray for Mary this afternoon?* No answer came for not doing it. What she hated the most, it was almost an afterthought.

With the last potato sliced and in the pot of boiling water, Betsy turned from the stove and announced, "It won't be long now...and we need to talk."

"But first, I'm ready for a snack. All this cooking made me hungry."

Betsy grabbed the bag of baby carrots out of the fridge and brought them over to the table. Before sitting down, she filled Matilda's water bowl. "There you go, Mats." The terrier mix bounded over to her dish and lapped up most of the water.

"Can I have some of your water, Matilda? I need something to wash down the rabbit food your mother is trying to feed me."

"Don't complain, sister." Betsy held up the bag of carrots. "We need to care. There are people out there without homes who would love to have these."

Once spoken, for all to hear, it made no sense to Betsy. And Rose's questioning look said, "You're not making a bit of sense."

"Let me rephrase that."

"Please do." Rose leaned in, putting her elbows on the table.

"What I was trying to say...*Oh this could come out so wrong.* Rosie, we're both self-righteous."

"What in the world do carrots have to do with the flood?"

"You said things come out of my mouth sometimes..."

"I did, but I'm still not tracking with you." Rose rested her chin on her hands and said, "Go on."

"What I mean is—we had an opportunity to pray for Mary and we gave a new believer the go-to Christianize mumbo jumbo, 'We'll pray for you.' Rosie, we haven't. I was more worried about my perfect potato salad than praying for Mary."

"What you meant was we're self-centered. Not self-righteous. And another thing, are you done spitting on me?"

Betsy could almost guarantee she hadn't expelled fluids on her friend, but handed her a paper towel anyway. "Whatever we are, we should have prayed?"

"The next time this happens, one of us needs to kick the other to get busy and pray."

"I'll look forward to it." Betsy grabbed a carrot and took a bite.

"Put that thing down and let's get to praying."

Betsy listened to her friend's prayer, wishing Mary could hear the compassion directed on her and her family's behalf. Tears spilled on the napkin Betsy had on her lap. Rosie dabbed at her own eyes and said a couple of "Amens". For good measure.

"Always have to have the last word." Betsy laughed as she reached over and grasped her friend's hand. "Great prayer, by the way."

"You know it and before your potatoes become mashable, you better check on them."

Betsy rushed to the stove and stuck a fork in one of the potato chunks. "Perfection. I'll let them cool then I'll work my magic."

"While we wait, I'll go over and take Baby out. Matilda, do you want to go for a walk?"

Rose barely had the request out of her mouth before the black and white dog started leaping around like she hadn't been outside in days.

"That would be a yes."

"We'll be right back."

Rose and the dogs weren't right back, giving her time to clean up her kitchen. By the time Rosie returned, Betsy had cleaned off the first layer of gunk. Ready for whatever else came their way.

"What do we need for this renowned potato salad?" Rose opened the refrigerator.

"The usual."

Rose got out all the ingredients and arranged them on the kitchen island. "There you go."

Betsy dumped the water off the potatoes, put them in a large bowl and went to grab a knife out of the drawer. Or she attempted the easy task, but the two ended up getting in each other's way. In the end, she retrieved the needed utensil.

"Okay, Bets, now that we've tried out for *Dancing With the Stars,* why don't you give me the knife and I'll cut up the potatoes?"

"That'll work." Betsy opened the jar of mayonnaise and put two heaping tablespoons into the bowl and added salt and pepper.

They worked side by side, neither making a peep. Betsy assumed Rosie stayed quiet so she wouldn't disturb her when it came to how much of each item to put in the pot, or large bowl, in this case.

Rose gave a little cough and said, "Hum."

"Hum...what?"

"Hum...think you're adding a tad too much mustard." Rose put the knife down and stood with her hands on her hips.

"Is that right?" With a smile, Betsy put her spoon into the jar and scraped the sides and bottom of it.

"You wouldn't?"

Betsy brought the spoon out and attempted to put the rest of the mustard on the mound of potatoes. But first she had to chase

Rose around the island a couple of times, after she'd grabbed the bowl off the counter.

"It'll add more color."

"You're a brat."

"And your phone's buzzing."

Rose put the bowl down and picked up her phone. While she chatted with Larry, Betsy put the potato salad away and smiled. Ben would be surprised at Rosie's and her culinary expertise for the day.

And their last-minute party planning. She hoped Rose would keep their secret until their hubbies got home.

~

"Hold on. I'll ask him."

"What?" Ben tried to hear the conversation, but only picked up a word or two.

Larry pulled the phone away from his ear. "Rose wants me to stop at the store. She wants…" He put the phone back up. "What do you want? Oh, she wants ice cream sandwiches."

Ben pulled into the King Soopers parking lot and shut off his truck. "What else do the ladies need? Or better yet, does Bets want anything while we're here."

Larry repeated Ben's question and waited. He pulled the phone away and said. "She hung up on me."

"Strange."

"We can assume they don't want anything else and we're having ice cream sandwiches for dessert."

Ben glanced over at Larry when he continued to sit in the truck. "Are you going into the store tonight, or are you hoping they walk out here on their own? It *was* your wife who asked for the goodies."

Larry got out and walked a few steps before he turned around. "Hey buddy, you're the shopper. Not me. I might buy out the freezer section, looking for the correct desserts."

Ben laughed as he stepped out of his truck and met up with Larry. "You got that right. Shopping isn't your forte. Unless you're buying coi—"

244

"You can stop right there. Since you have my...what did Rosie call it...my sin...whatever, I haven't bought anything online." Larry reached for the door to open it. "And you know what? It hasn't bothered me in the least."

"I'd say that's an answered prayer."

"I agree."

Ben walked into the store and got a cart, expecting Larry to follow him through the sliding glass doors. When he glanced back, his friend stood at the cleaning wipe dispenser, trying to get one out. All this while he's looking down at his hand.

"What are you doing?" Ben asked after he stepped on the sensor to reopen the sliding door.

"I'm trying to save us from disease and answer Rosie's text. She's asking where we are?"

"Tell her we're almost headed home."

"While I do that, why don't you go get what we came for?"

Ben didn't argue and off to the freezer section he went and got the ice cream sandwiches. For once, when he got to the checkout line, no one stood in front of him. He paid and went to find Larry, who still worked at getting a cleaning cloth out of the dispenser.

"You don't give up, do you?" Ben placed the cart next to the others and took the sack out of it.

Larry joined him. "No. That's why I became an engineer."

When the exit doors opened and the guys headed to the truck Ben asked Larry, "Did you fix it?"

"No, but I told one of the employees about it." Larry got in. "However, I'm not sure someone who doesn't look old enough to work at the store cares if the dispenser works or not."

Ben put on his seatbelt and headed out of the parking lot. "Don't underestimate the young people. Remember Christopher this morning. He cleaned up his act pretty well."

"With Jeff's help."

Ben made a right turn on Mulberry. "He did take Chris under his wing. Now it's time we did the same for Jeff and his wife. Let's talk to the ladies about what we could do for them."

"God does work in mysterious ways. All of us meeting the Miller's. Amazing!"

"Yes, He is amazing."

~

"Jeff and Mary please sit down. Here's some sweet tea for you." Betsy pointed to two lawn chairs. "Over there. The guys should be here any minute."

"Still can't believe you've worked with our hubbies," Rose said as she arranged the silverware next to the plates. "Unbelievable. And, Jeff, you are a tall drink of water."

"Yes, ma'am I am and I'd say we were all surprised when we figured out we all had met." Jeff stretched his long legs out in front of him. "As Mary would say, "It's a small world.""

"What do they call that...sixth degree of desperation?"

After the laughter died down from Rose's misquoted comment, Betsy corrected her, "It's 'sixth degrees of separation.'"

"I knew it was something like that."

Betsy smiled at Rose. "All I know is Ben and Larry will be surprised when they see our guests." She moved the bowl of potato salad to the center of the table. "And he'll be shocked I made one of his favorite dishes. Or tried to, at least."

Rose cleared her throat and gave Betsy a stare which left no question she was displeased. "Don't listen to her. She's a great cook, when she puts her mind to it."

Betsy left Rosie's comment alone and finished putting the food on the table. Everything, including the weather, cooperated with their last-minute party. Ben and Larry needed to hurry up.

"Are you sure there isn't anything we can do?" Mary attempted to get out of her chair, but Matilda had other ideas. She came and stood right in front of Mary with her paw raised as if to say, "Sit down and shake my hand."

"Looks like you've got a new friend." Betsy came over and attached the cable on Matilda's collar, which placed her a short distance from them and the picnic table. "There you go."

"Betsy, you didn't have to move her. Anyway, I could take this adorable pup home with me right this minute."

"That's if *we* had a home."

In Betsy's estimation of looks—the one Mary gave her husband would have won *her* an array of awards. Over the years Ben had accused Betsy of her 'Five Basic Looks', but this one she'd witnessed put hers to shame.

Right then Ben drove up and both men exited the vehicle. Larry lifted a sack in the air and said, "Not rude. Just gotta put the ice cream away."

Ben went over and shook Jeff's hand. "Good to see ya...Again. Where's your wife? I want to meet the person who puts up with you."

Jeff smiled, "Ben, I'd like you to meet my much better half. Mary Miller."

Betsy watched her. The daggers that had flashed from Mary's eyes had disappeared and love for her extremely tall husband took its place.

"Is it time to eat?" Larry said as he came out of the RV and stood next to Mary. "Hi, I'm Larry. Nice to meet you."

"He's harmless, Mary," Rose yelled from the table. "And, yes, it's time to eat."

They took their places and Betsy passed the food around. She'd checked out everyone's expression first before taking any of the potato salad. Rosie said, "Delicious" after tasting it. But Bets welcomed more opinions.

Ben took a bite of his and leaned over and gave Betsy a kiss on the cheek. "It's better than your mom's."

"Don't say those words in front of her. She'll write you out of her will." Betsy took the bowl, scooped out a helping and dug in. A thought came into her head and before she could catch it, it hit the open air. "I can cook."

"I'd say so." Jeff stuffed a spoonful in his mouth then added, "Don't change a thing."

To make sure he hadn't lied and her first bite wasn't a fluke, Betsy took another bite. Bigger than the first. The perfectly cooked and seasoned dish melted in her mouth.

When she swallowed, she could almost count that even her

little piggies smiled at how good the potato salad tasted. The grins on everyone's face at the table said they agreed with her assessment.

Rose stood, plate in hand, and announced, "I will never make a batch of potato salad again. As long as I live. Why eat slop, when you can eat this."

"Here! Here!"

Betsy wanted to quiet all the praise, but sort of appreciated the compliments. Not many came in the writer's life, so when you got some, milk it for all it's worth.

Except for when you've invited a couple to a get together who don't know all of you. Time to move the conversation to something with less of a chance of nuttiness.

"How about the women clean up? Give us time for our supper settle. We can have dessert later." Bets got up.

"No, you ladies have done enough." Ben came and stood next to her. "The guys will clean up, but first I'll start a fire."

"I like the sound of both of those things."

After Ben finished building the fire, he and the guys went inside their trailer. Rose and Mary moved their chairs closer and huddled around the brick surround. Betsy went and rescued Matilda and carried her to the RV. No need for their dog to catch cold.

Betsy opened the door and the three men stood behind the island in her kitchen. Larry had a dishtowel, drying silverware. Jeff held up a container and asked, "Where does this go?" Ben stood with soap running down his arms, pointing at the cabinet. "In there."

"Looks like you're having fun in here," Betsy said as she put their pooch down, who ran right over to Ben. "Hon, when you get finished, can you feed the princess?"

"Will do."

Betsy thought all three men answered her and left the camper, knowing Matilda wouldn't go hungry. Any more than the six of them had earlier. As she neared the fire pit, voices rang out in the cool night air. What Betsy heard and saw on her new friend's face made her heart sink.

"The foundation is it." Mary's eyes brimmed with tears.

Rose took her hand. "Dear, that must be awful."

Careful not to interrupt their conversation, Betsy picked up a lawn chair and moved it closer to Rose and Mary.

"Jeff should have listened to me. After the last flood, I felt the Lord told us to move...but noooo."

A piece of firewood popped at the moment Mary spat out the last two words, sending embers into the evening sky. Fireworks to match the hurtful words she'd spoken.

Ones, Betsy assumed, Jeff had heard more than once. *Father, how many times have I done the same thing?*

Too many times and Mary's sassiness reminded Betsy that belittling your spouse in front of others solved nothing.

"...now it's too late."

Betsy moved her chair closer to Mary. "It's never too late."

"You have no idea..."

"No, I don't and I'm sorry if what I'm about to say is too blunt."

"Remember what I said about her this morning? Interesting things can and will come out of Betsy's mouth." A snort escaped and even though Betsy wanted to crown Rosie for butting in, she saw a slight smile on Mary's face.

"Go on Betsy, I'm listening."

"As I was saying before Rosie rudely interrupted me...Mary...I don't know what it's like to lose a house to a flood. But I do know how much it hurts when you feel you've heard God's message and your hubby doesn't get the same email."

Betsy told Mary how well her announcement to write fulltime went over in the Stevenson's household a few years before.

"I'm glad you stuck with it, Bets. I've read your blogs and they've helped me. Made me understand things in a different way."

For some reason Betsy couldn't leave Mary's statement alone and added. "Are you sure you're reading *my* blog?"

Rosie stood and headed over to Betsy, giving her a menacing

stare all the way there. When she landed at her side, she gave her a swat on the arm and shouted, "Whatever is true. Whatever is noble."

"Not sure Jesus hit his disciples when they bad mouthed themselves."

"He should have. Then they—YOU—would have straightened up and not said any such things."

"Sorry."

"Now that I've 'straightened' Betsy out." Rose did imaginary quotes in the air and sat back down. "I want to hear what else she has to say."

"What are we talking about?" Ben spoke as he and the other two men came over to where the women sat.

"Some girl talk. Come over and join us. Oh, and while you're at it, bring some more wood. It's getting chilly over here." Betsy moved her chair away from Mary and smiled, hoping to convey to her they'd talk more later.

Mary's eyes brightened and Betsy settled into her seat. She watched Ben retrieve some wood and add them to the fire. The pieces ignited, causing flames to shoot high into the night air. The wood settled down and warmed those who took refuge near it.

Larry and Jeff grabbed the chairs closest to their wives, while Ben continued to play with the poker. Betsy chuckled—he even wanted to get the fire to burn just right. To some: he's picky. To her: he's endearing.

Thank You, Lord, for making him this way. I think...

Betsy's *I think* thought could go south pretty quickly, so she nipped it and asked, "Did you three solve all the world's problems while you washed dishes?" She almost patted herself on the back for such a great conversation starter.

"Men talking about anything meaningful?" Rose nudged Betsy before she turned to Larry. "All guys are interested in are cars and sports. In our case—RVs."

"Pardonnez-moi." Larry puffed out his chest. "There's other things we talk about. Help me out guys."

"Our wives, of course," Ben declared, while taking his seat

next to Betsy.

"Definitely a subject worth discussing. Who needs world peace when the three of us are the topic of discussion?" Rose grinned.

Everyone in the group nodded in agreement. All but one. Betsy. She thought she'd better steer their get-to-know-you chit chat into another direction. "Jeff, did Ben or Larry tell you how we ended up full-time RVers?"

"Despite what I said earlier, Bets," Ben took her hand. "This past week I haven't had time to discuss anything other than how to move mud and debris."

"And getting people to work." Jeff laughed. "After Ben scared Christopher, he made quite the transformation. He can work a front loader."

How the mention of a piece of equipment could liven up a conversation, Betsy did not know. Didn't care either. All she cared about—they'd gotten off of the subject of women. A hot potato, for sure.

"Isn't it time for dessert?" Larry got out of his chair and hurried to his RV. Almost to the door he asked, "Does anyone want coffee?"

A choir of "Yeses" and "You bet" sounded around the campfire. "Then coffee it is." Larry went inside.

"I'm right behind you."

"No, Rose, I'll help him."

While Larry made the coffee, Betsy went to the Wilford's coat closet/pantry and took out six cups, arranging them on the table.

"If you look under the dining room chair, you'll find one of those cardboard carry-out things." Larry pointed from the kitchen. "Rosie's new recycling bin."

Betsy got on her hands and knees and looked underneath the chairs. There stood empty plastic and glass bottles and a lone Starbucks holder perched on top of it. She got up again she asked, "Lar, when did Rose become eco-minded?"

"When she found out they had recycle bins here at the park, Rose said something about her being surprised they could do it with all the flooding going on."

"What does flooding and recycling have to do with each other?"

"Not sure, but I go along with keeping things out of landfills. We need to do our part."

"I'm with you. And, back to the flood, isn't it awful about Jeff and Mary losing their home?"

"I don't know about Mary, but Jeff's struggling. He...they need lots of prayers."

"They sure do. Let's pray for them before they leave."

Larry sat the coffee pot on the table. "Bets, I'm not sure he'll let us. He's pretty mad at God." He filled the cups and said, "But if the Lord leads the conversation that way, we'll have to obey."

Betsy saw the smile and little twinkle in Larry's eyes. "Absolutely. We ready to go do the Lord's work, Mr. Wilford?"

"I believe we are Mrs. Stevenson." Larry did a two-step around her. "But first I need to clear up something with you."

"Lay it on me."

"Bets, when you caught me in your RV compartment in Colorado Springs."

"Yes."

"I was putting my iPad away."

"I gathered that." Betsy reached over and touched Larry's arm.

"If you remember, I also paid you a compliment. Which I wanted to make sure you knew I meant. Betsy, I wasn't covering my tracks. What I said was, and is true. I'd love to have your attitude about life."

"Thank you. You're sweet." Betsy got up and gave Larry a hug. "How about we get the ice cream sandwiches?"

Larry grabbed the sack out of the freezer and they walked down the steps. Betsy wanted to tell Lar how much she appreciated his kind words, but she heard Rosie. Apparently, the discussion at the fire pit had gone south.

"...Jeff, you could be looking at this flood thing all wrong," Rose glanced in the man's direction then put her finger up to her chin, tapping it a few times.

Betsy distributed the coffee, but watched the group around the roaring fire. Complete silence enveloped the campsite. Almost like the old commercial, "When E. F. Hutton talks, everybody listens."

Only this time Rose Wilford had the floor and had caused the quiet around the firepit.

Oh, Father, here's another good time Your return would be appreciated. ASAP, if possible.

"We *are* looking at this all wrong, Jeff," Mary said as she got up out of her chair and faced her hubby. "Since we lost *everything*—we should do what these guys are doing and join the *Early Birds*."

The Second Coming didn't happen, but Betsy concluded with her new friend's statement the Lord had missed Mary when He'd handed out tactfulness. Betsy glanced at Jeff, his face took on the appearance of the ripe tomatoe she'd sliced for their BLT the other day.

Ready to explode. When or if it did, they'd all be covered. Not a pretty sight.

"Great idea. We can go around the country and I can tell other campers what the Lord did, or didn't do, in our lives." Jeff got up, knocking his chair over. "It's time to go."

Ben stepped up and blocked Jeff from opening his car door. "Don't think it's a good time—"

"A good time to do what, Ben?" Jeff leaned over and put his hands on his knees. "Is it a good time for God to let our house float down the river?"

"No, it's not. Can we go over and sit down?"

"Sure. Why not."

Ben led Jeff to the chair he'd overturned and sat it upright and said, "Sit. We need to clear up some things here."

"There isn't anything to 'clear up'. I got His message loud and clear about a week ago."

Larry put his chair next to Jeff and said, "Then you're listening to the wrong message, son. God doesn't sit up there, destroying people's lives."

"He could have prevented it?"

"Yes, but He didn't."

"Then why do I believe in all of it?"

"I don't know, but you're the only one who can answer that." Larry patted Jeff's leg. "One of the ways to find the answer is to ask yourself, 'What are you going to do now? Let the flood define the rest of your life? Put a wedge between you and your Savior?'"

"No."

"Then I'd say you've got your answer. The both of you better get on your knees tonight and thank Him for saving your lives. Trust me, material things don't matter, but you do."

Ben thought he heard sniffles in the direction of the women. Larry's to-the-letter theology almost brought a tear to his eyes too. He decided he didn't need to add anything else. Lar covered it.

Anyway, Ben reasoned that stopping a man, who stood almost a foot taller than him, from driving off in a rage, had put his system in shock. Another thing which amazed Ben, Rosie stayed completely quiet during her husband's spiel.

Rustling caused Ben and the other two men to turn around. Mary walked towards Jeff, kneeling next to his chair. "I'm sorry for what I said."

"I'm sorry too. I'm sorry for a lot of things."

"Can we pray for you guys?"

"What a splendid idea," Rose said before she took off and prayed a simple prayer. Her usual "Amen" at the end probably woke the saints in heaven and everyone at the RV Park too.

But the smiles on all the faces said they'd witnessed two very weary souls answering His call. For a second time.

CHAPTER THIRTY-FOUR

Betsy and Matilda strolled over to Rose's RV the next morning. When her friend opened the door she declared, "That was the most interesting get together I've ever been a part of. One things for sure, it was one of the tastiest."

"I'd say it rates right up there." Rose held up her coffee cup. "Come in and sit a spell."

Betsy unhooked her pooch's leash and let Baby and her tumble around the Wilford's living room. The sight of them made both Rose and her chuckle.

"They are a pair."

"Like us."

"Yep." Betsy grabbed a cup and filled it with the delicious-smelling brew. "What I need after last night's..." She let the rest of her sentence dangle and took a seat across from Rose.

"Last night's what? Revival meeting?"

Betsy wanted to laugh at the innocence written on her friend's face. "We did have a big praise moment last night. By the way, I loved your prayer. You're getting good at it."

"Thank you."

"You're welcome. However, there's more to last night. And

it's about us."

"Okaaaaaay," Rose elongated the word and wore a more confused look. Similar to the one the day before.

Betsy charged ahead—after she stopped and prayed for her words to make sense and didn't sting too much.

"Rosie, we're a lot like Mary."

"Yes, but we solved that one the other day."

"Uh huh. But last night made me realize we're—"

"Flawed?"

"Not flawed, Rosie. We nitpick. We point things out to our husbands, in front of others, what they're doing wrong."

"I'm not critical of Larry."

Betsy gave her friend a sideward glance, reminiscent of the one Rose gave her the night before.

"The look you're giving me tells me different."

"We're both guilty. What I need to do is pray for the removal of the log in my eye before I point out the speck in someone else's."

"Bets, I'd rather walk barefoot on hot pavement than admit a change is in order for...meeeeeee." A huge grin broke out on Rose's face. "And, even though it hurts—I appreciate your loving words. I'll work on being more like Jesus."

"That's a tall order, even for you." Betsy's laughter made it impossible to continue. When she caught her breath, she stood up and hugged her friend. "I love ya, Rosie."

"Even if I'm flawed."

"Even more." Betsy gave Rose another hug then asked Matilda, "You ready to go? Mama's got a couple of ideas for blogs and she needs to write them down before she forgets either one."

Matilda answered her with three leaps into the air. One almost taking out Baby, who had been quiet all morning. The Shih Tzu yelped and charged the Boston terrier mix.

"Yes, my friend, it's time to go. Talk to you soon." Betsy closed the door and walked over to her RV. "Come on, girl. We'll go for a walk later. Right now I've got to write."

Matilda bounced up the stairs with Betsy on her heels. After heating up a cup of tea, she sat down at her desk. It'd been way too long, but now two different blog ideas swam around in her head.

The one about friendship could wait. The happenings of last night shouted the loudest. Betsy went to work.

WHY, LORD?

How many of you have asked this question? I'm sure I'm not alone when I say I've inquired of Him more than once on this subject.

But last night, while sitting around the fire pit with a group of friends, the question(s) took on a whole new meaning when a baby believer asked, "Why did God let this terrible thing happen to me and my wife?"

Another friend answered him (and I loved it by the way), "God doesn't sit up there, destroying people's lives."

The new believer replied, "He could have prevented it?"

"Yes, but He didn't."

"Then why do I believe?"

My friend answered: It's between him and the Lord to figure that out, but not to let his life be defined by the disaster.

Can I get an "Amen brother and sister?"

We closed our evening in prayer, but the question the newbie asked bothered me. Could I define: "Why do I believe in God?"

Here's the list I came up with...

1) He died for my sins. Without Him I'm nothing. With Him I'm forgiven and know without a shadow of a doubt I'm loved from the tip of my head to the soles of my feet.
2) Which brings me to my next reason: He made little old me. All of me. My Father even knows the numbers of the gray hairs on my head.
3) He's the One who created the world we live in. Painting the sea and sky translucent blues. The only colors He could capture. Hues an artist only hopes to convey in his/her famous works of art.

4) Changing seasons—every year I marvel at the sights and sounds surrounding me. How does the elm or poplar know the exact time to throw (drop) their leaves? How do the geese know when it's the best time to fly south? How does the atmosphere know when it's time to snow? All three happen year after year.

5) But the main reason (along with #1) why I believe is: Babies and newborn animals. How does a wee bitty thing turn into a six-foot tall person or a tiny bear cub turn into a grizzly bear?

The only answer I can come up with is: A specific and divine design.

A Creator!!!! The one I believe in and the One who never questions me about why I do things.

So I shouldn't question Him since He gave me His instruction manual. The answers to everything we ask or need to know are within the pages of the Bible.

Words written over 2000 years ago, but ones still relevant today.

Search!

Find!!!

Look for His answers. You'll find them. And trust me, they may surprise you.

Love ya,
Bets

Betsy sat back in her office chair after sending the blog. Again, they were His words—none she could have penned on her own. She closed the lid of her computer and smiled. *Yes, Lord, You are amazing.*

She wanted to start the notes for her next blog, but glanced at Matilda. She needed to go on a walk. After a stroll around the RV Park, Betsy would call her mom and Camp Bow Wow. Matilda and Baby needed a vacation from them.

Oh, and I need to text Tina.

~

"Ben, we're taking the kids to C.B.W. today, before delivering sandwiches. I called them a couple of days ago." Betsy used their code word for Camp Bow Wow so Matilda wouldn't go bonkers. "Mats needs to run with her own kind. Look at her."

He glanced over the morning paper. "Seems so."

Betsy straightened the towel on the counter and smiled at Ben, knowing he didn't care if she took their pooch to her favorite place. But since they were on a budget, she needed to check with the money manager.

"She doesn't need the whole sppppaaaa treatment this time." Ben held up his phone. "It's only been a month since her last visit."

She laughed at the way he dragged out the word "spa".

"Have you told her she has to get a job to pay for the extra pampering?" Ben reached down and brought Matilda up on his lap, taking her face in his hands. "I don't know why you have to go get prettier."

"Oh, Dad."

Betsy didn't do the voice of Matilda as well as Ben, but her rendition still made both of them chuckle. And she, too, petted their pup. "She is cute, isn't she?"

"If she wasn't, she wouldn't stop traffic like she does at Starbucks."

Betsy nodded and her mind went to the one woman at their coffee hangout in Houston. The lady almost made a complete fool of herself when she stooped to Matilda's level and talked baby talk for a good two minutes.

Remembering the episode Betsy said, "Ben, please don't ever let me make a fool of myself like that one lady did."

"You have nothing to worry about," Ben said as he put their pooch down. "Now you go with Mom. She's going to take you to Camp Bow Wow."

Once the words came out, their dog jumped around before going to stand next to the door. Betsy watched the dance on her way back to the kitchen. "See what you've done. I'm not ready to go yet. Rose hasn't called."

"Sorry, hon." Ben picked up the newspaper again. "Better give her a call. She might have forgotten."

"I doubt it. She told me the other day Baby needs a break 'cause she's tired of them."

"Didn't know Demon Dog could talk. Thought she could only bark her head off."

"Be quiet. Rose or Larry might hear you."

"If the walls of our camper are that thin, we're in deep trouble."

Betsy grabbed the dish towel off the counter and swatted Ben with it, knowing full well what he meant. Without a mirror, she could feel her cheeks glowed from his innuendo.

"What's the matter, dear?"

"Nothing." Betsy fanned her overheated face with the first thing she could find—a pot holder.

Ben got up and came around the kitchen counter and gave Betsy a big smooch. "Have I told you I loved you today?"

"You did, when I was brushing my teeth."

Betsy heard a knock at the door and before she could unwrap herself from Ben's arms, Rose opened the door and peered in. "Well, what do we have here?"

"Hello Rose."

"Remind me to lock the door." Ben moved away, but put his arm around Betsy's shoulder.

"Am I interrupting something?"

"No, but I thought you said you were going to call me."

"If I had, I would have missed the peep show." A snort/laugh/unrecognizable sound came out of Rose.

Betsy laughed at her friend, but mentioned, "You do know when you knock, you're supposed to wait until someone answers their door."

Apparently what she just said brought on more laughter. No saving the situation, so Betsy picked up Matilda and her purse, kissed Ben goodbye and walked down the stairs. Right past Rosie and asked her on the way by, "Are you ready?"

"Uh huh." Rose followed, still chuckling. But instead of getting in the truck, she went to her own RV and said, "I forgot Baby."

That brought a round of chuckles while Betsy opened the back door of the dually. She put Matilda on the padded seat and said, "There you go. Here's some water."

Betsy waited for her friend, knowing she'd be out soon enough with the maniac in tow. In about a minute Rose came out with Baby in her crate, barking and carrying on.

"The C.B.W. in Houston knew us pretty well, but this one...I'm not sure they're ready for these two?"

"I'm sure they're ready for this one." Rose buckled her seatbelt and reached over and petted Matilda. "Baby's fine once she gets there and expels some energy. Before you know it, she turns into a bundle of joy."

Bundle of joy. Rosie must be hitting the bottle if she thinks that?

The ridiculous thought made Betsy giggle. Her sweet friend wouldn't even buy rubbing alcohol since it had the "A" word in it. She'd explained to her years ago they didn't use any hooch of any kind in it.

"I know my pet is the reason you're laughing. Fess up."

Betsy confessed why she laughed and before Rose's incessant snorts, which now included hiccups, caused more of a delay, Bets put the pick-up in gear and said, "If you don't shush, we'll never get these pooches to C.B.W. Remember we have a date with Mary for more fun in the kitchen."

"Well, then, put a foot into it."

All the way there, Betsy deliberated on their upcoming turbo cooking. Even though cooking sat in the middle of her favorite things-to-do list, putting sandwiches together and taking them to people in need brightened her day.

For the first time in a long time, her thoughts centered on someone else. Not Ben and her own troubles. Or dwelled on her faults—real or made up.

"Rose, I don't know about you but I've loved helping people.

It does a heart good."

"What makes it even better, they don't know who's doing it. Anonymity keeps the "me" out of the equation."

Rose had come up with profound statements before, but what she'd said could solve what Betsy had struggled with all of her life.

"Me."

Rose leaned up in the seat and stared at Betsy. "Huh?"

Betsy could feel Rose staring at her, so she repeated the word again. "Me. My problem has been 'me'. I'm too interested in *moi*." She pointed her finger at her chest and glanced over at her passenger – half expecting to catch her friend nodding in agreement.

Out of the corner of her eye, she glimpsed Rose squinching her eyes together. As if she tried to think of what to say in response.

"Go for it, Rosie. I'm man enough to take it."

Or not!

"Betsy, remind me if I'm wrong, but didn't you read *The Purpose Driven Life* a few years ago. I thought it changed your life when you realized it wasn't all about you."

"Touché. I'm finding out I'm a slow learner."

"No, sweetie, it's a head to heart thing. You have to live it, not read it in a book."

"Rose, I am saying you are on a roll today. Can I quote you in my blog on this one and the one earlier? Outstanding observations."

"Go ahead. I won't be using them. Anyway, I don't remember what I said." Rose opened her window and shooed a fly out. "Don't these things start to hibernate in October?"

So much for intelligence coming in threes.

Betsy made a mental note and repeated the two phrases in her mind, planning to write them down as soon as she parked at the doggy spa. Which happened a few minutes later. "We're here Mats. Are you ready to go to Camp Bow Wow?"

She watched Matilda. This time, instead of dancing around

inside the truck, she sat up like a statue on her haunches. Her front paws out in front of her. Before Betsy could get her phone out of her pocket to take a picture, their pup moved.

"She ought to be in pictures," Rose announced when she opened up the back door to get Baby's crate. "And Miss Noisy here could be her stand in. That is—after she's been to C.B.W. Come on girls. The court awaits."

Betsy jotted down what Rose said earlier. "Yes, there's a blog in those words, but they'll have to wait. Sandwiches are calling my name right at the moment."

CHAPTER THIRTY-FIVE

Ben watched Larry park his truck. Glad his friend drove and the job they'd worked on for the last two weeks had wrapped up. "How about we eat dinner, Lar. Then meet out at the fire pit later?"

"Nah. I'm going to bed. My hurts hurt."

"That's the truth. See ya later." Ben opened the RV door and an unfamiliar, but tantalizing, smell greeted him. He smiled. Someone must have abducted Betsy and taken over their kitchen to cook something with such an enticing aroma.

"You're home," Betsy said as she came out of their bedroom.

Ben didn't answer since the show in front of him had his full attention. He watched his wife as she tried to put her black jacket on while coming down their narrow hallway. The sight of her long arms, bending and twisting, made him wonder, *Which elbow will hit first?*

The carrying on took his mind off what he smelled. But not for long. He had to find out and taste whatever sat inside their convection oven and asked. "Did you kidnap someone who knows how to cook? Smells too wonderful for your cooking."

Betsy took a hold of Ben's face and patted each cheek. "Such a funny guy."

"And one who will be home with you for a while. We finished the job today."

Betsy wanted to jump for joy and scream all at the same time. She couldn't be happier to have him home. But what would they do with all the food they'd made today? Who would eat the cherry dump cake cooking in the oven?

She answered her own question when she said, "If you guys are finished with your job, this calls for a celebration. Are you hungry for some dump cake?" Betsy walked over and opened the microwave.

"There is a God in heaven," Ben said when he came up behind Betsy and kissed her on the neck.

"I never had a doubt, my love." Betsy brought the concoction out and sat it on top of the cooktop. The cherry pie filling bubbled in the middle and edges of the baking dish. If it hadn't been so hot, she would have stuck her finger in it to check how it tasted.

Betsy decided it couldn't smell any better than it did. She grabbed her phone and called Mary and Rose, inviting them over for the tasty treat. Instead of saying hello she said, "Always heard, 'eat dessert first.'"

Since Rosie always puts her phone on speaker, Betsy heard Larry shout, "I'm sure you've called the Miller's. We'll run and get the vanilla ice cream. That'll give Mary and Jeff time to get over here."

"They're on their way."

Less than thirty minutes later they sat around the fire pit chatting for a second night. This time they wolfed down the delicious dessert. How Betsy knew they loved it—no one said anything.

"I'm glad we're done at the motel and they got their permits to rebuild." Ben took a spoonful and almost got it to his mouth before he said, "It's a huge praise the Lord."

Jeff smiled, "I agree. Even I saw His hand in how fast the city worked. They usually sit on it for months."

"So what's next?" Larry asked after he wiped his mouth.

"I'd have to say—after making a dozen and fifty sandwiches, we should take them to the homeless shelter in Boulder or Longmont tomorrow," Betsy finished her sentence before stuffing the last bite of the cherry dump cake in her mouth. She sat back and savored every bit of it.

"Guess we won't be resting up this weekend?"

"Larry, old guys don't get that privilege. Since we retired, our wives tell us what to do."

"Ben, can you say that again. Jeff didn't hear you." Mary took his hand and kissed it.

~

"Baby, don't you make a fuss, I have you on film. I don't want you becoming a YouTube sensation."

Ben heard Rose giving their dog the what fors right before they headed to the shelter the next afternoon. He didn't have the heart to tell her you had to post the dog's mischief before it could appear on YouTube.

"Let Baby be and close the door." Larry opened the passenger door and Ben presumed his friend's frantic arm movements meant for the two ladies to hurry and get in with them.

"Okay, okay, okay. My short legs only move so fast." Rose got in and turned towards the rear. "Ben, if Baby makes a scene, we'll send you in again to smooth out the waters."

Ben kept his cool, but guaranteed his sideward glance spoke volumes. And from the look on Mary and Jeff's face, they had no clue what Rosie spouted off about.

I'm not telling them.

"So, what's with the comment?" Jeff asked the question when Larry got out on the highway. "I've heard you guys joking about it a couple other times?"

Guess I'm telling. If I want to or not.

Ben moved around in the back seat to look to his right. "It's time I, we came clean."

"Now you have me intrigued." Mary patted Betsy on the shoulder. "Is there something you haven't shared when we've been cooking up a storm?"

266

Betsy pivoted on her seat and nodded. "I did write about it in the blog, but it was before we met."

"Anyway, ladies, can I continue?"

On the thirty-minute ride to Longmont, Ben shared what had happened in Colorado Springs, concerning Baby and Matilda. Laughter filled the pick-up, but Ben made sure it didn't get out of control

"You see, I've been a Christian most of my life. Have I always lived the life Christ wanted me to—probably not, but He didn't call me to lie to anyone. Would Marilyn have known if we hadn't told her? I doubt it, but I would have. Along with the other three."

"I'm not seeing the big deal, guys."

"It does sound innocent enough, but at night, when I lay my head down on my pillow, I know I've tried my hardest to show others the love of the Lord through my thoughts, actions and deeds."

"And it isn't about performance either," Rose added in.

"No, it's because our heart is different. We look for opportunities to do for Him. What we did at the RV Park didn't reflect Him, or what I believe."

"The other night at your place is proof I haven't changed."

"Jeff, what you have been through...I'm not sure how I'd react. Don't be too hard on yourself." Ben reached over the seat and took a hold of Betsy's hand. "Like someone else I know and love. At times my wife is her own worst enemy. Never thinks she measures up."

"You?" Jeff and Mary said it together.

"My phobias are for some other time. Let's stick with Jeff. It's a better subject to talk about than me."

Again laughter filled the truck and before Ben took his hand away, he winked at her. Betsy made sure her smile told him she wasn't angry for including her in the proceedings.

"So, what you're saying, if we blow it and we will, God still loves us."

"Yes. And when we 'blow it', all we have to do is ask and He'll forgive us."

"Sounds so simple."

"It is, but as with the story I told you, we still screw things up. It's how we handle those times. Repent or remain in sin?"

"Lots to think about."

"Looks like we're here."

Larry pulled into a spot, but before they got out he backed up to the front door. Betsy got out with the others. Rose went around and opened the tailgate, handing boxes of sandwiches to those standing there.

Another vehicle pulled in next to them and the hatch opened. The smell made everyone turn towards the car. When the woman got out Betsy said, "Something sure smells good in there."

Unlike our P, B and Js.

The fiftyish-looking lady smiled and reached in the trunk and picked up a tin. "It's for the Harvest Celebration today."

"Can we help you carry it in?" Ben said as he hurried over. Betsy and the others joined him.

"I'd love that. I marked what's in each of the containers. By the way, my name's Claire." She pointed to her name tag."

Betsy and the others went in. The crew at the homeless shelter showed them where to put the food and they went to work when the people showed up. At one time, Betsy marveled at the line of humanity, which extended out the front door.

Later in the afternoon, Betsy thought they'd run out of green bean casserole and none sat in the back kitchen when she checked, but 15 minutes later she scanned the nine by twelve pan and it almost overflowed.

"Hon, we have loaves and fishes going on over here." Betsy put a roll on a young girl's plate. "There you go, sweetheart."

"Loaves and fishes? Ma'am, this is a meat loaf and a roll." The small child worked at lifting her tray of food, as if to prove her point, and showed Betsy.

Betsy wanted to laugh, but didn't dare. Instead she agreed with the tot, "You're absolutely right, little one. You're seeing one of the Bible stories at work here."

"Come on, Lyndsey. We're holding up the line."

~

"Here we go with another story about loaves and fishes."

"Huh?"

Ben laughed at Betsy's blank expression. "I'll tell you later."

"Might want to fill me in too." Jeff stepped over next to Ben and Betsy.

"It's a story in the Bible. I'll tell you about it on the way home."

"I'm excited. More teaching." Jeff smiled as he headed back to where he worked.

"Hey, you gonna put the gravy on those potatoes?" Larry tapped Ben's ladle.

"Sorry about that. The lull in traffic put me to sleep."

"Wake up. We have more people coming."

About forty minutes later Ben and the other five stood at the sinks, cleaning up the trays and putting them away. He looked at his watch and the time amazed him. 6:30. This meant they'd been there over four and a half hours.

"Time does fly..." Ben didn't finish the cliché when he heard the groans. Instead he lifted the last pan up on the shelf and threw away the paper towel he'd dried his hands on.

"And, if we want to stay for another couple of weeks, Claire said we could come as many times as we'd like." Rose laid out the dish towel on the counter. "She also said the next time we don't need to supply food."

Ben walked over to Betsy, who stood next to the exit. "We'll have to talk this over in the *Early Birds* weekly meeting."

"Weekly meetings? Have I missed something?" Larry untied his apron and put it in the garbage can marked *Laundry*.

Rose joined her husband. "They've probably had them and not told us." One of Rose's snorts filled the kitchen area.

"Bets, I knew we forgot something." Ben smiled as he took his wife's hand and headed her out the door to the Wilford's truck.

"You better not be having a meeting without me, Buster and Busterette Brown." Rose hurried past the others and scooted in front of Ben and Betsy and stopped. "Remember, I'm the brains in this operation."

Larry came up to Rose and took her arm, leading her towards their truck. When he opened the door for his wife to get in he said, "No, Rosebud. I'd say that would be me."

"Jeff and Mary, if you ever decide to join the *Early Birds* you better bring your boots." Rose tapped her foot on the parking lot. "It's getting real deep out here."

"I can see that."

Laughter filled the truck as everyone piled in. While Ben waited for Betsy to get situated, he devised a plan to continue the orneriness. He'd make smoochy noises and tell everyone he'd picked the particular seat so he could make out with his sweetheart.

Oh, shoot, I told Jeff I'd tell him the loaves and fishes story.

Ben hoped he wouldn't bring it up and they could talk about it when they got off by themselves. He didn't want Jeff or Mary to think every time they got together they'd have a church service. So far that's what had happened.

After Larry had gone a few miles and Jeff remained quiet, Ben implemented his planned kiss attack on his wife. Betsy's reaction went off as he thought it would, which brought more laughter from the occupants of the truck.

"Leave me alone. There are others here or haven't you noticed?"

Rose put her hands up, making it look like she had blinders on. "We'll keep our eyes focused to the front." She turned around and faced straight ahead.

"Don't encourage him." Betsy poked Rose on her shoulder.

"Ben, keep your hands to yourself. That is, when you are with company." Rose gave a short snort then added. "Is that better?"

"A little late, I'd say."

Ben did steal a few kisses on their way to Ft. Collins, but he kept them quiet so he wouldn't bring any more attention their way. Even though Betsy acted miffed, her kisses in return told him she welcomed them.

"We're home." Larry parked next to their RV and jumped out.

Betsy and Ben got out and he shut the door. On the way to their camper, he walked past the fire pit and his stomach growled. He tried to reason they'd had plenty of food at the shelter, but his sweet tooth didn't get fed.

"Would anyone else eat a *S'more* if I started a fire?"

He didn't need to say anything else. Betsy went in and a few seconds later brought out a huge bag of marshmallows and a box of Graham crackers. Rose went in and got their supply of Hershey bars. Jeff and Mary got the wood. In no time they sat and ate the gooey dessert.

"I'm a happy man." Ben leaned back on his chair and sighed.

"Got to kiss his wife all the way home then ends his day with his favorite snack." Betsy dragged her lawn chair closer to the fire and put four marshmallows on her hanger. "How about the 'loaves and fishes' story?"

Ben went in and got his Bible, giving Matilda a quick pat on his way out. He sat and read the passage in Matthew 14:13-21.

"I've heard the story before. Seems unbelievable."

"It does, but Jesus wanted to show them He had a plan. The end of the day arrived and He asked his disciples to go get food. They looked at each other and no one had a clue how to do it. Then the little boy gave Him his loaves and fishes."

Ben touched his Bible. "He raised the two items to heaven and asked the Father to bless the food."

"Sort of like saying grace for what we have?" Mary asked.

"My Sunday school teacher said, "Jesus gave thanks to God for what He had. Not to show them He could take it and multiply it. But He alone supplies our needs."

Ben put a couple of marshmallows on his hanger and continued. "Another example, the front loaders from the other day."

"Front loaders?" Mary said.

"I get it." Jeff stood up. "Makes sense. No way could two machines do what we got done. Without God in the mix."

"You're right." Ben stood next to him.

"Thus concludes the Bible study and it's late." Betsy got up and carried her chair and propped it up against their RV.

"Sooooo, when's the next *Early Birds* meeting." Jeff spoke up.

Mary's mouth dropped open and she asked, "What are you saying?"

"I'm saying we ought to join this group of wahoos. Why not?"

"I second, third and fourth the motion." Rose hugged everyone standing or sitting around the campfire. "Welcome to the *Early Birds.*"

"Can I fifth it." Betsy hugged the newest members too. "Can't wait to see what the Lord does next. But I do have one question...don't you guys need an RV to belong to the *Early Birds?*

CHAPTER THIRTY-SIX

On Sunday afternoon, the *Early Birds* decided to stay for two more weeks. The decision came after Ben got a call from Flatirons Church. The church they'd visited since their arrival in Colorado.

The gentleman on the phone had introduced himself as Tim, "Ben, I'm the pastor overseeing disaster relief. I was given the paper you filled out, wanting to volunteer at the church."

Ben smiled. "What do you need?"

"The church has raised over $50,000 and we've purchased seven ATVs. We need a crew to ride them into Lyons with supplies. You interested?"

"I've got three guys. Count us in."

The second Ben got off the phone and mentioned ATVs and the church's mission to everyone—Rose, Betsy and Mary jumped on board. Larry shouted, "Sign me up."

"Uh, I'm not sure. I've got something going on tomorrow."

Jeff started to pace, acting as if Ben asked him to go alligator hunting. But after a little good-natured ribbing from Larry and him, he agreed to go.

Larry walked next to Jeff and said, "Trust me, ATVs are a kick in the pants."

"They really are!" Ben added, hoping to convince Jeff.

"I'll take your word for it. Please take it easy on me."

Laughter came out before Ben could contain it. "Yea, right,

this coming from someone who makes running heavy equipment look like child's play."

"Yeah, I'm a pro."

"And I'm an authority of going to the store for supplies," Rose yelled from across the room. "Anyone want to come along?"

Betsy said, "You bet" and Mary nodded.

"When we get back, we'll fix a bunch of sandwiches again. Food, water and whatever else we come up with." The ladies left to shop.

Water. Hadn't thought of it. Then what they'd talked about the other night—*loaves and fishes*—Jesus supplied those sitting on the hillside with food over 2000 years ago.

And with some fortitude, and a bit of ingenuity, they'd 'feed' the needy in the 21st Century. Ben's phone beeped. He pressed the button without looking at the screen and said, "Hold on." He turned to Larry and Jeff and said, "Guys, when I get off the phone, we'll talk about our new gig." Ben went back to his phone. "Hello."

"Hi Ben. It's Brian."

"Let me sit down before I fall down."

For the next hour and a half, they caught up with life. Ben didn't leave out anything and he said, "You'll never believe what Bets and I are doing?"

"Knowing you, it involves work."

"You're right, but it's the kind of work I love. Hard work." He told him they'd retired and Ben waited for the bottom to fall out of the conversation.

It didn't.

"Congratulations. Great news, bro. I've made some changes too, I'm a commercial pilot and also teach flying lessons."

"You...the kid afraid of heights."

"Along with a few other things."

Commitment. To name one.

"How's—"

Brian coughed. "Not sure which one I was with the last time we talked. But no, she's out of my life. I'm married to Amy and let's say the Lord made me wait for a reason. How's Betsy?"

"Nuts as ever and congrats. Sorry we missed your wedding,"

"When we get together, I'll show you the pictures."

"I'd like to see them." Ben still couldn't believe fences could be mended so easy. He wished he'd done it sooner.

"Ben, I hate to run, but I've got to catch a flight to Denver. Then to LA."

"Too bad. Thought you might jet over to Lafayette, Colorado and go ATVing with me and the guys from Flatirons Church tomorrow morning."

"Sounds fun, but the airline would have my head if I called in. I'll talk to you when I get back to Chicago."

"Great talking to you."

Ben hung up and went into the RV. Betsy's back faced him, so he refrained from skipping around like Matilda. He'd wait until his wife turned around.

"Do you want a sandwich? I finished the ones you'll take tomorrow a while ago. Or, do you want leftover meatloaf?" Betsy spun around as she asked the last question.

"Neither. I'm taking us out to dinner to celebrate."

"The new job tomorrow?"

"No, the phone call I got. Brian called."

"Your brother. Oh, Ben. That's fantastic."

Thank you, Father.

~

Monday morning the church's parking lot looked like a cardboard graveyard. Boxes from the seven brand new ATVs lay in a pile next to them. Ben walked around and admired the shiny machines. He figured it'd been years since he'd ridden one of them. But thought it was like riding a bike—a skill one never forgot.

"Will these do?" The preacher he'd met asked when he came up to Ben.

"I'd say you've got a generous congregation."

"You have no idea. I'll tell you about them sometime."

"Look forward to it." Ben glanced at his friends. Larry had

hopped on one of the ATVs and rode it around. Jeff, on the other hand, stood straight legged and his face almost as white as the shirt he had on.

"Come on, city boy. Ready to try this puppy out?" Ben motioned for Jeff to come over. "Get on. It won't bite. I know you've ridden motorcycles...you have, haven't you?"

"Yes."

Ben heard the affirmative answer, but it didn't convince him. "Are you okay?"

"Yes."

"I've gotten two yesses, but nothing more. If you don't want to go. It's ok—"

"I know."

"Wow! I got a different answer."

Jeff grinned, but his face showed otherwise. "Ben, I'm not sure—"

"If you rode a motorcycle?"

"No, I rode them. It's not the ATV. I'm not sure I want to see...see what the flood did to other people's property. Ben, it's one thing to clean up the motel, but homes."

"We need to pray." Ben finished his prayer and patted Jeff on the back. "You sure you're good with this?"

"I am now. The thing I need to remember about ATVs, from past experience, when I put on the brakes, make sure I use both handles. Flipping over one of these is no fun."

"Don't imagine." Ben got on one of the machines. "Are you ready?"

"I'm on it, aren't I?" Jeff laughed as he adjusted the mirrors and played with the brakes. "Thanks, Ben."

"You bet. Now how about we do a few laps around the parking lot and see how they feel," Ben said the last word when Larry whizzed past them and waved. "Guess there's no problem with him. He used to have snowmobiles."

After testing the machines, they put some of the food and bottled water on them. The rest of the water went in the bed of the trucks and on the trailers. At 8:30, Tim stood up on his machine and announced, "It's time to pray, before we take off."

Ben bowed his head and listened to the preacher's words, asking for the Lord's peace and protection on them as they traveled today.

"And all the saints said, '"Amen."'"

"Amen. Now can someone show me how to work one of these things?"

Ben whirled around when he recognized the voice. "Brian? How? What? I never."

"What he's trying to say is, 'Good to see you.'" Larry shook Brian's hand. "It's been too long."

"Yes, it has."

Ben ran over and gave his brother a bear hug. "Thought you said you couldn't come."

"Perks of being a pilot."

"Glad you're here."

"Me, too." Brian stepped on one of the empty ATVs. "How about we get going? People are waiting."

Ben and the others followed Tim and they got as close to Lyons as they could. The piles of rocks, overturned vehicles and uprooted trees at every turn almost blew Ben's mind. And the fact his brother came along for the adventure, topped off the day.

Slow and steady got all of them through the destruction and to their destination safe. When they reached the end, Ben stared at his clothes. Not sure which flannel shirt or pair of jeans he'd worn that morning. Mud covered every inch of him.

"Why don't you take the food to the supply tent?" Tim helped Ben unload the back of his ATV. "It's over there. We'll wait for you two."

Brian grabbed one side of the 24 pack of water. Ben took the other end, along with the food. Once they got inside, Ben put the sandwiches out. He almost went out to get Larry and Jeff to see what their wives had done. They'd tied a bow with a Bible verse on each one of the them.

"Leave it to the ladies to go the extra mile."

"Like someone else I know." Ben realized having his brother, even for a few hours, meant everything to him.

~

During dinner, Betsy listened to Ben's retelling of their trek up to Lyons and his surprise visitor.

"Bets, he wanted to come see you, but he had to catch a flight. But he assured me, we'd see him sooner than later."

"We better. I want to meet Amy."

"So do I."

Ben continued talking, but Betsy zoned out. She couldn't quit thinking about Brian and marveled at another miracle in their lives. One neither could have fathomed. Yes, Ben had contacted him, but for once his brother put someone else first.

Her hubby.

"....and Bets, everyone appreciated the care packages you sent. Loved how you tied up the sandwiches."

"Wish it had been my idea." Betsy smiled. "Mary came up with it."

"Outstanding. I read some of the verses. I'm sure they'll touch their hearts."

"Hope so." Betsy took a bite of leftover meatloaf.

Ben put down the fork and wiped his mouth. "They've got a tough road ahead of them. Some have nothing left. Except for what they packed on their way out. Which wasn't much. But they're praising Jesus through the storm they've endured."

"I hope Jeff heard some of their testimonies."

"He did and I almost laughed out loud when I watched his eyes. They got bigger every time he heard the stories of survival. During one conversation, where the Lord's name came up a number of times, Jeff shouted "Amen!" I believe he found out what's important. Family and friends."

Betsy cleaned up the dishes, and after the news, they went to bed. Once again, sleep eluded her as she tried to settle in. One thought kept her wide awake. Betsy couldn't remember the last time they'd had a talk like tonight. Where Ben had shared his heart.

The words she'd longed to hear for too long. All the

counseling, the screaming (on both sides) and living apart hadn't opened their hearts to each other. What made it happen: a flood in Boulder. It gave them the ability to help others. Not always dwell on each other's faults and frailties.

Thank You, Father...for everything.

CHAPTER THIRTY-SEVEN

"Matilda, I can't take you out right now. If I do, I'll forget the muffins I have in the oven." Betsy leaned down and petted her pooch. "As soon as the dinger goes off we'll G.O. F.O.R. A. W.A.L.K." She spelled the phrase, but the dog's ears perked up.

"You know what I'm saying, don't you?"

"Talking to Mats again, are you?" Rose spoke, after opening the door.

"I am and I know she understands. Even when we spell the words."

"Baby stares at us when we talk to her and then does her own thing."

Betsy took a look into the convection oven at the cranberry muffins before she turned to her friend. "Rosie, I'm not a vet, but Baby's confused. One minute you're implementing the rules from obedience school. The next, you're nuzzling her. After she ate your shoe. Can you see why she's conflicted?"

"You have a point. Actually it's Lar who pampers her more than me. Anyway, they were cheap shoes."

"That's coming from somebody who's always talking budget. If the shoes are a quarter a piece, you'd still say it's monies spent."

Rose put her hand on her hip. "I'm thinking someone in this room got up on the wrong side of the bed this morning?"

"Could be." Betsy laughed as she turned to take the muffins out. "I did have some trouble going to sleep last night. The Lord must have wanted me to stay up and pray."

"Did you?" Rose reached over and grabbed a hot muffin out of the tin. "Ouch."

"I did and I thanked him for Brian surprising Ben."

"Like the Visa commercial. Priceless." Rose chuckled. "Larry said he's a lot grayer, but looks good."

"Aren't we all?"

"All, what?"

"More gray, but looking good."

"Glad your mood has improved and so you know, these muffins are OUTSTANDING."

"Thank you. Thank you very much."

"Elvis has just rolled over in his grave."

"I thought I did the king justice."

"Not so mu—"

A loud knock sounded, cutting off Rose's comment. Betsy went and opened the door. "Come on in, Mary."

"Hello, newest member of the *Early Birds*." Rose gave Mary the usual greeting...a hug when she entered.

"We're getting ready to whip up a batch of cookies." Betsy wiped off the well-used pan. "What'd you bring for us to throw in?"

"I've got some chocolate chips and raisins."

"Put 'em in and I'll take Matilda for a walk." Betsy watched her dog do her acrobatics, while she tried to put the leash on her. "Can you possibly sit for a minute, Mats?"

Betsy stood up, ignoring her pooch and said, "With all of Matilda's antics, she ought to be in pictures. But I'd have to drive us there. Don't think I'd get anywhere near Tinseltown with Ben. He's into quieter places."

"Jeff and I love visiting California. The wine country. Oh, but we went there before...you know...we found Jesus."

Betsy couldn't hold in the laughter. And after looking at Rose, who did everything but turn inside out to keep from laughing, squealed and hit the kitchen island with the wooden spoon.

Mary gave them a baffled look then glanced down at the front of her shirt and brushed something off of it. "What did I say? Do I have egg on my face? I'm going to look." She went up the stairs.

"No. No. No. Mary, you don't have anything hanging from anywhere. I, and I'm assuming Rose, cracked up at your comment about not doing the Napa thing anymore 'cause you found Jesus.'"

"That's one of the reasons Jeff fought religion for so long. He'd always say, "Nobody's going to tell me what I can and can't drink."

"I can see his point. The funny thing is, it isn't about the consumption—it's the importance of it in your life and the amount. The Bible states, "do all things in moderation."

"And the way I've been taught, it means in everything we do. Talking, drinking. Anything that takes our minds off where it should be. From what He wants us to do."

"Never thought of it that way. All I know, at one time, Jeff's moderation wasn't anywhere close to what Jesus had in mind."

Betsy chuckled again, but could tell her new friend didn't like her response and she said, "Mary, I'm sorry. I shouldn't laugh at your candor. It's how you put it. It made me laugh."

"Maybe the reason we've never seen this side of Mary is because we're the ones talking all the time. Not using moderation in our speech," Rose added.

Betsy stared at her new friend. Her cheeks flamed as red as a delicious apple. She also noticed Mary avoided making eye contact with her.

"We do talk too much, don't we, Mary?"

"Uh, I wouldn't say too much."

"We need to shut up and listen to this lady. She's got some wisdom under those salt and pepper curls of hers." Rose filled the cookie sheet and put it in the oven.

"I'm not sure you need to quit talking completely. I'm learning something every day from your jabbering."

"That's what I'm afraid of." Betsy slapped Rose lightly on her shoulder and then realized she might have sent the cookies flying. Fortunately, she'd finished shutting the oven door when the assault happened.

"How much time on this batch? I still need to take Matilda out." Betsy held up the leash. "I've been standing here this whole time holding it. Yes, I'm losing it."

"Go ahead. We've got this. Mats needs to go do her business." Rose shut the water off and opened the door for Betsy and Matilda.

"We won't be gone long."

With a bag in her pocket, Betsy walked down the stairs. On the way to the doggy park, Matilda stopped at every bush and leaf scattered about. Never tarrying long, but needing to check out where other pooches had been.

Betsy held the leash tight. The last squirrel sighting almost caused an ER visit. Betsy's shoulder hurt for days. "Mats, one things for sure—you're our entertainment. Life would be pretty boring without you."

She shortened the leash then realized a person, who walked their dog a few feet away, stared at her. Smiling.

"I talk to my pooch all the time too." The lady pointed down at her Chocolate Lab.

"I'm glad I'm not the only one."

"If I didn't have this guy to talk to, I don't know what I'd do. Have a nice day."

"You, too."

Betsy watched as the woman went up the driveway into a Montana 5th wheel. Only when Matilda tugged on her leash did she realize she stood in the middle of the street. Bets looked around, hoping no one else saw her idling there.

"All right, little one. We're going."

Betsy walked Matilda over to the doggy section. While she

waited, she prayed for family and friends. In the midst of praying for her mom, the woman she'd met a moment ago came to mind.

Wonder what her name is?

The thought made Betsy laugh. God didn't need names. If He knew the numbers of the hairs on our head, Betsy felt certain He knew her name and whatever she needed.

Matilda came over and stood next to her and Betsy put the leash back on. They headed to the RV. When Bets opened the door, the aroma from the muffins and cookies came out and greeted her.

Yummy!

Betsy took their dog's leash off and went to the jar to get a chew thingy for Mats. "You want a treat?"

"We thought you'd forgotten where you live."

"Rosie, when I'm on a mission for the Almighty, there is no timetable."

"What'd you find...or I should say...who'd you find to talk with this morning?"

"You are definitely on a roll, Mary." Rose held up a knife in one hand and a hot pad in the other. "Someone turned on your switch this morning and I'm liking it."

"Might be the new coffee we're drinking."

"No, I think the Lord's blossomed you into the person He created you to be."

"Always the poetic one, Betsy. And I agree with her. He is at work in both you and Jeff."

"I hope so, Rose." Mary smiled. "Jeff couldn't believe what he saw yesterday. What had happened to other people. He told me, "We don't have a house, but at least we have some of our belongings.'"

"How about we sit down and pray while we're having a goodie or two...or three? This will give us energy to navigate the trail He's put us on." Betsy grabbed her cup and filled it. "Want some more?"

Rose came over and poured a cup. "Bets, wherever He leads, I'm sure the *Early Birds* will follow."

"Amen," Mary said as she raised her cup. "I'll take some of it too."

Mary, are you talking coffee or the Father's leading?

Whatever her new friend meant, Betsy counted on the Lord to give them an adventure at every turn. But the one nagging question still remained and Rose brought it up before Bets could.

"Mary, back to what Betsy asked you the other night. You do know you need a camper to go with us. Don't you?"

"Not a problem, girls. It's the one thing that survived the flood. Only problem, the road's washed out so we can't get our camper out and over here to join you."

"You are full of surprises, Mary." Betsy raised her coffee cup. "Welcome to the *Early Birds.* Again.

"I second that."

CHAPTER THIRTY-EIGHT

Ben tried his best to sleep in the front seat of Larry's truck, but the bumpy roads made it difficult to accomplish. But after the day they'd had, he felt sure he could sleep on a bed of nails. Even something as small as Matilda's bed sounded good at the moment.

But tomorrow he and the rest of the crew could sleep in. Today marked the final day on the job up in Lyons and if Ben would have to pick the best part of the last five days, this morning would win the prize.

"Sheriff, Flatirons Church would like to present you with four brand new ATVs."

Ben and the crew watched a flatbed truck pull up. Hoops and hollers would have raised the roof, if they'd been in a closed building. But when Tim handed over the keys to the other seven they'd used during the almost-week long assignment and said, "These are yours, too.

Ben, Larry and Jeff left the church after a bunch of hugs and high fives. Even a few tears. The best part: Ben shared part of the adventure with Brian.

"Lar, I'm not sure anything can top what happened today. Or

the last two weeks." Ben buckled his seat belt as Larry got on the road.

"I agree. And I sure like working for a living again. Sweating's good for the soul." Larry turned on the radio and started to hum along with the song.

"All this talk about work made me tired. Could you quiet the music? I'm trying to catch a nap over here."

Ben almost had his eyes closed, but noticed Larry still fumbled with the volume button. Next thing he knew Lar's radio was full blast and he's belting out the poorest rendition of *Are You Lonesome Tonight* he'd ever heard.

"Hey, can you turn it down? I'm trying to snooze over here." Ben shouted over the noise coming from the speakers.

"Just trying to keep Sleeping Beauty awake."

"You need to keep your attention on the road, not the radio. A deer might jump out at you."

"The flood sent them scrambling—like the people."

"Is that what it is, oh Great Hunter?"

"Actually it does displace them. They go to higher ground to escape the rushing water."

"It's true. You are a know it all."

"Go back to sleep."

Ben took his advice and slept. Despite the road condition in what seemed like two minutes, Larry pulled into the RV Park and flung open his door. "Wake up over there."

"I must have died the last fifteen miles. After you left me alone."

"Your snoring kept me awake." Larry stood staring at him then added, "You do make a racket, my friend. Don't know how Betsy stands it."

"She doesn't, she pokes me in the ribs throughout the night."

"Rose and I will add this to our prayer list."

"Please do. See ya in the morning." Ben climbed out of the truck and went into his RV. Matilda came from wherever she'd been and greeted him. "Hello, little buddy. What have you and Mom been doing. Smells good in here again?" Ben picked up the pooch and went over and gave Betsy a kiss.

"Mats helped me with a new recipe. I'm not sure it's eatable, but we'll give it a try." Betsy stirred something in the crockpot that appeared a tad pale.

"Let me take a shower and change and I'll be ready for supper." Ben put Matilda down and she ran over to her bed.

"Take your time. I'm sure it's nothing to rush down for."

Ben gave his beloved a sideward glance and she put her hand on her mouth. A muffled "I'm sorry" followed.

"You need to quit putting yourself down." He leaned on the counter.

"I know. It's just—"

"It's just what?"

"You'd eat sautéed bananas if I sat them in front of you."

"Ooh, fried monkey food sounds good. Is that what we're having for dessert? Matilda, Mom fixed me a treat."

The minute the word came out of his mouth, their pooch went wild.

"I said it, didn't I?"

"Yes, and she's not eaten dinner yet. What do you think the chances are she's going to eat it now?"

"Slim to none."

"Better give her one and get it over with."

Ben did and watched their precious pooch devour the milk bone in less than 1.2 seconds. "She needs to slow down and savor those things. Instead of swallowing them whole."

Betsy had moved over to the crockpot and Ben watched her take the lid off. He stood there, expecting another remark from his bride and he didn't have long to wait.

"The looks of this conglomeration, you better gulp this down as fast as Mats does hers t.r.e.a.t.s."

"Bets?"

"Go take your shower."

"I will." Ben grabbed his towel and a change of clothes and walked to the RV showers. He'd found this easier than taking one at the camper and it kept their place cleaner. He climbed in under the hot water and all of the dirt and grime from the day washed down the drain.

Every muscle and joint hurt, but he classified it as a 'happy hurt'. Doing manual labor. When he'd sat behind a desk, pushing a pencil, he never ached all over. And as Ben watched the soap go down the drain, he imagined his previous life dissolving right along with it.

Ben no longer had to worry about schedules, or someone not doing their job. Or working until his eyes almost fell out of his head. But something bothered him. His wife's unsavory comments about anything she did. Never a positive slant on anything having to do with what she did. Constant put downs.

While Ben rinsed off the mud in his hair, he made a decision. He'd pray for the right time to talk to Betsy. Whenever it happened, he had to broach the subject.

Ben saw how hard she tried. But when it didn't work out, the first thing out of her mouth—a put down. His degree in Architecture didn't qualify him to diagnose Bets, but he figured it couldn't be good for a person to say those kinds of things all the time.

The water temperature changed and brought Ben back to where he stood. Under cold water. He shut the faucet off as fast as he could and grabbed his towel and dried off. "I do need to sleep in tomorrow. Pretty bad when you can zone out while taking a shower."

He got dressed and walked the short distance back to their RV.

~

"I thought you drowned." Betsy smiled when Ben came through the door.

"No, but I stayed in the shower so long I ran out of hot water."

"Bet that woke you up?" She took the lid off the crockpot and stirred its contents. "After the days you've had, I'm not surprised you ran it out. Are you ready for supper? I'm sure you'd rather…" Betsy left the rest to Ben's imagination.

"I'd rather have "what"?" Ben yelled from the direction of the bathroom.

"Nothing."

He came down and took his normal seat at the table, reaching down to give Matilda a pat on her head. "Good girl. You ready for dinner too?"

"Already fed her." Betsy brought the plates over and set them in front of the two places. "Dig in."

"Looks good."

"It's true. Love is blind."

Betsy noticed he gave her one of those "you're doing the self-deprecating thing again" then watched him pick up his fork. "Probably should tell you it's pork chops. In case you haven't figured it out."

Ben took a bite and chewed. After he swallowed he said, "I...have to say..." He put down his fork, cleared his throat and wiped his mouth with his napkin. "Hon, you might be right on this one. It's the most intriguing taste I've ever had before."

He picked up his fork again and took a bite. The expression on his face meant one thing—she'd rather eat liver than take a taste.

"So you are verifying it's terrible."

"No, I'm saying it's unique. The texture and the flavor. Betsy, it's delicious."

"Delicious. Are you kidding me? You don't have to eat it if you don't want to."

"Oh, I'm eating it and when I'm done I'm taking some to our friends."

"Why, so you can get rid of it?"

Ben put his fork down and stared at Betsy. This time she could tell he didn't see any humor in her. She could also tell he tried hard not to come out of the gate yelling, which she appreciated. But, 'delicious'. Not!

"I don't get you. Compliments don't work. Praising what you do falls on deaf ears. Betsy, this humor, if that's what you call it, isn't funny. Might get lots of laughs, but you truly believe what you're saying...but it's not true. Hon, you are loved. You have to start believing it."

"Wow, I should have made this recipe a long time ago." Betsy squeezed his hand then reached over and picked up her own fork and took a bite. "Hey, this *is* good." She took another taste and savored this one, instead of swallowing it whole. "Bub, you ain't sharing this with anyone. This is a keeper."

Ben started laughing. Then choked. After he took a drink he said, "Did I hear you say something nice about yourself?"

"You did. And it didn't kill me."

"Try it more often. It's more becoming."

"I will. But if I get too big headed, you have to promise me you'll call me on it."

"You can count on it."

Betsy had to admit the new recipe hit it out of Royal stadium. She also assessed she had little to do with its success, but kept quiet. Ben made a good point. Over the last couple of weeks, she hadn't spent much time reading the Bible. When that happened she went back to her old ways, forgetting to dwell on whatever was true, honorable, just...

"You're in deep thought."

"The verse I read a few weeks ago. I'm finally realizing how important what I think about is."

"And what you say about yourself."

"I'll work on that. I promise."

"It's not you working, Betsy. This one is too big. You need His guidance on this one. We'll pray, but you also need to ask Him to help you with this during your quiet time."

Ben's words confirmed she needed to spend more time in the Word. And when Betsy finished cleaning up the kitchen, she'd stop and do it. Only problem, she couldn't remember where she'd put her Bible the last time she'd used it.

"I saw it next to your recliner the other day."

"Oh, are you reading minds now?"

"You had that look on your face, so I thought I'd save you from hunting." Ben got up from the table and took his plate to the sink. "I'm going outside and start a fire. You can join me, if you want."

"Maybe later."

Betsy went to the sink and in no time she'd cleaned the kitchen and sat on the loveseat with her Bible. Matilda snoozed beside her. She opened to Philippians 4: 8-9 and reread her favorite verses, drinking in the Lord's words. His ointment of truth and restoration rushed over her.

Her mind lingered on the last verse. *Whatever you have learned or received or heard from me, or seen in me—put it into practice. And the God of peace will be with you.*

But Betsy knew it wouldn't happen unless she believed what she read. "It's the head to heart thing again. Yes, Lord."

~

"Larry and I are going into town this morning." Ben put his cereal bowl in the sink and grabbed his jacket. "He needs to get some stuff for his camper before we take off again."

"Speaking of taking off. What about Jeff and Mary's camper?"

"Jeff said the highway department has rebuilt enough of the road they can get their camper out whenever they want."

"Sounds like a plan. Guess I'll see you later. I'll be slaving away at the computer. Got a great idea for a blog."

But first I'm going to make a trip to the grocery store.

"See you in a couple of hours. Noon at the latest. Might have to run to a couple of places." Ben walked over to Betsy's desk and leaned down to give her a kiss.

"Love ya."

Betsy heard her hubby leave, but her mind had already left on her shopping trip. After a quick goodbye to Matilda, she went in search of the items on her list: ground chuck, zucchini, green onions, Pico de Gallo, sour cream and a type of bread she'd never heard of.

Along with those items, Betsy picked up their normal weekly staples. If she kept surprising Ben with cooking dinner, she might as well shock him with getting the other groceries they needed, so he wouldn't have to.

On her way home, she devised a plan of getting the items

into the house without her friend seeing her. Betsy had seen the laundry bag she'd left in the backseat. It would work brilliantly. If Nosey Rosie came around, she'd tell her she'd forgotten her clean clothes.

Betsy made it home and got all the food inside, unnoticed. Which made her happy. Once she put the food away, off to her desk she went to start her blog. With her fingers poised on the keys, she typed three words: *Is There Change?*

Hoping the rest would flow as fast as the title, Betsy waited. Fragments of content floated around in her head, but nothing seemed to materialize as one sensible phrase to put down.

Hello, up there. Could I get some help here? I'm not hearing Your voice.

The nothingness continued until Betsy wrote a random thought down, which turned into somewhat of a paragraph. Not sure any of it made much sense. Instead of causing one of her blood vessels in her brain to burst, she closed her computer and went to the kitchen.

Stepping behind the island, Bets chuckled. "Father, I may not have it in the writing department today, but if this is Your idea of change then I'm ready to spend time doing this cooking thing."

And spend time she did. Along with slicing and dicing, Betsy watched the Food Network show she'd taped last night. With Bobby Flay's instructions, she created a meal from the items she'd purchased earlier.

While the ingredients simmered on the stove, Betsy cleaned up her mess and kept lifting the lid to her latest attempt at cooking. "If it smells, tastes and looks appealing – I might consider sharing it this time. Unlike last night. Wallpaper paste looking stuff that ended up tasting good."

Betsy laughed. "Hey, if something doesn't taste right—I'll throw...no, we're on a bud...get. I'll put it away and eat it for lunch when Ben's gone to work somewhere."

"There you go talking to yourself again?" Rose came up to the screen and almost scared the spoon right out of Betsy's hand.

"You could knock before you holler at me next time."

"Wouldn't be as much fun as watching you stirring the pot and talking away to no one in particular."

"Glad I could entertain you. What do you want?"

"I want to know what the wonderful smell is?"

"Something Ben fixed before he left." Betsy fibbed, but wanted to keep her secret a while longer. "And I've spent the whole day stirring it."

"Smells wonderful."

"If you promise you will NEVER come over and frighten me ever again, we'll share some of this with all of you."

Rose opened the screen door and came up the stairs. "If you give me a bite of what you're stirring, I'll never so much as think about startling you."

Betsy turned and faced her friend. "Who are you kidding?"

"I promise."

When Rose said she'd do something—or in this case, not do something, Betsy believed her. She grabbed a clean spoon, spun around to face the stove and took out a tablespoon of the Beef Stroganoff and fed it to her friend.

Betsy couldn't figure out if Rose wanted to get rid of what she had in her mouth, or if she'd swallow it. Whatever the case, she got a paper towel ready.

Rosie hates it.

Or did she? Rose managed to swallow and wore a grin the size of Texas on her face. All at the same time. With the approval of her friend, Betsy wanted to lindy hop all over their 350 square feet of living space.

Betsy almost told her she'd made it and how it all occurred, but decided she'd wait. Didn't want to toot her horn prematurely. Her hubby might suggest she feed it to the dumpster.

Oops! I did it again. Sorry.

CHAPTER THIRTY-NINE

Ben didn't suggest anything of the kind, after he'd tasted the tiny bite Betsy gave him when he got home. But sharing it, he had a problem with that. Rose stared at him until he relented.

"Okay, you can have some more."

Rose picked up the pot, wiggled past Betsy and proceeded down the stairs. Ben followed close behind. Didn't want the food to get too far away. While he kept watch of Rosie, he noticed Jeff pulling in with their travel trailer.

"Hey, look who's here."

"I see who it is. Jeff, park it and fast. We've got good eatins' here." Rose grabbed the bowls out of Betsy's hand and ladled out six dishes. "Let's hurry it up over there."

Ben guided Jeff into a spot as fast as two men could park the pull-along camper. If they hadn't gotten it accomplished, their friend, Rose would have taken the wheel and put it wherever it fit best.

Thank the good Lord that didn't happen and Ben and Jeff came over and joined the party in record time. Right when Rose said, "Attention, everyone. This delicious meal came from no other than Ben Stevenson."

"Glad you guys could make it before it's all gone," Larry said as he glanced over at Ben. "I thought you said, on our way to Camping World, you needed to go to the grocery store. No food in the house." He held up his spoon. "This doesn't taste like you're lacking anything."

"Ah huh." Ben continued the façade, enjoying how Betsy's color went from baby-bottom pink to a shade of off white. Not on any color chart he'd seen. Ben sat down and took a taste of the Beef Stroganoff and decided he'd spill the beans on the actual cook.

But before he could, Betsy stood at the head of the picnic table and told the group. "I can't tell a lie either. It wasn't Ben. I'm the one who made it."

"Keep doing whatever it is you're doing." Mary reached for her spoon and took another taste.

"Amen." Jeff's garbled one-word sentiment made everyone around the table laugh.

"You're all too kind." Betsy did a little curtsy then took her seat.

"All I have to say, hon, is why have you kept this talent hidden for all these years?" Ben took his second helping. Smaller than the first and took a bite.

"Guess I had to wait for Bobby Flay to woo me away from HGTV."

"And that, Mr. Stevenson, took some work." Rose took a drink of her tea and set it down. "Especially those fix-it shows. Never imagined anything or anyone could end their relationship."

"Sometimes you have to let go of something you love. If it comes back to you, it was love. Or something like that." Betsy smiled and shrugged.

Ben had heard the saying before, but he didn't think it went quite the way his wife recited it this time. The previous time Betsy said it to him, it rang out a few octaves higher while he packed his clothes to leave her.

Ben nudged Betsy's arm and she turned his way. Her smile and nothing in her expression told him she recalled saying the words to him years before.

"I don't know about you guys, but I'm freezing." Mary stood up and wrapped her arms around her middle.

"If you hang around us for much longer you'll have extra padding to keep you warm." Ben went to grab his midsection, but his coat covered his extra poundage. "In my case, I'm working on having enough around here so when we hit the beaches I won't need an inner tube."

"How we can go from enjoying a delectable dinner to a discussion about tonnage." Rose put her hand over her mouth. "Sorry. I wasn't saying any of us weigh a ton."

"No problem. Mary's right. I'm getting a little cold myself."

"Which is a great segway to an *Early Bird's* meeting about where we go next." Rose stood at the head of the table.

"But first, can I go get my coat?" Mary ran to her camper.

"Me too."

After Betsy and Mary returned, with their coats on, Rose started the meeting. "I vote we move the *Early Birds* to a warmer climate. No use staying around here. Our work is done."

"Early November in Ft. Myers Beach is still in the 90s." Larry turned his phone around so everyone could see.

"If you hadn't noticed, we moved in today." Jeff glanced over in his wife's direction.

"Doesn't matter to me, sweetie." Mary snuggled deeper into her fleece-lined jacket. "We've filed all the paperwork. No reason to stay here."

"I like her logic. What do you guys think?" Larry eyed Ben and Betsy.

"You know me, I'm ready for an adventure whenever it calls."

Rosie shouted, "Hallelujah" then moved her hips around, looking as if she'd break out in a hula at any time. Blessings to the saints she changed her mind when some of the other campers walked by their spot.

"Rosebud, sit down." Larry remained standing. "Can we get a vote?"

All six raised their hands and everyone talked at once. The

commotion went on for a good five minutes before a voice of reason, Jeff, brought the party back to order.

"How about we leave Tuesday morning? That way we can go to church on Sunday. Tell Tim and the other guys goodbye. Then Monday, Mary and I can get everything finished up. Next day, we'll get on the road."

"You guys are going to fit in fine. Hope you have a CB radio." Rose winked at Betsy.

"We do. Why?" Mary asked.

"You'll need it when we sing Betsy's favorite song, *On the Road Again.*"

Larry sat down. "Please tell me we aren't going to sing the song again?"

The country song took over most of their conversation, but at 10:30 Betsy announced, "It's bedtime."

"Couldn't agree more." Ben got up and carried the pans and dishes from their feast to their RV. Before he stepped inside he said, "See all you *Early Birds* in the morning."

Ben closed the door behind Betsy and before she had a chance to run the water in the sink, he scooted her away and told her he'd take care of it. "Go read a book. Turn on the Food Network Channel. Do whatever hits your fancy. I've got this."

Ben checked around the kitchen. For the most part Betsy had done the work before he got there. Always the tidy one in the kitchen, following him around with a washcloth or towel, or rinsing out a pan right after he finished with it.

As Betsy said, "When Ben cooks, even the ceiling needs to watch out."

After one of his more exuberant experiences in the kitchen, she'd found tomato sauce above her head. Ben couldn't explain how it got there. He simply went to the garage and brought in his eight-foot ladder and cleaned it up.

Ben came over to the loveseat when he finished the dishes. "What ya watching?"

"Jeff Mauro. He won *Food Network Star* and makes the most delectable looking sandwiches."

For the next half hour, they sat in silence while the chef did a Sassy Ham and Cheese sandwich. Ben watched Betsy jot things down. He had to admit the sandwich looked good. "And it looks like a lot of work to me."

Betsy muted the sound of the TV. "Perfection in anything takes time and effort."

"You are quite the quoter today." The minute the words left his lips, he regretted it. He knew she'd give him her questioning look, since she might not recall what she'd said earlier. Then he'd have to remind her.

She did as he'd predicted.

"You know the one. About letting something go." Ben gave as vague of an answer and hoped it would satisfy her.

No such luck. Perplexed was still Betsy's middle name and she said, "What are you talking about?"

"Am I going to have to take you to the doctor. It only happened about twenty minutes ago and I'm paraphrasing now. 'Sometimes you have to let go of something you love. If it comes back to you—it was love.'"

The stunned look on Betsy's face told Ben she remembered and he'd pretty much said it verbatim.

"So that's why you nudged me."

"Uh huh."

"Wasn't a real good memory to bring up, was it?"

"Not exactly, but it all worked out."

Betsy reached over and touched Ben's arm. "Yes, it did. I didn't want to let you go, but I loved you too much to make you stay where you were miserable."

"Oh, hon, I took the miserable with me. I found out it wasn't you. It was work and how I reacted to it. You didn't do anything to deserve what you got. I'm so sorry."

Betsy started to cry and flipped the TV off. "Thank you."

"No, thank you."

"For what?"

"For putting up with me and for wanting to give me credit for the wonderful dinner you made. But I have one question. How did you get it done and your blog too?"

"I didn't. Well I got the title and first paragraph finished."

"Can I read it?"

Betsy got up and handed him her laptop. Afterward, she fixed them some decaf coffee. Ben opened the lid and waited for it to come alive. While it churned, he read a saying taped to the side of her keyboard. The one they'd talked about earlier.

> *"If you love somebody, let them go,*
> *For if they return, they were always yours.*
> *If they don't they never were."*

He turned and looked at Betsy as he pointed down at the words. "You do know I love you with all my heart and I will never leave you again."

Betsy smiled. "I know. I love you, too." She came and sat on his lap. "You better not leave me. You might miss out on some good grub."

"Don't want to do that." He turned and planted a kiss of the century on her lips. Again.

~

"Wake up, hon."

How could Betsy sleep with Ben in one ear and Matilda bouncing around her legs? She blinked her eyes a couple of times and squinted to see the clock. "9:30? Why'd you let me sleep so late? We've got lots to do today." Betsy scrambled out of bed and pulled the covers up.

"You didn't get much sleep last night, so I let you sleep in."

Betsy opened her side of the closet and got out her outfit of the day. Blue jeans and a Bronco sweatshirt. "Did my tossing and turning keep you awake?"

"You didn't toss and turn much, but your talking kept me up half the night." Ben came over to her side of the bed and gave her a hug. "Who were you chatting with at 2:30 a.m.?"

"I missed a couple of people when we prayed, so I wanted to get them in." Betsy finished getting dressed, pulling her shirt over her head. The last part of her sentence came out muffled.

"I'm sure whoever you prayed for appreciated the late-night get together with God." Ben walked the few steps to their bedroom door then turned towards Betsy. "Are you ready for some pancakes? I stirred up a batch and was waiting for you to get up."

"I'm up and I'm ready for anything you cook." Betsy chuckled. "I'm tired of cooking."

"You are kidding, right?"

"Yes. Now let's go down and see if I can make your pancakes better. I'm sure I've learned something from watching the Food Network Channel to spice them up a bit."

"You're not touching my pancakes. When I'm in the kitchen, your job is to clean up. Nothing more. Nothing less...Sweetems!"

Ben laughed as he worked on breakfast. And, as usual, Betsy gave her hubby's pancakes rave reviews. Fluffy and down-right stupendous and ones you better enjoy when you're eating them. Since her beloved never made the same thing twice.

A little of this and a little of that. No recipe needed.

Oh, how she hated when something tasted so divine. Betsy had tried to write down the recipe, but when Ben used the directions the next time the meal didn't taste the same. Good, but not superb.

"Ben, I have a new name for you. You're a 'one hit wonder'." Betsy had her fill of pancakes and wiped her mouth.

Her husband tilted his head, which told Betsy she'd had a large part of the conversation inside her head before she said something out loud. Instead of leaving him in the dark she said, "I was talking to myself again. Shouldn't come as a surprise to you."

Betsy cut a tiny piece off of the pancake left on Ben's plate. "And, anyway, the one-hit wonder name came because when you cook—you never duplicate the same meal twice."

"I think another name would fit even better. I'd call it mastery." Ben got up and put his plate on the pile in the sink.

Betsy stared at her husband then to the stack of dishes. "And 'mastery' should come with fewer dishes, so the wife doesn't have to clean up after him."

"Oh, contraire! That's the 'mastery' part. Make a mess—make a masterpiece. And with that the master will leave you." Ben went to open the door.

"Not so fast, master of the griddle."

Betsy's comment got them laughing and neither moved from where they stood. Whenever she wanted to add something, fresh laughter erupted. In the end, the only thing left to do—throw a towel at him. Then out squeaked. "Help me."

"Hon, that's not possible."

Betsy would almost bet it took them a good half hour to clean up their small kitchen. They'd have to stop and contain their amusement after one of them made more funnies.

At one point Betsy said a big, *Thank You, Lord.* She couldn't remember when she'd had so much fun or loved her hubby more.

~

Ben still chuckled when he walked down the stairs. When he looked out, both Larry and Jeff stared at him. He could only imagine what they thought since he'd left the door open when Betsy made him help with the breakfast clean up.

If they heard, it's a good possibility the whole park heard their carrying on. Larry laughed as he opened the tailgate of his truck and said, "Sounded like there was a party going on in there."

"Sort of. With Betsy, every day is a reality show in the making. This morning she wanted to include me in the festivities."

The two guys nodded their heads, but Larry's bobbed the most. Then he asked, "Is the world ready for the *Early Birds*?"

"It's not the world we have to worry about as much as the parks we stay at," Jeff said as he moved closer to the truck.

"I'm never going to live Colorado Springs down, am I?"

Larry looked at Ben. "Probably not."

Ben finished tying down the bikes for their departure in two days. Another journey to help people. Wherever the Lord would lead them.

For some reason not knowing what they'd be doing scared him a little. But why? Ben had no clue what they'd run into when he came up with the crazy idea to full-time RV. But never in his wildest dreams would he have believed what the *Early Birds* got done while in Colorado.

"Whatever you have in store. Bring it on, Lord."

"Have you started talking to yourself now?" Larry shut the tailgate.

"Maybe I have."

"I knew Betsy would convert you to the other side."

"The other side?" Jeff joined them at the rear of Larry's vehicle.

"When the Father handed out right braineyness. Not sure that's a word, He gave my wife an extra helping. Her brain never shuts down. She's always thinking, planning, doing something creative."

"I thought she'd changed religions."

Ben laughed at Jeff's illogical comment. "My wife wouldn't deviate from her beliefs in her heavenly Father and isn't afraid to share her faith with others."

"Like my Rosie."

"I've noticed. One of you is always preaching at us."

"What he means." Mary smiled when she walked up. "All of you have blessed us beyond measure and shown us the love of Jesus."

"You have no idea what that means to me." Ben gave Mary and Jeff a hug.

Larry stepped up. "From me and Rose, too."

"I think the *Early Birds* are ready to hit the road." Ben took out his phone.

"Are you putting the date we're leaving in on your calendar?"

"No, Larry, I'm inviting my brother and his wife to Florida. Brian and Amy need to soak up some sun over Christmas break."

"Great idea and I better call Mom and warn her we're coming." Betsy laughed as she walked over and joined the other five.

Rose added, "Larry, did you make reservations at Ft. Myers Beach? Remember the snowbirds are arriving about the time we are."

Larry's blank stare told Ben, and pretty much everyone else who looked in his direction, he'd forgotten to call for reservations.

"Rosebud, can you hand me my phone?"

"No need to worry, Lar." Betsy held up her phone. "Mom texted me. She's reserved three spots at Cypress Grove RV Park in Ft. Myers."

"Florida here we come."

The End

ABOUT THE AUTHOR

This is Janetta's debut novel
To see more wonderful stories, visit www.forgetmenotromances.com

Sign up for Forget Me Not Romances newsletter and receive a cookbook compiled from Forget Me Not Authors!

Janetta Fudge-Messmer is an award-winning inspirational author who resides in Florida, or wherever the wind blows, with her husband of 34 years. She's received Honorable Mention for an article from Writer's Digest Magazine. Her article, "A Working Relationship" was published in Guideposts Magazine. Guideposts Books published, "Shorthaired Miracle". Janetta and her husband Ray, along with precious pooch Maggie, became fulltime RVers in 2012 and enjoy traveling around the USA in their Minnie Winnie.

Social Media:

Blog: www.nettie-fudges-world.blogspot.com

Facebook: Janetta Fudge-Messmer

Twitter: Janetta Messmer@nettiefudge

Made in the USA
Charleston, SC
17 October 2016